CW00687633

ZIAN

SCHAFER

BLOOD MOON SANCTUM

A CURSE
OF OBSIDIAN
&
SILVER

BOOK ONE

Blood Moon Sanctum by Zian Schafer

Published by Zian Schafer

Visit the author's website at www.zianschafer.com

Copyright © 2022 Zian Schafer

All rights reserved. No part of this publication may be reproduced, distributed, or transmitted in any form or by any means, including photocopying, recording, or other electronic or mechanical methods without permission from the publisher, except in the case of brief quotation embodied in critical reviews and certain other noncommercial uses permitted by copyright law.

This book is a work of fiction. Names, characters, places and incidents are the product of the author's imagination or are used fictitiously. Any resemblance to outside events, locales, or person, living or dead, is entirely coincidental.

Cover by Saint Jupiter
Gideon chapter art by Errol Exner
Dex chapter art by Zian Schafer
Editing by Ashley Oliver
Map created with Map Effects
Formatting made with Atticus

ISBN ePub: 978-0-473-64349-2
ISBN Kindle: 978-0-473-64350-8
ISBN Soft Cover: 978-0-473-64348-5

First Edition

TRIGGERS AND WARNINGS

Note: This book is not suitable for persons under the age of 18.

WARNING: This book contains sexually explicit scenes, adult languages, and violence. It may be considered offensive or disturbing to some readers. It is intended for sale to adults only, as defined by the laws of the country in which you made your purchase. Please store your files wisely, where they cannot be accessed by underage readers.

Triggers:

Death, violence, blood, gore and sex, groping (occurs once), poverty, thoughts of suicide, self-harm (palm is cut open for a spell), alluding to a miscarriage.

This is for everyone who wouldn't survive a single day in a fantasy setting.

PRONUNCIATION GUIDE

Acele - *Ah-cell-aye*

Aditi - *Ah-dee-tee*

Aywin - *Aye-win*

Callaia - *Call-eye-ah*

Callpaith - *Call-payth*

Dehran - *Day-raan*

Devereux - *De-ver-oh*

Ealrin - *Eel-rin*

Faeus - *Fae-yus*

Haemir - *Hay-mer*

Hadeon - *Hae-dee-on*

Hinixsus - *Hi-nix-sus*

Icoden - *Ee-ko-den*

Kaliak - *Ka-lee-ack*

Kikii - *Ki-kee*

Kriotz - *Kree-otz (rolled 'r')*

Kselia - *Ke-say-lea*

Mediel - *Ma-deal*

Mirya - *Mir-re-ya (rolled 'r')*

Nodisci - *No-dee-see*

Pater - *Pay-ter*

Rhaelson - *Rayl-son*

Rielway - *Reel-way (rolled 'r')*

Saeya - *Say-a*

Satrina - *Sa-tree-nah*

Vareso - *Vah-ray-so (rolled 'r')*

Vencen - *Ven-sen*

Volducan - *Vold-oo-can*

Xonas - *Zo-nas*

Zarlor - *Zar-lore*

PANTHEON

Acele - *Goddess of Love*

Aditi - *The Great Mother of All*

Callaia - *Goddess of the Moon*

Dalthorn - *God of War*

Dehran - *God of the Sun*

Hadeon - *God of Destruction, the Missing God*

Kriotz - *Goddess of Trickery*

Mediel - *God of Sports and Communication*

Pater - *The Great Father of All*

Rielway - *Goddess of Life and Agriculture*

Satrina - *Goddess of Hell, Queen of the Dead*

Vareso - *God of Wisdom*

GLOSSARY OF TERMS

Ama - *A Sarioan term for 'mother'*

Black Bloods - *A part orc, part ogre species that lives in Renlork and protects the hole into Hell*

Blue Surud - *A mouthless creature that communicates telepathically.*

Callpaith - *A species with a third eye that can sense when a lie is told*

Crystal Spear - *An elite force of soldiers within Hinixsus*

Ealgate - *The closest kingdom to Renlork*

Hinixsus - *The Kingdom of the Moon, home of the lunar elves, Callaia's kingdom*

Kaliak - *A monster of pure chaos*

Kikii - *A small, harmless creature that eats rubbish*

King Haemir - *King of Lodaxo*

King Rhaelson - *King of Hinixsus*

King Nodisci - *King of Volducan, the "One True God" or the "False God"*

Lodaxo - *A kingdom built along a mountain, also known as the kingdom of ice and snow*

Onaf - *A poisonous creature that lives in the woods*

Paragon Dawn - *Believers of King Nodisci, followers of the self-proclaimed god*

Renlork - *Home of the Black Bloods and the hole into Hell*

Sario - *A kingdom on the west*

Taravene - *The Kingdom of Wealth and Riches*

Volducan - *Home to the Followers of the Paragon Dawn*

Voren - *Descendent of ogres, a large humanoid creature with tusks*

Zarlor - *The Kingdom of Lawlessness*

PROLOGUE

"She'll bring us back, on the last blood moon," the Great Mother whispers in the darkness, echoing through the minds of the gods and goddesses willing to listen.

The time is coming: the death of the Divine, and the reign of kings. Chaos will bleed through the eight kingdoms until the only sound tainting the air will be the cries of those dying in battle. It will be a war with more than one end in sight.

"There must be another way." The objection of the gods rumbles through the winds, traveling to each corner of the earth, meant only for the ears of the divine. "It is done," the Father of Gods' voice pierces through the protests, silencing them. "Only eleven of us remain. Hear me when I say: *When the Kings come, they will serve your head on a platter. They will drain your blood into their gilded chalice, and you will die.*"

"My people will protect me—the moon will not let me pass," Callaia's harmonic voice sings, but for once it does nothing to fill their veins with peace, something that will soon become foreign. Though her words are filled with confidence, she knows that the greed of kings is greater than their loyalty to the divine.

"I have seen your death, dear sister," Vareso speaks before the havoc brewing amongst them can erupt. "As I have seen the inevitability of all our deaths." For Vareso sees all; he has seen the death of every God time and time again, even his own. He has felt King Nodisci's claws gouge out Vareso's own eye, and still, he will stand before Nodisci—a mere fae—and let him draw the god's last breath. "We need not be afraid, my brothers and sisters, for she will save us. *The Daughter of the Blood Moon*."

DEX

CHAPTER ONE

"If you're going to kill someone, try to do it tidily. You just ruined my new dress." I scowl, watching the crimson beads seep into the indigo fabric.

There's something about Vencen's face that triggers me. My rage knows no bounds when it comes to him.

Since I escaped, he has become one of my greatest regrets. Loneliness, boredom, and rebellion are toxins that plague the mind into doing wretched things. No one tells you how to cope when you keep making the same mistakes over and over again, even once the toxin has left your system. He's an ex-lover that never seems to stay in the past.

Over the neatly stacked books, I can see the satyr's life drain from his face as his blood soaks into the worn carpet.

"The bastard made me go into Black Blood territory for some book, and then he tries to tell me that it's the wrong one?" Vencen hisses, cleaning his bloodied blade with the creature's fur. "He was offering big money for it, but now he doesn't want to pay up."

I school my features into nonchalance, the same look I've plastered on my face since he told me about the book of spells. I've been itching to get my hands on it, to go through the pages to see if it has a spell to break my curse or summon the witch who cast it. But I haven't, because that's the only thing Vencen is capable of respecting: the goods he procures, and the money that comes with them. We don't play show and tell during a job—we never let the other person see our client's goods unless they can't or won't pay.

I try to distract myself from the Kingdom of Zarlor's humidity, twirling a knife between my fingers to stop from peeling the fake baby bump from my skin. The horrendous thing is the perfect disguise in such a wretched place. Rising from the settee, I leave the knife on the table and take another look around the study and at the book that caused the satyr's death: plain, simple, dull. It doesn't look like something worth going into Black Blood territory for. It looks like it belongs here, sitting neatly atop stacks of paper, perched just next to a scroll detailing some philosophical theory.

I stare at the dead creature, studying the crystal hanging from his neck, the silver on his horns, and the chains dripping from his wrist. I've stopped feeling sorrow for the dead, only pity. The sign on the door said he's just an academic. No one on an academic's wage working out of their own quarters can afford such fine things. The only explanation is that he's an informant. The main question is, who tasked him with finding the book?

"If he has so much money, then you shouldn't have killed him." I snag a gold bracelet from a shelf and tuck it into my bustier. I may not be a princess anymore, but that doesn't mean that I've stopped liking pretty things.

"It's a matter of principle, Dex. They ask for it, I get it, they pay for it." As he moves around, the black feathers of his wings barely catch the stack of books piled haphazardly on the floor.

"Principle doesn't mean shit when Zarlor is crawling with Black Bloods and you're here with something you stole *from them*."

I should judge him for killing a non-paying customer, but I'd be a hypocrite for doing so. Non-payment is just bad business. Not to mention he knows what would happen to me if *any* of the kingdoms caught me. I'd be dead by sundown—or worse: married.

I take a deep breath in an attempt to soothe the red cornering my vision caused by his very presence. Vencen may be a fully grown man, but he acts like a child when someone tells him that he's wrong.

"Besides, non-paying customers deserve a fate far worse than death," I say, and he flicks me a smug grin in response. I admit, I've cut off a finger or two in my time out of the palace.

He starts rummaging through the room, ignoring the scrolls and going straight for the things that shine, shoving it into his spelled satchel that never fills. The book he stole catches my eye like a temptress far more enchanting than a siren drenched in diamonds. Like a moth to a flame, it simply isn't a call I can ignore.

Running my fingers over the frayed leather binding, a low hum ripples through me, vibrating through my hands and down my back as the smell of sage fills my senses. I don't know what the book holds, but whatever is within the pages is potent and worth the money the satyr was willing to pay. At least I would have thought so.

"What were you contracted to get?" I question with newfound curiosity, forgetting all about my schooled boredom.

He looks over his wings, baby blue eyes wide with bewilderment, like he's completely forgotten why we're here. Digging my nails into my palm, I have to stop myself from tapping the table as he tests my patience.

He shrugs. "He called it the Book of Twilight, or something about a Weapon of Kings. I'm not sure. I stopped listening after he told me the 'what', 'where' and 'how much'."

This could be it. I might have finally found a spell that I've spent the past eight years looking for. None of the other spells I found were strong enough to summon the witch who cursed me. A book powerful enough to be a weapon for kings *must* have a summoning spell.

It has to.

I could stop running. I could stop hiding from every follower of the Paragon Dawn and Hinixian that I see. I could finally be my true self.

"But it's a fake," he sighs, turning back to the shelf.

Shutting my eyes, I lean against the desk. I should've known better than to get excited. Hope is for fools. And fools get caught. Just once, I'd like to have a lead, to see the light just within my reach. Instead, the weight of the prophecy threatens to suffocate me with each passing day.

"I almost died because of that bloody thing," he mutters. "Some Black Blood tried to eat my wings as soon as I got through the pass." He shudders at the thought. "The book is yours. I never want to see it again."

Yanking the book off the table, I shove it into my bag before he changes his mind. Whether it's fake or not, a spellbook is still a spellbook. If I'm going to pretend to be a witch, I might as well know some of their charms and invocations to really sell the act. We elves don't need the grandeur of incantations just to throw someone out of a window, however, being a witch would solve all of my problems.

As soon as the book leaves my touch, the smell of sage disappears, replaced by the stench of fresh blood clinging to the back of my throat, and I swear I can taste its tanginess. There are many things people deserve to die for. This was not one of them. I did nothing to stop Vencen, so the least I can do is let the satyr rest in peace.

The fake bump twists against my stomach as I lower myself to my knees next to the satyr. I should feel sorrow, guilt, or even pity that he died. But all I see is a man who didn't play the right cards, and all I feel is a deep fear that one day I may follow suit, and everyone I've lost would have been for nothing.

My thumb touches his skin, closing his eyelids. He feels as warm as a living person. I can't help but wonder who the satyr got involved with, where he was willing to pay someone to steal from the Black Bloods, especially when he lives so close to Renlork, their territory.

Placing my hand on his still warm forehead, I close my eyes. Dipping my head down until it touches the floor, a sign of respect for the corpses withering beneath the earth, then raising my head to pay homage to the moon, I whisper, "In the shadow of the light, and the tides of the deep, through sundown shall you find peace."

Opening my eyes, I rise to my feet, ignoring the way my necklace buzzes from saying the Lunar Elves' prayer for the dead. It's the only practice of my people that I still follow.

"You know you don't need to do that anymore, right? Your god is dead. All the gods are dead, so nothing matters anymore." Vencen shoves a porcelain jar into his satchel.

I shake my head. They died long before I was born, but still, every day I wish for Callaia to return, the Goddess of the Moon. Not just because she kept my father in check, but so she can kill him for his betrayal of her.

Even though only eleven of the twelve Divine remained after Hadeon's disappearance, how that deplorable man managed to kill a goddess is beyond me.

There's only one cure for all of my troubles: the death of kings.

"You can keep your religion. This is mine." He grins, pulling out a knife from his scabbard and pointing it at the creature's silver-tipped horns. "If you help me saw them off, I'll give you a pretty penny for it."

I don't bother hiding my scowl. "I want no part of your black-market filth." Admittedly, it was a poor choice in words because I trade in black-market goods. My morals may be slim when it comes to the trades I do in my line of business, but I draw the line at dismembering a creature for coin when their body is still warm.

He shrugs, squatting down and wrapping his fingers around the silver-tipped horns. "Hate it all you want, but the fact of the matter is that black-market trading is the right place to be with the war between Volducan and Renlork. You won't need to mess around with procurement if you get a month's wages with one of these." He taps on the horn.

"With all the Black Bloods and their hellhounds crawling in from Renlork, you won't make it far before they sniff you out. Especially with gods knows what you have in that bag." I genuinely wonder what ungodly things he holds in his satchel.

What I want to say is that he's a selfish prick with zero modicum of decency for anything. I would have let someone kill him long ago if it weren't for the fact that my adoptive mother would be heartbroken if he died.

"Then I guess I'll need a strong *princess* to keep me safe," he mocks. "I've booked myself a nice inn for tonight. It would be such a shame for lonely ol' me to have it all to myself. You can do that thing you do with your tongue again."

Bile makes its way up my throat. The man doesn't cease to make me ill. I can't believe I used to fall for that—and that I fell for it more than once. Regardless, he knows that I will never go back with him if I get my hands on a new spellbook. He's always known where my priorities lie.

"I'm doing this for you, not me," he says with a wink. "You're in Zarlor, the Kingdom of Lawlessness. That's all the more reason to come back to my inn. None of the Black Bloods will bother you if they see a simple man walking his pregnant wife—might I add that you always look dashing with a bump."

A shiver rolls up my spine from the thought of ever raising a child in this political climate. "I hate kids."

I want all thoughts of my disguise out of my mind. Especially when my mother is such an *exemplary* vision of everything a mother *shouldn't* be. It's one of the many reason I hate the baby bump disguise, but out of every trick in the book, this is by far the best one. Most people in Zarlor stop seeing a person as soon as they see any kind of bump. In truth, if there's one thing I hate more than children, it's the thought of any part of my body going near him again.

"That was a long time ago, and my tongue will never do that again," I say through gritted teeth.

"It's your favorite inn. Remember we tried—" he starts to speak, but my hands snap to cover his mouth before he can utter another word. My ears perk up from the sound of wood creaking under slow heavy footsteps.

Someone's here. They must have smelt the blood.

Fucking Vencen.

"Run," I hiss.

The room erupts into a flurry of movement as we snatch our bags off the table, attempting not to make a single sound. I run toward the back door on quiet feet, a pointless attempt at escaping undetected when Vencen knocks over a pitcher as he tries to get to the back door.

My heart thunders against my chest as the creaking grows louder. More frantic. More erratic. There's more than one person coming.

This can't be how I get caught. I refuse to let that winged male be the cause of my demise.

He pulls the door open, slipping out the door without sparing me a single glance. The footsteps grow closer, and mine move faster. A waft of humidity stains my skin as I make it out of the door, giving up on being silent and slamming it shut behind me.

Sand and stone crunch under my boots, skidding through the alleyway as I sprint in the opposite direction of Vencen. I don't turn back. Not when the door crashes open just as I make it onto the main street. I want to look. I want to know who it was and what they wanted. But I can't let them see my face. No disguise will work if they know my face.

My hands snap to my bag, feeling for the outline of the book. Even through the fabric, I can feel the hum of its power, but I just can't tell if it is a beautiful melody or an ear-piercing screech. It's an unnecessary distraction from my immediate peril.

Moving my hand away and pulling the strap onto my shoulder, I join the flow of civilians heading toward the market. I swallow the lump in my throat as I fall into character: a pregnant maiden.

I can hear footsteps pummel onto the street behind me, and it takes everything in me not to turn around to see who almost captured me.

Slowing my pace down and cradling the cushion beneath my smock, I try to sell the act, grimacing from the feel of the moist fabric pushing into my skin, soaking up my sweat.

I strain my senses, listening for the sound of their footsteps and the urgency of their breaths. I can hear them, standing there, searching the crowd for me. For us.

Walking to the closest food stall, I barely look at the horned male as I hold up one finger and drop a coin in his hand, asking for whatever it is he's selling.

Don't turn around, I remind myself as every part of me aches even for the slightest peek. Maybe just one look won't hurt?

The horned stall owner shoves something warm into my hand and turns to the patron next to me. "Lamb wrap," the vulture-like man squawks at him.

I look down at the warm flatbread in my hand, and deeply inhale the aroma of the roasted lamb... *gross.* I hate lamb.

I'll still eat it, though, once I get back to my temporary home.

Shoving the wrap into my satchel and merging back into the flow of people, I can no longer tell if the people from the satyr's study are still on the prowl. It could have been Black Bloods in there, but their kind doesn't believe in stealth. Whoever it was at least *tried* to sneak in unsuspected. I guess they didn't expect elf ears to pick them up.

Though clouds cover the sky, I can still feel the weight of the sun battering me down. Sucking my life force bit by bit. After eight years of living in the daylight, it still doesn't get any easier. My kind wasn't born to live under the sun, but to thrive in the moonlight.

I keep walking until I find a shaded area on the outskirts of the market. People tend not to notice someone standing in a corner, especially when there's never a dull moment in the center of the market. No one bats an eye when a group of kids snags fruits off a stall, or when a vendor gets into a knife fight with a customer.

My hand touches the rough wall behind me, and I let what little magic I have course through my veins and tickle my fingers, burning the wall with a half oval and marking the spot where I'll meet my client tomorrow. She wants to be inconspicuous, and this place is beyond her husband's suspicion. He would never question her going to the market.

I stay there, watching as patrons argue with merchants, and spot children pocketing their latest treasure from unsuspecting bystanders. Then I hear it. The familiar swishing sound that haunts my dreams rings through my ears, turning every fiber of my being cold. I press against the wall as if he might not see me if I stay flush to the stone surface.

The man who smells like ice yet tastes like fire. The man who lives in the shadows of my nightmare and taints my sweetest of dreams.

He's found me again.

DEX

CHAPTER TWO

I DON'T KNOW WHO he is or who is paying him. Whether it's my father or the self-proclaimed god, neither of them are good news. Each day is a guess as to whether he will finally decide to make his presence known by confronting me. Maybe father will send Aywin after me, and the elf could let me down all over again.

Though they contradict, I believe in fate and coincidences, but neither of those two things are what his presence represents. Regardless of which of the eight Kingdoms I have been hiding in the last eight years, he finds me. Since that first time, he has been the most constant force in my life. Every few weeks, I hear him again.

I creep back around the corner of the building, watching him from across the market. His dark hair is always pulled taut in a bun, and he always wears the same dark gray robe. The only reason I know that he is of Sario lineage is because of his narrow, hooded eyes.

Our eyes have never locked, and as far as I am aware, we have never been in the same room. I'm not simple enough to believe that my disguises have been so convincing that he has never spotted me when I have spotted him a thousand times over.

He's waiting for something. Orders from a king perhaps? It has crossed my mind that maybe he's following me because he, too, is hunting down the witch who cursed me into becoming the Daughter of the Blood Moon, and therefore made my life a living hell. If that's the reason, then I only ask that I can have the killing blow. Whatever his reason, it would be in my best interest *not* to be in his vicinity when he decides to act.

Wiping my clammy hands on my dress, I slink into the closest alleyway with the single goal of putting distance between me and my 'stalker.' Or as Ico, my mentor, says, "It's time to make like Hadeon and disappear."

The streets of Zarlor are always packed, which makes slipping away easier. Staying hidden, on the other hand? Not so much. People in my kind of work can spot anything hidden.

Flattening my hand on my lower back and leaning into it, I lead with my hips and let myself relish in as much wincing as my body allows. Kselia always calls this walk 'selling the fantasy,' because the fantasy in this instance is getting ignored for long enough to make my escape. Wincing is an easy feat when I am defying my species' very nature by being out in the sun.

As I walk, people look at me with pity, disgust, or lack of interest, then turn away instantly. *Welcome to Zarlor*. All eyes go towards the bump and nothing else, so my face is never registered in their memory. Perhaps they take notice of my brown hair color, but it's dyed often enough that by the time they see me again, I'll be another woman, except with black hair, or even red.

The disguise is foolproof until it comes to actual confrontation, especially if I have the misfortune of interacting with a creature that can hear heartbeats. I've learnt that the hard way.

The people crowding the streets begin to dwindle when I reach the outer part of the city. Quiet, but not peaceful. This is where real lawlessness begins. If I could get to the forest without passing such an area, I would. I'm simply not interested in spending a quarter of my day trying to get there.

My disguise falters as I walk past stacks upon stacks of cartons sitting atop a carriage, taunting me, and I stop in my tracks. Burnt into the side of the boxes is the emblem of my people: a crescent moon pierced by an arrow.

Hinixsus.

Without thinking, my hand reaches for my neck, looking for the opal necklace hidden safely under my dress. My fingers graze the outline to convince myself that it's still there, and that no one knows who I am or *what* I am. My entire lie hinges on the necklace.

Taking a step closer to the carriage, I twist my ring around my finger to stop from reaching out and touching the emblem. Each carton is rectangular in shape, and I know well enough that any goods from Hinixsus coming to Zarlor aren't food or decorations. It's weapons. And if there's a carriage full of Hinixian weapons, then there will be Hinixian soldiers nearby—or worse, there will be Black Bloods watching the whereabouts of the weapons. Our weapons are powered by the moon, perfect for anyone wanting to be well protected in the night. I should've known better than to stop.

My feet start moving without a second thought, springing into step faster than a person trying to be unsuspicious should. I can't let a Hinixian catch me. *I can't.*

"Ay', Miss," a graveled voice shouts from behind me, followed by a low, unearthly growl.

Shit. Shit. Shit.

I force myself to ignore my rapidly beating heart which twists in pain and exhaustion. I should never have stopped. I haven't been back since I was fifteen years of age, I shouldn't be as fazed as I am about seeing their symbol.

"Yes," I stutter as I turn to face the two Black Bloods and their hellhound. I was aiming to sound like a strong woman who had every right to be there, but what comes across was the far more truthful, anxiety-infused voice of a fearful woman.

They don't need to don any symbols of Renlork for me to figure out that they're Renlork's soldiers. If they're male and of age, they'll be a soldier if not a noble, and there's nothing noble looking about these two. They watch me with their black, pupil-less eyes that blend seamlessly into their obsidian-colored skin riddled with scales and bumps. Every time I see them, I think that it's only fitting that a creature so ghastly guards the Hole into Hell in Renlork.

"Empty yer sack," the taller Black Blood soldier orders, pointing a scaly brown finger at me.

Zarlor has changed.

They never used to be allowed to give out orders. But I guess that the Zarlorian King is so greedy that he will bend the knee to any usurper willing to fill his pockets with enough gold.

"He said empty yer sack," the shorter Black Blood barks when I don't react immediately. He steps forward, drawing his sword. The hound growls, stalking toward me in time with its master.

I can feel the book weighing heavily in my bag, reminding me of its existence. I rack my brain trying to recall exactly what it looks like. Could it pass off as an ordinary reading book? Will they sense its power as well?

They'd kill me on the spot if they thought I was a witch. They hate every creature that has access to divine power. Well, really, they hate fae, elves, and witches.

"Please, my husband is waiting for me," I beg, running my hand over my cushioned stomach to draw their attention to it. If they think I've been 'claimed' by a man, maybe they'll go easy.

"Now," the tall one snaps, and the hound barks at me, lunging so close that its head is a step away from ripping my chest out.

It stalks my every movement with blood red eyes, the hunch on its back accentuating the vicious curled horns atop its head. Up close, it makes sense that a creature so hideous crawled out of the hole in Renlork—or the more correct term: Hell.

I nod quickly, pulling the bag off my shoulder and saying a silent prayer to the dead gods that they won't pay the book any mind. I keep weapons on my person for reasons just like this. Discarding the contents onto the graveled ground, I suck in a sharp breath, watching as the two creatures laugh like they've won the lottery.

They step closer to inspect the items. I try studying them to see whether their gaze lands on the book, but their black eyes reveal nothing. The hound is instantly drawn to the lamb wrap packed tidily in a cloth. One man's nose twitches in acknowledgment, as well.

Thank you, Callaia, I mutter in my head.

The smaller one hisses at me, and I step back, grinding my teeth and fidgeting with my hands in anticipation of their next move.

Please don't notice the book. Please don't notice the book.

A throaty laugh grates my ears as the short one yanks the wrap off the ground, kicking the vegetables and the books to the side. His sharpened teeth bite into it, and the hellhound whimpers, begging for a bite as well.

The tall one snatches the wrap out of the other's hands, taking a bite as he steps toward me, standing so close that his stomach almost touches the bump. "Nex' time, I won't ask twice," he spits.

"Yes, sorry." I stumble back and bow my head to make them feel like they've won. They turn away to squabble over who should get the last bite. My breath catches in my chest as the hellhound loses interest in the wrap, and slowly strides toward the books with its ears perked.

"May I go?" I say loudly to catch the Black Bloods' attention before they notice the hound no longer cares about the wrap and its suspicions are clearly elsewhere. I try not to look at the beast in case I betray my intentions.

Both men snap their attention toward me, and it takes everything not to flinch. "Did I say yer could speak?" the smaller one snarls.

I shake my head quickly, hanging my head low and stepping to the side, *away* from the hound as it starts to sniff the book. I need a distraction, but the beast will be able to smell any magic I use. The necklace is the only reason that the hound doesn't smell the magic on me. It's one of the only things stopping them from realizing that I'm the Daughter of the Blood Moon.

As they start to turn away again, my eyes dart around the street trying to figure out another distraction before the hellhound alerts its master.

Now would be a good time for the elven soldiers to arrive so the Black Bloods can take their torments elsewhere and leave me be so I can finally see what powers lie in that book. Despite such things, I'd rather fight a Black Blood than any of the fae or elves. The orc lineage within the Black Bloods means they're brutal fighters, but they don't fight dirty like the fae. Or elves. When we fight, there are no rules, attacking from the shadows.

A roar echoes through the street, and the beast starts to growl only to whimper away, scurrying behind its masters with its tail tucked between its legs. It looks no more fearsome than the average dog. I spin in my spot, blood rushing through my ears, searching for whatever it is that managed to make the beast scared.

The two Black Bloods draw their axes, rusted with dried blood, searching the windows and roofs around us. My fingers wrap around the cold hilt of my knife sheathed within my dress.

This isn't good. Only something big and ugly could scare a hellhound.

"Come out," the taller one growls, and I realize this is the perfect opportunity to take my leave. I'll let the Black Bloods deal with whatever monster skulks in the streets.

Moving faster than a pregnant woman would, I shove my belongings back into my bag: an apple, bag of coins, a jar of poultice, a scarf, and the book. As soon as the last item is pushed into the bag, I throw the strap across my body so it sits next to the cushion. With each heartbeat, my blood runs colder and colder. The Black Bloods don't spare me a second glance as I leave.

What really causes prickles to rain over my skin is the look of fear the hellhound gives me. Not me, my stomach. Spinning on my heels, I search, gripping the blade tightly in my hand. But all that stands in my way is a broken door and a bucket of piss.

I scramble away before the Black Bloods change their mind about letting me go. I want to run, but now is not the time, especially if there could be something roaming the streets. I don't want to be anyone's target unless I've intentionally made it so.

As I walk, I scan the street, analyzing every piece of material hanging across balconies, every piece of rubbish that floats past, and every creature that I can see. Even as I walk through the forest and make it to the smaller settlements, I still search my surroundings. Something doesn't feel right. I can't quite grasp what it is. Everyone I walk past seems calm, like it's an ordinary day, but I can feel it in my bones. It doesn't feel like I'm being followed. I've never felt anything like it. The only way I can describe it is that something is here.

I take deep breaths, trying to dispel the tension rising in my chest. Only when the streets change into greenery and the leaves hide the fleeting sun does it feel like I can breathe again. Still, the sensation follows me deep into the forest.

Pulling out another blade just in case, I keep all my senses open. As the sound of running water fills the air and the feeling remains in place, my only option is to rationalize with myself about how something is *not* here. Because I would have seen and heard it already. If someone or something were following me, they'd have attacked.

The weight sitting on my chest could be from the fact that I dealt with the people in the satyr's study, my stalker *and* the Black Bloods. That's more than anyone should deal with in a single day. I may well just be spooked by the hellhound, nothing more. Maybe the hellhound was having a bad day as well?

Passing the last settlement before the thick of the forest, I try to ignore all the possibilities and focus on the present. There's no point stirring over 'ifs' and 'buts' when my stomach is grumbling and the layer of sweat that once coated my skin has turned into a sticky mess.

I need to focus. There are too many poisonous plants around here, and I can't risk stepping on one of them.

In truth, I don't really need to focus, I know this path like the back of my hand—every branch, fallen tree, and poisonous bush. I could make it safely to my cave with my eyes closed, but it's a good enough excuse to forget about the hellhound.

The sound of running water turns into violent crashing. *Home.* A soft smile dances across my lips when the waterfall comes into sight. At the very top of the waterfall sits a red tree filled with the most luscious fruit that I've ever laid my eyes on, its vines climbing down the rocks sprouting flowers and thorns. When you're under the tree, all you hear is silence. No birds have made a home within the branches, no bugs burrow within the fruit.

Nature knows when things are poisonous. Yet somehow my mother has managed to keep a whole garden alive.

All around the waterfall, poisonous plants intermingle with safe ones. Only those with keen eyes and a background in herbology can tell the difference. Spotting the bush filled with green flowers that smell like acid, I hold my breath and jump over it to make it to the beach.

It's the very reason I've chosen to make the waterfall my home in Zarlor. Even monsters know better than to dare step on one of the plants and get impaled by a venomous thorn. Insects are another matter entirely. Their ability to adapt to their surroundings has always astounded me.

I drop onto the sand right on the edge of the lake with a sigh. As I dip my hands into the cool water, the cold bites my skin, but I welcome it with open arms. I cup the water, splashing my face as a small groan leaves my lips. Pressing my now frigid hands against the back of my neck, the tension disappears from my shoulders, and all memory of the "feeling" leaves with it.

Cold. That's what I needed.

Staring at my reflection in the water, I can just make out the darker layers of red-tinted hair at the nape of my neck, while the top leaves a silver glow. The silver and red hair combination are reserved for the Daughter of the Blood Moon, and unfortunately, there's only one of those—me. Most people are only so fortunate to have a prophecy associated with them, and only the rarest few are cursed as well.

Fear ripples through me that someone might have noticed my true hair because of the fading dye. But also, a tinge of excitement. There's something therapeutic about dying my hair.

Orange light casts the forest in an ethereal hue. Shadows dance along the ground, and birds chirp in the wind. I can feel my energy pick up as the sun starts to make its final descent across the sky. Which means the light will soon disappear.

Yanking my boots and socks off, I dip my toes in the water to calm myself. Shoving my hand into the bag, I suck in a sharp breath before wrapping my fingers around the book. Only this time, power doesn't thrum through me from the contact. It feels like any other ordinary book.

I pull it out and my fingers find their way to the light brown ribbed spine. Chuckling to myself, I open the first page and a waft of must hits my nostrils, as though the book is as old as time. Of course I wasn't going to be so lucky. Why did I think I'd find the one book that contains the spell I want?

My defeat only stings more when I turn the page: drawings of plants. Another page: poultice jars. Another page: healing crystals. Another page: cures for poisons. Snapping the book shut, I shove my face into my hands. Of course the book was useless. I shouldn't be surprised I didn't find a spell.

The only reason I felt any semblance of power from the book must have been because there was something else in that study.

"I need to stop getting my hopes up like this," I whisper to myself.

Talking to yourself out loud isn't normal, I admit. But it helps me cope.

My stomach grumbles for attention. The lost lamb wrap would have been the perfect thing to help me devour my defeat.

In the morning, I'll find someone to trade the book with. Its only selling points are that it's old and in a good state. There are enough books relating to healing out there that no one will really pay it any mind. I'll probably only get a single coin for it.

Jumping to my feet, I head to the closest non-poisonous berry bush with the book in hand. Fruits and nuts won't be enough to quench my insatiable hunger, but I'm in no mood to hunt for anything. I'd rather sleep.

Passing the juicy red berries, I head straight to the sickly brown ones that could be confused as rotten. One thing I learnt about Zarlor's forest is that the more revolting it looks, the safer it is to eat. The issue is when poisonous and non-poisonous berries grow on the same bush, like this one.

My fingers maneuver between the branches, carefully plucking the berries from its stems so as not to get pricked by a thorn. It is one of the few bushes with thorns that won't kill or seriously harm me. Still, I'd rather avoid scrapes.

Piling the berries on top of the book, I snicker to myself thinking that the book finally has some use to me. It almost feels like some kind of payback for all the trouble it has caused.

After some time, I look down at my makeshift plate and consider the fruit in my bag. I probably have enough food for tonight, but I keep piling so I can sleep in tomorrow and not worry about needing to forage. At least that's the excuse I'm sticking with, and not because the sun is minutes away from setting and the moon is now high in the sky, filling me with power that itches to be used, a power that I haven't accessed to its full extent in years.

With the moon's help, I pluck a hard-to-reach berry from its stem and watch as it floats in the air and lands in my hand. The residue of the lunar magic hangs faintly in the air from the small task, but not so much that hounds could smell it. Drawing power from the moon means that our well of strength is only available to us depending on when the moon rises and sets. The stronger elves can draw from her regardless of where she is in the sky. But still, even my father's powers are limited to the progression of the day.

The power of the blood moon on the other hand? The chasm that feels as if it has its own heartbeat, thumping besides my own. The kaleidoscope of stars and the oceans of tumbling blues and purples, a galaxy of untapped power. That? There is no end or beginning to the raw magic that pumps through my veins as if I might be equal to the moon.

So much potential is lost on me. I have no interest in it. More importantly, I can't use it. If I did, I would be a beacon for all eight kingdoms to track down. Either way, sticking to my hands keeps me feeling mortal. Whether that is a good or bad thing, I've yet to decide.

I keep picking until I have more than I actually need. My knees click when I stand back up to readjust the pile.

"Gods," I hiss through my teeth when a thorn pricks my finger. Bringing my pointer finger right up to my face, I watch as blood beads to the surface, and the dusk light reflects off the crimson. It's deeper than the average prick, but it'll still heal within a matter of minutes.

Wiping my finger on my dress and swapping the book into the pricked hand, I go back to my spot right by the water and watch the clouds swim across the sky, covering the full moon. Eating the berries, I bask in the moon's rays as I feel my necklace fight against my being's urge to glow silver.

My fingers skates over my chest, over where my mark should be. I can still picture the white crescent moon on the spot above my heart; one of the indications that I'm who the prophecy is about.

Through dusk and dawn, the shadow of the silver light will crack through obsidian and bring destruction to kingdoms. The heart of the crescent moon will win the war, in mayhem and in death.

Couple the prophecy with the curse—in which, somehow, I will bring the gods back to life—I become the biggest target in all eight kingdoms. It's only a question of whether the kings want to marry or kill me. Depending on how one interprets the prophecy to win the war, of course. And depending on whether one wants to utilize my curse by killing me to bring back the dead gods and end the war once and for all.

Either way, whether a king wants to win the war or end the war, both will likely lead to my death. King Nodisci of the Paragon Dawn, on the other hand, is one of the few that doesn't wish me dead. Yet. My betrothal to him is a sure sign that he wants to use me as a symbol, 'win my heart' and somehow win the war with it. I guess it's his way of keeping me alive, since the last thing he wants is for me to somehow bring the Divine back with my death, since he's the one who basically killed them all.

But I really don't see how I have the power to bring them back or win the war. I don't particularly want to find out.

The Black Bloods, on the other hand, do wish me dead. And they wanted me dead yesterday. They want to bring back their Goddess, Satrina, the Queen of Hell. Unfortunately, that means I have to die in order for their wish to come to fruition.

Looking back down at the book, my lips form into a tight line.

Oh great, now it's worth less than a coin, I think when I notice the dark patch near the top of my book. It's going into the fire now, not some pathetic trade. I'm not stupid enough to let someone have anything with my bloodstain on it. I've read of enough spells that could be used against me if I didn't destroy it.

"Screw this." I put my boots back on, push myself onto my feet, and walk towards the waterfall while carefully placing the remaining berries and book in the bag, hoping that they don't get crushed.

I can barely make out a puddle up ahead. Though you can't see them, there are always baby crabs in there. Jumping over it and making the last few steps to the rock, my fingers find their grip on the moist stone, and I pull myself up. It may be dark, but I can see everything perfectly as if it were daylight.

The jagged stone threatens to tear the skin off my fingers and rip through the cushion of my fake bump. With each weary pull, I readjust my footing and my grip, careful not to slip on algae as I angle myself toward the waterfall. Eventually, it roars at my back as I climb behind it. Water dampens my dress and hair, and a cold chill ripples through my body, which almost relaxes me. Pushing myself as close to the stone as I can, I start shuffling sideways to make the final few feet to the entrance of the cave.

I stumble inside to find the wondrous sight of my makeshift bed. Squatting down, I study the sand I poured at the entrance of the cave to catch any footprints. There's nothing but the pattern of my own boots. I sweep the sand until it's even before moving deeper within, my fingers glide over all my hidden spots, ones filled with coins, a client's necklace, and the odd filched jewelry within the cave, to make sure they've stayed undisturbed.

Dropping down onto the pile of blankets, I finally take the bump off and inhale deeply, relishing in the freedom my stomach is feeling. I change into tomorrow's dress and leave my boots on, like I always do when I sleep outdoors, and I shut my eyes, listening to the sound of the water.

Within seconds, sleep takes me.

DEX

CHAPTER THREE

AN EARTH-SHATTERING SCREAM ESCAPES my lips. My skin feels like it's being torn apart from the inside. Like something is trying to escape—power trying to break free.

"*Who are you*?" booms a voice.

Sweat coats my body, and I drag myself out of the thick blankets, trying to find the voice. But nothing moves in my cave. No figure. No noise. No smell. Just emptiness.

Screams that sound like they've been birthed from Hell rend through the night air, and more follow.

Slapping the ground next to me, my hand finds my bag and I throw it across the cave to get to my weapon beneath. I wrap my fingers around a short sword. Each movement feels like I'm being *granted* the right to move, like this body is only on loan to me.

"*I said, 'who are you'?*" the voice roars again. It sounds like it's here, everywhere and nowhere.

Clawing at my chest, I try to scream, but my words are taken from me. My lungs squeeze, and a sharp pain pierces my head. I can't see anyone. Surely, I'd *see* someone.

The sword drops out of my hand, and I try to reach for it. My fingers fumble for it, reaching for some semblance of protection. But my body doesn't move. It doesn't obey my own command. I can't even feel the power of the moon within my bones.

Maybe this is just a bad dream, like I'm falling and will wake up any second. I haven't had a bad dream in years. Maybe the hellhound affected me more than I realized.

The book catches my eye in the center of the cave, just out of my reach. A phantom wind turns page after page. Only this time, there are no flowers or spell jars. This time, symbols that I've only seen in temples drench the pages in the deepest crimson. I can just make out the symbol of an eye with arrows pointing up and down. Then I smell it.

Blood.

My blood.

"*How did you get that book?*" the voice bellows.

I inhale sharply, concentrating for the briefest moment, feeling something heavy seated in my mind. Not something, *someone.* My body starts to move of its own accord. Crawling sluggishly toward the book and pulling it into my arms.

I try to speak, but nothing comes out.

As my body nears the book, I realize that the pages aren't the only thing that has changed. Black vines crawl across the cover of the book, flowing and pulsing in time like it has a heartbeat. No, not vines, *veins*. They radiate out like thorned spirals from a crimson spot near the top of the book. The spot where my blood dropped.

"*What have you done, mortal?*" Each word the male voice says is filled with utmost horror.

"What are you?" I rasp. If I know what he is, I should be able to dispel him from my body. *Should*.

None of this should be happening. I'm the Princess of Lunar Elves. I'm wearing a necklace to protect me from tracking spells *and* possessions. Nothing—no one—should be able to possess me. That can only mean that whatever he is, he's far more powerful than I am.

"*Release me,*" he roars. My body vibrates, feeling as light as air, as something warm drips from my nose.

What? Release *him*?

My body starts to move again, and I can see every single thing in the room clearly–every hiding spot, every stone, and every drop of water.

It feels like I'm a passenger in a carriage, watching things go by even though I'm not moving. I can feel every bump, every turn, every breath. But none of them are mine. Nothing about my movements feels natural. It's like a child trying to walk for the first time.

"Let me go," I manage to whisper, but the male doesn't respond.

My head moves, forcing me to look at the blade lying on the floor, and my body homes in on it. My fingers wrap clumsily around the hilt like it might drop if I move too quickly.

I can hear his thoughts. But I can't make out the words. They're a torrent of panicked and rage-fueled murmuring, like the buzzing of angry wasps. His wrath seeps into me, mixing in with my fear as the hunger for death coats my tongue.

He wishes for my death.

No, no, no. Stop it! I scream inside my head like my body might listen.

Panic tears through the walls in my mind as I picture the man forcing the blade in me. Only he doesn't. He focuses on moving each step in front of the other like it isn't muscle memory for him.

With each step, my slouch disappears, and my movements become surer. The ground beneath my boots shifts from stone to sand as I make it to the entrance of the cave.

"Stop. Let me go," I croak.

"You first."

I try to fight against his hold, but nothing works, and I can't help but feel imprisoned in my own skin.

Before I can register his plan, water crashes from above me, drenching my hair and clothes. Then it's gone in an instant. Air rushes past me, as we make our descent. What is he doing? What is happening? There are rocks down there. He's going to kill me.

Only then do I realize that the jump was calculated. Executed with precision. We're heading far from the jagged rocks that jut out of the sand. My arm sticks out, aiming toward the ground with my forearm. Tucking my head down, sand rolls over my back and I find myself on both feet before I can blink.

Despite the terror, the first thought that crosses my mind is that I need to learn how to do that. The second thought is far worse: He's going to expose me. He may not know who I am, but if he finds out, he could ruin me, or he could be so reckless that he captures the attention of a Hinixian soldier, and it'll be over for me.

"Stop it," I try to say. He's learned how to control my body better now, and he's fighting my attempts at speaking.

"*You're the one who has trapped me,*" he says through my mouth. It's my own voice, and it's like I'm going crazy, talking without meaning to.

My head angles toward the sky, and I can feel him calculating something. The moon sits proudly in the center of the sky, and I can feel my eyes water. I can't feel her. I can't feel the moon. *Why can't I feel the moon?*

My body jolts into action at once, stomping over to a bush to pick the flower of the dead, then running my—our—eyes over the forest until it lands on whatever it is he's looking for. Breaking into a light jog, my damp dress catches the sand, weighing us down as we head in the direction of the thorniest bush in the clearing.

Don't you dare, I think when I can no longer speak.

I'm helpless, completely at his mercy. The harder I try to fight him, the stronger he becomes. My body feels lighter than it ever has, filled with a power that feels completely foreign to me.

It's his power; raw, chaotic, destructive.

It feels like I could control all eight kingdoms with it. If only I was in control.

As we near the bush, I spot the mushrooms scattered on the forest floor, tucked safely within the moss. My fingers plunge into the cool dirt, curling around the roots of the poisonous mushroom and scooping it out. Its yellow ooze coats my fingers, leaving a trail of pain in its wake.

Jumping back up, he takes us toward the widest part of the clearing. Laying the book, dagger, flower, and mushroom tidily in the middle, a single foot drags along the sand in a straight line, pivoting once we are twelve steps away from the book. He moves my body again, dragging my foot along the sand for twelve more steps, then pivots again, heading straight back toward the book.

A triangle.

I try everything I know to stop him and take back over: elven prayers, incantations, even reciting random spells I've seen in books—none of which will work unless the moon hears me say it.

He moves again, this time curving from one corner of the triangle to the flat line on the other side. Then he repeats the process and adds more curves, circles, arrows, and lines.

I may not be a real witch, but I've seen enough spellbooks to know that this is not a sigil used by witches. It's something else entirely.

Standing back, he studies the sigil, nodding to himself before turning toward the lake. I hiss internally as the chill of the liquid bites my skin. We stare intently at the water that ripples the reflection of the moon as we wade through it.

We stop, holding our breath for reasons beyond my understanding. We stand there for minutes that feels like lifetimes, leaving me to stew. Without warning, our hand spears through the water, wrapping around the slippery body of a fish. Yanking our hand out of the water, the fish struggles within our grasp, threatening to slip away, but we hold firm.

He moves us through the water quicker this time, increasing our speed the closer we get to the shore. Walking around the symbol, he drops the fish on the ground, exchanging it for the dagger before moving to the center of the sigil. Pulling it out of its holster, my soul ignites with a fire of renewed desperation.

No. What is he doing with the dagger?

He begins chanting in a language I don't understand. It doesn't sound familiar at all. But as he speaks, I can feel *his* power within me thrum rapidly, coursing through my veins in a crescendo. It gets stronger and stronger, suffocating my soul like it's kicking me out.

Like *he* is kicking *me* out.

No! Don't! I try to scream, *This isn't a body that you want. You'll be a target!* I don't know if he can hear. but I scream them all the same. Begging for mercy.

Bringing the tip of the blade to my open palm, my necklace heats. It's trying to fight his magic; a power that wants my blood. He can use any magic *but* blood magic. As long as my necklace is on, my blood will be tainted. There's no telling what will happen to the spell.

Stop it. You need to stop!

We don't even wince as the tip pierces my skin so deep that blood instantly pools at the surface. In the back of my mind, relief soothes some of my worries, but only makes others grow. I'm bleeding plain red, which means the necklace is holding true, and my identity is kept hidden. *No*, my blood will be false. If the necklace were broken, silver specs would glitter in the crimson.

Shit.

Shit. Shit. Shit.

Angling our hand so that blood drips into the sand, we stare up at the sky as his—our—chants echo through the forest. Monstrous screams that don't belong to us breaks through the night, yet they sound dull compared to the chants which have ensnared my soul. Clouds begin moving through the sky rapidly, darkening the lands, and with it comes a storm that engulfs the moon. Thunder brews within the obsidian clouds, and silver bolts crackle through its void.

The darkness is calling me. The chaos is summoning me with its claws. I know that it is tricking me into believing that I might have a choice about submitting to it.

But I won't let him take me. I would rather die than let him turn my body into his permanent vessel. I don't know what he is, or who he is, but I'll find a way to kill him if he does.

His chants continue, and my wound stays wide open, unhealing. The power of the spell is hungry for more blood, drawing it from my hand until it starts pouring onto the ground as violently as the waterfall. Spots dance in my vision and my body becomes weightless.

Lightning tears through the sky and blinds my vision, striking me directly in my heart, burning my lungs until it sears into my soul. The single split-second feels like an eternity. Everything that has happened in my life reverberates through my mind in a series of heart-wrenching images: my father's betrayal, King Nodisci's proposal, my brother's death, my sister's execution... I'm living through the pain all over again.

My blood boils. My flesh feels like it is ripping from my bones until my body splinters and fuses back together. I can't scream. I can't breathe. I want to forget all the suffering. I want the pain to end.

When the lightning leaves my body, I drop onto the cold sand. The agony isn't there anymore, but the memories still remain.

My body reacts to my wild emotions, and I instinctually clutch my necklace, rubbing the smooth unharmed stone over and over and over and savoring the image of my sister's smile—the last time she ever smiled.

My muscles tense as a shadow flickers from the corner of my vision, and my fingers curl into a tight fist. Ignoring the blood creeping between the gaps of my fingers, I revel in the feeling of my skin stitching together layer by layer.

I have my body back.

The moon's energy slams into me. It feels like home, but somehow so foreign at the same time. It has been a long time since I've felt its power flowing through me when the moon is at her peak and most potent. It isn't as intoxicating as his power, but even the moon can still be savage.

It's time to see who will be the recipient of my wrath.

I leap onto my feet, pulling out the knife hidden within my boot. Ready for someone else's blood to be spilled tonight.

Lightning cracks through the sky as the clouds tear to let the harsh glow of the moonlight rip through. Hair darker than obsidian cascades across his face, and light descends down his cheeks, curving like a scythe across his jaw, chiseled by the God of War. Every breath barrels into his broad chest, consuming the air around him as warfare rages across his savage stare.

Before me stands a man who looks like he can make entire kingdoms crumble into ash. A hurricane molded into being to become the most beautiful of disasters.

Before me stands the man who possessed me.

DEX

CHAPTER FOUR

HE DOESN'T LOOK AT me, straining his shoulders and clenching his fist so tightly that his trembling knuckles turn white. His ragged breaths stumble upon themselves like he has forgotten how to breathe.

"Who are you?" I growl, repeating the same words he first said to me. Only this time, my knife is drawn, held in a death grip as the dagger he used lies bloodied and discarded behind me.

The pale skin of his forehead creases, and his lips curl into a venomous scowl. He pays my movement no mind, undeterred by the weapon in my hand like I'm pointing a spoon to the base of his throat.

Anger starts to glimmer in his eyes—eyes that stare intently at his tremoring fist.

"I said *who are you*?" I step closer to him.

The raw power of the moon ripples through my veins, itching my fingertips in a dangerous dance of control and absolute carnage. My necklace hums peacefully against my chest, reminding me that I'm the one who chooses when to harness the power, not the moon.

I am not the curse.

I am not the prophecy.

Deep concentration etches his face as he starts puffing his chest, bringing his arms away from his side and back down as his chest deflates. Almost like he's trying to summon something.

Screw it, I think. Letting the magic seep into my muscles, I pounce, aiming straight for his throat.

I move fast, but he moves faster, jumping to the side like a shadow chased out by the light. His fingers spread wide to summon energy to attack me. A flicker of confusion darkens his eyes, and I take it as my opening. With the moon's strength coursing through me, I lunge for him with all my might, shoving him until his back hits a tree.

The blade catches the light as I push it against his throat and relish in the thought of splitting his skin open just as he did to mine. His frame towers over mine and it takes everything in me not to cower in response.

"Let me say this *one* more time," I hiss through my teeth, glaring up at his unamused eyes. "Who are—"

The world around me spins as the knife is jerked out of my hand, tumbling across the beach until it skitters into the water. A breathless grunt forces through me when my chest hits the coarse surface of a tree. A calloused hand wraps around my throat while his other arm pushes me into his headlock against the tree, but halts before my face makes contact with it.

"You're mistaken if you think you're in any position to be asking the questions, little witch." His chest rumbles against my back with each word that he snarls in my ear. It shudders through me more powerfully than when he was possessing me.

My gaze casts to the rocks edging the line between the forest and the beach. Stretching my fingers, tendrils of silver power ripple within me.

"I don't make mistakes." I flex my fingers. Grinning while watching as several rocks hurtle through the air towards us. But he doesn't flinch when each rock misses its target, flying straight past his head.

"Did you just try to throw rocks at me?" he says in disbelief.

How did every single rock miss? Gritting my teeth in frustration, I summon the moon's power into my muscles once again. The fabric of my skirt struggles against me as I shove my knee into the space between me and the tree. Using my free leg, I push off with the full power of the moon.

We barrel through the air with my head firmly in the crook of his inner elbow. His hold doesn't loosen until we are parallel to the ground. With the amount of power used, I expect us to land in the middle of the lake, yet we don't make it more than a couple paces from the tree.

I scramble away from him, heading straight for the knife. My fingers find comfort in its familiar weight, and I spin on the balls of my feet to find him standing and readjusting the collar of his coat.

Aiming the knife at him once again, I say, "If you won't tell me who you are, then at least tell me *what* you are."

"I believe I'm the one entitled to those answers when you are the one who woke me." I don't miss the raw edge of his voice, a clear indication that his patience is dwindling when he's the one who ruined *my* night.

"No, you woke *me* up."

He looks at me for a brief moment like he's debating some kind of strategy. "This is a waste of my time," he grunts before turning away from me with ethereal grace and marching into the forest without sparing me a second glance.

I stare at his receding figure with dismay. What just happened?

He possessed me, drew a symbol that I've never seen before to conduct a spell using *my* blood, then he accuses me of waking *him* up.

Eying the book, I blink a few times to ensure I wasn't hallucinating when I saw what had happened to it. At a glance, it looks exactly the same with veins stemming from my patch of blood wrapped around the book. Except it isn't pulsing anymore. The blood within the veins remains idle, waiting to be fed to create havoc.

I won't approach the book, not until I'm certain he won't come back. I can't hear the leaves beneath him crunch under the weight of his footsteps, which causes my skin to prickle from the eerie silence. The muscles along his back are still taut as he strains like he's trying to summon something.

Just as he is about to disappear out of sight, the blood drains from my face. A cloud of smoke swallows him whole. Gripping the blade tighter, I bring my hands up in front of me, shifting my feet into a fighting stance. In a blink of an eye, the same smoke appears beside me, bringing with it the man who possessed me.

"I thought you were leaving," I say through gritted teeth, but it doesn't stop the surprise from leaking into my voice. There are very few creatures and people I know of that can teleport, and he is none of them. He's far too 'pretty,' and his ears aren't pointed like the fae.

He opens his mouth like he is about to say something, when he seems to spot the book from the corner of his eye. "I forgot my book." Uncertainty lingers behind his confidence.

His book.

What could he have to do with it? Has he been after it just like the men at the study? The satyr said it's the wrong book, but clearly neither he nor the people at the study believed that.

He notes my weapon this time, walking backward toward the book as if he finally perceives me as a threat. Snatching the book from the ground, he marches back into the forest like he is about to set it aflame. The book appears so miniscule in his hand that it's hard to believe it holds any real power.

It isn't lost on me that the answers I seek could be written in my blood on those pages. Is it worth the fight trying to pry it from his hands? Is the attention the book will gather worth a glimpse at those pages? The answer I seek might not even be in there. Not to mention that the book is now written in symbols that I don't understand.

The critters in the forest come out from their hiding spots, filling the air with harmony that breaks the ghostly silence. His figure starts to dwindle out of sight and my form eases slightly, only to be reignited when a plume of smoke engulfs him, and he appears beside me.

This time I don't leave my safety to my knife. Power courses through me ready to blast him with energy.

"Don't play games with me." My patience is wearing dangerously thin. I should be asleep in bed, dreaming about what I could have bought with the single coin I'd get from the book.

"You speak when spoken to, mortal." He doesn't look at me when he talks. However thin my patience might be, the look in his eyes tells me that his is far thinner. The muscles in his jaw ticks in time with his footsteps as he marches through the forest once again.

I bite my tongue to stop myself from saying something that will make me lose any more sleep than I already have. The sooner he leaves, the sooner I can get on with my life.

Just as he's about to leave my line of sight, shadows engulf him, and he reappears right next to me.

He throws his hand out at me, fingers spread and palm toward me. The vein in his forehead throbs along with the fury blazing in his eyes. I fling my arm up, blocking whatever magic he casts my way, but nothing comes.

Throwing another hand up, the sound of his frustrated groan fills me with misplaced joy. My shield holds firm, and I can't help the amusement spreading through me from his attempts.

"What have you done to me, witch? Where are my wings?" he roars, and the critters of the forest go silent.

He thinks that I am a witch? Good. Let's keep it that way.

"You possessed me! I didn't do anything." Except of course bleed on *his* book.

"Oh, you did *something*." He takes a step toward me, and my soul seems to fold in on itself from his presence. "No one in possession of the Book of Twilight is innocent." Each word oozes with raw disdain.

"It was just a random book of tonics," I retort, knowing that it is anything but a "random book." The look of offense is enough of an indication to confirm my suspicions that the satyr died for nothing, and Vencen did exactly what was asked of him.

"This book is more important than anything in your *measly* life," he spits.

If only he knew.

"You have your book, now leave." Waves crash along the shore, reacting to my emotions that twirl in a dangerous dance with my and the moon's power.

Breathe, I tell myself, *calm down.*

"I'm not going anywhere, *darling*." His voice is low. Lethal. It is sharpened to precision.

That could mean two things, neither of which are good. One, which is the lesser of two evils, is that he makes me his prisoner. I have a fighting chance if that's what he means. The other possibility is that he possesses me again.

Or option three, I take him down before he gets the chance to do either. He has strength and speed, but no offensive magic other than possession. I have all three.

I like the third option best.

The feeling of euphoria washes over me as I release the power brewing within me. It rips through my hands, aimed directly at him. I want to roar with surge and scream from the release. The sand around us swirls between our legs and the trees rustle in the wind. Yet nothing happens. He stands there, unmoving, unaffected by the moon's power.

He seems to realize this before I do.

Shit.

He lunges and jumps to the side. His hand wraps firmly around my arm. Then I leave the power to my knife, using it when it becomes a dance between a warrior and a thief. Each of his attacks are intended to remind me that he could do far more damage than a light tap. Every swing of his arm is sharp and calculated like a battle strategy that he has spent years perfecting.

He catches my wrist and uses it like he's a puppeteer, twisting it behind my back.

"Asshole," I mutter, kicking him to the side of his knee and causing him to loosen his hold.

Spinning, my fist buries itself into the side of his stomach, and he doesn't flinch. Yet I do. The impact sends pain up my arm, convincing me that the only semblance of success that I'll see is from running. Even with the moon's assistance, I'm no match for him. I have speed on my side and nothing more. I barely dodge his attacks fast enough.

A light wind kisses my sweat-stained forehead. Dipping below his swinging arm, my fingers find comfort in the cold sand. Scooping it up in my hand, I swing the sand right into his face and jolt to my feet. It's the only opening I'll have.

I don't make it two steps before arms wrap around my core, yanking me down onto the sand with him. His body hits the ground with a thud, taking the brunt of the fall before rolling over so that his frame towers over me, and I'm forced to stare up into his spotless face. Above him, the sight of the moon is obstructed by branches bristling in a light breeze.

Pressure builds at the side of my hips as he straddles me, and a gust of wind carries his scent to my nose. *Sage.* Buckling my hips beneath his weight, warm hands wrap around my throat, but it isn't to hurt me. It's to restrain me.

"I wonder if killing you will mean that I will be free of you." A sinister smile unfurls on his face.

The moon's energy might not work, but the earth's will. Flicking my hand, I brace myself for the loosening of his hold as the magic ripples through me and into the earth. The branch of the tree whips through the air, aiming directly for his head. But the sight fills me with short-lived victory.

My lips part as the branch goes straight through him, completely unhindered by the man on top of me. His hold around my neck loosens, and I momentarily forget about my desire to escape. The rage from his face dissipates, morphing into one of shock that matches my own.

"Do that again," he says breathlessly.

I stare up at him, unable to process the logic behind his request. Taking a deep breath, I flick my hand again, and a different branch swings through the air going straight through him as if he were a ghost.

I forget how to breathe, trying to think of all the things he might be. The silence of his footsteps as he walked, the rocks that never hit him, the lack of sand covering his body.

I flick my hand again. And again. And again. Watching as branches, stones, sand and leaves fly through him. Not one catches or slows.

"That's enough," he snaps, jumping off of me as if I harbor a plague.

I do the same, keeping a healthy distance away from him. His name isn't important to me. "What are you?" Part of me wonders if he even knows the answer.

He glares at his empty hands with slightly slouched shoulders. Though he wears all black, he seems to be illuminated in the darkness. The image of unbridled defeat.

"I am the darkness in the night that destroys everything you love. I am the light of a lunar eclipse. I am everything you fear and everything you want."

This is more than I bargained for. All that I wanted was a summoning spell and some berries.

"I asked what you are, not for a dramatic speech to fuel your ego." I stomp to the book that has brought me nothing but problems. "Just take the cursed book and leave me the hell alone."

"You have no idea what you've done." He finally looks up to meet my unfettered gaze. "You have ripped open a lock without a key. Now you have no way of keeping the monsters from opening the door."

DEX

CHAPTER FIVE

I STARE AT HIS silver eyes—so similar to the eyes of a lunar elf.

"That's poetic and all, but it means nothing to me. I just want to know when you're going to take your book and leave," I fume.

"I've been left forgotten, gathering dust on a bookshelf a hundred years before the Divine fell, waiting for the day someone *uses the key* to set me free," he starts saying as if the story is meant to ring a bell.

What he says finally dawns on me. He was inside the book. *He* is the power I felt within the book. He is who those people in the study were after. How was he inside of my head? Gods, what have I just unleashed?

No, what happens to everyone is not my problem anymore. I want to get rid of the curse for this very reason. I don't want the fate of the world to be on my plate.

There are enough creatures spelled into objects that it doesn't surprise me. The only thing this knowledge does is pique my curiosity as to why he's been cursed to such a fate. A criminal perhaps? Maybe he was caught lying with someone he wasn't supposed to.

"Pity that you're not still on a bookshelf," I grumble to myself.

Noting the book in his hand, I start to question whether I want him leaving with my blood. My chances of besting him are slim to none. I'd have to take a page out of Vencen's book and resort to common thievery.

"Congratulations on your newfound freedom. If you head in that direction, you'll eventually make it into the city." I point in Zarlor's general direction.

"Maybe you didn't understand me before," he whispers darkly, taking another step forward until his chest almost hits mine. But I refuse to give him the satisfaction of stepping back. "I'm not going anywhere anymore. I'm in your head, witch."

"Like a hallucination or a headache?" I drawl.

"Like a nightmare." His voice sounds like it belongs to death himself, intended to make me shrivel and hand over control.

Instead, I don't bother biting back the laughter that shakes through my chest. And I only laugh harder when I see the combination of shock and confusion plastered across his face. His flair for the dramatics is rapidly losing its allure when all it does is evade my questions.

"Laugh all you want, *witch*. Where you go, I go. It is embarrassing enough to have people see me walking with some mortal," he says the last part more to himself than to me.

My laughter quickly disappears as I finally take in the gravity of the situation. My blood on the Book of Twilight opened a door, leading him straight to me. He can't leave my line of sight without appearing next to me. I can't use my magic on him...

"My blood... We're linked." I file through my mind in an attempt to recall any unbinding spells.

He nods with an ominous grin. "Smart girl. Needn't worry. I shall be free once I kill you." His fingers curl, about to attack.

"If I die, you'll just go back into the book," I say quickly. Before we were fighting for the sake of fighting. We weren't fighting to kill. I know in my heart of hearts that if he were trying to kill me, I'd be long dead. So, I continue, "My blood created a portal between the book and me. You just said that we're connected. If I die, the portal will close," I say, hoping he can make sense of my words. Because I'm not even sure what I'm trying to say.

Fae magic can't do anything more than allure, telepath, and open portals in some cases. It's possible this is the work of a demon. Truthfully, I don't know enough about their kind of magic to make that conclusion.

It seems foolish to have such an allegedly powerful book that should be opened with some key, become compromised by a drop of blood. Did whoever or whatever casting the spell not consider papercuts?

He breathes in sharply, making sense of my own words. "You've become my tether to this place, and if you die, then I will go back into the book for it to host me." He drags his hand down his face, then rubs his temples as he stares at the lake deep in thought.

"Yes," I say, keeping the uncertainty out of my tone. "How do I get rid of you?"

He starts to pace along the shore, tapping his chin with his finger. The look of utter confliction sears his eyes, making my skin prickle in fear of what might be going through his head. Because whatever he is thinking about will very likely involve me.

"What?" I sound more confident than I feel.

I don't want this to be my last night alive. If he tries to kill me, I won't go down without a fight. I can't run from him, because he'll only appear by my side. I don't want to lie to myself by saying that I can actually kill him before he kills me, especially when I don't know if he is capable of dying.

"I'm thinking," he lashes.

"Well, think faster. I want to go to bed," I retort in an attempt to fool myself into believing that I actually have control in the matter.

"Take me to where you got the book, right now," he orders as if I were a soldier under his command.

"At this ungodly hour? I don't think so." His eyes darken, and he opens his mouth as if he is about to say something. "Walking the streets of Zarlor at this time of night as a woman is *not* advised if I don't feel like getting blood on my hands. Anything goes there, but contrary to popular belief, I try not to kill if I can avoid it."

That isn't the real reason I don't want to go. I simply don't know enough about what is happening to risk it. Yes, I may find the answers I seek in the satyr's study, but what then? Will he do another spell that draws the attention of every hellhound in Zarlor? Could he have done some kind of damage to my necklace which means that the hellhounds can smell the full strength of my magic? What if he possesses me again?

His voice rises, dripping with intimidation. "I have waited hundreds of years to—" I cut him off with a dismissive gesture before he continues.

"If you've waited hundreds of years, then you can wait a couple more hours," I say over my shoulder as I walk back toward the cave entrance.

Truthfully, I don't think it's sleep that I need. I'm more awake than I've ever felt. I want to feel the comfort of my own presence. Maybe it's cowardice that my waking thoughts consist of fearing change. It's always been easier to hide away than face the darkness.

A hostile hand lands on my shoulder, and my reflexes kick in. I spin around, and the sand all around me floats in the air, responding to the power flowing through me—another reason why I've forced myself into living in the daylight. Flicking his hand away, I step back before I reveal more of my powers.

"Now," he growls.

"Tell me, if trees and rocks go through you, does that mean that another person's attack will do nothing to you?" I realize how little I know about him or what the book has done to me.

He pauses, frowning at me while deep in thought. "I don't know."

"If I go out there, and a group of Black Bloods corner us, it will be just me against them. You don't have any powers and I don't think your broodiness will scare anyone off. Everyone will see you standing there looking all pretty and dainty." He flinches so dramatically that I might as well have slapped him. "If I die, you'll be back in that book." I say a silent prayer to Callaia, hoping that he doesn't see through my false confidence.

I've been attacked by a group of Black Bloods in the dead of the night, and I got out with a gnarly scratch. But a hellhound was tracking my scent for weeks. I don't want to be put in that position again, especially if people are on my tail about the book.

"Would you like to wait a couple more hours or go back in that book?" I cock my head and cross my arms over my chest. Kselia, my adoptive mother, would be in awe if she saw that I mastered her passive aggressive scolding.

The deep creases on his face mark his venomous scowl, but his body screams hesitance. I can tell that he doesn't like knowing as little as I do about our situation, and it's eating him up inside.

"Good decision." Spinning on my heels, I march back to the rocks next to the cave. A question plays at the back of my mind wondering if he will appear next to me in a cloud of smoke because he isn't in my sight, or just how much space I can place between us to get any semblance of privacy.

"I am as old as time itself. Sleeping is for the mundane."

"Then you can stand there and scare off the fish."

"We leave at first light," he yells to my back.

I don't respond, not because I don't know what to say. Rather, that there's so many things that I should say but can't bring myself to. How did my blood do that? What's his name? What is that book, and why is it so important? Why was he trapped in there? There have been so many opportunities to ask all those questions, but I can't bring myself to.

There is a voice whispering a delusional idea in my ear that if I don't know the answer, then maybe I can pretend it didn't happen. I can go back to Taravene and Kselia can tell me that it was all just a bad dream.

All I'm doing is fooling myself. Through knowledge, there is power. But there is no power in willful ignorance.

I pause, just before the puddle of crabs. "What's your name?"

There's power in a name. It can be worshiped or feared, or a way to control and manipulate. Yet, at the same time, it can mean nothing at all.

"Gideon." He hesitates for a moment. "And yours?" His tone is rough like he couldn't care less about my answer.

"Dex," I say. Because I'll never say Princess Devereux of House Hinixsus again.

I can feel a presence in the cave watching me in my slumber. Despite the crashing of the waterfall, there's an unnatural silence within. Their breath doesn't echo through the rocks as mine does. The cave feels smaller in their presence, yet at the same time it's as if they don't take up any room at all.

The time of the sun will rule the lands soon. The last whisper of the moon's power will trickle away, leaving me with nothing but my own power that's suppressed by the necklace.

"Get up. The sun is about to rise." Gideon's voice vibrates down my spine, and with it any shred of hope that last night's events were a lavish nightmare.

"Five more minutes," I grumble, turning my back to him.

I glide between the space of sleep and being completely lucid, relying on nothing but my gut to inform me of any looming presence. He's as silent as the night, a shadow creeping in the edges. Fear takes, and every second that my eyes closed is another second he might kill me. Still, I cower in my blankets and can't bring myself to face the truth. There's bliss in pretending.

"Now," he barks, making me sit bolt upright with murder thrumming through my veins. I don't like being denied a sleep in.

"Speak to me like that again and I'll—"

"And you'll what? Talk back? *Attempt* to injure me? There is *nothing* you can do to hurt me. The only sort of punishment you could dole out is keeping us linked together for a second longer than is necessary." Each sentence is spoken with unfathomable disdain.

Hatred oozes from every one of his pores as if I am the bane of his existence, and the fate he faces now is worse than being trapped in the confines of a book.

I stare with utter loathing at his righteous posture, his arms crossed as he looks down his nose at me as if speaking to me is beneath him. He stands by the entrance of the cave, but it isn't nearly far enough. He takes a step toward me in warning, and I catch a glimpse of the sand behind him, completely unaffected by the trails of his weighted footsteps.

He felt so real last night. I could touch him, feel his warmth, smell him. If he wasn't real, would I have been able to feel him? Or has my loneliness truly taken over that I've conjured a man of shadows?

"How do I know this isn't a bad dream?" I'm losing the fighting spirit I had moments ago.

"Because no one wants to dream of me. When we go out, and you see people cower at the sight of me, you will have your answer"

It isn't an answer to my question, but I'm beginning to learn that any information I ask for will be delivered in nonsensical riddles. Although, he does have a point.

"Get ready."

Smoke envelopes his body, and he disappears from sight in the blink of an eye before I get the chance to respond. I guess he spent the night learning a new trick.

Sighing, I collapse back onto the pile of blankets and stare at the grooves of the ceiling. There's something so enchanting about staring at it. The reflection of light from the moisture of the rocks makes it seem like I'm lying beneath the stars. Every time I look up, there's a new constellation to explore, and I get lost in it. Nothing on land matters in comparison.

It is said that the stars are Callaia and Dehran's broken children; offspring of a love that could never happen. The power of both sun and moon, chaos and healing, tore the children from inside out. Even though the kings killed the gods and goddesses, the sun, moon, and stars remain. Night changes to day, rain falls from the sky, and crops break through the surface of the soil. The world continues as if the Divine don't exist.

The only difference now is that without the peace and order the gods brought to the realm, the kingdoms are fighting to see who will reign supreme.

Groaning, I pull myself upright and rummage through the cave for the gods forsaken fake baby bump in case I run into the Black Bloods from yesterday. Strapping it to my body and righting my dress, I assess the rocks, looking for the exact ridge that hides my client's ring. Once I spot it, I pull the leather pouch out of the hole then hide it in the concealed pocket of my dress.

Spotting the gold bracelet that I nicked from the satyr's study, I bend over to pick it up from where it lies harmlessly on the ground. As my finger touches the cold metal, a sour taste coats my mouth. It doesn't feel right wearing something I stole from a dead creature while its body is still warm, only return to the place where my 'friend' killed him. That, however, does not mean that I won't feel inclined to slip some more of his things into my pocket. It just means that I can wear the bracelet tomorrow.

Shaking my head, I grab the bag off the floor and a sharp pain rips through my stomach from how wrong the bag feels, like it's tainted somehow from carrying the book. I try to ignore the sensation as I continue with my morning routine. Yet the nausea remains as I pat myself down, doing a count of all my weapons; knives in each boot; one sewn into the dress; pins in the hem of the dress in case I need to escape; one tucked into my bustier; a dagger strapped to my thigh; and there should be pocketknives…

My hands slap against my dress, furiously searching for the second pocketknife. Rushing to the pile of blankets, I wait to hear the sound of clanging as I rustle through the fabric. But the sound never comes.

The last time I used my pocketknife was… shit. The satyr's study. *How convenient that I'm already going there.*

Sighing in frustration, I right my dress once again. The weapons usually bring me a sense of comfort. I didn't think of them as armor, more so just a part of my clothing that stops me from feeling so naked. Even with one weapon down, I'm still 'dressed' enough. But today feels different. Today I feel as naked and vulnerable as the day I escaped Hinixsus. I was charging headfirst toward a foreign enemy without armor or protection. I didn't know what I was facing or how I was going to get through it, fight it, and still have my wits at the end of it. Back then, my enemy was the whole world, and they already took away the person I loved most: my sister.

I feel as naive as I did back then. Except now my entire issue stems from accidentally pricking my finger and summoning some man named Gideon.

I can never tell Vencen that this all happened because of a damned berry bush. I'm grateful that Vencen won't be up at this hour, so there's no chance that he'll run into me and see my new shadow.

As I tuck my hair behind my ear, my finger brushes the silver hoops and studs that climbs up it. I take a fortifying breath as I stare out at the running water, trying to make sense of my reality. The sun starts to peer over the horizon, and I can still feel the last remnants of the moon before it fades away for the rest of the day.

A large part of me doesn't want to go with him to the satyr's study. It isn't because I don't want to be rid of him. It's the fear of the unknown that frightens me. Since I was born, my fate was written and drilled into me. I always knew what steps I needed to take, and what I would achieve. Now, I'm dealing with an unknown magic, with a man of an unknown species, and with absolutely no idea what to look for except maybe an unbinding spell.

I consider jumping through the waterfall like Gideon did when he possessed me, but I know I won't be anywhere as graceful as he was, and I'll just end up making a right fool of myself.

"Callaia, please help me," I mutter under my breath before taking a step out of the cave for the waterfall to swallow me whole.

DEX

CHAPTER SIX

"THAT WASN'T THERE EARLIER," Gideon says, eying my stomach completely mortified.

"It's fake." I am too ashamed to think of something snarky.

"I have waited all night for you. Hurry up."

"Congratulations. Now look how well-rested you are." I sound more miserable with each step.

Mornings are never easy. It always feels unnatural like I'm lost out at sea and nursing a hangover at the same time. When I first started to unlearn my elven antics, I made myself one of many rules that I follow to this day:

Never look up in the morning, because it will only make me grieve for what I can no longer be. I haven't broken that rule once.

I don't regard him or the book as I pass, heading straight toward the forest. Without the sound of footsteps, I can't be sure if he's following behind me. Turning my head, I bite my tongue to contain my startle to see him a few short steps behind me.

We continue trekking through the forest in complete silence, and uneasiness burns the air. I have to stop myself from constantly glancing back at him to see if he has finally decided to test his luck and attempt to kill me. I wouldn't hold it against him if he does, not when I would do the same if our roles were reversed.

Last night, I was too much of a coward to ask questions, and I won't let that happen today. Knowledge is power, and I intend to be as powerful as him.

"What is the Book of Twilight, and what does it do?" I say to break the silence. "And don't bother answering in riddles."

"It doesn't concern you." There isn't the slightest hint of emotion in his tone. His response vanquishes the tension rising in my chest, replacing it with pure annoyance. This is going to be a long day.

"Last I checked, it's my blood in your hands. I would say it is *very much* my concern," I snap, nodding to the veined book that appears miniscule in his hands.

"When we get the key, you can take your blood back and we will part ways. This isn't the concern of a *common witch*," he sneers like saying the words make him nauseated.

I suck in the inside of my cheek to stop myself from correcting him. I should be used to being called a witch or a mortal, but the royal blood within me bares its teeth every time. I'm starting to regret ever speaking.

"What are we looking for?" I try to speak quickly and sharply, not leaving any room for debate.

"I'll tell you once you need to know."

"Tell me now."

"No."

"I want you gone, so tell me everything I need to know to make that happen."

A disapproving look crosses his face. "Your wants are of little concern to me, *mortal*."

A warm arm wraps around my torso, pulling me against a thick tree before I can react. Hard muscle pushes against me, pressing me harder against the tree as his hand clamps down over my mouth. I let the remaining power of the moon strengthen my muscles to the point of euphoria as I ready to get him off me at any cost necessary. How *dare* he man-handle me.

He presses his body against mine, and my spine threatens to groan. Even with my power, he feels like an immovable boulder crafted by the gods. Looking up at him, he raises his index finger to his lips, signaling for me to stop moving and stay quiet. The moon's power trickles back out under the weight of urgency in the air, dissipating the fight in me.

I nod begrudgingly, wary of his motives. He drops his hand slowly, but he doesn't step away, keeping his body flush against mine. I try to arch my back and push myself further against the tree, searching the forest to find what has him on edge.

A high-pitched whistle crawls through the air, dragging its piercing melody over my skin. It's barely noticeable for a human to hear, but if it weren't for my necklace, I'd hear it as clear as day. Nature knows when danger is around, and when the insects turn silent, death will surely follow.

The whistle hangs in the air, holding the forest hostage. I've never heard anything like it. The creatures of the forest are never scared of anything, yet since last night, they've turned silent twice. As witches say, bad luck comes in threes.

My fingers inch down to the pocket of my dress, pulling out my one remaining pocketknife as the whistling grows louder with each passing second. My heart pounds rapidly against my chest, beating faster when thoughts of the creature hearing me starts to bombard my mind. The whistling seems to come from right next to us, and with it, the scent of death. Gideon moves nearer, closing his arms around me and blocking my sight. I don't fight his hold in case the whistling creature notices us, and we've walked too far from the cave to seek shelter in its poisonous bushes.

My chest burns as I hold my breath, hoping and praying that the beast doesn't notice me. The thought of fighting it isn't the reason that my blood runs cold. No, this is just another bad omen, another signal of change—a change I don't want to be a part of.

The forest floor squelches as the monster lurks past, like the leaves are being impaled rather than crunched beneath its step. It sounds unnatural. I don't notice the shivers raking through my body until Gideon tightens his hold around me, pulling my face closer to his chest. His woolen coat is soft against my face, bringing me more comfort than none. I can see shadows move, and a chill showers over me as a raspy hum feathers through my hair from the *thing's* closeness. Even Gideon's warmth does nothing to combat the beast's icy breath.

I inhale deeply and instantly regret it as the putrid smell of acid and decay burns my nostrils. The beast makes a sound eerily similar to a man taking their last breath. Then, a more chilling thought moves through me; it can smell me, but can it see me?

My body seems to understand the gravity of the situation because even my shaking hands go still. I tell myself that if I squeeze my eyes shut, the nightmare will go away. I start to list the names of all the dead gods in my head—a coping mechanism Kselia taught me; *Aditi, the Mother; Pater, the Father; Hadeon, God of Destruction, and the missing god.* The monster's raspy breathing moves closer. *Kriotz, Goddess of Trickery. Vareso, God of Time and Wisdom. Satrina, Goddess of Hell.* Gideon's body molds into mine, and his thumb circles my shoulder in slow motion in an attempt to comfort me. Of course it's in an attempt to comfort me, or else I will be dead and he'll be back in the book.

I'm not sure if I'm besides myself because there's a monster, or if it's because the beast even has Gideon on edge. It's a foreign foe. It means that I have no idea how to kill it before it kills me.

Focus, I scold myself. I take a deep breath and continue, *Dalthorn, God of War. Rielway, Goddess of Agriculture. Acele, Goddess of Love.* The muscles in my body start to relax into Gideon's hold, and my racing heart starts to steady. *Mediel, God of Sports and Communication. Dehran, God of the Sun.* My breathing becomes even, calm, and composed. *Callaia, Goddess of the Moon and Healing.*

Gideon's presence disappears, leaving me a cold shell, and my eyelids flutter open. The smell of blood is thick in the air, and the remnants of my fear continue to weigh on my heart.

"Are you alright?" Gideon's silver eyes bore down on me as I start to taste rosemary.

"What was that?" My voice is barely above a whisper, afraid that the beast might hear and return.

"A monster that walked through your unlocked door."

His answer frightens me more than the beast's presence. Whatever that was is my fault? What else escaped because of me?

"Come," he says with a quiet urgency. "We should hurry."

I nod hesitantly before picking up my pace to a light jog. The insects' songs resume, but it feels like it's only temporary. My eyes dart to every shadow and movement within the forest. The stench of death only grows stronger as we proceed, and Gideon's demeanor becomes tenser as the smell of blood grows stronger.

"Gideon." I stop dead in my tracks.

Carnage.

Absolute carnage. That's the only way to describe the scene before us. This is where the smell of blood is coming from—the same direction that the monster came from.

"Dex, wait," he shouts at me as I run headfirst into the bloodbath with my knives drawn.

I don't listen to him, I just run. Someone might still be alive. All that's left of Callaia's power is mere specks of dust, but it could be enough to save someone—let them live for another day. "Dex, stop!"

The monster isn't around. We would have heard it. But other creatures will come to feast on the remains. I have to hurry before it's too late—before anything else gets there.

Blood. It's everywhere. Four human-like beings: three men, one human in a dress all lying on the ground with a hole in the center of their chests where their hearts are meant to be. I can only assume the one wearing the dress is female. The skin of her face has been ripped clean off, I can see the whites of her skeleton that has cracked under the force of the creature. My stomach churns, threatening to spill its contents. One of the men's severed head stares at the sky through milky eyes. A sickly pale blue hue paints their cheeks, and green veins climb up their exposed skin.

The pattern of the green veins is what breaks me. I can't stop my stomach's reaction or the way my body shakes violently as I stare directly at the slaughtered beings, retching until there is nothing more for my body to retch. The veins look like the thorned spirals filled with my blood that's on the book.

I'm the reason they're dead.

That *thing* killed these people because of me. I left the door unlocked.

Bad luck comes in threes.

"More will come if we don't go now," Gideon says from somewhere behind me.

He's right. More will come. More of whatever that *thing* was—the thing I brought into the world. But I can't leave them like this. I can't just serve carcasses on a silver platter to any starved when their souls haven't moved on. I have to do something. *Anything.* I owe it to them.

My legs tremble but I manage to pull myself onto my feet with the taste of bile and blood in the back of my throat. Slow, hesitant steps make their way to two men that still have their faces attached to their bodies.

"We need to go, Dex," Gideon urges.

Anyone who dies within these forests will never be found again. Leaving them here means that their families will never know what happened to them. By the time the forest is done with them, they'll be nothing but nameless corpses with nothing left to show except their bones.

"I have to." Salty tears make their way into my mouth, mixing in with my whirlwind of emotions.

The moisture of the dirt seeps into my dress, as my knees fall onto the ground. I take deep breaths, trying and failing to control my shaking hands while holding back a sob. I know there's nothing I could have done about this. I know that I didn't intend for any of this to happen, or even had the slightest idea that something like this could happen. I still feel at fault.

I have to hold back the bile lurching in my throat as my fingers touch the warm blood around the men's eyes. Shutting their eyes, I say the lunar prayer of the dead in my head. It isn't nearly enough. It doesn't make up for what I've caused. But maybe it might mean something. Maybe their souls will find some peace.

As I walk back to where Gideon stands, my eyes are firmly set on my fingers and the men's blood that has embedded into my nails and the grooves of my skin. I can sense Gideon sending me wary glances like I might break again at any second.

I can feel myself inching closer and closer to blaming it all on him. It would be easier to put their blood on his hands. I already loathe him for the nuisance he's created. It wouldn't be hard to hate him for the destruction he is causing. But it isn't his fault. I'm the one who summoned him.

"Stay here," I whisper when I can no longer stare at my fingers, and the sound of a stream coaxes me with its cleansing waters.

Following the noise, I use the water to scrub off the evidence of my recklessness. Threads of red float down the stream, trailing around stone and moss like a winding river. Though I long to have this moment alone, I can feel Gideon's eyes on me, watching my every move.

Shaking off the last drop of blood, I can't bring myself to look at him or the book in his hands. But I force myself to anyway, force myself to take responsibility for what I've done.

"What was that?" To my surprise, my voice doesn't crack like I thought it would. Instead, there's a desperation in my words that could be mistaken for determination.

"It isn't any—"

"No," I stop him. "Just tell me. Don't mince words. Don't tell me that it's none of my concern. Four people are dead because of me—because of that *thing*. Please. I know you don't give a shit about me beyond keeping me alive. But please, answer the question." My voice is broken, defeated, desperate. It doesn't sound like it belongs to the Daughter of the Blood Moon, or even a procurer.

The way he looks at me is almost pitiful, yet under the shadows of his brutal demeanor, there's a mirror of the same pain I feel, like he, too, is broken, only he's learned to live with it.

"Kaliak."

I stare at him, lips parted with tears welling in my eyes. I quickly blink them back, refusing to succumb to my emotions. "I have no idea what that is."

"Before the eight kingdoms were established and civilization consisted of warring tribes, this was a land of monsters and Divine." I stare at him weakly, searching his eyes to find meaning in the havoc. "Aditi and Pater, who you know as the Mother and Father, wanted more for their children and the rest of the creatures."

I nod along, having heard this story a hundred times in the Temple before I ran.

"Aditi and Pater ordered the gods to eradicate the monsters; some became extinct, while some were forced into Hell." He takes a deep breath as a feeble attempt to hide the strain hidden within his soul. But for the life of me, I can't figure out why this story would distress him. "But even the Divine are no match for nature's need for balance. With good comes evil. The wicked cannot be destroyed without killing the kind. The only promise anyone can make is that when scales tip, death will follow."

My forehead creases with both concentration and confusion. Witches speak of balance in spells and incantations. They think the elves and fae are unholy because we can take and take and take, but never give. Balance amongst the populous through the treachery of creatures is a concept I've never read in scripture. What does *balance* have to do with that creature?

"The kaliak are among the most *vile*." The word hangs in the air, clogging my ability to breathe.

"Why have I never seen or heard of them? Why are they back?" I try and fail to fill in the blanks of the story.

He hesitates like he's unsure of how to answer the question. "Once the twelve gods that you've come to know walked the land, they discovered a way to control the monsters."

"And now that all of the gods are dead, kaliaks can't be controlled. At least not until someone brings the Divine back to life," I whisper, finishing his sentence for him.

"Yes." He nods, failing to hold back a scowl. There's more to his answer than what he's saying, like a secret he's strategically trying to keep from me. I know he won't tell me even if I ask.

"There has to be another way."

"There is."

I stare at him, waiting for him to say more. He did what I begged of him; he told me what they are without speaking in riddles.

"How do we get rid of them? How many are there?"

"Even one of them is too many. Be grateful, witch, that those are the only things that have come out," he says, returning to his riddled answers, shaking his head as he stares at the sky. "Let's continue. We need the key. The sooner we're rid of each other, the sooner you can stop worrying."

But I won't stop worrying. I'll only worry more. If kaliaks start attacking cities and the kings discover the only way to control or get rid of them is by bringing the gods back, then I should be scared. I should be terrified. Kingdoms will want me even more than before, and it won't be for some political gain. No, they'll want me because it will be a matter of life and death for their people.

Now, more than ever, I need to find a way to break the curse.

"What sort of spells are in the Book of Twilight?" I whisper, careful not to speak unless I'm confident that no one can hear. Constant tension curls on my shoulders from the knowledge that the Book of Twilight is hidden within my bag. Now that we're in the city, we can't risk anyone seeing it in Gideon's hands, especially when his foreboding presence screams attention.

"Nothing that you can use," he responds dryly, paying no mind to anyone we pass.

"But you can use it?" I try to keep my hope from seeping into my voice. An elderly woman sends me a suspicious glance as I speak. Out of habit, I instantly fall into character. Rubbing my stomach and leading with my hips. I give Gideon a disapproving look when he scowls at her, and she quickly turns away.

"I can, just not for you."

My nails pierce the skin of my palm as I curl my fingers into a tight fist. *Arguing with him will only bring more unwanted attention*, I tell myself as I suck in my cheeks.

If my sister, Ameria, were still alive, she'd tell me to take a deep breath and be the bigger person, because "Princesses are calm" and "strike with their silence."

"What language is it written in?" Soon, I'm sure he won't answer at all.

"Not yours." There's an evident warning in his voice to stop asking questions.

"Yes, I gathered that," I snap, causing the people around us to give us a wide berth while eyeing me suspiciously. So I whisper, "What type of magic?"

"The powerful kind." His words are short, sharp, and dismissive. He makes no attempt at decreasing his volume.

Spinning on my heels, I turn to face him as passersby stare at me disapprovingly. I'm not liking the attention, but it's early in the morning and they'll forget about me soon enough. "Other than whatever the hell was back there, you haven't told me much of anything. Whether you like it or not, this involves me now. You can be an ass if you want, but don't think that keeping secrets will help your cause." I poke his chest.

A woman watches us with utter bewilderment, but I can smell the fear dripping off her. Fear for the man before me. Gideon pays her no mind.

"You have mistaken me for someone who cares about what knowledge you wish to learn. Do not fool yourself into believing that I need your help getting out of *your* mess. I will never need your help," he says each word with deadly grace. "The fact that you are awake and speaking is an utter inconvenience in and of itself. You should be thanking me that you still have your wits about you. It would have been easier if I put you to sleep and dragged you by your feet to get me where I need to go."

Asshole.

His threat is loud and clear. He is right about one thing: I'm a fool for believing that I have an upper hand in any of this. I need food, water, and sleep, which already makes me weaker than him. The only positive side to any of this is the comfort in knowing that he can't possess me again just because he can't gather the ingredients he needs: the book.

At least I hope that is the case.

Crossing my arms, I challenge him. "So take us to where I found the book."

The challenge delivers the intended response as the side of his lips curls into a wicked sneer.

I shoot him the widest grin that I can. "Why? Is there a problem?"

He doesn't respond, staring at me with eyes that promise death.

"Oh dear, do you not know where it is?" I say with sickly sweet innocence.

"Stop wasting my time." He turns away from me to continue down the path.

I tsk, failing to contain my triumphant smile as I eye the red wooden sign above the door, with the hoof of a goat painted on a scroll. "Pity. Because I was just about to say that we're here."

DEX

CHAPTER SEVEN

His body still lays in the middle of the study, emitting its ungodly smell into the room. Not a hair has moved since I saw him last, and I'm eternally grateful that the satyr's milky eyes don't stare aimlessly just as the men in the forest did. Instead, they remain closed.

But everything else has changed; papers are scattered across the room, shelves of antiques and collectibles lie broken on the floor, and books have been thrown haphazardly everywhere. Amongst the mix, a single pocketknife discarded on the floor. My pocketknife.

"I'm back, baby," I whisper, retrieving my lost weapon and returning it to the safety of my pocket. I expect to feel like a completed puzzle with the knife tucked safely at my side, not the vulnerability that aches in my heart.

The people yesterday completely ransacked the study, looking for the item I now keep in my bag.

"Friends of yours?" Gideon scoffs with disgust, eying the disheveled room.

"The mess? No. The satyr? No, I wouldn't call him 'friend.'" I say the last part a little too quietly to remove suspicion. "What are we looking for?"

He doesn't respond, bending down to inspect the papers that are soaked in blood.

"If someone was here, then what we need won't be here anymore," he says, running his eyes methodically along each sheet of paper like the answer he seeks is on one of them.

"So we failed before we even started. Shall we go home then?" Bitterness clouds my voice.

Ignoring my comment, he continues, "Someone would have hired him to locate the book."

"Which means we're stuck with each other for even longer until we either find who tore this place apart, or find who hired him? Great." I lean against the table to stare at the ceiling.

Zarlor's humidity has already caused sweat to build under the fake bump and down my back, making this entire situation even more infuriating. Apparently Zarlor's weather never used to be so awful, the blizzards in Lodaxo never used to be so frequent, Sario used to be greener. The teachers at the temple say that everything has been going downhill in the past 300 years.

"Or, the third possibility is that he has never been in possession of the key, and was in the process of looking for it," he corrects. "There must be something in here that will point us where we need to go."

Raising back onto his feet to start filing through the books on the desk, his hand moves to pick up the ledger, only to slip right through it. His entire body tenses, and I can taste his anger as his nostrils flare. He attempts to pick up a scroll this time, gaining the same result. He tries again, and again, and again. Each time, nothing happens.

"Would you like some help?" I perk up, unable to suppress the mischief in my grin. "Oh wait, forgive me, I forgot. You don't need my help with anything," I say, mocking his deep voice.

The energies of the room vibrate with fury, and the taste of whiskey bombards my tongue, distracting me from the way his jaw ticks when he grits his teeth. It's as if I'm drinking the liquor; oaky and dry, yet filled with a spice that could burn my system. Inhaling deeply, I try to locate the smell, but all that fills my senses is the satyr's blood.

I can practically hear Gideon's teeth grind as he tries to pick up the ledger again. His hand goes through it as if he were a ghost. The taste of whiskey only grows with each attempt he makes, as does the taste of herbs. I can't make out what herbs they are, but they blend with the whiskey, creating a smoky flavor that becomes so rich that I fight back a gag.

A roar thunders through the room, and the taste multiples as he tries to throw the table. The glasses seem to clatter and shake with his power, except they don't move at all. His breathing is anything but calm; it's ragged and deafening, filling the otherwise silent room. But with each breath, the taste slowly dissipates.

My feet move before I can think better of it, and my fingers find the ledger lying upside down on the table—the ledger he first tried to pick up.

"Do you need help?" I say slowly and calmly. There's no humor or rage written on my face. I'm taunting the beast by playing on his weaknesses. It makes me an awful person for saying something I know will hurt. If we are going to spend more than a day together, I will not be subjected to further disrespect on his part. When I turn the other way, he's welcome to whisper profanity about me, but I refuse to allow him to treat me like little more than an object of inconvenience, especially since the inconvenience goes both ways.

"Just show it to me" he growls.

"Say it." There's no emotion in my voice.

He huffs like I said the most ridiculous thing he's ever heard. But I know it's just a show to downplay the anger he feels for himself. Maybe even the rage for all of the situations that led up to this day.

The taste of whiskey vanishes along with the storm within his eyes. He closes them for a brief moment, inhaling deeply to dispel the tension. "Help," he says as if it pains him.

"You can do better than that." It's likely that I'm asking for more than I deserve to get, especially when I've done nothing kind to him. Instead, I asked him to stay up all night while I slept.

He sighs with everything he has in his chest. "I need your help, Dex. Please." A pang of guilt squeezes my heart to see defeat spread over his features.

Satisfaction ripples through my bones as a sense of power blossoms in my chest. I make room on the desk to lay the book down and open to the first page, and a knowing weight rests on my shoulder—my triumph will be short lived. Someone is going to need to turn the page for him.

I murmur, "It will help if I know what I'm looking for. Should I just keep an eye out for something that says 'important key'?"

"Look for the Hell's Quill or Ring of De—"

"Did you just say that the key is a quill? A *quill*? Of all frightening and daunting objects to exist, they chose a *quill*?" I struggle to contain my laughter, but it resonates through the room. My hand slaps over my mouth to dampen the sound so as to not to alert anyone else of our presence, and the taste of herbs returns to my tongue for the briefest moment.

I expected the key to be a dragon's tooth, maybe an enchanted mirror, or even a legitimate key. The last thing I expected is a feathered writing tool. It's ridiculous to believe that a book and something as innocent looking as a quill could unleash the kaliak into our world.

"The quill holds Satrina's blood," he says through gritted teeth, but something twinkles in his eyes.

His statement stops my laughter; anything that has the blood of the gods in it is capable of unspeakable things, especially something that holds the blood of the Goddess of Hell.

"I thought it made sense. You need a quill to write," he mumbles under his breath like he's trying to reason with himself.

"It does make sense. I just wouldn't associate you with something as dainty as a feather, but I suppose it's fitting." I eye him up and down obviously.

"I am anything *but* dainty," he growls.

Huffing sarcastically, I take a step closer so our chests are a breath away from touching. His closeness makes me want to shrivel in on myself, but I pull my shoulders back and look him straight in the eyes. The thought of actually knocking him onto his back brings me a strength I can't describe. "That's yet to be seen." I throw my hair over my shoulder as I return my attention back to the ledger, flicking through the pages like his proximity doesn't bother me.

Triumph flickers through me when he steps away with a grunt that sounds eerily like he's gagging.

"Wait. *You* chose the key? So *you* put yourself in the book?" The pieces start to fall into place to make an incomprehensible picture. Why else would anyone pick out the exact objects that would free them?

"Your feeble mind wouldn't understand."

I grind my teeth, taking several slow deep breaths. There's no point pursuing this particular line of questioning. "You mentioned something about a ring and a quill," I say without looking up. "Do we need one of them or both of them?"

I can sense him pause, considering my question. "My ring controls me, and the quill frees me from the book," he says. *His* ring.

From the corner of my eye, I can see him reach for something on the shelf only to pull his hand back in stiff resentment. It's going to be really awkward when someone accidentally walks through him. I'm sure Gideon will want to start a fight with them. He was already angry enough as it was when people looked his way.

I nod, moving the ledger to the side and carefully stepping around the fallen objects to make my way to the wooden drawer that now lays in splinters on the floor. Grabbing the notebook closest to me, I quickly thumb through the pages.

Gotcha.

Journals. At least one thing is going my way today. Shuffling through each notebook, I try to gain a general idea of what each might hold. Some concern medicine, while others are about politics. After scouring through each notebook on the floor, I manage to find a few journals relating to magical objects, another on previous acquisitions, a couple of diaries and books of spells.

I've been in the industry long enough to know that anyone dabbling in matters relating to powerful people will keep some kind of evidence of their clientele as a failsafe in case things go sideways. But I can either go on a wild chase to try and locate his failsafe that may or may not be in this building, or I can focus on what I already have—while also breaking the news to Gideon later that we will need to pause for my meeting with my own client later.

If my assumptions are correct, the satyr researches and collates data on objects then hires someone like me to procure the item. He's the middleman.

Carrying the pile to the table, I drop it down with a thump. After pulling down the two books sitting at the top, I open them both to the first page.

Gideon stands in the corner, quietly observing what I will do next. "The fun has just begun," I grumble, motioning for him to stand on the other side of the table as I slide the open book in his direction.

He spends less than a second looking at the page before saying, "Next page."

"Read it properly or you're going to miss something."

"Next page," he repeats, a threat in his voice.

Suppressing an irritated grunt, I turn the page as he asks.

"Next," he says as soon as I look down at my own notebook.

I hiss, turning the page for him. How am I meant to focus or read through any of this if I'm too busy flipping to a new page every second?

"Next," he says again in a monotone voice. I do as he says. "Next," he states again.

Slamming his book shut, I pull it away from him and exchange it with the biggest book in the pile, but also the thinnest. Opening it to the front page, I shove it right in front of him.

"That satyr asked my friend to procure your book from Renlork. The day we got here to do the exchange, we're told that the book is fake. Next thing we know, people show up here and ransack the place looking for what I can only assume is the Book of Twilight. A book that had *you* locked in it. And somehow, a kaliak appears for the first time since civilization started and it's all because I didn't write something with Satrina's blood," I list, raising my voice. "What *exactly* are you?"

I'm not sure how I will react if he tells me that it isn't any of my concern. Throw the Book of Twilight at him perhaps? It's evident that it's the one object that he is capable of holding. Instead, he does something far more infuriating. He says nothing. He stands stoically, staring directly into my soul. With each heartbeat that passes, rage heats and boils within me, and the urge to scream becomes overwhelming.

"There are two things that we can agree on. Do you know what those two things are, *Gideon*?" I'm getting closer to the point of complete hysterics. He doesn't respond, just scowls at me. "I guess I'll answer for you. One, we *despise* each other for very evident reasons. The fact that you wanted to kill me is one of those reasons. Two, I want us unlinked just as much as you do." By this point, I'm speaking in screaming whispers. "You may be old, but you aren't wise, that's for fucking sure. Because if you had any sense of self-preservation or wisdom you would know that keeping things from me, things that will help us get rid of each other, will only mean we're stuck with each other for longer."

Magic bubbles beneath the surface of my skin, threatening to be released onto the room. The desire to set the curtains ablaze and unleash a blizzard within the room becomes all-consuming.

But I'm not going to. I won't let myself. I'm allowed to be angry, but this level of rage is completely unfounded. There's something about him that agitates me more than it should. If I had to guess, it would come down to the fact that I know he's hiding more than he should. With every piece of information he tells me, there will be another side to it that he will keep to himself.

That's one of the only things I give my parents credit for; they never kept anything from me. It didn't matter how horrific the truth was, or how frightened I might be by the knowledge, they *always* told me the entire story. It wasn't like I could ignore the whispers about my fate, especially when I had it stamped on my chest and when I was born on one of only two blood moons in history; on the day the last god died.

I suppose it was also to their detriment that they were so 'open,' because I did end up running away after all.

Taking a deep breath, I tear my gaze away from him with the hopes that I'll calm down. "Look, you can hate me. You can be disgusted by everything that I am. But respect that our interests are aligned. For now. So answer me this; why are they after you?" I watch him with a helpless stare, feeling the rage slowly turn into a low simmer.

"I am a weapon." It isn't a doubt or a question. He says it like it's a fact that he is certain about.

"What kind?" There's almost a hesitancy to my question.

"The kind that no one will ever forget about." A dark cloud seems to hang over his shoulders as he says it, like what he is pains him. "I am a weapon that can be controlled with just the ring, but it was intended that all three be used together."

His words play at the back of my head as I stare at my bag sitting innocently atop a pile of books. Inside the bag is one part of a supposed weapon, one that brought the kaliak back. What happens if he gets all three? What will become of the world if we get the quill and ring and he's free from the clutches of my mind?

"My hands may be covered in blood, but I am not so black-hearted to become a weapon against humanity once free," he says as if he knows exactly what I'm thinking. "There is enough death in this realm, and it does not need me to make it worse. If I get the ring, no one can use me against anyone else. I want to be free so I can see my family."

He has a family? Would they still be alive? I didn't expect him to be the kind of person who has family, let alone the type of person that holds said family to a high esteem.

There's another question buzzing in my mind: Would they still be alive? Gideon said that he's waited 'hundreds' of years inside a book. Many creatures can live for centuries, but it's still possible they could have been killed when King Nodisci and my father killed the gods.

Will he choose to become a weapon if he finds out his family no longer lives? Could he use his powers against the people that took their life? Better yet, how many people would be caught in the crossfires? Then again, it's possible that Gideon's family are gathered around a table grieving their son, or husband, or father.

It upsets me that I believe him when he says that he won't try to destroy the realm once he's free. But also, no one gets trapped for centuries if they're actually *genuine*.

"Can someone control you if they have the ring, but not the Book of Twilight and Hell's Quill?"

He nods, raising his chin in unchallenged confidence. "But I won't let that happen."

I look at him in complete bewilderment. "Again with the wisdom. You've been in that book for 'hundreds' of years. It is highly possible that someone has your ring. Hell, as far as you're aware, a noblewoman could be slipping that ring on before she heads to a tea party with all the other ladies."

I know the thought will upset him because of his sensitivity toward the artifacts. But I get a sick enjoyment from egging him on.

A sudden sharp whiff of herbs spreads across my tongue. "No one would dare. The ring is made from the bone of a dragon, forged by—"

"Oh, okay. Not a noblewoman then. Let me correct myself," I say quickly, basking in Gideon's chagrin. "Your ring might be on the finger of a royal," I add, a fraction louder than I would normally speak.

Whiskey heats my tongue as his gaze burns holes into me. Biting the inside of my cheek to stop myself from smirking and aggravating the 'weapon' even more, I force my attention back to the book. Gideon is a weapon that has no power and can cause no harm to anyone but me. I snigger internally at the irony.

My nose scrunches of its own accord as the satyr emits foul-smelling gas. "Hurry up. Getting out of a room with a dead body is my main priority now," I grumble, with a finger on his book, ready to turn the page for him.

DEX
CHAPTER EIGHT

"This is useless. Let's go," Gideon orders when he's halfway through his last book, still standing with his hand behind his back.

I look up at him through heavy lids, clicking my stiff neck. I love reading, but reading to retain information? Not so much. I would rather try to make it through another battle than spend another morning shuffling through stacks of books in the hopes that we might get some inkling of an idea as to where the quill is.

"Thank the Divine, my stomach is telling me that it's lunchtime." His statement brings the same amount of relief as taking your corset off after a long day.

A pang of guilt tenses my system for giving up on the books so quickly, and not pulling the room apart to find the answers. There's a small voice inside my mind telling me that by admitting defeat, I'm letting him stay in my head. However, the guilt is short-lived. I'm hungry, bored, tired, and sweating. Frankly, any longer, and I'm certain I'd be capable of committing war crimes.

"The last time I saw the quill was in Taravene. We'll go there and follow the trail." He readjusts his coat so that it isn't out of place.

I shake my head, using the back of my hand to wipe the sweat gathered on my forehead. "We'll speak to Vencen first. He was contracted to retrieve your book. He might have more information that will lead us to the satyr's employer."

"Who's Vencen?"

"Your feeble mind wouldn't understand," I mock, wanting to use the line before I forget about it. Also, because I have no idea how to describe who Vencen is.

He snarls, walking toward the door without waiting for me. I could run after him to keep up. But it's a rather comfortable chair, and I wouldn't mind watching him storm back into the study in frustration. So, I take my sweet time. According to the clock, I have half an hour to get to the market before I make the trade with my client. The market just so happens to be in the opposite direction of the inn Vencen is staying at. So I walk briskly to my bag with my morals trickling away as I slip random knickknacks into it to make some extra cash or just to add to my treasure trove.

It has been one night already. The mourning period is over. Whatever is left in this room is free for all.

I can *sense* Gideon approaching, the taste of herbs thick on my tongue. I've never been one to taste things that I'm not eating or smelling, so it's yet another item to add to my never-ending list of things that I don't understand.

Whiskey burns my mouth as he storms back inside, walking straight through the door. If he could actually touch things, I'm sure a tremor would vibrate through the building with the ferocity of his searing gaze. It must be a bewildering sight to anyone standing outside.

"Are you coming?" he snaps in warning like I've heard my father do many times, 'encouraging' me to hasten in my steps to catch up to him.

I don't respond, delicately placing a tourmaline at the bottom of the bag. The spellbooks say that it's a good crystal to 'dispel and shield from negative energy.' It didn't specify whether it included a six-foot-something 'weapon' that was enchanted into a book for unknown reasons—another question that I'll be needing to ask should he feel so inclined to answer.

Maybe if I throw the crystal at him he'll disappear?

He folds his arms over his chest, a tell-tale sign of his annoyance. "Spouting nonsense about wisdom, yet you act like a petty child." I'm not sure whether he's referring to my silence or for making him wait. Either way, both are indeed petty, and I would have chosen to do the same thing again if given the option.

"I have an appointment, or should I say *we* have an appointment, and *we* have time to spare." The innocence in my voice does nothing to mask the anxiety building in my chest. This is my life *for now*, and it's highly possible that it could become worse.

"No, we see this *Vencen* first."

I take my time to braid my hair off my face as I do another walk around to see if there's anything else I might want. To him it probably appears that I'm taunting him, but in reality, to me this is like taking a sip of water before speaking.

"*I* will be seeing Vencen while *you* wait downstairs. He won't talk otherwise. Plus, you've ruined enough, I don't want you ruining my career in the process." It's taken a long time to build my clientele; though small it may be, everyone in the industry has heard of the Diamond Echo, the procurer that can get you what you want without being noticed. The expediter that has never been caught.

I really do hate the name, *Diamond Echo*. It barely even makes sense; what's echoing? Why is a diamond making noises? Echo implies that I'll be heard, which is contrary to what I'm known for. Saeya, Icoden, and I had a too much to drink one night and we thought Diamond Echo was a great name because I could say, "I'm Diamond Echo, the 'X' is just silent," and I can finish it off with a wink and say, "So call me D.E.X." Ico refused to let it go, and now he tells all his patrons about the 'Diamond Echo and Vencen,' because apparently, we're an inseparable pair.

My attempts at separating us as the procuring duo is making me lose money and making him gain more now that he has more freedom to pick jobs I would never agree to. His inability to say no to anything makes him well-loved by the masses.

"Get on with it then," Gideon huffs like a stubborn child, and I roll my eyes saying a silent prayer to the dead gods in thanks that he didn't decide to start an argument.

Tying my hair off with a leather string, I feel the pocket of my skirt to double-check my client's ring is still in there. In that moment, the keening sound of my stomach rumbles through the room, and an unreadable expression crosses Gideon's face. If I had to wager, whatever look he wears is somewhere between disgust and confusion.

I wonder what Ameria would think of Gideon. I'm sure she'd gush over him and call him dreamy, then look at me with pity because she knows I'm betrothed to another. She'd then probably ask about Lysander and whether I received another letter from him. She would always tell me about all the other noble boys and how she'd freeze whenever they looked her way, but she was always so excited about the big wedding she'd have. Always talking about the grand white dress she'd wear and the bouquet of lilies she'd hold. But I guess that will never happen. We have our father to thank for that.

Gideon trails closely behind me as I make my way to the door. Only now do I notice the various sigils engraved into the wooden doorframe. Coming to a stop, I drag my eyes over the symbols that I recognize. Some of them are for protection, a couple are to stop the smell of magic from leaving the property, and the last one I recognize is a sigil to ward off evil—which obviously doesn't work if Vencen and Gideon are capable of coming inside.

But there's one more that I don't recognize. Bringing my finger up to the symbol, I trace the dips and curves etched into the wooden frame.

"It stops people from entering the premises without invitation," Gideon's voice chimes from behind me.

"What?" Either he's confusing the sigil with something else, or the sigil is botched. Whoever walked in on Vencen and I yesterday definitely weren't invited in.

"Once the satyr allows someone inside, the invitation cannot be rescinded," Gideon adds.

So the satyr knew whoever it was that came inside yesterday? Another thought crosses my mind that I hadn't considered. What if yesterday's intruders were actually his employers and they ransacked the place in search of what they paid for?

Packing that thought away to another part of my mind, we exit the threshold into the familiar alleyway. Vencen's inn is to the left, and the market to the right. I can't begin to imagine the nonsense he will spout when he sees Gideon with me, and I most definitely do not want to explain to Vencen how we came to be. Worse yet, Gideon doesn't strike me as someone that would be willing to wait in the hallway.

He says nothing as we file through the smaller streets packed with people. I take a different route from yesterday just in case someone recognizes me, especially when my stalker is in Zarlor as well.

I always feel claustrophobic down this street. With the balconies and awnings and the clothes hanging across buildings, there isn't a single inch spare for sunlight to seep through. In the humidity, the smell of shit and piss is unbearable, I don't know how the locals can live with it.

No one pays Gideon any mind even though he towers over everyone around him and looks like he could kill someone with a single glance. He looks offended by the fact that no one is shying away from him. I know I should be grateful that somehow, he is managing to avoid attention, but a quick glance his way tells me that underneath all the anger, he is also as confused as I.

As the hustle and bustle of the small street spills into a large one, a soft sigh leaves my lips from having room to breathe. I throw another backward glance to check that Gideon is still following me, and I halt in my steps.

I suck in a sharp breath and stare at him; standing in the center of the street with his eyes closed, face angled up to the sun like he's basking in its rays. He looks majestic—godly even—like this. Somehow, he doesn't look so pale when cast in the golden light, almost like he has a perfect tan from his acquaintance with the sun.

His chest rises slowly as the taste of vanilla consumes me. Rage doesn't dance in his eyes as he opens them. The taste of cinnamon mixes in with vanilla and I swear I can see the slightest hint of sadness cloud over him, like reality pains him.

My feet start to move against my will and my fingers ache to touch the light that glistens against his skin. The intensity of his gaze on me causes my breath to hitch, distracting me for the briefest moment before reminding me of who the man is to me: an absolute nuisance.

"I haven't felt the sun in so long," he whispers, breaking our eye contact as he takes in the sun once again. "The moon may have many faces, but the sun has more. It is chaotic and destructive, yet without feeling the burn of its touch, you can't feel truly alive. Life grows on everything it touches, and despite its power, it shares the sky with the moon on even the brightest days." The softness of his voice is at odds with the man who had his fingers wrapped around my throat just this morning. How can someone who sees beauty in the sun bring with him a darkness like the kaliak?

His words may be poetic, but I wholeheartedly disagree. I have turned a bright shade of red because of that thing one too many times. But the sun doesn't stop there. After it burns you, your skin peels and flakes regardless of how much salve you lather on.

Alas, I say nothing. He needn't know that I am a creature of the night. I may have what Vencen calls 'sun-kissed skin,' but I yearn for the shade.

The silence still feels comfortable as he sighs and begins his trek along the street in the same direction of the palace, all the while an uneasy expression dances across his face. Prickles crawl all over my skin as we move closer to the palace. My muscles fight against my orders, tensing and spasming. I usually do all things necessary to avoid even glancing at a castle, let alone walking past one. It's like my bones hold the memories of my time in the Palace of the Moon and they shiver at the thought of being inside once more.

I walk closely beside him as we pass a group of Black Bloods that just stepped through the gates with a look of complete smugness. There never used to be so many Black Bloods crawling around Zarlor. I can only assume that they've probably won more freedom of movement. It seems to be a trend in kings: being a complete sell-out. It's either their gods or their people. Or both.

"Since when has Zarlor been in bed with Renlork?" he says, like the mere idea is scornful. A flicker of shock resonates through me that someone would even ask such a question, but of course, he doesn't know. He hasn't needed to live through the realm turning upside down.

"When King Rhaelson of Hinixsus killed Callaia, and King Nodisci of Volducan and his followers killed the rest of the gods and rose to power—which the Black Bloods of course hated. Now, them and the Followers of the Paragon Dawn have been at each other's throats ever since. All the other kingdoms have been forced to pick a side." At least that's part of the current political climate. I'm not about to mention that even though some of the kingdoms have picked a side, they would turn on each other in a heartbeat if it meant getting their hands on me.

"Zarlor's king has always been a greedy bastard." He shakes his head, scowling at the palace like the king might actually see it.

"The Black Bloods won his favor by—"

A tall merchant jumps in front of me, waving some ornament in front of my face. "Miss, half price, today only!" he bellows, invading my comfort zone.

"Not interested." I swat his hand away from my face and clutching my bag closer. He may well genuinely want to sell me his product, but I've done a trick like this enough times; one person distracts, another picks their pocket.

I try pushing past him, making sure he doesn't squish against my stomach and realize that the bump is fake, but he sidesteps to stay right in front of me. "It's handmade with the finest oak in Zarlor, safe for babies to chew. For a pretty lady like you, I'll—"

Gideon pushes me aside, hurling his hand out to get the man's throat, only for it to slip right through him. Pain lances through Gideon's features as he stares down at his hand helplessly. The merchant doesn't even flinch at the attempted assault, training his eyes on me, hellbent on selling me some ornament.

"She said she's not interested," he growls, replacing the pain with utter irritation.

The merchant doesn't react to him and continues speaking. "Come, miss. I have more shapes and sizes." He tries ushering me toward his little stall. I could easily get rid of his incessant pestering and get away without anyone batting an eye here, but there's a feeling in my stomach stopping me: curiosity.

Shadows flicker in the corner of my vision, calling to me. They feel so familiar and so foreign at the same time, like they're almost part of me and something else entirely.

"Are you deaf? She said that she isn't interested." The danger in Gideon's voice sends my blood curling in on itself, but out of the three of us, only I seem to be affected by it.

The shadows grow thicker, taking shape. Its obsidian shade is darker than the space between the stars on a cloudless night.

"I don't think he can hear you," I say under my breath as the blood rushes to my ears

The shadows reach out, seeping beneath my skin, dragging its claws against the walls of my mind like it's trying to find a way in. It feels as if it's pure chaos, like if I falter in my control the shadows will consume me whole. My heart thumps loudly as I try to find where the shadows are coming from. What are they? What do they want?

"What did you say, miss? You want to see more? Yes, yes, come with me. I have a good discount for you," the merchant says, placing a hand on my shoulder. In that instant, every single inch of my being screams, and my breath lodges in my throat.

The shadows sink its teeth.

He's touching you, the shadows whisper as darkness drips to my soul. *He shouldn't be touching you.*

I stop breathing.

No.

He can't—I can't—he's touching me.

Kill him. Make him pay for it.

My body takes over on behalf of my faltering mind. Spinning on my heels to face the merchant, his hand flies off my shoulder. My fingers curl just above his elbow, as my other arm wraps around his until his frame is buckled over to my will. Adrenaline surges through me, each breath coming out heated and uneasy. The merchant whimpers and withers beneath my hold, struggling to break out of it only to find himself in more pain.

The shadows snap back, disappearing from sight and the air slams back into me at once. Still, remnants of those carnal whispers remain at the edge of my frantic mind.

"Touch me again, and I'll break every single finger on your hand. Do I make myself clear?" Each word is low and deadly, just like my father's when he sentences another elf to the hands of Volducan. I sound nothing like a princess. No, I sound like a commander of death. "I said, 'Do I make myself clear?'" I snarl when he doesn't respond.

The merchant nods his head frantically, looking at a passerby for help, but no one so much as glances in his direction. "Yes. Please, Miss, I'm sorry."

I can feel his body shaking with unshed tears. This man doesn't belong in Zarlor; no person that can't hold their own and breaks under such a small threat is a true Zarlorian. He won't survive one week here if he crumbles this easily.

Stop it, you're causing a scene, I scold myself.

"Good." I let go of his arm, watching as he scampers back, clutching his robes like they're hanging on by a thread. "Now get out of my sight."

He doesn't waste another breath before running off down the street with his tail between his legs.

I spin, looking for the darkness, yet it's nowhere to be found. But the touch, the *shadows*, they're the least of my concern at the moment. Gideon is a ghost, a man who can't be seen. He's incapable of picking up an object, able to walk through doors and become a completely soundless being. That's why everyone was sending me strange looks. Could he be a figment of my imagination? Did my mind doctor a person in order to cope with the lonely nights and the constant travel?

The only sure sign that my sanity is still intact is the blood shed from the kaliak. My mind is not one to bring up images of such carnage. Nor is my mind creative enough to imagine being possessed. There is not a shadow of a doubt that he's real on one astral plane or the next, the dark power I felt brewing within him is real. Gideon is real.

I turn back to him. The golden glow of his skin has disappeared; all that remains is a ghastly hue that mirrors my own. I don't know how I would react if I were him. I feel broken every time I can no longer feel the moon, but at least I still have my own power. Gideon? He has nothing anymore.

No power, and no ability to touch things. I can't imagine the loneliness he would feel after spending hundreds of years inside of a book, only to come out to find that you are invisible to everyone.

Everyone except me.

"Are you okay?" I question softly.

"Let's go." He storms past me toward the market.

Well, that's the last time I'm asking him that question.

As we approach the market, the smell of cinnamon buns fills my senses, and my stomach responds to its sweet calling with a loud groan. I start walking in its direction, opposite of Gideon, and an exaggerated huff comes from behind me. Turning around, I bite my tongue to stop from saying something snarky to an invisible man in a place full of people. His arms are folded firmly across his chest, and he stands in his spot like a stubborn mule.

Shrugging my shoulders, I continue my journey. I refuse to let anyone get in the way of my lunch. Dropping a coin into the baker's hand, I take a big bite into the warm crust before making a beeline straight toward the wall I marked yesterday.

I start to chew the bread. Dry, over-salted, and overcooked. I'd be inclined to describe Gideon in the same manner. However, I'm sure the inanimate object would give me far less grief if I asked it how it felt.

Ignoring Gideon's foreboding presence, I search the crowd for my client as I walk. Sometimes I like to watch the people flit by, studying the way the vendors hunch when they think no one's looking, only to slap on a wicked grin when someone approaches. Or the way some people try to hide their winces as they drop coins into the merchant's hand to buy another garment they probably don't need.

This market isn't just for goods. Zarlor is the Kingdom of Lawlessness for a reason. It's where the rich send their henchmen in search of a person to do their dirty work: bounty hunters, procurers, assassins. Which means that this is my hunting ground.

I wince dramatically, clutching my stomach and eying the mark on the wall. I can just see Gideon grow wary of my fake pain, and I force myself to wince and flinch with every step until I make the last few steps to the wall. This trick only works in Zarlor because selflessness doesn't exist here. No one will help someone in pain. Usually, at least. They prefer to look away.

I stop myself from moving to the balls of my feet to get a better look. I may be short for an elf, but I'm tall for a mortal; just over the crowd of bobbing heads and frantic customers, I can see the pacing head of my client. As I get closer, I spot the bag of coins clutched tightly in her hand. They hire me to be discreet when they stick out like a sore thumb. It's times like these where I reconsider whether I want to make the trade. I'm about to give this woman a ring that kills any individual that the wearer kisses. Apparently, this ring makes the cause of death untraceable, I just hope she's smart enough to hide the ring afterwards. If she isn't discreet then I could be dragged into the crossfire.

I don't always have murderous clients, but the murderous ones tend to get my heart racing and it makes me feel alive for one sick moment. Sometimes they tell me about their vendetta and what made them so murderous, and it's like I live vicariously through them because I won't get the chance to take down my own enemy. My father. One day, he'll be on his knees, and I will teach him the meaning of pain.

Leaning against the wall, I rub my stomach as if it might miraculously heal it. The woman's gaze locks with mine, and she watches as my hand slips into my pocket to pull out the small bag with the ring. She scampers toward me, jerky in her steps. Then, as if she suddenly realizes how suspicious she looks, she walks slowly—regal almost—like the commander's wife that she is.

Call me a villain, but there's a small part of me that loves this kind of anarchy.

"You look ridiculous." Gideon appears next to me, burning his gaze into the side of my head.

"No," I whisper under my breath as the woman approaches, "I look like someone who gets the job done."

"Are you okay?" she says in a sickly-sweet voice, reaching her hands toward me. One of which holds a pouch full of coins—more than what the item is actually worth. But she doesn't know that.

I grin at the scorned wife. They aren't afraid to pay for 'good service.' She doesn't look like someone who would murder her husband. I'm not sure what he did, but I'm on her side already.

"Thank you, Ma'am." I take her outstretched hands into my own.

The sweet sound of coins clinking together soothes whatever phantom pain I feel, and I drop the pouch into her partially open purse before pulling away, tucking the coins into my pocket. It would have been a safer idea if we had a drop site where she drops the payment, and I leave the ring in the coin's place. Unfortunately, I don't trust her, so we are doing it in the open.

She nods sharply, walking away a little too quickly to be casual. It isn't my problem anymore.

"So you're a procurer." Gideon's voice travels to me, with intrigue lurking beneath the surface of his words.

My features remain neutral as I say, "Yes, and I'm also tired and running low on patience. Now let's see what that stupid angel knows."

DEX

CHAPTER NINE

BREWER'S BOOT, HOME OF ale that smells like leather and food that looks like death—both of which taste like regret.

I cringe every time I see the sign. The 'B' and the 'r' on the sign has been partially rubbed so that it says 'ewer's Boot.' Saeya dared me to rub off one of the letters with my powers when we were younger, and Vencen took it upon himself to rub out the 'B.' He found it hilarious, and really that should have made me run. But I was young, and thought he was the gods' gift to me, so I laughed along with him and told him that he was the funniest man I'd ever met.

Disgusting.

I can't count how many times I've pushed that front door open, pale with shame, smelling like the sins from the night before. Every time we'd come to Zarlor, we'd stay here; get blackout drunk downstairs, then go upstairs to do things that I don't want to be sober to think about. Saeya told me that it's normal to have an ex-lover that you keep going back to, but when your ex-lover is Vencen, you really start to question just how desperate you are.

The windows have a brownish tint to them from the lack of cleaning that goes on here, and it's times like these that I'm grateful I only have my partial elf hearing thanks to my necklace, because I can faintly hear the distinct sound of a headboard banging and the fake moans of a woman.

Please don't tell me that's Vencen.

"How do you know that he will be here?" Gideon's voice interrupts me from my stewing. His voice is the spark that lights my anger. I need to step into this inn, *plus* see Vencen, and to top it off, I have a shadow magically bound to me.

"Because he's a prick that doesn't leave bed until after lunch," I grumble, stomping toward the green door. I consider asking him to stay outside, but I quickly change my mind; if I am cursed to see Vencen in compromising positions, then so is Gideon.

Entering the tavern, the smell of must and bodily fluids wafts into my nostrils, and I gag on reflex.

"Dex." A voice bounces through the tavern from behind the counter.

She is used to seeing me leave in the early hours of the morning, not enter in the middle of the day. My eyes meet hers from across the tavern, the ocean blue stark against her iridescent skin. I can just make out the thin white lines of scales that never quite formed properly. She said that her mother is an elf and that's why she's opted for life on land rather than with the nymphs out at sea.

Her eyes bulge as they drop to my stomach, and despite the mortification plastered on her face, all I can think about is how she's far too beautiful for this place. Maybe I should just give her all the coin from that woman, so she finally has enough money to leave Zarlor.

"Whatever you're thinking, it's not *his*," I say far too quickly, hoping the overwhelming amount of brown furniture and walls in the room will detract from the heat rising to my cheeks. "It's fake," I whisper, winking at her.

"Good, because if Vencen were, I'd beat him to a pulp." She grins as she says it, nodding at my stomach, but something tells me that she isn't joking.

Her warm laughter sends stars shooting through my stomach. What I wouldn't give to lean my head against her chest and feel it vibrate as she fills the place with joy—joy that only seems to be reserved for me.

I know that deep down I'd never forgive myself if I dragged Ealrin into my mess. As far as she's aware, I'm the daughter of a merchant that goes from kingdom to kingdom trying to find the best products. I'm surely not about to tell her that my real father is a king.

Laughter dies in an instant, and the soft scales on her neck harden as a jet of water heads in my direction. A warm hand grasps my arm, pulling me out of the line of fire and hitting an unsuspecting patron in the back of his head. My head snaps up to find Gideon staring at Ealrin like he's ready to declare war.

"You didn't pay your tab," Ealrin bellows, low and lethal to someone behind me as water wraps around the patron's wrist as he tries to sneak past and out the door. Her voice is nowhere as powerful as Gideon's, but somehow it still gets my blood pumping all the same.

The man mutters something incomprehensible, and with a wave of her free hand, the sound of coins clattering onto a random table fills the air, and the water disperses. I think I make out the words to the extent of "keep the change," but I can't be sure with the mumbling.

The man exits the threshold, and the warm smile returns to Ealrin's face. Gods, I should have gone home with her, even if just for one measly morning. Despite her silky-smooth skin, the rugged edge of her jaw tells me that whatever she does beneath the sheets would go down in history.

Yet again, another regret associated with this inn; for some unknown reason I instead went under the sheets with Vencen rather than her. I never used to like the dirty looks she'd send him, but now, I live for them.

"I don't trust her aim. Let's go before she misses the next one," Gideon says with a tint of annoyance that I can't quite place my finger on.

For that briefest moment, I forgot all about Gideon. It was a truly blissful moment. But it was never meant to last. The sooner I can get rid of Gideon, the sooner I can take my time staring at Ealrin's hypnotic eyes.

"And is the prick here," I question, before quickly adding, "alone?"

Her face goes tight, like it's something that she would rather not think about. "The usual room," she says, slightly quieter.

I hesitate, worried that she might be disappointed in me. But I nod, muttering my thanks and climb up the crooked stairs to the side of the room, wincing as the wood creaks beneath my steps but stays utterly silent beneath Gideon's.

I wonder if he can hear how quickly my heart is beating, and whether he knows what is causing my dread as we head closer to Vencen. Could he have seen fractions of my memory when he was inside my head? Does he know what we are about to get into?

The only silver lining is that there's some level of comfort in knowing that I won't walk in on anything. Every time I know I'm about to see Vencen, my body screams, fighting each step that leads me closer to him. But as soon as I lay my eyes on him, something snaps, and I'm ready to fight him tooth and nail.

My feet stop on instinct just in front of his door, and I can feel Gideon's presence right behind me. The air burns with hostility, but it doesn't feel like it's toward me. The hallways are empty save for the occasional oil lantern hanging on the ceiling. I know for a fact that most of the rooms are windowless, and my best guess is that it became too costly to keep replacing the windows after every 'incident.'

Taking a deep breath, I prepare myself mentally and emotionally. I know he's going to say something crude, and truthfully, I am not sure how I'll take it now that Gideon will be in the room as well. He could think I'm weak for letting someone speak to me the way Vencen does. Or he might think that I'm just like Vencen.

No, it doesn't matter what Gideon thinks. I'm not letting myself feel lesser just because I'm worried about what some man might think. He's invited to form his own opinion of me, just as I've developed my own opinion of him.

"Is there a problem?" Gideon's voice is snide, and it only solidifies my previous thought: Screw what he thinks.

Banging on the door as loud as I can, I hear a groan come from the other side. "Get up," I order, attempting to use the same vigor that I hear in Gideon's voice.

I can just pick up on a string of mutterings and curses, followed by an exaggerated thump and stomp leading up to the door.

"What?" Vencen bites, swinging the door open.

I can't help my eyes that travel down his bare not-so-muscular torso, down to the bottom half of his body, naked and exposed for all to see. Bile lurches in my throat, leaving behind a putrid taste that will last the whole day. My muscles react faster than I can tell it to stop, apparently disturbed by the sight as well. I spin around with a yelp, bumping my shoulder into Gideon and slapping my hand over my eyes trying not to blanch.

"Put that thing away," I snap as though I might lose my sight if I see it again.

"You never complained about it before," Vencen chuckles, which only makes the muscles in my body protest more.

I can hear his footsteps retreat from me, until the sound of the bed squeaks and dips under his weight. Only when the rustling of his sheets fills my ears do I feel safe enough to drop my hand from my face.

"I seem to remember you had a different reaction to *Lord Hardwick* last time, sweet cheeks. A much *wetter* reaction if I do say so myself." He winks at me, and I all but hold back a gag. Gideon's hatred tinges the air, staring at Vencen's wings with a look that conveys deep rooted envy.

"Have you come to take me up on my offer?" Vencen grins.

Disgusting. My face contorts without hesitation. Does he not understand the meaning of *no*?

I look around the room in an attempt to dampen my irritation. It is no surprise that the room is just as dirty and rundown as the rest of the tavern: stained sheets, partially ripped curtains, a nightstand balanced by three books, and a fireplace that doesn't work.

My own reflection catches my eyes, and panic rises up in my chest. Silver strands peek through my braid, just a few days ago it was a vibrant brown, but now it's a dull grayish brown that sends me questioning how much of my silver and red hair has come through the brown and how many people noticed.

Ginger burns my tongue as I snap, "I'm here on business." Casting a sideways glance at Gideon, I note the combined fury and confusion darkening his gaze. Whiskey trickles onto my taste buds as Vencen chuckles, and my teeth start to grind on their own accord.

"I don't like him," Gideon growls, taking a step forward like he's trying to intimidate Vencen.

"Forget what you heard, you can in fact mix business with pleasure." Vencen drags his eyes up and down my body. This time I don't hold back my gag as the urge to crawl out of my own skin fills every inch of me.

"I'm here about the book the satyr paid you to get." I pull the knife out of my pocket, twirling it through my fingers so that maybe he will drop the childish act and focus on why I'm really here. Intrigue plays in his eyes like it's a ridiculous question though he's curious as to why I'd ask. "Tell me more about it."

Gideon leans in ever so slightly, waiting to hear what the winged man has to say.

Vencen shrugs, edging toward the end of the bed to grab a jug of questionable liquid and take a deep swig. "Not much to say. He wanted the Book of Twilight. I got the Book of Twilight. And now you have the fake Book of Twilight."

"He's useless," Gideon scoffs, folding his arms dramatically.

It's an odd sight, seeing one man react with such vigor, while the only other person in the room barely bats an eye. Pretending that I'm not aware of Gideon's existence is something that I doubt I'll ever get used to.

I try to focus on the conversation. "Where did you find it?"

Pride twinkles in Vencen's eyes, and his lips curl into a smug grin. *Here we go.*

"I stole it from some Black Blood general's place—the guy was practically ancient. He left it on a bench just for me. I put the hounds to sleep, slipped something in the Black Blood's drink, and the rest of 'em had no idea what hit them."

Gods, he had better hope no one saw him, or else he'll be as good as dead. It doesn't make sense though. Surely, they would put a book that is harboring something so deadly somewhere safer? If Gideon wants to go to Renlork to see exactly where his book was, then he's on his own. There's no way I'd get into the city as a lone female traveler.

"Wait, how did you know what the book even looked like?" That was the part that never made sense to me. When I first saw the book, there was no writing on it to suggest that it's the Book of Twilight.

"Didn't," he yawns, ruffling his golden hair. "Just had a gut feelin'."

Again. More holes in his story. I turn slightly to study Gideon's face to find his eyes narrowing in on the male, belittling him with his gaze.

"I guess you could feel the power coming from it." I suppose it partly makes sense, except I didn't feel its power until I touched it.

"What do you mean? It feels like an ordinary book." There's no lie written on his face. I think about prying further but remember that even the satyr didn't feel any of its power. The only other being that noticed was the hellhound.

"Did the satyr tell you what it's about?"

"Give me a kiss and I'll tell you." He puckers his lips, blowing me a kiss and a seductive glance.

I pull out a knife. "This is the only thing of mine that will be touching you." Each time I see him, I can't help wondering what in the gods' name

I saw in him. If Callaia were still alive, I'm sure she would not give her blessing to any such matrimony.

"You're no fun." He pouts like a child, looking at me expectantly like I might change my mind. He sighs. "Flicked through the pages, but it looked boring." Vencen snuggles into the bed as Gideon tenses. *Sore spot.* "He said he was after 'Hell's Gate' or the 'Book of Twilight' or something. Something along those lines. It just sounded cool, so I took the job."

Hell's Gate? Gideon certainly did not mention that. So far, nothing is pointing me in the direction of my freedom. "Did you see or hear any mention of a quill?"

His face twists in confusion. "Nah, I don't know if you saw, but he had enough to write with." He looks at me like I asked the most dumbfounded question.

"What about Hell's Quill?"

His features morph again as he eyes me suspiciously and asks, "Why are you asking me all these questions?" He pauses for a moment as if he somehow answered his own question. "Did that book have what you're looking for? I asked my contacts in Renlork about your spell, and no one knows where to find it. Does the Book of Twilight contain one? We can keep searching for it if it does." His tone shifts into one of hope and excitement.

I've never once doubted his devotion to breaking my curse. It's one of the few things that I can always trust him with. Maybe that's why I haven't killed him yet.

I shake my head quickly, momentarily forgetting about Gideon's presence as I sheath my knife. Telling *him* the truth about who I am will not make matters progress faster. Especially when I don't even know what he is beyond a 'weapon'. After one too many wines and someone looking at me the wrong way, I consider myself a weapon too. That doesn't mean that I'm going around saying that's my kind.

"No," I whisper, "it's just a book of tonics and spells." Guilt pinches my heart for lying to him, especially when I know how much he cares about ending the curse. But the truth will only confuse matters. How can I even begin to explain that I have a 'weapon' as my shadow, but no one can see, hear, feel, or touch him? "We both should leave Zarlor soon. There are more and more Black Bloods here every day, and I don't like it."

"But I haven't finished exploring everything Zarlor has to offer," he whines.

"Then stay. Do you or do you not know where the Hell's Quill is?"

"Unless you're talking about the brothel in Renlork, I wouldn't have a clue."

He throws the blanket off the lower half of his body without warning, exposing his *area* to us. I cringe back, squeezing my eyes shut and throwing my hand up in the general line of sight of his bits. "Put that thing away!" I wanted to sound forceful, like a command. Instead, it comes out as a strangled yelp.

"I'll protect you from the scary Black Bloods, baby girl," he purrs like he's about to be my personal escort. My teeth grind, holding back the need to vomit from such a thought.

"He needs to learn to shut his mouth." Gideon's clothing rustles as he takes another step toward the winged male.

I stumble backward, turning on the balls of my feet as fast as I can, and only then do I open my eyes. I thought I'd only want to gouge my eyes out if I saw him in compromising positions. As it turns out, there are a lot of things that will make me want to never see again.

I barely turn the handle before swinging the door open. "Goodbye, Vencen," I yell over my shoulder, slamming the door before Gideon walks out.

Vencen's never been one to ask questions, or even have a drive to acquire more knowledge. What I do know for certain is that he isn't lying. It's one of his few endearing qualities. There are many stories he fabricates out of nothing, but I know with every inch of me that he's telling the truth.

My footsteps echo through the hallway, and I'm still hot with disgust and mortification. A cloud of black smoke appears at the bottom of the staircase, and from it, Gideon emerges wearing the same revulsion that I feel.

The tavern is busier than it was before despite the fact that it is well past lunchtime. Angling my head as I descend the stairs, I try to spot Ealrin's hypnotic eyes, but her back is to me, rummaging through cabinets and drawers to keep up with the 'after-lunch' rush. The taste of whiskey on my tongue isn't so odd when I'm inside of a tavern, but it brings back bad memories when I taste it during the daytime.

Gideon's gaze locks with mine. I've been around him less than a day, but from the slight twitch of his nostril and the tensing of his jaw, I know for a fact that he has something to say. What I don't know is whether he will speak poetically or in another way that ignites a fire within me.

Sidestepping him, I push through the front doors before someone sees me talking to no one. I breathe in Zarlor's fresh air, relishing in the fact that I no longer smell piss. Still, I prefer the musty chill of the tavern than this humidity.

"I don't like how he speaks to you," Gideon says through thinned lips.

When we're out of earshot, I say under my breath, "Don't pretend to be protective of my honor."

His lips curl into a sneer as offense burns hot in his eyes. "I am not. Like you said, it is no longer *you* or *me*, it is *us* now, darling."

"Only when it's convenient."

DEX

CHAPTER TEN

"Well, isn't this just *splendid*," Gideon spits as another person in the market walks right through him, despite standing as close to the stall as he can without touching someone. "I'm bound to a weak witch with a spending problem. *Let's go.*"

The mention of being 'weak' makes me wince, but I know that it is far easier to get under his skin. "I may be weak, but at least I can actually use my powers," I say, earning wary looks from strangers. The stall owner is too distracted to notice that I'm speaking. I'm not too worried about people remembering me and thinking I'm mad. People generally want to forget about things that make them uncomfortable.

I can feel him flinch as the taste of whiskey appears in my mouth. I should ask Gideon why I'm starting to taste things, but it could be a form of opening in my mind that might allow him to possess me once more. The benefit of knowing the truth does not outweigh the risk.

Dropping the fifteenth beetroot into the sack that already holds two bunches of carrots and a jar of oil, the stall keeper finally drags their attention back to me.

"Are you afraid that you'll mess a spell up?" Gideon scowls as another person steps too closely to him, brushing through his arm.

The logical assumption for any person to get this much of the same vegetable is that it will be used in a spell. I don't respond, holding up my items to the shopkeeper.

Six coins, their voice barks in my head.

I don't like their kind, the blue suruds. All twelve of their eyes bore into me like they can see into my soul. They're conniving creatures, communicating telepathically, making you wish that you could block them out when they start screaming and yelling inside your head.

It was only three coins a few moons ago. I throw my hands wildly.

It's harder to get stock. Take it or leave it. Their voices are threatening, and the last thing I want is for them to start screaming in my head. Again. I'm not exactly their favorite customer, but I keep coming back because they sell the brightest beetroots.

Muttering curses under my breath, I dig out the coins from my pocket and drop them into their outstretched hand with fervor, saying, *This is just bad business.*

They don't acknowledge my retort, turning to the next customer that wants to argue with them about the price. Snatching the sack, we head back in the direction of the satyr's study.

As we continue, my skin tingles, a natural indication that the moon will soon wake from its slumber and the sun will be laid to rest.

Another person walks through Gideon, and he stops in his steps, gritting his teeth as his chest expands in time with his deep breath. The busier the street gets, the sourer his mood turns. I don't blame him. In truth, I would react much the same.

"There is no spell that you can do that will get rid of me, *witch*. Not that you will be strong enough to perform it either way." There's so much animosity in his voice that makes me want to snap as well.

Instead, I wonder how to get under his skin. He may not be able to kill me, but who knows what he might be able to do to make my life even more of a living hell?

I consider responding with something snarky but think better of it after mulling over his words. At day's end, people can still see me. They can hear me, touch me, *smell me*. I can still touch objects and use my magic, and I don't turn into smoke when I walk too far. This pains him far more than it pains me.

He sneers at my lack of response, continuing on our track and enjoying the silence between us. We pass several beggars who look up at me with sorrow written in their eyes. Zarlor has always cared very little about their homeless. I can't help but think back to what it was like to truly be a princess: throwing away things as soon as I got bored, not finishing a meal because 'I'm not in the mood,' prancing around in dresses that would have cost more than what some people make in a year.

Despite all my father's faults, I can at least say that he isn't the type of king who will let his people go hungry. He would always let the maids bring any leftovers back home to their families and he does his best to make sure every person in Hinixsus has a roof over their head. Father insisted only because it makes people respect him more. He's a 'good' king; he's just a bad person.

Now, I am a princess fallen from grace. What would father say if he knew how I spent my first year of freedom? Mother would be mortified to hear that I was one of them, roaming the street, sitting in front of a tin jar and going days without food. I remember the difference a single coin could make. I remember the feeling of the first bite of food in days—all because of a stranger. Then Kselia took me in. She kept me fed and made sure that I always had a roof over my head.

Living life in royalty and poverty changed my perspective. Because the truth of the matter is that it all came down to sheer luck.

I reach into my sack, giving carrots to children tucked closely to their mothers and dropping coins into the tin jars. A single item will not change their situation, but it will do *something*. I would be a liar if I did not admit that the simple act makes me feel good about myself, like perhaps I am a *good princess*, the same way that my father is a *good king*. Maybe it's also a selfish way of making me feel better for not playing my part in ending the war.

Every time the coin rattles in the can or a child wraps their little fingers around the carrot, I can feel the weight of Gideon's stare heavy on my back. As the last carrot disappears from the sack, and all that remains is a single coin that is enough for my dinner and passage to another city, I turn to Gideon and ask the other question burning in my mind, "Who put you in the book?"

He doesn't respond as we turn a corner and spot a group of Black Bloods marching in our direction. My hand jumps to my necklace, feeling the rapid thumps of my heart beneath it. They're armed to the teeth in axes and clubs, even the hellhounds are adorned with chainmail that rattles as they prowl the street, sniffing the air in the hopes they can catch a whiff of my kind of magic.

The sight of them dissolves any reservations I have about leaving Zarlor tomorrow. I wanted to comb through everything in the satyr's library in case he held any information about my curse and prophecy, or how to break it. Or even try to find where the quill might be. But having one or two Black Bloods order Zarlorians around is a bad sign in itself. If there is a battalion here, then that is very, *very* bad news, and this may well be the last time I will step foot in this kingdom.

I suddenly become very aware of what is in my bag. The book is no longer plain. Without a flicker of a doubt, they will all know that it's the Book of Twilight. They will smell its magic in an instant, and if they don't smell it now then they will if they ask me to empty out my bag again.

A pair of beady black eyes land on me, and I have to hold back a gasp. *Keep it together, Dex. Nice and easy,* I try to say soothingly in my head.

I can't turn in the opposite direction without drawing his attention more than I already have. I'm not about to outrun a hellhound, and I'm also not about to reveal that I am the lost princess of Hinixsus.

The blood rushes to my ears as more questions filter into my mind. What if my necklace is damaged from last night and they smell *me*? What if the hellhound can spot Gideon? It reacted strangely to the book yesterday when it wasn't unlocked. What about now?

A warm hand finds its way to the small of my back, making me jump out of my skin. My feet pivot, about to turn around to see who it is that dares touch me. But a low thrum of *his* power heats up at the back of my mind—a reminder that I have a shadow that no one else can see.

"Keep walking." Gideon's deep whisper vibrates through me.

I turn slightly, trying to read his expression. It's as if a blanket has been thrown over his anger, leaving his face devout of emotion to focus on the task at hand: keeping me alive, just as he did with the kaliak. Or maybe it's a reminder that I'm not alone in this anymore?

I do as he says, becoming completely conscious of his hand on me. I start 'selling the fantasy'; holding my stomach protectively as I lead with my hips walking quickly past them. I can still feel the Black Blood's stare on me. I can still hear their restless feet and searching eyes, desperate to wreak havoc. It feels like the calm before the storm, and I am in the center of it.

Don't look at them. Don't look at them. Just breathe. One foot in front of another. You're just a pregnant maiden returning home from the market. No one can see the real color of your hair, I repeat, like if I think about it hard enough then it might come true.

"Not much further." The words flow smoothly over his lips like warm honey. They ground me, making me feel like I can take another breath without worrying that it might be my last. And I forget about the blanket he has thrown over his irritation. Only then do I become acutely aware of his breath that is in sync with my own as if he's helping to calm my frantic lungs.

I want to push him away and tell him that I don't need his help, but I can't, not without causing a scene. I can do this on my own, just as I've always done. But I let his hands stay where they are, because it's *us* now.

I try to block out the sound of the Black Bloods, focusing solely on putting one step in front of the other, and feeling the way my ankles bend as I walk along the graveled street. Gideon's hand leaves my back, and I can't help wanting it back where it was, like it was a crutch that kept me going. Forcing the feeling aside, I avert my focus to getting out of the Black Bloods' view.

I can just make out the sound of several hellhounds whimpering, but I don't look, too afraid that the Black Blood might see right through my disguise. And too hesitant to see what effects Gideon has on the creatures. Clutching the fake bump harder, I pick up my pace. I can still feel his eyes on me, stalking my every move. Any rational pregnant woman would start running at this moment, and walking slowly would be the odder choice.

"You're almost there. Just two more blocks." Gideon's voice is deeper now, almost as if he's urging me forward like it's the last few paces of a foot race.

Just two days ago I could walk past Black Bloods without batting an eye and breaking into a cold sweat. I wasn't fool enough not to worry that they might smell the elf in me, but at least there was an element of confidence because the chances of getting caught were small, close to nil.

Now? Gods, now it feels like there's a timer attached to my life, like each second I breathe is a gift, except it's getting closer to expiry. All this because of a fucking book. Gideon's fucking book. This is what my own desperation has led to. Or maybe this is payback for treating a book badly. Either way, Gideon is in the center of all my *new* worries.

When the Black Bloods are no longer in sight, we both take a step away from each other as the memory of his touch on me poisons the air. I open my mouth to mutter my thanks when my arm is yanked back toward the building. The last thing I see is alarm burning in his eyes and whiskey hot on my tongue before spinning to see the culprit: a male with a beak. My mind instantly reels, weighing up whether to use my freehand to protect my stomach like one would in the circumstance, or reach for my knife like one *should* in the circumstance.

The wind is forced out of me as a new pair of hands pushes me against the walls with a thud, giving me an opening to see my assailants. Four males:

a dwarf, a human, a horned male with a single wing, and a bird-like male with a beak and no wings.

Easy enough to take down. I bite down a grin as my fingers itch for what's to come.

"Step away from her." Gideon's voice booms through the street, bouncing off the walls so forcefully I fear the windows may crack. None of the males reacts to the sound, yet all I feel is the urge to jump out of my skin and step away from *me*. I watch as his nostrils flare and the fire in his eyes starts to extinguish, the taste of whiskey goes with it until all that remains plastered across his face is helplessness.

"I be takin' this from you," the mortal starts to pull at my bag. The same bag that is holding the Book of Twilight. Rather than fear, a giddy feeling builds in my chest.

"What's a prett' lass like you doin' lone?" the dwarf says, and I find myself squinting like it might help me understand him better.

Then I make my decision.

My stomach.

I'll hold my stomach. It will be far more satisfying ruining them with my bare hands.

"I strongly advise that you run along, and we can pretend none of this ever happened," I say, flashing them my winning smile. Vencen has always said that I look deranged whenever I get pushed into a corner like this, and I always respond saying that this is just a way to show strength. Rather than admit that I sometimes like violence, I tell myself that it's because it will distract me from the Black Bloods. Also, because common thugs are some of the few people I can fight without any real repercussions.

I don't stop the chortle that leaves my lips as further excitement builds, because I'll be able to prove just how wrong these people are for continuing to stand in their spot. The males look wearily at each other, which only adds to my giddiness. The angel steps forward, his skin is the same shade of brown as his single wing, paired with a sinister grin that is trying to force me into submission.

Little does he know that all I see is a challenge.

My eyes travel along the faces of the four males. Though the dwarf looks like he knows how to pack a punch, he will be slow. The mortal will go down like a bug. The winged male will be the most fun to punish. But the beaked male? Oh, I want to make him squawk. Maybe I'll even take Gideon down for dessert?

My body stiffens, waiting, ready to pounce as the winged male's hand lifts, edging closer and closer to my face. "Last chance. I should warn you, I'm in an awfully *foul* mood." I cock a threatening brow at each male, becoming consumed by the excitement pounding in my chest.

The single-winged male, the cockiest out of the bunch, moves so close that I can almost feel his finger graze lightly along my chest. "And I'll take this," he says, touching the chain of my necklace.

Am I not in the Kingdom of Lawlessness? What kind of visitor would I be if I didn't take part in what Zarlor has to offer?

"Oh," I gasp. A wicked smile forms on my lips, and my voice darkens like I am the night itself. "You've done it now."

He staggers back a fraction, and I can just see his mind ticking like he's trying to comprehend my response. In Zarlor, a woman who knows how to fight is no surprise. However, his first mistake is underestimating a woman. Their second is underestimating her so much that they haven't even drawn their weapons.

Before my heart can take another beat, my fingers release the sack and I lunge forward with a speed unknown to witches and mortals. My hands curl around the smooth feathers of his wing and my face comes inches from him. "I told you to run."

The color drains from his face, and before he can move, I collide my fist with the bottom of his chin, forcing his head to swing back. The angel's body lifts off the ground with the force of my punch, and I use that moment to yank. And yank hard.

His cries fill the air, and I sprint towards the other males, dropping to the ground to kick my leg out and bring the birdman onto his back. Sparing a glance at the pile of feathers in my hands, I'm back on my feet. My featherless hand grabs the human's collar. I swing beside him and throw him onto the ground next to the beaked male, ripping the mortal's tunic in the process.

The dwarf wraps his hand around the short sword sheathed at his back. *Too slow.* I lunge forward before he gets the chance to pull it out. Grabbing him by the hair, I whip around to stand behind him, pulling his head back to shove the remains of his friend's wing into his mouth. Throwing him to the side, I head straight toward the beaked male standing firmly on his feet with both arms out in front of him in a fighting stance. Meanwhile, Gideon stands back with an unreadable expression on his face as he watches the events unfold.

I step toward the beaked male, with an innocent smile plastered on my face and my head tilted to the side like a child eying up a treat. His battle cry tears through the air as he lunges for me, arms out in front of him.

Rookie mistake.

I stand perfectly still. When his arm comes a hair away from touching me, I pivot to the side and curl my arm around his so that his throat runs straight into my curled fist. He staggers back with a delicious squawk.

Two arms wrap around my torso. Before the human can pull me to his chest, the same fist that brought the angel down hurtles down until it buries itself deep within his groin. Another cry fills the air as he drops, curling into a ball as his hand covers his now-damaged goods.

Gods, I need to do that to Vencen one day.

With slow, predatory movements, I spin on my heels to take in the damage. Smirking with deep-rooted satisfaction from watching their chests heave as their minds struggle to register what just happened. The winged male cradles his wing in his lap, gawking at the fresh patch of missing feathers at the center of it. The dwarf hasn't even bothered plucking his comrade's feathers out of his mouth, too busy staring at my stomach to actually move.

"Down boy." I turn to the dwarf with a wink. "You're right, I do think I'm quite a pretty lass. So unfortunate that none of you put up much of a fight, really." The blood rushes from my face as I stare down at the pool of men, and a new taste bathes my sense: mulled wine. It tastes rich, sweet, and spicy all at the same time.

Through the mortal's ripped clothing, a red mark that doesn't belong in Zarlor is stamped proudly in the center of his chest: the mark of the Paragon Dawn.

DEX

CHAPTER ELEVEN

Burnt into the mortal's skin is a crown sitting atop a warrior's helmet. This skin is a bright red, still raw from when they branded it into his chest. He's a worshiper of King Nodisci, leader of the Paragon Dawn. He's one of the delusional people who believes that Nodisci is the one true god—or the False God, as some call him—and that he should be King not just of Volducan, but of all eight Kingdoms.

No one from the Paragon Dawn travels this far into the realm, not since it's become clear that the Black Bloods have laid their claim to Zarlor. Death will follow if the Black Bloods and the Paragon Dawn are in the same Kingdom. Why would the Paragon Dawn choose to start a war in the kingdom next to Renlork? It doesn't make sense, especially if Zarlor has already been bought.

Is this human a spy? What if he's been sent to find the Daughter of the Blood Moon and I've walked right into his trap? Maybe he'll follow me to the waterfall, shove a white dress on me, and drag me to Volducan to marry the False God. I take a deep breath, forcing myself to reassess the situation. He might just be visiting Zarlor because he's a bounty hunter looking for jobs. Maybe he's the only follower in his group? That question can easily be answered by searching the other three men, but that will only raise suspicions.

I need to get out of here and fast.

I can feel their eyes on me as I rush to get the sack from the ground and step over the groaning beaked man. My gaze meets the human's, and I raise my chin to him in challenge and say, "There are 27 bones in a human hand, and I will take great pleasure breaking each and every one of them if any of you so much as *thinks* about laying a finger on me again."

Gideon's heated stare is heavy on me, but I don't look at him; I'm too focused on walking away from the mess that I made. I can hear the men cursing and making empty threats to 'make me suffer.' They may well act on those threats, and frankly, if it weren't for the mark on the mortal's chest, I'm sure I'd still be there having my fun.

Even if Gideon saw the mortal's mark, would he understand the seriousness behind it? The last time he would have roamed the realm freely, the Paragon Dawn would have been nothing more than a cult following a heretic king who believed there should be one true ruler of the realm. The Black Bloods would have been under Satrina's control, busy crawling into Hell and doing whatever it is that they do in there.

The sky slowly turns orange as we make our way back to the waterfall, and I can practically hear Gideon shifting like there's something he wants to say. "So you can fight?" He frames it like a question, but it comes out like a statement.

"Did last night not give it away?" I say a little too harshly. The sky is too bright, the weather is too muggy, the material of my dress is too rigid.

"I was going easy on you." He clicks his neck.

He's probably right. He could have easily killed me or wounded me badly enough to stop me from fighting. However, my ego is willing to test that theory out once more.

"As was I," I hum with confidence, "You looked sad about your missing wings, I didn't want you to feel worse by getting beaten in a fight by a *witch*."

I expect whiskey to coat my tongue because I always seem to taste it when anger burns within him. Instead, there's a taste that I can't quite put my finger on. From the corner of my eyes, I can just make out the tick in his jaw and the tight line of his lips, but the amusement in his eyes gives away the angry exterior he's attempting to portray.

"Unlike your *friend,* my wings aren't at risk of any plucking," he says the word 'friend' with so much disgust.

"What wings?" I return the look of amusement. A woman passing by starts whispering to her husband when she sees me talking to Gideon. This is attention that I don't want. Albeit being on the outskirts of Zarlor, I'm sure this area is used to seeing all sorts of people.

"People would cower in their homes when they saw my wings. With a single flap, armies would lay down their arms and beg to be spared." He closes his eyes to summon a fond memory.

"Even though you're all grown up, I think it's cute that you still have a wild imagination." I smirk and the taste of herbs fills my senses as he bares his teeth. "Don't worry, Gideon. As long as we're together, I will support you and your dreams." I place a soft hand over my heart.

"I am not dreaming," he mumbles under his breath like a child that has just been scolded, angling his head away from me. "Out of all my brothers and sisters, my wings were the most fearsome. Except for my ex—" He stops himself like he just slipped up.

"Sorry, what was that?" I push with amusement still bright in my eyes.

"One day you'll see my wings, and you too will fear me."

I roll my eyes and repeat my question as I lift my skirt to step over a discarded carton. "Who put you in the book?"

He hesitates like he's unsure how to answer. Turning slightly to face him, his lip twitches as he stares at the ground, pain seeping through his every pore. Anger, betrayal, love, and grief all tangle within his eyes.

When he notices me looking, he stares straight ahead, as if the question doesn't faze him. "My family," he says, like answering is an afterthought. "Who is Vencen to you?" He tries to steer the conversation away from his family and pretends he couldn't give two shits about the answer. But there's a raw edge to his voice that casts the question in darkness.

If he can avoid talking about his curious family dynamics and still wants to see them after they shoved him into a book for a couple hundred years, then I can get away with not talking about my relationship with Vencen.

"Why did they bind you to the book?"

What sort of monster must he be if his own family trapped him with the kaliaks? A better question would be why he would agree and go so far as to choose the object to be used as a key? I do suppose my own parents would do something similar without my input. My betrothal is a clear example.

But what does this new information mean to me? I do not feel any less inclined to rid myself of him by any means necessary.

"If your family finds out, would they put you back in the book? Is the book damaged in some way so that you will be bound to me again? Can we find them and ask them where the key is?"

"You ask too many questions," he bites, speeding up his steps to avoid being within talking distance.

I can't shake the feeling that he's hiding something; he has to be more than just a weapon. With the war, it makes sense why everyone would want a weapon. But it doesn't make sense why his family would put him in a book that can be unlocked using a key made from a dead goddess' blood, then also have a ring that's capable of controlling him.

"Just—" I start with irritation in my voice, before he abruptly halts his steps, spinning around and cutting me off with a wave of his hand.

"You have no leveraging power over me, little witch," he spits with a menacing smile. "But please continue with your feeble threats. This is the most entertainment I've had in hundreds of years."

Fury is hot on my skin as I stomp on ahead of him, and his chuckle makes it apparent that this is the reaction he hoped for. Another woman watches me with concern in her eyes and I return her stare with a soft smile, rubbing my stomach lightly and cringing as the material sticks to my sweat ridden skin.

Shouting and the pounding of hooves erupts through the air when we turn a corner. There aren't many Black Bloods in this part of Zarlor, so the sounds can't be coming from them. A fist fight rages in the middle of the street between a few satyrs with yellow stripes painted on their faces, and brown humanoid creatures with tusks painted in blue protruding from the center of their foreheads. With the paint, I can only assume that there was some sort of sports game lost and one side cannot handle losing.

Passersby skirt around the ruckus and continue on with their day like nothing is happening.

"Come back here, mutt!" a satyr screams at a centaur, as he tries to fight off the tusked creature. The centaur smiles from ear to ear as she gallops away with her stolen goods held tightly in her hand. Her hair flows with the wind, exposing her bare chest that glistens from Zarlor's humidity.

"Zarlor is more lawless than I remember," Gideon mutters, scowling when a satyr gets pushed out of the fight, landing a few steps in front of us. A bracelet around his left wrist catches the light, and my eyes zero in on it.

I rush up to the satyr before he can get back up. "Let me help you, young man." I wrap my hand around his forearm.

He grunts in response but accepts my assistance. I grip him tighter as he moves to stand, and my hand reaches out to lightly touch his wrist in *assistance*. He doesn't bother steadying himself before launching back into the brawl.

"You're welcome!" I yell at his back.

When the fight is no longer right next to us, I slip the bangle on, lifting my hand up to the sun to admire my new piece of jewelry. It's much too large for my wrist, but I can still fetch a decent amount of coin for it.

"Seriously?" Gideon grinds.

I shrug, smirking back at him. "I'm just fitting in."

~~GIDEON~~
CHAPTER TWELVE

MORTALS ARE CURIOUS THINGS, fretting over mundane matters that are boring to everyone's eyes but theirs. It seems that a short life span has a direct correlation with attempting to prove something; either by collecting knowledge, or by pouring all of their money into looking like they are a walking jeweler. It is as if their lives are nothing without the things that others can see.

Then there's her, and whatever ungodly mess she has intentionally brought upon herself.

"You're dyeing your hair instead of going to Taravene?" The impatience in my voice rolls from my tongue easily after watching her slather her hair in paste for almost an hour. She can hold her own; there's no need to wait until morning to travel.

Her concentration doesn't falter as she stares intently at her own reflection in the water as if she is trying to find a single strand that is out of place.

The little witch looks at me with gray eyes alight with mischief. She sucks in her bottom lip for the briefest moment, and I can feel her concentration transform into amusement like she's contemplating refusing me the luxury of her response. In a split second, the emotion written on her face changes into pride as her brows raise ever so slightly. "Well, at least one of us needs to look pretty."

She turns, suppressing the smug grin that touches her lips. There truly is nothing 'pretty' about the sight before me. Whatever she is doing is borderline sickening on every level there is.

Scooping the maroon paste with her stained nimble fingers, she smears the mixture onto her scalp. Brownish red chunks trickle and fall as she massages it into her hair, and the bangle drops down her arm, tucking itself into the crook of her elbow. I can feel the way the bracelet causes a flicker of annoyance that dampens her mood.

In my experience, those who pour their earnings into appearances would never stoop so low as to sleep in the hollow of a waterfall or paint their own hair with a vegetable paste that will likely wash out within a week. It would be far easier for her if she simply cast a beautifying spell on herself, unless she's too weak to do so.

"Stupid thing," she mutters, covering the stolen item in the paste as she slips it off and drops it into the sand next to her, and the flicker of annoyance becomes one of relief.

Her actions are practically incomprehensible. Why steal only to damage and disregard it in such a manner? I sensed the darkness that emitted from her pocket and later dropped into the hands of the woman who dressed in riches. It would not have been easy for Dex to procure such an item, and then she drops the earnings into the hands of beggars? My life has revolved around those that pray for the death of their foes and destroy lives for their petty greed. None of those people would do something as benign as steal and donate it to others, especially to their own detriment.

I heard the rattling of her coin purse. She has far too little left if we intend on making leeway on our plan to get out of Zarlor and to get her out of my own mind. I can feel her emotions shift again in the span of seconds, turning to one of grim seriousness with an excitement that feels intoxicating.

The she-witch feels far too much. I struggle to hear my own thoughts from the vigor of her erratic emotions. I am surprised her head hasn't combusted with all of the things she feels.

A wet slap fills the air, and my features curl into a firm scowl. Deplorable witch. It perplexes me that someone who can move with such regal grace can act like a barbarian.

"We're going to the Kingdom of Wealth," she says as if I can read her mind and understand the purpose of this beauty regime. She rolls her eyes impatiently. "Red equals rich, and if you look rich then you're blending in just fine." She looks up at me through her lashes as the paste drips down the side of her chin. There is almost an ethereal glow to her. The evening light catches the smooth skin of her face, tarnished by the splotches of beetroot that have escaped their place in her hair.

I remember Taravene as the kingdom that caused the most delicious kind of chaos because money is the true cause of destruction. My brother and I used to see who could become the most intoxicated and attempt to climb up the golden obelisk without getting caught.

"If it isn't there, then we go to Hinixsus"

Her raw fear thrums through me at the mention of the lunar kingdom. When she spoke about Hinixsus by the palace, I felt a barely noticeable spike in her anxiety. I thought nothing of it at the time, but it appears the little witch is hiding more than I initially suspected.

"My family lives in Taravene. They'll find us a lead," she says in an attempt to dissuade me. "I'll tell them that it's for a job." By now, her panic is acidic in my chest as she ties her hair up and out of her face.

Curious.

"There's an elf in Hinixsus, tasked with tracking the whereabouts of the book." It isn't up for debate. Another tremor of fear wrinkles in my chest at the word 'elf.' Even if the matter were not up for debate, I would find a way to drag her to Hinixsus to see what it is that causes the same unbridled fear I felt in her when she looked at the mortal on the street.

If this fear is hindering our ability to reach our goal, then it's time I begin schooling her on *her* communication skills.

"Why do you not want to go to Hinixsus?" I fold my arms.

"Your elf is probably already dead, and I don't want to waste days of travel for what will likely be a dead end," she snaps, washing her hands in the water and leaving a red hue behind.

My parents cast me into the book for a purpose, and that purpose does not involve watching a witch play with her hair. She may make a mockery of the lock and key, but if she knew the truth, she would not waste my time in such a manner.

"And if he is alive, then his days are few."

The longer we stay idle, the closer someone is to finding the quill. My brother did well at keeping the items a secret, but kings like to talk. Eventually, knowledge of my existence will slowly leak to the masses. Then the hounds will be set upon her, and she will not have the power to stop it.

I cannot let anyone get their hands on the ring; all will be lost if I don't reach it in time. Being controlled is not part of the plan, but it could not be done any other way. I've hidden the ring in a temple, and I do not trust Dex to take me there.

"I need a summoning spell. Can you do one?" she asks abruptly, placing her hands on her hips.

The blood-red book peeks from within her bag, and a fire ignites in my chest. Nothing should have been able to unlock the book, not even the blood of a witch. I haven't stopped thinking about it since stepping back into the light, yet still, I have been unable to figure it out.

"What do you intend to summon?" I uncross my arms and walk closer to her. Dex's jaw tightens, and her body tenses ever so slightly. She looks at me like I'm a predator prowling toward my prey, only I don't sense any fear in her.

"It's a yes or no question." She crosses her arms in turn.

A small smile plays at my lips. *The little witch wants to play.* "Let me rephrase my question; *who* do you intend to summon?" With each word, I step closer to her, and her body tenses more and more, but she doesn't cower. The smell of beetroot tickles my senses as her head comes mere inches from my own, and I can practically feel her rapidly beating heart. Pulling her shoulders back, she cocks her chin in challenge, but her own emotion betrays her: fear.

Break her, the shadows of my power laugh. *Make her scream*. I ignore the voices, pushing them back down to the darkest depths of my being where it belongs. It's unfortunate that all that remains of my power are the sinister voices that crave chaos.

"That is irrelevant," she says with nonchalance, closing what little distance there is between us until only an inch remains. She cranes her neck almost all the way back just to look up at me. Despite the clothes between us, I can feel the heat of her body emitting from her, warmer than the sun's rays. After all the people I was surrounded by today and the lack thereof for the past two hundred years, being able to *feel* someone else is truly unexplainable. Even the joyous sensation that brews in my chest from being able to speak to another person does not compare to the finest of wines.

Alas, the person in question is a thief. Still, there's something about her that feels familiar like I have met her before. In fact, it goes beyond a sense of familiarity. Unbinding me from the confines of the book should not cause such a feeling. Perhaps the reading of her emotions is a consequence, however the reaction my soul has when I see her is not part of any such unlocking.

"Quite the contrary, darling," I whisper darkly, "Because if you had any sense of self-preservation or wisdom, you would know that keeping things from me—things that will help us get rid of each other—will only mean we're stuck with each other for longer."

She winces when she realizes my words are stolen from her own. "You ask too many questions," she mutters, pulling away and taking all of the warmth with her. "You keep your secrets, and I'll keep mine."

"Come now, shall we light a fire and talk about everything that's troubling our minds?" I suggest, letting the chaos of my power trickle into my mind. The response is out of character for me; she just makes me feel alive. I have been deprived of conversation for so long.

She sets her ferocious gaze on me, warning me to drop it. Little does she know that I can see into the witch's heart; she's enjoying the witty responses. Yes, she is irritated beyond comparison, but she hasn't yet admitted to herself that she gets a thrill from it.

"We can talk about our deepest fears and—" My mind falters as she begins untying her overskirts, dropping them into a heap in the sand. "What are you doing?"

"I'm about to bathe, and you're being a prude." Venom laces her voice as she grips her tunic, about to lift it over her head only to freeze when it is at her sternum. "Turn around." She raises her brows in disbelief that I haven't yet.

I can still feel her irritation bubbling through her, while joy builds deep within. It brings me no greater pleasure than to be the one to light that fire in her and see just what she can burn with that tongue of hers.

Folding my hands tidily behind my back, my features remain cold and distant. Her gaze jitters, reading my face as if attempting to determine what I'm feeling.

She huffs, granting my challenge and raising me another. Pulling the tunic over her head, she places heavy hands on her hips, staring me down in nothing but her brassiere and thin underskirt. *The little witch wants to play indeed.*

My fingers graze over the silver button of my coat; a dragon head—the most chaotic and beautiful creature that I've ever laid my eyes on. They have more morals and values than many of the men I have had the misfortune of interacting with. How I have missed those beasts.

Pushing the button through the loop, I move to the next, undoing it as well. Her gaze never once leaves mine as I pull the coat off with practiced ease.

Her eyes protrude, but she shows no sign of backing down. Her hatred seeps into her veins, engulfing the exhilaration she feels from our game. Good. Her hatred will fuel her to move faster so I can be free of her sweeping emotions.

"Your turn, little witch. I still have much more to lose." I nod down to my remaining layers of clothing and the few that remain on her.

She shakes her head while her lips twitch into a sneer. "No, thank you, keep your clothes on. I have no interest in seeing more of you than I already have. Now be a good little boy and turn around."

She dares speak to me like that? Me? I am the most powerful person she has ever had the fortune of casting her eyes upon. She could stare at mountains and look into the eyes of kings, and *nothing* would compare to my very presence. I have made kings cower behind their thrones, brought armies to their knees, and *she* calls *me* a little boy?

I step forward without noticing that her brassiere has found a home amongst her discarded clothing, and I shut my eyes, turning around to make sure I do not see any more than I already have. What little I saw of the way the golden light cast deep shadows over her skin, tucking around her curves, making me forget all about the monstrosity on her head—all caused my breath to seize and send my mind reeling, tucking away the memory so it doesn't see the light of day again.

She is a witch, I must remember that.

Yanking my coat off the ground, a shallow pain aches in my chest from the way the sand leaves no evidence of my existence. The sound of water rippling becomes my cue to wander into the forest with the coat held firmly in my grip. Once I'm free, I'll burn it. I've worn the same thing for 232 years, and it did nothing to keep me warm inside the darkness of that *fucking book*. Now, as I stand in the sun, I can only feel mere prickles of its rays. I never used to be one to rejoice in being in the sunlight; it was always too calm and predictable. But in the dead of night, the possibilities of destruction are endless.

In all my years of existence, I never looked down at my feet as I walked because I *was* power. I *feared* nothing. I've become nothing more than a ghost of my past, stuck in an endless cycle of grasping onto my days of glory and yearning for them. That is but a distant dream. The formidable power I am—was—is left rotting in that cursed book.

Now, I watch my feet move through bushes and branches without a single sound and walk over patches of moss without leaving a dent behind. It's as if I don't exist at all, and I'm still inside the cold book, letting my mind take hold and taunt me with my worst nightmares.

A scream rips through the air in the direction of the beach, paired with the lethal screech of the kaliak. *Dex.* My body moves before my mind does, tensing my shoulders as I run in her direction, waiting for wings that never come. The shrill sound of a sword being drawn pierces my ear, and I can just see the light reflect off a short sword. The weapon won't be enough to stop it unless she can behead it or kill it with fire.

My eyes squeeze shut, and I reach out for the rope that tethers us; hers a blinding silver and deep red, mine an obsidian darker than night itself. Grasping onto the rope, I pull. My body and soul expand, morphing into vapor and traveling along the silver rope, all the while thinking that she *mustn't* die. My soul contracts, and my body shatters into a million pieces before becoming whole again.

My feet are planted on solid ground, but it takes a moment longer to get my bearings. A gruntled cry sounds over my shoulder and an ear-piercing scream that I can *feel* follows suit. Spinning and clenching my fist I try to summon the power fermenting in my core. But nothing comes except a low, static hum that warms my fingers.

"You stupid bitch," Dex grunts, kicking the kaliak in its stomach as sand flies everywhere and she wrestles its claws away from her face using her sword. Patches of fur and whiskers spread sporadically over its body, swaying and shuddering with its rigid movements.

It towers over her fallen form, double in size. Bones from old and new victims protrude from it in all angles, pushing aside what remains of its droopy skin. The poison from its claws drips down her arms, leaving the skin crimson in its wake.

"Don't fucking dribble on me," she spits as it wails, shaking its head from side to side, causing its melting skin to sway. Green venom splashes along the sand, hissing and sputtering in a plume of smoke.

It won't go anywhere—not when all eight spikes coming out of its two long legs are plunged deep within the ground.

"Get off!" I yell at the monster, but it pays me no mind. "I command you to stop!"

Magic fills the air as she lands another kick to its ribs, cracking a bone and making it pierce through its own skin. The beast flinches back ever so slightly, and she takes the opening to throw it off balance, losing her hold on the sword in the process, she attempts to dash out from underneath the kaliak. A deadly shrill rips through its web-like mouth before she has the chance to leave its hold. The sound can kill a mortal in seconds; a witch in not much more.

Nausea swells in my stomach from the ringing of its cry. It has been a long time since I've heard it. Dex's mouth opens to scream as her hands move to cover her ears, but she stops herself, using the sand to try and scramble away.

I've never been so helpless before. People used to turn to me when they needed something. Now, I have to stand and watch my string of freedom die right before my eyes.

"Dex, run!" I try to yell over the monster's cry. Blood starts to drip out of her ears and her fingers shake, attempting to dig into the sand to pull herself up. "It can't hear you when it screams, run!"

The metallic smell of power mixes in with the smell of rotting flesh and the hum in my fingers grows louder like it is trying to make me do something. But I won't. Not again. I won't give into that darkness.

Dex falls onto her side as blood gushes from her nose. Her arms shake as she tries to pull herself back up. We won't be able to outrun it—it will only make her death more imminent. The kaliak continues to scream, warning any other monsters nearby that the kill belongs to it.

She throws her hand back at the monster and the silver rope between us coils and shudders from the weight of her power. The forest descends into a silence more deafening than when the beast screeched its bloody cry. It flies through the air and across the beach. Cracking fills the silence as the beast's bones sprawl across the sand—it looks like it would be dead. Only those bones belong to its previous meals, and Dex slowed it down.

A soft groan breaks the tension as Dex struggles to get back on her feet. Red gushes from her arm as pain decorates her features. I expect to feel her hurt, but all I feel is annoyance and exhaustion. She starts, "The bloody—"

"Dex, no!" I scream when the kaliak leaps and lunges toward the sound of her voice.

Time seems to slow as I watch each point plunge into the ground for barely even a moment before it uses its long legs to sprint with its claws raised, dripping with a fresh sheen of venom. Dex's fear drowns my own, and I let the darkness take over.

At a pace faster than the beast's, my power has me sprinting to the spot between Dex and the monster. The dark magic spreads through me, covering every inch of skin until it all hums with violent hunger; a hunger to kill, hunger to feed, and a baseless need to protect her, even if it kills me.

Bones splinter and crack as my fingers penetrate the kaliak's weak skin, moving through rotting flesh and matted fur until my hand curls around its spine. The beast stops in its tracks, and the chill of its skin flickers surprise in me, but the darkness has no room for mortal emotions. Fate is playing a cruel joke; the two things I can feel are a witch and a monster of death.

Power starts to flood my mind, pumping rage into every corner of my body—rage that it *dared* harm her. It seeps from my fingers, into the kaliak.

"Die," I snarl. My darkness shudders through the beast's system, and it disintegrates into a pile of ash.

DEX

CHAPTER THIRTEEN

THE REMAINS OF THE kaliak drift along the beach on the feeble wind. Gideon's chest heaves and his black tunic pulls with each ragged breath. His fingers that wrapped around its spine moments ago hover in the air with a tremor, and the smell of his remaining power lingers. It smells like chaos.

Whiskey burns my tongue and scorches my lungs. His rage only worsens the ringing in my ears. I swear I can still hear the monster's scream ripping my mind to shreds until I can barely tell which way is up and which is down.

My own shaky breaths become more in sync with his, and the last drop of blood trickles from my nose.

"How did you do that?" I can barely say the words. I've never seen anything like that *thing*.

He stares at his raised hand for a moment longer as if he's trying to rein something in. I can only see the side of his face, yet the look of hatred is unmistakable.

His fingers curl into a tight fist, and he whispers, "I guess it and I are both monsters."

My mouth hangs slightly ajar, unsure of how to respond. He could in fact be a monster and I wouldn't know. "Thank you." I place my energy into keeping my breath even and my body steady as the moon does quick work of returning me to my natural state. "For saving me," I add.

"If you die, I will go back into the book."

He drops his hand to his side and shifts his weight, turning to face me. All signs of his hatred evaporate, and his gaze moves from my legs to my undergarments, dragging up with a slow burning intensity as his eyes trail the curve of my silk camisole where it sticks to my damp skin. Gideon's eyes land briefly on my chest before snapping up to meet my gaze. Mulled wine seasons my tongue, warming something deep in me.

Heat rises to my cheeks and molten need floods my veins from the simple act. *It has been too long since I last got into someone's bed.* I wrap my arms around my body to hide my important parts. Elves are no strangers to being nude by a lake under the moonlight, but even though I have a camisole on, his gaze makes me feel like I'm walking exposed through the streets of Zarlor. The thin fabric does nothing to stop the feel of his eyes that seem to undress me.

Another feeling morphs in me: nauseating, sickening, and embarrassing. His presence is making me feel self-conscious. I can't imagine what I'd look like with all the sand stuck in my sodden hair. Somehow that unwanted feeling makes me want to be the most beautiful creature he has laid his eyes on, so that he never thinks of another again.

I shove all my emotions down my throat because that invisible "weapon" does not deserve it. Not when the smell of rotting flesh lingers in the air. As soon as I heard the sound of spikes plunging into mud, I ran back into the water. Except the kaliak heard the movement of the water. I almost died, yet here I stand with a racing heart, not from my brush with death, but from the weight of his stare.

Gideon clears his throat, running his hand through his hair. He turns away to face the forest like he's keeping an eye out for more kaliaks, and something akin to disappointment flickers within me. As he shifts, the moonlight reflects something shiny on his chest. Only then do I notice the onyx amulet hanging around his neck, tucked neatly beneath his tunic.

That could fetch some heavy coin.

Turning my back to him, I can't help but clear my own throat. "So," I drag out to break the awkward silence as I zip over to my pile of clothes. "Tell me more about the kaliaks," I finally say once I manage to form clear thoughts in my head. I'm telling myself it's because of the near-death experience, and it has nothing to do with the way his eyes darkened when they landed on my almost naked body.

Peeling the wet camisole off, I can hear his clothing rustle from behind me, stretching the uncomfortable silence between us.

"The longer I'm in this form, the more kaliaks will come," he says like I was imagining his prior hesitation.

"Right." I fasten my undergarments before slipping into what I consider my traveling clothes: cotton breaches, a loose tunic, and a thin overdress to make me appear a fraction more 'innocent.' "We better get going then."

The last thing I want is for more people to die. I'll even risk running into a Black Blood for it. I have more than enough energy to travel through the night thanks to the moon, and the attack has disbanded any need for sleep. All I need to do is steal a horse and we will be on our way to Taravene.

"No." We both turn at the same time. I look at him with my brows raised in silent disbelief. "The kaliaks prefer to hunt at night."

The answer only makes me more confused. "If they rely on their hearing to hunt, would it not be better for them to hunt during the day, when it's loud?"

He shakes his head. "Typical witches, they refuse to learn the history of any other species but their own," he all but spits. "The kaliaks' hunger knows no bounds, yet they find pleasure in the darkness of the night."

Sounds like another species I know. Mine.

"What is with your vendetta against witches?" My patience with his incessant attempt at insulting me with the word is running out.

"Because they like to use power that isn't theirs for them to use." He pauses like he's considering if he should explain further. "If you read your history books, you will know that out of all the races, witches and warlocks are the ones who like to play god." The look he gives me tells me that there's more to his distaste than what he's letting on.

And fae, I want to add.

"Fine." I yank my belongings from off the ground and walk to the waterfall. If I'm traveling during the day, I'm going to need my fair share of rest. Despite the threat of potentially being killed by a kaliak at any given moment, I'm surprisingly comforted by the fact that Gideon can kill any that wishes to devour me in my sleep.

As he said, he has a vested interest in keeping me alive. Keeping me 'well' will simply be my own concern, because I doubt he will care if I rest or not, so long as it doesn't impact on our ability to find the quill and ring.

Jumping over the puddle of baby crabs, I look over my shoulder and say, "Wake me up at first light." And under my breath, I mutter, "And not a moment earlier."

Screams rupture the air, and I can still feel the moon.

"Dex, get up!" Gideon's voice roars through the clearing, and he appears next to me a second later.

Sleep still clouds my heavy eyes as I try to riddle out his words. My nostrils twitch as the smell of smoke stains the running water. Just behind Gideon, a light flickers.

Not just any light, a fire.

"What's happening?" I scramble to my feet—already booted and laced— readjusting the position of the weapons hidden on me.

"Zarlor is being attacked. We need to go, *now!*" He grabs my arm and pulls me to the entrance with the book in his other hand.

They've found me. They know I'm here. They're going to kill me, and it will all be Gideon's fault.

I pull against his hold, reaching for my bag as an excuse to free myself from him. "Wait." I have to run *now*, but I need more than just a sword if I'm going up against an army of fae or elves. I won't be able to take my necklace off and use my powers to their full extent in case it turns out that they weren't after me at all.

"We don't have time," he snarls with raw urgency.

I don't let him try to pull me again before I yank myself out of his grip and snatch the bag off the ground, running to the closest hiding spots. Pulling the stone out and grabbing my coins hidden within, I don't bother fixing it before moving to the next compartment to take a crystal necklace and clip it around my neck. Grabbing my cloak, I throw it on as well.

"Move back," I hiss as I prepare myself to recreate the motion he did just the other night. Running to the back of the cave, I take a deep breath and imagine the exact spot I want to land on; not the water and not the rocky parts. The moon's power starts to flood into my muscles, making both necklaces buzz, and I ignore Gideon's urgent mutterings.

Pushing off the wall with the help of the moon, I sprint right for the waterfall. Stones scatter, and my boots slide across the sand as I gather momentum. The waterfall splits down the center, and I push off the cliff of the cave. I aim for the thin line where the water laps against the beach and descend headfirst toward the sand. Putting my arm out, bending once it hits the sand, I curl into a ball and roll onto my feet.

Gideon appears beside me as hellhounds howl nearby. We start sprinting in the opposite direction of Zarlor.

Volducan's red arrows and Hinixsus's glowing blue arrows spear through the sky like fireworks. Their colors. They're here. Volducan and Hinixsus are here. My father's army is here. My betrothed's followers are here. And they're fighting the Black Bloods in Zarlor. Why would they attack the city closest to Renlork? Did my stalker tell them that I'm here?

Callaia, please. If you're listening, please don't let them catch me. Please guide the way, I repeat over and over again, because it's all that I seem to know how to do right now, apart from running.

Jumping over a fallen tree, we go in the opposite direction of the sound of the fight, but it seems to be coming from everywhere. My heartbeats thrash as my breathing goes sharp and short with panic and bloodlust. Red curls around my vision and a sick, twisted part of me wants to join the fight, to annihilate anyone I see. But it isn't just my own power that is fueling my desire for death; it's his. A flicker of the darkness that possessed me yesterday remains, poisoning my mind with its whispers of chaos.

Drawing my sword out, the moon's power fills my veins ready to defend—or attack. I need to rein it in or else I'll become a beacon for the hellhounds.

The orange glow of the fire spreads from tree to tree as the roars of warriors rage louder than the flames themselves. My feet barely touch the ground as I sprint through the forest. Gideon knocks me off my feet, taking the brunt of the fall when an arrow lands right where I stood. He pulls me back up just as the smell of blood and rotten flesh stains the air.

They're hunting.

The high pitch hum of the kaliak starts to mix in with the screams of dying soldiers.

Fuck it, I think, letting my own power consume me, and I start running faster than any witch could. Bile builds in my chest as my own power fights my necklace. It feels like it's only a hair away from cracking the gem into smithereens. I've known that my power has been getting stronger, and the ache to *become power* grows.

Three Black Bloods charge toward us with raised clubs and axes just as another stray arrow drops from the sky, glowing blue under the reflection of the moon—the weapon of my people. I flick my hand, changing its course to plunge into one of their eyes, and he drops to the ground with his ax still raised in the air, leaving two for me to kill.

Sheathing the short sword, I move my hands to my hips, drawing out two knives. From the corner of my eye, I can just make out a new set of black eyes focusing on me in the distance. And he charges. Four Black Bloods; I like my odds. When the two remaining Black Bloods are close enough to swing at me, I roll onto the ground between them, missing their attack as I tuck the knives close to my chest. Stopping myself before they move out of my reach, I land with one knee on the ground and my arms back so the knives penetrate tough skin and scrape the bone from the back of their knees.

I pull my knives back out. Like flies, they drop onto a single knee, crying out in pain and rage. Pivoting to kneel next to them, I spot another Black Blood heading my way while the other makes his way to me. Crossing my arms in an 'x', with the moon's power, I push my arms out again. Lodging my blades into the sides of their heads and yanking it out, they drop to their sides.

Three down, two to go.

The closest Black Blood roars, lunging through the air with sharpened bones in each hand. A sadistic smile curls at the corner of my lips, blocking out the fear that still lives inside me. Gripping the knife, I swing my arm up, harnessing the moon's power, and at the same time, the root of a tree breaks through the ground, piercing the Black Blood's stomach. When I lower my arm, the root slams him to the ground, pulling him deeper into the dirt until his spine releases a pleasurable crack.

Four down, one to go.

Releasing my hold on the tree, I throw my weapon directly at the neck of the last Black Blood. When the blade finds its home in his soft throat, black blood wells around the hilt. Wide-eyed, he drops to his knees and grabs at his neck, attempting to stop the bleeding.

"Down boy." He lands on his face with the knife still lodged in his throat. The sound of hooves approaching drags my attention away from the dead Black Bloods. *What a waste of a perfectly good knife*, I think as black feathers and a black mane come into view.

Vencen.

I sprint to him. "Dex!" he yells. Behrman the horse rears and trumpets next to me from the abrupt stop. "Get on." Vencen holds out his hand, and I grab onto it as another Black Blood comes into view.

When he tugs me up onto the back of Behrman, I summon the moon's power again, using it to throw the Black Blood across the forest to crash against a tree. Gideon sprints alongside us as we gallop.

"Watch out!" Gideon roars just as we're thrown off Behrman.

Claws latch onto me as a hellhound snaps its maw to sink its teeth into my flesh. With a single hit to its stomach, the hound rips its claws off me, whimpering as it's thrown against the tree. Vencen grunts, clashing his sword with a soldier in red armor.

A priest of the Paragon Dawn.

The crimson scales of his armor ripple as the priest blocks Vencen's attacks with practiced ease. But I—I can't move. I can't breathe. All I can see is *his* face. King Nodisci's face. The emblem of the thorns and the helmet stares back at me, taunting me, sniggering like it's telling me that *he* is here. It's whispering that he has come to take me and make me his bride.

I can hear someone shouting a name that is not my own. Dex. I know it's meant to be me, yet I don't *feel* like I am her. I can see the other version of myself staring back at me in the reflection of the follower's helmet. Scared, getting fitted in white in preparation of my sixteenth birthday, or as everyone else liked to call it: my wedding day.

The same voice keeps calling that name. How can I respond when I no longer have the right to call myself that? Diamond Echo. She's strong. Smart. Powerful. And I'm weak, frozen in place by my own fear.

Warm hands wrap around my shoulder, shaking me out of my own mind. "Dex, you need to run!" Gideon shouts, staring at me with an urgency that makes my breath hitch.

A hiss sounds from behind him, and the mask of 'Dex' slips back into place, hiding the scared little girl.

I spring into action just as an elf with snow-white hair and crystal blue eyes comes running. I can taste the moon's power coursing through her—strong, but nothing compared to mine. The hellhound comes running straight for her instead, and I turn my attention to the priest. Flicking my wrist, the fae flies into a tree just as Black Bloods, fae and elves start to appear.

My ears pick up a short huff behind me, and I spin around, drawing my sword and plunging it into the elf. Another Hinixian comes running, her sword powered by the moon; my weapon is no match. Leaping out of the way and dodging the oncoming attack of a follower, I kick my leg out, burying it in the follower's stomach while using my own magic to scatter dirt into the elf's face. I can't let them smell the moon on me or else they'll see right through my disguise. He stumbles back, and the elf smirks as two more elves circle me.

"Oh, you want to dance?" I say breathlessly. "Then let's dance."

A woman as tall as Gideon charges first. Our swords clash, sending violent vibrations up both my arms as I try to push back against the power in the Hinixian weapon. I send the vibration back tenfold—it travels through my own sword into hers and she drops her weapon with a bloodied cry. Spinning, my own blade slices her throat open, and the next elf comes running.

They attack one by one, crying out as they charge forward. *Amateurs.* In the face of a fight, they seem to have forgotten all they learned: to fight as a team.

From the corner of my eye, I see Gideon taking care of the hellhounds and keeping Behrman safe. As they run to attack, his hand pierces their hides, and they turn to dust. Just as the last elf goes down, a sharp pain rips through my stomach.

I look down to see something sticking out from the side of my belly button. My blood pumps with lightning and I pull the arrow out with a hiss, running toward Vencen as he stabs the last orc. He turns to me, wings tucked closely to his side as we both make a beeline to Behrman with my hand in the air creating a shield as arrows start to rain down on us.

He flaps his wings to make it onto the horse first. His hand wraps around my forearm, hauling me up as Behrman starts to gallop.

"We'll go to Ealgate!" Vencen roars over the sound of the battle nearby, and the screech of a kaliak brings even more fear into his eyes. "What the fuck was that?"

"It doesn't matter." I shake my head as I keep a lookout for oncoming attacks, my magic hot in my hands. "We ride to Taravene."

DEX

CHAPTER FOURTEEN

WE DON'T STOP MOVING until sunlight breaks the sky and stares down at us, oblivious to the carnage unfolding in Zarlor.

I can no longer hear the sound of fire crackling, though I can see smoke polluting the air just by the mountains.

Truthfully, I'm not sure how far we are to the borders of Zarlor, or if we'll even make it to Taravene's territory.

King Nodisci would rather flatten an entire kingdom than let the Black Bloods have it. I can't help but think that I should have left sooner. I should have known as soon as I saw that wagon of Hinixian weapons. That was close, too close. What would have happened if Gideon didn't wake me up?

I might have been safe in my cave, but it doesn't matter who wins. Getting out would have been impossible.

Gods, I hope Ealrin made it out of Zarlor. She can hold her own in a bar fight, but drunken men are nothing compared to a trained follower of the Paragon Dawn.

Gideon follows along next to us the entire time, but none of us have uttered a word since we made it out. The wound at my side hasn't healed, remaining at a dull, steady ache. I can feel my blood pumping, trying its best to dispel the poison, but I know it won't be enough. Somewhere in the woods between Volducan and Hinixsus lies a bush of yoles, a flower that can kill any creature if left untreated. The same flower that the arrow was tipped in. It's an eight-day ride to Taravene from this direction, and the next settlement won't be for another three.

Elves and fae have been known to die from yoles sooner than that, so I can only hope that being the Daughter of the Blood Moon gives me survival points. At least it's stopped bleeding even though the wound is still yawning. I guess if it's oozing pus, that means my body is trying to get rid of the poison, right? At least that's what I'll tell myself to feel better.

Glancing at my cloak to make sure my injury isn't showing, I run my hand along Behrman's smooth neck, finding her coat is damp to the touch. I remember stealing her from a farmer who didn't pay Vencen and I. She was our client's prized possession; the largest of all his horses with a coat as dark and silky as the night sky. When we looked at her, we thought we'd be ensnared by her golden eyes, and truthfully, we were. She went from pacing four corners of a stall to running headfirst into a battle with a winged male on her back.

"We should give ol' girl a break." My voice comes out hoarse from the poison draining into my bloodstream. Walking will only make it spread faster, but it's unfair on her to push her over the limit for us.

I could tell them both that I didn't come out of Zarlor unscathed, but what will that do? We can't turn back to Zarlor, and *knowing* I'm injured won't make our trip any shorter. All it will do is make Gideon worried that he's going back in the book and Vencen will just freak out. He might be good under pressure, but he doesn't know how to handle situations like these. My only option is to make sure they *don't* find out and wait to see if I can pay someone to heal it at the next settlement.

"I agree. You can walk." Vencen pulls the reins back to bring Behrman to a halt.

"He's lucky that I can't pull him down by his feathers," Gideon hisses. "Tell him to count his days." His glare could burn holes into the side of Vencen's head. The taste of whiskey is a welcomed distraction from the acidic tang of venom.

I start to shake my head, only to stop when the wound protests to any form of movement. "She has been running with the both of us on her back for hours. Just give her a break." The combination of exhaustion from the fight, my lack of food, sleep, my injury, *and* the fact that the moon is nowhere to be seen only makes the situation far worse than it has to be.

Vencen lets out an exasperated sigh, jumping off in one swift motion. "I'm only doing this because it's a good idea, not because you said so," he says and begins walking without waiting for the rest of us.

Okay, I tell myself, *you just need to swing your leg back and land on your feet. It's just one and a half movements. No one will be none the wiser.* Taking a deep breath, I try to do exactly that; I pull my legs over with rigid movements and land less than gracefully on my feet. Letting my hair drape over my face, I try to hide my wince from Gideon's studious gaze. Try and fail.

"What's wrong?" Gideon's voice is filled with deep concern, as rosemary replaces the strong taste of whiskey.

I turn away from him to hide my pain as I pull Behrman's reins down her head. "Fine. Just tired." The wound screams when I take my first step. The pain thunders down to my toes, and all I can think is that I should be grateful that at least my mind is still intact.

One glance at Gideon tells me that he doesn't believe me for a single moment. My side screams louder when I try to hurry my steps to catch up with Vencen.

"Sorry, girl," I whisper, leaning my weight onto the horse only to feel sickened from the added heat emanating from her. The sun may be hiding behind the clouds, but the weather isn't appropriate for wearing cloaks. But I keep it on to keep my wound hidden.

"Tell me," Gideon insists, lightly touching my elbow. Sparks crawl through me at the innocent touch.

Pulling my arm away from him, I speed up my steps. I shouldn't be feeling those sparks, and he can't know that I'm on my way to an early grave. Still, I can feel him watching me.

I haven't forgotten the real reason he's asking; if I die, he goes back in the book. His concern isn't genuine, it's purely selfish. It was me who sowed the seeds in him that he needs me alive for his own good, but I can't help hating that I'm nothing more than a pawn.

We all continue our journey, looking at the peaceful scenery as if war doesn't rage, taking turns riding Behrman until the moon starts to appear in the sky, and the sun gets closer to setting. We move through fields and forests with Gideon constantly watching for predators. Now I've found myself back on Behrman, seeing as it's "my turn" to rest. Most of the walk has been spent with us listening to Vencen speak, me making a noise to pretend that I'm listening, and Gideon talking about how much he dislikes the "useless feathered idiot."

The parts I did hear was him boasting about how much coin he received from plucking the wing off a dead pixie, or about the time a nobleman let him into his home and the daughter paid him to sleep with her. With the taste of whiskey on my tongue the whole time, I'm surprised that I'm not drunk.

"You know," Vencen starts, popping a berry into his mouth. I brace myself for whatever he has to say. At least it takes my mind off the pain in my core and the ache in my thighs from straddling the horse in a way that doesn't make me wince. "You shouldn't have left yesterday. My best performance is in the morning." He winks up at me.

Bile makes its way up my chest from the comment and the slight sway in Behrman's steps. Its bitter taste consumes the whiskey, and I can't help but long for its sharp bite.

"I don't like him," Gideon growls for the hundredth time. "His name sounds like venison."

If I wasn't in so much pain, I'd chuckle. If I ever see Ealrin again, I'm telling her that we're changing Vencen's name from 'prick' to 'venison.'

"Not a chance," I grumble in response to Vencen.

"His wings are useless and flammable. Light a match and he'll soar like a burning chicken," Gideon sneers.

Throwing a berry as high as he can, Vencen leaps into the air, flapping his wings to catch it in his mouth before lowering himself back to the ground. Sometimes I feel bad for him when I watch him fly. After all, his poor flying skills are the whole reason he found himself in Kselia's care as well. You don't win popularity contests with your clan when you refuse to learn how to use your wings well enough to carry you any real distance.

"If he actually cared about you, he would have flown you out of there without a second thought." Gideon watches the winged male twirl and spin in the air.

"Dex." Vencen dives back down to the ground. "I need to take a leak. There's a stream up there for us to stop." He points towards a bushed area between two trees.

A slight sheen starts to glaze over my eyes, and all I can think about is sleep. Too tired to answer, I nod, steering Behrman in the direction he pointed in. Vencen jumps up, flying in the other direction as I fight the urge to slump onto the horse and let her take me wherever she wants to go.

"I don't trust him." Gideon's animosity snakes its way into my mind, making me flinch. "I don't want you anywhere near him."

Behrman whinnies and snorts as we come up to the stream. She drinks like she hasn't had water in days. By now, I've improved my ability to get on and off without feeling like I am tearing my innards apart.

"It's not for you to decide who I spend time with," I mutter, making my own way to the stream. I drop onto my knees, biting my wince.

"He's selfish and will throw you in the fire just so he doesn't mess up his hair."

"What? And you aren't selfish?" I snap, my miserable condition taking over my own emotions. My loose hair drapes into the stream as I bend over to scoop water. I shiver from the cold sweat and the icy chill of the liquid that bites my skin. I snatch my hand away, holding it close to my chest like it might freeze.

"I—" he starts to say but I hold up my hand limply before he can say anything else, and he scowls at the motion.

"You only care because it means it *might* inconvenience our goal."

The dark power I felt in Zarlor stirs deep within me, drawing up my spine as shadows seep into the corners of my vision and bringing with it thoughts of chaos and destruction. *Kill the angel,* they whisper as the weapon in my pocket feels as if it were vibrating.

Squeezing my eyes close to shut them out of my mind, I focus my attention on 'the weapon.' "Rest assured, Gideon, you'll be free of me one way or another." At this rate, his freedom from me will only drag him back to the book. Which in truth, shouldn't make me feel a speck of guilt, but my traitorous mind does when he has done nothing substantial to earn the thought.

"Who are you talking to?" Vencen's voice bellows from above us, and both of our attention snaps to the male.

"No one," I growl, grabbing a nearby tree to pull myself up. My grip slips, and though I know that I'll hit my head on something on the way down, my bleary mind can't seem to process that I need to stop it from happening.

Something wraps around me before my face pummels against a tree. "I've got you," Gideon whispers as he pulls me up onto my feet.

I don't need help, I think to myself, pushing against him with staggering steps. Blinking back the haze, I can just see and feel the tension that suddenly appears on his features.

You clearly do, a voice that sounds like Gideon's rumbles through my mind, sending my soul into a frenzy. It seems to reach for him, connecting and entwining itself with the remnants of his voice. The sensation of having him in my head is so similar, yet so different to the night he possessed me. This time, it's almost comforting.

I'm going mad, I think, focusing on putting one step in front of the other. *I'm hearing voices again.*

Gideon chuckles as I wrap my hand around the horn of the saddle. *You can only dream of it. But I will gladly be the nightmare whispering wicked thoughts into the darkest depths of your mind.*

I want to curl in on myself. It feels like he's poking and prodding at my mind, uncovering my every secret to leave me exposed, but all he's doing is setting his gaze on me. *Get out of my head,* I squeal as I try and fail to pull myself onto Behrman.

A deep thrum vibrates through me—his voice—covering my skin in goosebumps. His hands cradle both sides of my waist away from the wound, lifting me onto the saddle. I want to squirm beneath his touch, to push his hands away and pretend to be stronger than I am. I shouldn't enjoy the feeling of his hands on me, it feels like I'm committing a sin. As soon as he lets go, something in my soul whimpers for his touch to return.

And yet, you're the one haunting my every waking moment, little witch. But alas, you aren't a witch at all, are you now? His words come out smooth and silky, but beneath it lies an undeniable jeer.

I wince as I squeeze the side of the horse, and she jolts into a gallop, leaving the men at my back. I need to get out of here; it all feels too much for my aching mind to deal with. I don't have the energy to respond to Gideon or listen to another word from Vencen. I need to breathe.

"Dex, what the fuck?" Vencen yells.

"You can't run from me forever," Gideon's voice booms at my back.

I may not be able to run from the truth, but I'll hide it away for as long as I can.

Unease is in the air, only I can no longer smell it. I can feel the moon high above, but her powers aren't flowing through me—another side effect of yole poison: It makes you truly human. My own magic is just a weak glimmer, and the road ahead is but a blurry haze. I squint my eyes, trying to block out the stars twinkling too brightly.

Hours have passed since we stopped at the stream. Vencen is somewhere up ahead. He stopped talking when I stopped responding in empty noises. I know he's angry, but I couldn't care less.

It's too cold to care about anything. So cold.

My fingers shake, pulling my cloak tighter as I look down at the ground. *Left foot. Right foot. Left foot. Right foot.* I repeat over and over because I've stopped trusting my body's ability to know what to do. With each step I take, I'm sure it'll be my last, I'm certain my knees will finally give out. Still, the left moves after the right.

Walking isn't the only thing I can think about, not when I can feel *him* beside me. The warmth of his body whispers through his clothes like a siren's song. *It will make me warm,* I think, then sway my head side to side like I've consumed too much ale. *No, it won't,* I respond back to myself.

Angling my head sideways, I catch his worried stare. And each time, I swallow the imaginary lump in my throat and look straight ahead like it never happened.

My left never makes it in front of my right when my knee finally buckles beneath me. But like before, he catches me. My footing steadies and again, I repeat the same words until the fog covers my mind, lulling me to sleep. I could just drop here, fall asleep amongst the moss. If I don't snore, then maybe a kaliak won't find me. Slowly, my mind becomes silent—a silence so peaceful. If I just rest for a second...

Ask me something. Gideon's voice stirs in my mind, tugging enough of the fog away to realize that my eyes have fallen closed. I pry my them open, focusing back on my footing.

I close my eyes again because they're too heavy to keep open, and the sound of the battle cries from the night before deafens me for a moment. I try to think of what he says between my own instructions to my feet, and I don't know how long passes until I can finally think of words to say. *Zarlor, the attack, was the attack for you?* Even my own thoughts come out breathless, and with another blink, the fog creeps back making me forget about my own question.

No, it was a long time coming, he pauses for a brief moment. *The kaliaks and their search for me likely accelerated it.*

I listen to his words, folding them in my mind and reopening it to try and process what he said. No matter how many times I reopen it, his answer doesn't settle within me. I'm not sure whether it's because of the poison or because his answer really doesn't make sense. *A weapon,* I whisper, dragging out the word and trying to string together a sentence. *I've never heard of you.*

A soft chuckle buzzes in my head, almost leaving a giddy feeling in me. *I am the secret of kings and gods, little elf. The—* my knees buckle again, and his arms wrap under my shoulder, pulling me to him.

Warm. He's so warm. I lean into his touch. My soul nestles into the contact like it wants to wrap around him and keep him there. Somehow, someway, it feels like a ship coming to shore. *Little elf.* He's figured it out. Was it the fighting that gave it away? Maybe when I jumped out of the cave? Maybe my necklace stopped working?

We're almost there. Keep going; left foot, right foot, he says encouragingly in my mind, moving his thumb over my ribs in slow, tender motions.

"Almost where?" I sputter, keeping my sight trained on the lush grass beneath my feet.

He squeezes my arm. "Look up."

I do as he says and stifle a whimper as lights blare back at me. Oil lanterns encompass a two-story tavern in the middle of the fields. Only then does the sound of a woman yelling something while milling around outside fills my ears. I can just make out a winged male leading a black horse around the back of the building.

I stop in my tracks with renewed vigor. "No, that's a bad idea, there could be soldiers there."

"It doesn't matter," he responds. "You need to rest."

By Callaia's grace, a trickle of the moon's power makes its way into my system, washing away some of the cloud from my mind—with just enough power leftover to kill someone if need be.

DEX

CHAPTER FIFTEEN

"THREE BEDS." MY HANDS slap the wooden counter and lean my full weight against it. A green hue enshrouds the wooden interior, and the treelike woman blends in with her surroundings. The whole place seems to sway and spin ever so slightly as I stare right at her.

A cold hand wraps around my waist, narrowly missing my open wound. When Vencen pulls me from the counter and squeezes me tightly against him, my soul doesn't jump the way it does with Gideon. In my disorientated state, I expect his hold to hurt—maybe I'd cry out from the pain. Yet I feel nothing, not even the warmth from his skin. It doesn't hurt.

My ears ring from Vencen's nasal laugh. "Aren't you a cute lil' thing?" Vencen chuckles arrogantly. He taps my nose at the start of his sentence, but I don't react until he's moved on to a different line of conversation with the innkeeper. "Don't mind her, she's crazy at the moment." He leans over the counter, covering the side of his face like he's trying to hide it from me as he whispers, "It's *her time*."

The woman watches him with a sour look on her face as he shakes with laughter, and I can't understand why. Whiskey melts onto my tongue as Gideon mutters some form of curse that I don't understand.

Still, the added rage is a mystery to me.

Realization barrels down on me when the meaning of his words settle into my slowed mind. *How dare he.* The room darkens and shadows creep in around the corners. I narrow my eyes, ignoring whatever else they're saying. The shadows seem to have faces; some are screaming, some are crying, some are smiling ear to ear.

Kill him, they whisper with a unified voice. *You don't want to be friends with someone like him. Ruin him.* I can feel every syllable of their words in my bones, crawling through me with iced fingers, letting that darkness come alight. *Destroy him,* they command again and again. *Kill him,* the faces giggle and scream. Until eventually, the shadows words are all that I can think about.

They're right, he's a sexist pig with no concept of boundaries. I'd be doing the world a favor if I took him down once and for all. Power starts to thrum and build in my fingertips like a dance with death. Everything around me becomes a blur, and nothing else matters but spilling Vencen's blood all over the wooden floor.

Dex. Gideon barges into my mind and the tendrils of that dark fire gutters.

I'm getting sick of him waltzing in and out of my mind. My head snaps toward him and the voices fall silent. I start to aim my power at the man who has made my life far more difficult than it needs to be. But something whispers that I won't be able to kill him. The whispers tell me that my own death will be far worse punishment for him.

As I stare at him, something starts to simmer in the back of my mind like a cold shower that extinguishes my fire. Something else whispers, not the voice of the faces, but my own: I can't kill him, because I don't want to.

I turn back to the faces, waiting for their next command, but the room is bright once more. Where there were once faces lies bags of linen and produce. The need to destroy and ruin is gone, only the rage still burns within.

Vencen's cold hand tugs at my numb torso, steering me into a hallway lit by a single oil lantern. He slots the key into a black door, pushing the door open and tugging me inside. "We can finally make up for some lost time—I miss the way you would scream," Vencen purrs, dropping his hand to my backside.

Destroy, the darkness whispers, extending its tendrils to caress my mind.

My body moves faster than it has all day, my hand snatches upward, fisting the male's damp collar and slamming his body against the wooden wall. I drag him up until my wound cries for me to stop, but the voices urge me to keep going, urge me to make sure that when my knife finds skin, I make the kill. His throat bobs against my fist which only makes me push harder until he starts choking for air.

Let me make one thing clear, *angel*," I hiss inches away from his face. The word may not be an insult, but it's a name that can shatter him from the inside out. "I don't give a *shit* if it was an act. Call me crazy one more time,"—I push harder against his throat, moving in closer so my lips touch the shell of his ear—"and I'll show you just how crazy I can really be."

Dropping his whimpering form, I step back with disgust as he falls to his knees, clutching his chest for breath.

"It's been two years. Get it through your thick skull that you and I will *never* happen again. So take this as your one and only warning, *Vencen,* if you touch me like that again, I promise you that it will be *you* who screams until your throat runs dry."

I look up, sizing up the one bed in the room and then back to the angel. Vencen pulls himself up. "It was just a joke, princess." He wanted the title to hurt me, but that isn't going to bother me tonight.

"And you're the only one laughing."

Something in my chest softens, and the fire pulls back its tendrils as I watch guilt start to seep into his eyes like years worth of pain has finally surfaced. Gritting my teeth, I hold tight onto the rage. I shouldn't feel sorry for him; he brought this on himself.

"Take the bed." He opens his mouth to protest, and I silence him with a glare. I've no interest in bleeding or seeping poison all over the linen, not that I care about his level of comfort. The innkeeper might decide to tell someone that we ran out of Zarlor, and I'd hate for more innocent blood to be spilled in this war.

He mutters something under his breath, apologies perhaps, but I can't hear beyond the buzzing in my ears. Then I blink, and suddenly I'm staring at the clumps of dust floating beneath the bed and listening to Vencen's soft snores.

I don't know how I ended up on the floor with my cloak covering me like a blanket, when my bag turned into a makeshift pillow, or when my teeth started to clatter. I'm lying on my side—the side I think the arrow hit. But it doesn't hurt.

I'm going to die. I'm hallucinating, shivering, I can barely walk, and I've lost feeling in my toes—no, I've lost feeling everywhere.

Elf. I need to find an elf. Or is it the fae that can heal? I can't remember anymore. Sludge has muddied my mind. No one is here but the innkeeper. Can she heal wounds? What type of creature was she? A mortal?

"You're awake." Gideon's deep voice rumbles up my spine.

Each movement is stiff yet painless as I angle my head in the direction of the sound. Squinting, I try to make out the face of the person sitting on the floor. Silver eyes catch the light, and an unwanted sense of comfort floods through me. *Stop watching me sleep,* I respond breathlessly like even thinking it was too strenuous.

"You look so peaceful when you sleep. Less vicious," he says with a tone of indifference. "It's rather boring when you aren't annoyed."

Guard the perimeter or something, I breathe, dragging the skin of my face along my bag to block his presence.

"I'm not a dog," he bites.

You're right. Dogs are far less irritating, I fume and take a deep breath.

I don't have the energy or the willpower to suppress the groan that leaves my lips as I pull my arm from under me to bring myself onto my hands and knees. My stomach buckles, bringing nausea hurtling up, and I bite my tongue to keep it back. My fingers touch the side of the bed, fumbling along until they find something to grab onto, and when I do, I grip it limply. Using the last bit of energy I have left, I heave myself onto two feet.

The room spins, and I stumble back until my legs touch the bed. *No, I'm fine. I just need to clean the wound and it will be fine until we find a healer,*

I think to myself in an attempt to block out my impending doom, hoping that Gideon didn't hear it.

I think I hear him stir from his spot. But I can't be sure.

"Stay." I don't look at him in case he sees through my lie. "I need to use the washroom."

I force my feet forward, grabbing the door to keep me upright as I slip into the cool hallway without waiting for a response. I don't bother closing the door, leaning and dragging myself against the wall to make it to the entrance of the inn. My eyes adjust to the darkness, and I glance around, checking if Gideon is following, but nothing catches my eye. I think I saw a stall outside, or maybe even a stable to clean the cut out.

Time. That's all I need.

Stumbling into the night, the stars seem to spin and explode as my breath starts to evaporate in my chest. *One step, two steps, three steps,* and I don't make it to the fourth before falling onto the clay ground as pain thunders through my whole body. Tears well in my eyes, stinging my cheeks as I retch. And retch. And retch. Yet nothing comes out, and I still need to throw up, but everything hurts again. My chest contracts, attempting to hurl the contents of my stomach.

I retch until I don't notice the warm hand rubbing circles on my back. I retch until I forget about my hair that's being held out of my face. I retch until I can't hear a male's soft whispers. I retch until my body gives out, and I stop making a noise, lying against a mass of solid chest, breathing slow, shallow breaths, staring at the moon with cold tears streaming down my face.

I feel nothing.

No power.

No pain.

No fear.

Nothing.

For the first time in years, I feel at peace. Content.

With Satrina dead, no longer directing the souls of those who have passed, where will my essence go without her to judge my fate? Will I be like Gideon when I die? Walking along the streets with people going right through me, being alone with nobody but myself as company?

The moon seems to come closer as warmth moves beneath my knees and around my back. Suddenly it's out of sight and all I can see are the shadows cast along Gideon's face, curving against his cheeks and hiding the glisten of his eyes.

"Where are you taking me?" I whisper, unsure if he heard or if I even spoke.

His face angles down to me with an intensity that almost brings back tears. Pain lances every edge of his face, and the only twinkle in his eyes is one of grim sorrow. "You've been poisoned. You shouldn't have walked at all; it has spread even faster."

He should be mad. He should be furious that I didn't tell him, that I risked his freedom by keeping the wound hidden. But he isn't. Not at me, at least. Pain bleeds from every word like a knife to the chest. I've never heard anyone so worried about me before, so angry at me about my own pain.

Trees come into view just above his head, and a whimper escapes my lips as his hold releases me, placing me with gentle ease onto the overgrown grass.

"I will be right back." He hesitates, tucking a strand of hair behind my ear before moving away quickly. He disappears into the night, leaving me to stare at the green blades that seem to stretch well beyond my vision. My eyes drift shut, lulled to sleep by the gentle buzz of the insects of the wild.

Peace, that's what this feeling is. Peace that I'll finally be free.

A soft caress glides across my skin before the sound of clicking, slapping, and grinding stirs me awake. Peeling my eyes open, I blink slowly, unsure whether the poison is affecting my mind once more.

Gideon kneels beside me, and I just make out soft green fur and a small round face. He's holding each of the onaf's arms with both hands. The venomous creature stares ahead in a confused daze, watching its small hands get controlled by another; moving flowers, nuts, and berries from the forest floor onto a big leaf, mashing it in with whatever else is on there. I huff breathlessly, unable to laugh at the sight. I wonder what is going through its head, dangling in the middle of the air as an invisible man guides its limbs?

The onaf's long fluffy tail flicks back and forward, lightly touching my cheek in an almost soothing motion. The green and blue fur of its rounded belly is stained with dirt and berries like he was carrying the supplies on its stomach. The area around its eyes is the deepest blue, changing into a soft turquoise where the eyebrows are meant to be. I've always thought that if they weren't so deadly, I would have wanted an onaf for myself.

Are you trying to kill me? I joke tiredly, and his gaze returns to mine. Though his face is emotionless, the darkness disappears from his eyes like he's happy to see me awake. A shiver ripples through me, and I pull the cloak around me with an empty numbness.

If I wanted to kill you, I'd make it fast and painless. The corner of his lips tugs into a barely noticeable smile as the rest of his face remains passive. The animal clicks its tongue again, struggling against his hold and trying to lick the paste it made. *They won't harm you unless you harm it,* he adds, noticing my concerned gaze as it licks the air wildly. He adjusts his hold on the creature, carrying it from under its shoulders to let it lick the paste off its hands. *The common perception is that their saliva is what is deadly, but it's quite the opposite; it's a cure to a select few poisons. Its fear is what can bring down even the strongest kings,* he continues.

Strands of red hair stick to my sweaty face as I nod, not quite understanding what he means. *How are you holding the onaf?*

He doesn't respond, and I find that I've lost the energy to say it again.

"A lunar elf," he mutters to himself as the sounds in the background grow more frantic. "A lunar elf that shines brighter than the moon herself," he says it quietly, like his words aren't meant for me to hear.

The tip of my fingers lightly glide along the grass, feeling the friction of the serrated edge of the blades prickle against my skin. The onaf's frustrated click is almost rhythmic, like I'm being rocked to sleep, swaying my mind back and forth, back and forth.

"Stay with me." Gideon starts to work faster, anger in every single one of his movements. "I forbid you from dying on me, little moon."

Opening my mouth to speak, it hangs open, and I lose the energy to say more.

Sparks tickle my skin as his warm hand presses against my cheek. My soul tugs at him, wanting him closer to me. The place where his skin touches mine ignites with a spectacle of fireworks like every touch is meant to be. My eyes flutter open to meet his, and a soft gasp escapes my lips. Above him, the branches claw at the sky and extend their boney fingers toward us. Between them, the stars flicker in and out of existence; the goddess' children. Yet it isn't the brightness of the sky that consumes my attention, it's the man who stares back at me with the whole night sky in his eyes, filled with the most overwhelming pain.

He hesitates. "Do you trust me?"

The question throws me off. Do I trust him? I don't know if I'm capable of answering that in this state. I know that he won't kill me and nothing in those eyes tells me that he'll hurt me. *Right now.* I can hear the shadows laugh and cry.

I nod and watch as his hand moves down to my feet, tugging my outer dress and tunic up until the night air kisses the skin of my stomach. The material peels off the wound, but I feel nothing but the chill that rakes a shiver down my spine. I don't need to see the extent of the injury; his eyes say it all.

"This is going to sting," he says with an air of calm, but I think I catch pain snaking through his features. Or it could be my mind playing more tricks on me.

He holds the onaf with two hands again, using the creature to pick up the paste and spread it evenly over the large leaf. Slowly, he places the leaf over my wound, and I groan from the bite of the cold. My reaction makes him freeze in his movements, swallowing the lump in his throat before pressing the leaf onto my skin.

Gently placing the onaf back on the forest floor, he releases his hold on the creature, and it scurries away like its tail is on fire.

I watch with tired eyes as he studies me for a brief moment before moving about in a flurry. "Your heart needs to be above your wound," he mutters like he's annoyed at himself for not realizing sooner.

Strong arms lift me upright, and another wince contorts my face as pain rips up my torso. He leans my body against a tree that feels like jagged rocks against my back, and then he yanks off his coat, folding it neatly. Dropping down next to me, he places the folded coat in front of him, and he gently pulls me into the space between his legs. His hands move with the utmost care, positioning and angling me so his coat sits comfortably beneath me. And slowly, he leans me back onto his solid chest, and I welcome the reprieve from the sharp edges of the tree.

I watch his fingers spread and move, running my gaze over the trail of veins bulging in his forearms, shirt pushed to the elbows.

The effect of the paste is almost immediate as I start to feel the tenderness of my stomach muscles while the storm of nausea settles. Despite feeling returning to my toes, a fog still hangs over my mind, numbing my thoughts. But not so much that I miss the sound of sniffling and hopping as a jackalope peeks out from between bushes, sprinting across the path into the next bush.

His feather-light touch pulls every strand of hair off my face, tucking it neatly behind my ear.

"Why can you touch the creatures?" I ask again.

"All those creatures come from the same cloth that I was cut from. They all have a darkness lingering inside of them that calls to me."

"Are you a monster?"

He doesn't respond for a long moment. "I've been called worse."

My breath hitches when his hand moves to my chest, tugging at the strings of my tunic. We both seem to stop breathing as we watch the threads unlace. He pulls away quickly once the last lace is undone. Moving my head from off his chest as he runs his hands through the knotted mess of my hair, carefully untangling it and creating order before he parts it into three at the top of my head with the string still in hand.

Why can you touch my clothes? I finally ask when my eyes drop to the dress that is hiked around my hips.

Like calls to like, he says after a brief moment of hesitation. He pauses again as he tilts my head forward, pulling the hair from the side of my head before elaborating further. *Anything that is a part of you, becomes a part of me. Just for a fleeting moment.*

I sit there, absorbing the warmth of his body and ignoring the giddy feeling of my soul, basking in the serenity of the moment.

How can you see into my mind?

It's the same reason that I cannot touch mortals, he starts. *When you have full control of your consciousness, I am unable to see into your mind or touch you.*

So you can touch a drunk person? The premise confuses me.

Not quite, he chuckles lightly, easing my body before his anger becomes thick in my own throat. *Dex, you were nearing the brinks of death. Your mind was completely open to me. You should have told me earlier that you were poisoned,* he scolds, wrapping the string around my hair, tying it off in a tight bow.

I didn't want to worry anyone. I thought that there was nothing that could be done, and it was more important that we got far away from Zarlor. He drapes a tense hand lightly on my waist, grunting in response. *Where did you learn how to cure yole poison anyway?* I wondered. Cures for poison aren't common knowledge.

You could say that my sister had a gift when it came to healing, he laments gruffly, and the taste of turmeric rolls over my tongue. His words come from a place filled with heartache and sorrow, and my chest squeezes with familiarity.

What happened to her? Flashes of Ameria filters through my mind; her infectious laugh, the way her nostrils would flare every time she ate something she liked.

His muscles underneath my back tense from the questions. *She's dead.*

It's as if a wall has risen, and he's become closed off all over again. And it's like at the same time, we both remember who we are: a weapon imprisoned to a girl, and a girl running away from imprisonment. The only thing we have in common is that we both have a vested interest in keeping me alive.

D E X

CHAPTER SIXTEEN

EVERYTHING HURTS. MY BACK hurts from falling asleep awkwardly on Gideon the other night. My stomach hurts from almost getting killed. And my thighs scream from sitting on Behrman since we left the inn five days ago. Letting me ride Behrman is Vencen's attempt at an apology.

I glance at Gideon, and our eyes meet for the briefest second before he snaps his attention away. We haven't spoken to each other beyond simple requests like 'look away' and 'make sure there's no kaliak that will kill us in our sleep' since the mention of his sister.

There was a part of me that thought that he might genuinely care about me from the gentleness of his touch or the way he braided my hair. But it meant nothing to him. All he wanted was to make sure I didn't die so he doesn't need to go back into the book.

Fresh poultice is slathered on my stomach, only without the onaf's venom this time. With every move, I can feel the medicine slither in a way that makes my skin crawl. All of the poison has already disappeared from my system, and the wound has almost completely sealed. But still, nothing compares to the feeling of the moon's power coursing through my veins again.

The air turns colder, and the forest starts to thin, taking with it most of the edible fruits as we head closer in the Kingdom of Lodaxo's direction. The further north we go, the less daylight we get, which means that I'm stronger for longer. But it also means that we are now galivanting around during the kaliaks' feeding time.

We walk through the thickest part of the remaining forest in comfortable silence. Out of nowhere, laughter rings through the air. Every fiber of my being becomes alert to each aspect of my surroundings. My heart thumps against my chest as my gaze jumps from tree to tree to find the source of the sound. Vencen hasn't noticed, but Gideon moves into a fighting stance, spreading his fingers wide in preparation to wrap it around whatever monster that wishes us harm.

What is it? his voice booms in my head.

I heard laughter. I pull the reins back to bring Behrman to stop.

Then all three of us hear it: the soft sound of hooves and boots marching through the forest ahead of us—it sounds like an army.

Vencen's attention snaps to me with wide eyes, and I stare back with a jittering heart. But I can't see anything.

"Run," Vencen mouths, and all of our bodies spur into action, throwing strategy out the window, only to dig our heels in and freeze in position when a deep, crooked voice speaks in my head.

That won't be necessary. His voice is so loud that the male might as well be screaming in my ear. Based on Vencen's reaction, he heard it too. But there's something almost bubbly in the voice as if he's a...

Shit. A callpaith. Of all the creatures we could run into, we come across one of the few creatures that can smell lies.

Vencen turns away from me, directing his attention to the callpaith at my back, then looks back at me with worry more fearsome than when Gideon held me like I was going to take my last breath. The look makes the night air colder than it already is, and the desire to run hisses at the back of my mind. There must be more than just the callpaith.

Taking a deep breath, I pull the reins to the side, directing the horse to turn, all the while the sound of marching grows louder and louder. What would have Vencen that worried? It can't just be the callpaith. My mind starts to spin and boil down all the possibilities of who I might find when I turn: the marching, Zarlor, the resting of the sun... All at once, the blood rushes from my face as a sickening feeling in my stomach floods my system. I try to grip the reins tighter to stop my hand from shaking, but all it does is make the leather strap vibrate beneath my grip.

"Get down." The callpaith wraps his fingers around the sword at his side in warning. The moonlight bounces off his silver armor, casting shadows over the emblem embossed on the chest plate: a crescent moon pierced by an arrow. Unlike the emblem I saw on the cartons in Zarlor, this one has a six-point star in the center.

It's the emblem of the Crystal Spear, the deadliest soldiers of Hinixsus: a faction within the Hinixian army that breed people like mares to make the perfect soldier. It's the only reason King Nodisci was so willing to form an alliance with father long before my fate came to light—he was never much of a fighter, but he has always had tools in the art of war.

If there's one solider here, that means that there will be more. He won't be alone. He'll just be the one tasked to travel ahead first. How did we not hear the marching sooner?

They'll know.

They'll know it's me. They'll see through the necklace.

It's over.

It's all over.

No, stop it, I scold myself between hiccupping breaths. *They don't know anything yet. Think of a plan. Focus.*

I take heed of my own warning and wrack my head to figure out the best disguise that will stop him from smelling my lies. Throwing my leg over the horse, I move in slow, rigid movements, wincing from the pain that still remains from the wound—all while assuring myself that the callpaith can't read my thoughts, just my lies. I need to get out of my own head.

All three of his eyes watch me intently, and I can feel him summon the moon's powers to his fingers, perceiving me as a threat. *Good, that means he's only half callpaith.* Full callpaiths have nothing to do with the moon. Hopefully, that means that he'll only *half* smell my lie.

"Be careful," Gideon warns, and I shrug off his unhelpful comment.

My feet land on the ground just as my plan forms. We've been through enough messes to know the drill; Vencen stays quiet, and I take the lead. His hand snakes around my shoulders, pulling me tightly to him as soon as I take a step in his direction. He hugs me so tightly that it doesn't feel like an act. It's the type of hug that you give someone when only fear runs through your veins.

"It isn't safe to be in the forest at this time," the callpaith taunts dangerously. "What brings you to these woods?"

I can feel the intensity of Gideon's gaze on me as the taste of ginger rolls onto my tongue when Vencen's fingers entwine with my shaking hand, rubbing it in a soothing motion. I swallow the lump in my throat as the sound of boots becomes clearer. "We're traveling to Taravene. We have family there," I stammer.

Glancing back, I watch as the first batch of elves break through the trees. They're nothing but a sea of silver and white hair, all staring at us with light eyes. Each one of them smells of the moon, whether it's from the power they've brought to the surface or the glowing weapons by their side.

I wonder if they, like the rest of the realm, believe that their Lunar Princess was taken from her own home by the Black Bloods. Or did they see through Father's lies and figure out that I ran away?

One by one the calvary stops as the callpaith raises his hand.

"And where did you come from?" He pauses to sniff the air, and I hold my breath. "Human."

Hold onto that thought. I'm definitely a human. Whiskey mixes in with the ginger and almond, and I let my emotions come out to the surface: fear and sorrow. "I had a—" I graze my hand over my stomach before touching the site of the wound, whimpering in pain. "The other night, I felt a pain in my stomach and there was,"—I pause for dramatic effect, searching the ground as if I were trying to find the words to say—"so much blood. *So much.* I just want to be with my family in Taravene." I let my voice shake and tears well in my eyes. Vencen pulls me closer to him, hugging me tightly. The taste of ginger, whiskey, and almond grows to the point that it burns, and my mouth starts to dry.

Good. Sell the act, lover boy, I think to myself.

The callpaith's gaze looks up to someone behind us, and I fight the urge to turn as well in case anyone recognizes my face, but that doesn't stop Vencen. The Hinixian nods and says in a softer voice, "We have a healer with us. You are welcome to see her before you continue on your travels."

"Thank you." I smile weakly. "But there's nothing more that anyone can do." The sound of more Hinixian approaching fills the air and the need to get out of here becomes more prominent by the second.

"Very well." The callpaith nods, and the tension in Vencen's and my shoulders eases only to tighten again as the sound of footsteps close in on us.

Vencen turns to look at the callpaith, yet I don't dare to. I want to touch my necklace just to make sure that it's there, but doing so will only draw their attention to it.

The sound of a blade being unsheathed scrapes the air from behind me, and I spin to face the sound with my fingers curled into a tight fist at my side. But at the sight of him, my whole being screams for me to run.

Commander Aywin, one of Father's most trusted men.

No. No, no, no.

He knows me. He watched me grow up. Against my father's wishes, he taught me how to throw a punch. He taught me how to grip a knife and throw one—not well, but enough to defend myself before running for dear life. He'll see through any hair dye.

His eyes are blue, and he continues to fashion his hair into three long braids that reach the middle of his back. But there's something different about him. Though his elven blood will let him live well beyond his hundreds, the past eight years have aged him far beyond natural comprehension. His tired eyes now sink into their sockets, and faint lines etch his forehead from too much frowning. A tinge of guilt flickers in me that it might be my fault the life behind his eyes has disappeared.

Maybe it's also the fact that he's commanding the Crystal Spear—a faction he hates. He used to be one of them, bloodthirsty and deadly, but despite all his years serving there, he never lost his humanity.

His and the moon's power roll off him in waves, drowning me in it, and my heart aches in yearning. That could be me. I could hold that kind of power, flaunt it whenever I wish and instill fear in people just by standing there. I bow my head, shielding my face and cowering back into Vencen's arms as if I were threatened by his presence. At once, his power lessens into a slight shimmer.

Gideon flickers into existence, standing in the space between Aywin and I. Though Aywin is tall, Gideon is half a head taller than him. He looks down his nose at the elf as if daring him to take another step. At first, I think that it's anger surging through him from the way he holds himself and the whiskey rage on my tongue, but it doesn't account for the almond I can taste. My gaze follows the trail of his arms, down to his hands and a foreign warmth settles inside me. One of his hands curls into a tight fist at his side, while the other arm is behind him with his fingers stretched wide like he's trying to protect me. He won't be able to do anything, but I have to stamp down the warmth budding all the same. I'm just a means to an end.

Then the pieces fall into place. I know what the taste of almond is: It's when he feels protective.

"Blessed be the moon. Here." Aywin offers the Hinixian knife to me. I don't say it back, afraid he'll recognize my voice. I look down, and fury burns through my core as I catch sight of his hand that's burnt with the symbol of the Paragon Dawn. I don't live in the palace anymore, and still my father hurts the people I care about. "War is coming, and there are things lurking in this forest that I pray you will never come across."

Tears prickle my eyes, and all I want to do is run up to him and wrap my arms around him. He's the closest thing to a father that I've ever had. He never said that he didn't approve of my union with Nodisci, but I could always tell it didn't sit right with him.

Does he recognize me? What would we do if he did? Would he drag me kicking and screaming all the way to Hinixsus, or would he turn a blind eye?

Gideon doesn't shift from his position despite the elf's offer.

"Thank you." Vencen takes the glowing weapon from the elf when he realizes that I'm not about to move.

A long bout of silence hangs in the air, and the elf's intense gaze stays on me. He knows. There's no way that he doesn't know.

"We should be off," Vencen finally says. "We've been riding for a long time. We were about to seek shelter to rest."

I know Aywin well enough that he would ask us to rest with them so the Crystal Spear could keep us safe.

He steps to the side to let us pass, and with hesitant feet, we do. I refuse to look Aywin in the eyes. I'm telling myself that it's because I don't want him to see through my disguise, and not the fact that my mask might break if I do. I bow my head in thanks to the elf and the callpaith, clutching Vencen tightly to me, while Gideon stays in place.

Just as we pass him, Aywin clears his throat, and we pause. "Move with caution. Though the moon is out tonight, there is always blood on the horizon."

"Thank you," I mutter, bowing my head once more while silently urging Vencen to pick up his pace. I don't bother jumping back onto Behrman as the soldiers part to let us through. One of the elves says something, but I can't hear them beyond the pounding in my ears.

Moon... Blood...

He knows.

~~GIDEON~~
CHAPTER SEVENTEEN

"He knows, Vencen, he knows," she says frantically, attempting to fight off Venison's little arms that try to hold her down. "He's going to turn the Crystal Spear around. He's going to get me. He'll take me back to Father. We need to go. We need to run."

His arms wrap around Dex tighter, pulling her to him, and the gnawing within my chest that has been eating at me all night roars once more, loud enough to make me deaf to the terror I feel within her.

Jealousy: a despicable sensation reserved for mortals too weak to attain their heart's desire. I am well acquainted with the destructiveness of greed, however, I am beyond jealousy—it is such a feeble concept that poisons the mind into becoming nothing more than one's basest desires. I refuse to accept that the *anger* that plagues me when men or women glance at her is anything more than something as simple as because she is my only ticket to fulfilling my purpose, and they are mere obstacles that may get in the way.

Kill them, the voices rasp. *Bathe in their blood.*

The chaos of my power claws at my chest, snapping, whispering its hunger for blood. And that elf... Rage burns brighter within me in memory of the feeling that blossomed in her chest when she saw him: a toxic mixture of fear, longing, and love. No, it is not jealousy; she simply has terrible taste in men, and it's getting in the way of our goal. Plus, he is too old for her. If what she wants is to find love, then she needs to quash all thoughts of that elf or that selkie maiden, and especially that winged male that should thank the divine he continues to breathe.

But I have no care *or interest* in her love life. There is no room for such things. *I* have no time for it. This is all just a mission, nothing more.

Dex knows the elf somehow. Because of the Hinixians, her fingers have not ceased to still in their tremors since the encounter. It is not the right time to pry for information about it, not when asking her about her fear will not solve the problem. She needs her worries soothed.

"Deep breaths, Dex," he whispers slowly, softly blowing into her hair and sending that primal being within me into another inferno. This time, I know the purpose of my rage: it's him. Such simple words meant to be filled with patience and comfort, and yet, his words are dipped with poisonous impatience. "It was an innocent statement. Blood and moon just so happen to be in the same sentence."

"We don't have time to rest. We need to keep riding." She glares up at him.

Kill them, the voices taunt, darkness swirling in the shadow. I grit my teeth, stamping the chaos away as the harsh glow of the moon filters through, taking the space where shadows once occupied.

Listen to her, stupid mortal, keep walking, I try to communicate into the male's mind knowing I won't break through. It is not my preference that we travel at night when the kaliaks are hunting, but I can walk ahead to ensure that none lurk nearby—so long as she feels safe from the past that is haunting her.

It's what I should have done to begin with; use my gifts to keep her safe. But I failed her. I missed a whole army because I didn't want to leave her side—not after she was poisoned. If I missed an army, what about a kaliak? If not one kaliak, then it could have been a group of them. More would follow as well, because Venison looks like he will be a screamer.

You didn't look on purpose. You want her dead. She is meant to die by your hands, the voices whisper from inside me, straining against my hold. With a final surge of energy, the chaos disappears completely.

I don't have complete control over the darkness in this form. I have never felt so weak. One day, they will sink their teeth in me and succeed in making me snap. I only fear that it'll be her that I will break.

Venison shakes his head. "We're both tired, and so is Behrman." His eyes tell me that this isn't a discussion that he wants to entertain.

The fire in her ignites at his comment. She has a plan.

Her muscles go limp as she stops struggling in his grasp that looks tight enough to hurt her. Several heartbeats pass before he loosens his hold carefully like he's afraid she might topple over. Taking a deep breath, she stares straight into his eyes and says, "Fine, I'll continue without you."

I grit my teeth to suppress the grin that wants to form from seeing his jaw drop as she pushes him away and continues marching in my direction.

"And what do you think is going to happen when you run into another army *by yourself?*"

She stops in her steps right in front of me, and her scent carries to me in the faint breeze. Her gaze moves to the ground briefly as she considers something while fear rampages through her.

"Do not underestimate me, Vencen. You'll find that people live to regret it," she says, then continues her path in Taravene's direction, tugging her cloak around her from the drop in temperature.

Venison grunts, throwing a sleeping sack on the ground to get ready to sleep for the night. Even the sight of the sack angers me beyond any reasonable comprehension. He has refused to share his blankets with her despite the chill. She shivers in her sleep from having nothing but a thin cloak to keep her warm. He has left me no choice but to drape my coat over her as an added layer of heat every night once she falls asleep. But as we near the Kingdom of Lodaxo, it isn't enough.

Last night, she almost woke up to find herself curled next to me because my own body heat seems to be the only thing that stops her teeth from clattering. I vanished into smoke before she woke. I'm sure the little elf would cause a fuss, and I simply cannot be bothered proving to her that I don't want her to die. Even though I have never heard of an elf dying from being cold.

The winged male plops onto the blankets with a sigh, which sends another wave of anger crashing in me, and I focus on the thread that binds us to lead me to her. But as I walk, I realize that I can hear Dex's clattering teeth before I see her.

Unbuttoning my coat, my pace quickens until our strides are in sync. I slip the coat over her shoulders and the slightest bit of tension seems to disappear from her face, causing something warm to flutter in my chest from her ease.

"Thank you," she mutters, continuing on her trek.

I watch her carefully, studying every inch of her skin, her light steps, shortened by her heightened anxiety. She was dying and I could not feel her pain. I could not feel the life draining from her. All that I felt was her hollow rage, crippled by exhaustion.

"There is a stream over there," I start. "Drink, breathe, and let us continue." She looks at me with the same frustration she looked at Vencen with, and something in me shifts. I don't want her to think that she cannot trust or speak to me about things that trouble her. She almost died from it. I'll be damned if I let that happen again. "Your power will react to your fear. Though your necklace may block it, I would imagine that elf can detect it. So rest, and when you are ready, we can continue at your pace."

Her fingers pull my coat around her as she pauses, contemplating my words before heading in the direction of the stream. Nearing the stream, I realize the mistake that I have made with just how cold the water might be. She's shivering enough as is, and the water will only make it worse.

I have never done anything so reckless and ill-planned. It's pathetic. My time in the book has weakened me, turned me into a man that I do not recognize. I had no fears. I had no weakness. Now? I care about the temperature of the water and how warm a mortal is as she sleeps.

This is not who I am.

I look away when she drops to her knees before the stream. I can hear her hiss when she plunges her hand in the water, yet it works to lessen the fear that terrorized her. She rolls back on her heels to sit, and I follow suit, sitting close so that some warmth might find its way to her.

"Why is it that you fear the lunar elves?" I ask once the angst within her begins to subside. I study the lines of her face intently as they jump and squirm from her thoughts. I look away, already accepting that it is not a question that I will receive an answer to.

"My father, he uh—" The dread bubbling in her makes its way to her voice, and she refuses to look at me, searching the ground for the answer instead. Then she clears her throat and straightens her back before she says with indifference, "When I was born, my father arranged for my marriage to a very powerful, violent man. But I ran away a week before my sixteenth birthday. Now, I've brought shame on my father, I've pissed off my betrothed, and all I have to show for it is a dead brother and sister."

Tension releases from her chest and moves into mine. Power crackles beneath my fingertips as rage blinds me. The hollow cries of the shadows echo through the forest, and I want nothing more than to find these men and show them just what hides within the shadows. A growl threatens to rumble through my chest at the thought of anyone laying a hand on her.

So long as I live, I vow to do everything in my power to keep her free from their hold. Both her father and her betrothed's. If they harm her, I will make them pray to their dead gods for mercy in death, and I will make sure that the afterlife brings them right back to me.

Who? I want to ask, but I know that I may not stop myself from hunting them when I am free. Mission be damned.

"I see." I don't let anger steep my voice because this moment is not about me.

A heavy bout of silence lingers between us as she gazes out into the distance, eyes devoid of emotion. If not for the fact that my eyes were on her, I would miss her say, "May women make thrones from the severed heads of men."

"Has your *betrothed* laid a hand on you?" I say the words with more disgust than I intended, and it takes more effort to rein in my rage. If that elven male had anything to do with her suffering, I hope he comes back, and I hope she kills him.

Dex shakes her head. "I met him once when I was young so he could *assess* his goods. His... *friends* on the other hand?"

The chaotic power roars, begging me to change course to this male that would treat her in such a way, and a sick thrill courses through me from imagining all the ways I can make him scream. Grinding my teeth, I realize that I need to change the direction of the conversation because I'm not meant to care about what happens to her.

She's a means to an end, I tell myself.

Kill her now. Kill her to end it all, the wicked voice laughs from my momentary lapse of control.

"Who was the elf?" Every whisper is telling me it isn't my business, yet it doesn't feel like I will be able to breathe until I know. She flinches from my scorn, but I hold firm. She knows who I am referring to.

"I guess you could call him a friend of my father's." She looks away like she feels guilty for running into him.

I break the weak hold I have over myself and reach out to cover her small hands with my own. Her skin is colder than the night itself, and I squeeze harder. "Do *not* feel guilty for that man. Those who support men who do abominable things are just as complicit. They are not good people if they stand aside to let the obscenities unfold."

She looks at me like she wants to defend him, but she stays quiet, then she stares at our hands. The rope between us tightens and glows, and as does my soul, encouraging me to do more than just touch her there. She snatches her hand away tucking it beneath her cloak as she stares off into the distance once more.

"Then we continue on our journey. However, if the winged male is left alone, it's possible that a kaliak reaches him. There is, unfortunately, strength in numbers in this instance." I hesitate to speak my true thoughts because I would much rather that he dies.

Sadness seeps through her fear as she starts to play with her fingers, which have become an unhealthy shade of blue. Digging my nails into my palm, I focus on something else to distract from the urge to cover her hands with mine to keep them warm and feel the way my soul comes alive. And like each night, I remind myself that keeping her alive does not mean keeping her warm. Had she not minded her own business and kept away from the book, our paths would be very different.

Despite it, I can't help but think that she did me a favor. I have yet to hear about the existence of the one who is meant to unlock the door. For all I know, they have not yet been born or they're long since dead, and I could very well end up controlled by one of the kings, and I am of no mind to ask her about it.

"I will stand watch while you both rest," I say.

"Right, because you want to keep me on track." She nods her head, agreeing with herself. "I guess I can trust you to keep me alive for the sake of your own freedom."

Her comment causes a pinch in my stomach that doesn't sit well with me. It shouldn't offend me that she believes that my care for her is limited to my desire for freedom. In reality, it shouldn't offend me because what she said is the truth. Well, it should be the truth at least, because it should not bother me as much as it does to see her cold or upset.

Instead of responding, I look at her emptily in some attempt to keep her at arm's length. I have made the mistake of developing a fraction of affection for the little elf, and it would be best if she continues on her path of hatred for me. I'm grateful she can't read my emotions as I do with her, or else she might see right through my facade.

Pain lances her face, turning the pinch into a dull ache. "Whatever." She moves to her feet. "Just get on with it."

Vencen gets to live another day. For now.

It's been two nights since our encounter with the Hinixians, and since then, Dex has refused to meet my eyes. Every time she glances my way, I can feel the pain shift in her chest, adding to my own. The more she hates me, the easier it will be to reach our mutual goal. Maybe soon she could hate me so much that I may stop concerning myself with the things that bother her.

"Once we get there, I don't care what you say, we're drinking tonight," Venison says for the third time in the past hour. Yet each time he says it, light gleams from her eyes as she looks at him with a smile going from ear to ear. I have to look away to staunch the fire that blazes in my stomach every time I see it. It becomes harder by the second, because the closer we get to Taravene, the more infectious her laugh becomes.

"As long as I get to have Madam T's raven buns, I'll be happy," she laughs back at him.

"And tonight, we drink." Venison has become more bearable since he's stopped making crude comments.

End him, or he'll disappear into the night with her in hand, the voices whisper from the darkest depths of my being. *You'll be forced to watch him take her. He'll laugh at how meek you've become.* Their taunting comments pierce my skin, poisoning me with unbridled hatred for the angel.

For a moment, I consider it—pulling on that thread and forcing my essence upon her—making her bend to my will as she did the night I woke.

I could do it.

It would hurt her, but I could make the male take his last breath. I would smile as her hands become painted in red, organs spilling between her fingers. We'd both laugh as his mouth hangs open in in a perpetual scream and—

I suck in a ragged breath, blinking away the tendrils of darkness clouding my mind. The chaos has never been able to take hold of me before, not even for the briefest moment. The corner of my lip twitches into a sneer. Only thoughts of *her* could weaken me into such a state.

"First one to pass out wins." Venison grins.

His voice deepens the twist of my lips. Partying is not the plan I had in mind when our sole purpose of traveling here is to find the quill. But I say nothing, not wanting to feel her eyes upon me or the power she has over me to silence even the voices.

I stay behind them, disappearing ahead and to the side every so often to make sure the path continues to be safe from creatures that could kill her. I don't like that she has kept the Hinixian blade hidden in the saddle and not at her waist, but I know she is powerful enough without it.

As the moon begins to rise higher in the sky, she starts to walk with more bounce and vigor in her step like she does every night. Once Taravene comes into view, a soft giggle leaves her lips that will forever be imprinted on my mind. I disappear into smoke and reappear at the very edge of the thread so that I can't hear her laughter anymore.

Taravene has always been one of my favorite kingdoms. Thousands of years ago, Taravene, Lodaxo, Zarlor and the like, were all nothing more than large cities with idle kings and queens. The villages in between were run by whoever the chosen leader was. The royals learnt of the power that can come from greed, so they began conquering lands and taking over villages. Until eventually, they could call themselves a kingdom, and the main cities became the capital.

Even though we are still miles away, the gilded city is brighter than the moon herself, and the palace at the center of the city towers over even the mountain. As we get closer, I can hear the faint laughter of patrons and the sound of coins clattering against each other.

By the time we reach the city, Dex's excitement becomes all that I can think about as she eyes everything with eagerness. A look I've begun to know all too well steals across her face as her eyes land on a shop filled with crystals and jewelry. Her fingers start to tap against her side like she's itching to knick something, and I find myself having to suppress a chuckle. I've been around thieves my whole life and much of what they do I find appalling, yet it's completely acceptable when she does it.

My eyes narrow as I walk behind her to watch passersby carefully to see if they look her way, but none of them pay her any mind. A lunar elf comes into view, and I find our thread, readying to step in the way, only to falter when her emotions go unchanged when she sees him; she feels safe here.

Taravene is neutral territory for a reason, and she knows this. She thinks of this place as her home. Before the Divine died, the only rule of this kingdom was that there is to be no conflict by way of rival clans or warring gods, or else one will be cast out. I assume that continues to be the same.

The air is filled with laughter and patrons who gather around tables to eat while their children run and play about. The streets are free from rubbish, lights blaze everywhere, reflecting off the marble and tile buildings. Everyone here seems so innocent to the war brewing just beyond these walls, and it makes me doubt that they know of the bloodshed in Zarlor.

Both Vencen and Dex's stomachs grumble when the smell of food hits the air, and she starts walking even faster to the source of the smell. She bumps into a woman with hair the same shade of red as hers, and I tug on the thread to appear by her side, only to spot her slip something shiny into her pocket. *Little thief.*

I turn to the guards stationed in pairs sporadically along the street, but none of them notice her act of deviousness.

An all-consuming hunger appears on her face as soon as she sets her sight on the purple sign that says 'Talavell's Cookery,' and in the shop window I can just make out the silhouette of a raven.

I remember her. *Madam T.* Hundreds of years ago, the old crone used to have a cat stamped onto her buns *after* she tried to use her magic to disguise her age and woo gods. It almost worked, until the goddess Kriotz used her trickery to lure Madam T into one of the goddess' more lucrative clubs and restricted Talavell's magic to be forever elderly.

"Gods dammit," Dex groans, while the look of hunger is replaced by annoyance as she stares down the line of customers that wraps around the street, all with the same emotion drawn on their faces as they tap their feet in wait to get their hands on the spelled treat.

You know, her food tastes truly horrific once the magic is removed, I whisper in her mind and watch as she shudders in a way that makes me feel victorious.

It's a good thing that I have no intention of getting rid of the magic then, she bites, folding her arm as she leans against the wall at the back of the line. From here, we can't even see the shop.

You aren't a woman with renowned taste. The spell-less treat may taste exquisite to you.

I have an exquisite palette, thank you.

What do you call Venison?

Her gaze snaps to me with annoyance glaring in her eyes. *Don't start.*

I chuckle, and we revert our attention to the surroundings. As the line progresses, the pavement beneath our feet shifts and dips; a perfect rectangular shape slightly beneath the ground. Everything is as it was before I was in the book, yet everything is different at the same time. Stepping aside and turning toward the square, I look at the empty space where the statue of Goddess Rielway once stood, at my back. Before me is another rectangular shape beneath the ground, the place where a statue of Acele used to exist.

I still remember how people tended to gardens beneath Rielway's feet, and by the Goddess of Life's blessing, there was always fresh fruit on the trees. Her outstretched arms mimicked the statue of Acele, the goddess of love on the opposite side of the square. *Kindred Square*, that's what the Taravenians used to call this place, where young doting couples came in the hopes of receiving the goddess' blessing.

Rielway always gave out blessings whenever she could, as she was always a being of love and light. No one realized that Acele was one of the most spiteful gods from too many failed loves. One should only pray to her when one wants a love to end. Most mortals don't realize this.

Vencen leaves to go somewhere else with the horse after several minutes. Once we get to the front of the line, Dex has an argument with the server that she should be allowed to buy eight buns because 'she's buying it for a friend,' and she walks out with only three and a sour look on her face. A look turned more scorned when she sees my amused expression. And as soon as she bites into the black bun, the annoyance melts away and a feeling close to lust begins to heat the corner of my mind attuned with her emotions. I try to keep my distance so as not to feel the sensation's tendrils, but she only speeds up her pace to match mine. I sigh, steering my thoughts in the direction of the quill and its potential whereabouts.

The city's light makes the silver undertones of her crimson hair stand out, giving the appearance that she's glowing, especially with the *emotion* that she's feeling plain on her face to anyone even without a bond. We pass shops and homes tucked tightly next to each other, some reaching up to six stories while others stand only on two stories. Unlike Zarlor, Taravene is much tidier, and the people are more likely to cut each other's wallets than their throats.

We continue to walk in silence side by side, all the while my teeth start to ache from the force of clamping down to ignore the insatiable need to watch as she licks the sugar off her fingers like some barbarian. This elf really does not have a shred of manners.

We're going to see my Ama who isn't actually my mother, she says, and I look at her curiously. *She took me in when I ran away, and she's taken care of me ever since. She took Vencen in, as well.*

I nod and wince when another person walks through me. *And does that make Vencen your brother?* My response will only rile her up, but I can't help but poke at the destructive fire that burns within her.

As I expect, she snaps her attention to me with a look of embarrassment and annoyance. *No, obviously not. He's just like a teammate with the same team leader. There's a difference,* she bites, turning her attention back ahead.

Whatever you say, darling. She looks at me with unrivaled irritation, which only makes me smirk.

You're such an ass. Her embarrassment disappears under the overwhelming wave of excitement as soon as a large white sign comes into view, making her almost skip. Golden threads decorate the background to form a large circle, filling in the space to form the Sarioan symbol of longevity. The words 'Magic Seam Couture' are written in bright red letters in front, where buttons are used in place of the 'o'. In black cursive letters just below, it writes 'No Loose Threads.'

You're taking us shopping? I did not intend to sound bewildered, rather, I intended to sound irritated. She doesn't need to know that I'm fascinated by the cause of her excitement and *why* exactly she has taken us here.

She stops in her tracks, spinning to look at me with a serious gleam in her eye. *When we are in there, I don't want your unsolicited comments to ruin the mood. I haven't seen them in months, and I would like to actually enjoy my time with them without your constant presence.*

So your family lives in a boutique? I query with a raised brow, knowing that the response will make that fire inside her burn.

What did I just say about unsolicited comments? She turns away and stomps up the concrete steps and pushes the door wide open, leaving me behind on the street.

A high-pitched screech sounds from inside, and I grab onto the thread as I sprint up the stairs four steps at a time, summoning what little power I have to the surface.

If anyone hurts her, I'll kill them.

~~GIDEON~~
CHAPTER EIGHTEEN

I LEAP INSIDE ONLY to stop short to see that the screeching is coming from another woman in Dex's hold. They wrap their arms around each other tightly, swinging from side to side as they giggle. Her thick black hair is fashioned into a single long braid down her back that swings like a pendulum when she moves. The petite woman pulls back to hold Dex at arm's length and gives me a better view of her in the process.

Chameleon.

To the normal eye, her bronze skin appears almost human, but I can just make out the faint glimmer of iridescent scales and the golden flecks in her round eyes. She looks about the same age as Dex, if not older, with a yellow bindi on her forehead to match her lehenga.

The entryway is small enough to feel crowded even though only two corporeal people stand inside it. On one side, there's a beaded curtain that hangs over the entrance of a door that appears to lead into a room full of fabric and half-dressed mannequins. On the other side is a raised platform with racks upon racks of dresses and suits. In the corner, I can just make out an area sectioned off by a red velvet curtain for people to get changed. Straight ahead, a set of wooden stairs hugs the walls as it climbs up into the top floor. Orbs of light hang from the ceiling in each room, no doubt powered by one of the fae in this building.

"You should have sent word that you were coming, I would have made us matching dresses," laughs the woman with the smooth voice.

"It was a bit of a last-minute decision." Dex smiles back. "Where's Ama?"

"Here," a short Sarioan woman says gruffly as she walks through the doorway with beads draping down like a curtain. Her pointed ears tell me that she's fae of some sort. Sniffing the air, her aged skin creases as she frowns. "Smelly. Go bathe then come back," she mutters, waving her hand.

I glance at Dex to see how she reacts to the woman's rudeness, but she grins like it's a comment she expected. The woman glances around through her heavy-lidded eyes, and as she moves, her short salt and pepper hair stays perfectly rigid. "Where's the boy?"

"*Vencen* has gone to collect payment from someone," Dex corrects.

The old woman grunts, sizing her up in a way that has me fighting the urge to step in between them. "You're too skinny. You need to eat more." She shakes her head. "Saeya, go feed her. You,"—she clicks her fingers at Dex—"bath. You're scaring my customers with your stench."

I look around, but there is not a customer in sight. I expect Dex to plunge into an explanation that she's just been poisoned and has eaten next to nothing in the past eight days. But without another word, the beads clatter as the woman disappears into the other room.

"A warm welcome as usual." All of our attention moves to the sibilant voice of the sepia-skinned gorgon woman standing at the top of the stairs. Her green eyes shine with Dex's mutual excitement as she stares down at the pair, but the many sets of cautious eyes that stare in my direction doesn't share its owner's amusement. The woman frowns as the white snakes on her head curl and slither in the air, sniffing and flicking their tongues to taste the change of energy in the air.

The gorgon pats the flour off her apron before she runs down at the same time as Dex runs up and meets her in a tight hug. The snakes hiss at the impact, trying to keep their distance from Dex just as the woman pulls away as well.

"Gods, Kselia wasn't wrong. You *do* smell." Her forked tongue flicks out in disgust as she holds Dex at a distance.

Dex rolls her eyes. "It's lovely to see you too, Mirya."

I thought her name would start with 's', I add, smirking up at her. The joke isn't the best of taste, but it's something my brother would have said, and saying it is keeping his memory alive.

Silence, she grits.

"I'm going to Ico's tonight," Dex says, looking between Saeya and Mirya. Mirya looks back at Dex disapprovingly, and Saeya's lips twitch downward. "There's no, 'let's get drinks' or 'we can play board games like old times'? You haven't seen us in months and you're getting straight to business?"

Dex's shoulders hunches ever so slightly to match her grim expression dampening the excitement she felt. "It's important," she starts, but the gorgon waves her off and heads back up the stairs. Dex stares at Mirya's back, and I can feel the ache that shrouds her chest as her lips twitch like she's debating adding more. With a defeated sigh, she turns back to Saeya.

"Ignore her." A reassuring smile warms her face. "She lost her job and hasn't been taking it too well."

The pain in Dex morphs from guilt into sympathy as she walks back down the stairs. "Singing at that fancy tavern?"

The chameleon nods, holding out her hand to Dex. "But I *am* happy to see you, sister. Ama let me use the expensive fabric that you've always wanted. I didn't know you were coming, but I finished it. You *must* wear it tonight."

The excitement returns to Dex at the mention of 'expensive' like it's a trigger for her. "I'm not the only one getting dressed up. You are, too. We're mixing business with pleasure tonight." She winks at the chameleon.

"Please, for the love of all the Divine, bathe," Saeya laughs, pinching her nose and swatting the air.

Dex raises her hands defensively. "You are all being dramatic. I do not smell *that* bad," she says loud enough for the whole house to hear, taking slow steps up the stairs. "If you think *I* smell bad, wait until you smell Vencen."

Kselia, or Ama as everyone but me calls her, comes charging out with a straw broom, pointing it straight at Dex who scrambles up the steps with a mischievous grin and a giggle ringing through the air. "You dare yell in my house, eh? *Eh*? You dare, *huh*?" Kselia's nasally voice booms as she waves the broom about.

Saeya giggles, holding her nimble fingers in defense as she steps clear of the swinging.

So this is where you get your penchant for violence? I say, and watch as Dex's grin grows into a full-blown smile. I can't help but smile in return.

In all my years, I've never once known what it means to be a family; to grow up with everyone else, laughing together at what has become an inside joke, to always have each other's back and genuinely care about what is happening in the others' lives. I have always known that this level of joy exists behind the closed doors of happy homes. It makes me envious. My mind has become honed on the single idea that families involve bloodshed and tears, where you never know when one of your siblings might pine for your seat on the throne.

Dex climbs the stairs on all fours like a child trying to get away from a scolding, and Kselia just shakes her head. "You kids are going to be the death of me," Kselia mutters under her breath, going back into the workshop.

I can see why you call her Ama, I muse, following the thread while I walk up the stairs.

You don't know the half of it.

I follow her up to the second floor where we pass a storage space doubling as a lounge area. The next floor holds a kitchen filled to the brim with sacks of flour, spices, and a wide variety of vegetables and meats. In the corner, a door sits ajar, opening into a cupboard that has been turned into a bedroom with male clothing folded neatly atop the shelves on the wall. Mirya doesn't acknowledge Dex from where she is sitting cross-legged on the floor in front of trays of different half made Sarioan dishes. She is scooping up a mixture and rolling it into a ball before placing it in the center of a circular piece of rice paper and folding it into an elaborate shape. The entire floor is filled with partially made street food and meals like they are street vendors.

Then at the very top of the stairs we come upon four doors.

Dex opens the far left one and walks straight inside. I follow along, stopping on the threshold. Dresses and fancy blouses are strewn around the room, piling on top of each other in a disarrayed mess while jewelry and other trinkets are scattered atop dressers and tables.

Barbaric little elf.

A bunk bed tucks up against the wall, and the bottom bed is unmade with questionable stains all over the sheets and covers. The top one is tucked to perfection while various crystals and gems are glued to the ceiling.

All over the walls are sketches of a winged boy and a silver haired girl. A couple of the drawings have a girl wearing a crown with a moon on it, and one even has her with streaks of red hair. Some of the drawings right by the bottom bunk depict the black-winged boy with muscles larger than his face and wings bigger than a house. It pains me to admit that Venison has talent.

I have to question Kselia's parenting if she paired you with Venison, I say.

It's Vencen, she corrects. *And that's only because Saeya won a bet when we were younger, and we had no choice but to share a room. It's taken years to get the smell of his body odor out of here.* She shoves a pile of dresses off a chair and on top of another pile. *It's worked out well either way. Vencen doesn't like to stay here, so Saeya and Mirya can share one of the other rooms.*

She makes her way to a spot by the wall and squats down to an area where the drawings are sparse. The room hums with magic as she waves her hand, opening up a section of the wall to reveal a hidden cupboard. As soon as it opens, more magic burns through the room. Hints of darkness linger in the air, far more potent to the measly light objects that she has stored in her hidden compartment.

Edging closer, I can just spy a bag of coins sagging in the corner next to another Hinixian blade. Dex reaches into her bustier to pull out the bangle that she pinched from the satyr and drops it atop a goblet. She unclasps one of the necklaces from around her neck and drops it into the disorganized pile of jewelry. Then she drops the bracelet from the red-haired woman over a serpentine dagger. Amongst the chaos, I struggle to figure out which of the objects is emitting the dark energy.

Pulling the book out of the bag, she shoves it into the hole, forcing it to stand upright just so that it will fit.

It will be safe here, she says.

From you or from the others? A scowl plasters her face, and I hold my hand up in defense, just as she did before. *You said, 'no unsolicited comments around your family.' I do not believe I am mistaken in saying that they are currently not 'around.'*

With another wave of her hand, the wall closes and all that remains is the smell of the residue of her power. *No unsolicited comments ever.* If her glare could kill, then I would be dead a thousand times over. But the little elf still doesn't realize that her emotions always betray her.

I agree with your family. You could use a bath. I don't add that it's because she stinks; I think I've become immune to whatever it is that they are referring to. I am not sure when I began longing for her quips and wit sharper than a dagger. Yearning to feel her bite has come as desperately as my need to breathe. The truth of the matter is that anything I feel is fruitless and against the course nature has made for me.

I've slaughtered vicious beasts, led armies into battles and came out victorious. And yet I don't have the strength to remove myself from her presence. It's a forbidden whisper in my chest that feels so foreign, and at the same time, like it belongs. A light breaking through the span of endless darkness, a figure in the shadows.

She shakes her head as she moves to a dresser, rummages through it while mumbling something nonsensical under her breath.

Who's the assassin in the family? If I had to hazard a guess, it would be the gorgon, I say with a tone of indifference.

She turns slowly to look at me with her hands midair like she's still going through the dresser. *What?*

Magic Seam Couture—No Loose Ends? Venison is too arrogant and loud-mouthed—she rolls her eyes at the nickname—*you are too messy. Saeya is too timid, and Kselia is the leader. Which leaves the grumpy gorgon or the nameless boy that lives in the kitchen cupboard. Are you saying that with a store name like that, there are no assassins?*

She studies me like she knows my intentions. *It's a play on words. And the nameless boy is Faeus, and he happens to be very lovely.* A glint of admiration flicks across her face at the mention of the male, and she turns back around to rummage through her dresser.

Is he another 'teammate'?

She spins to look back at me and throws a tunic at me. It flies through my body, unhindered by any means, and she stares at the fallen fabric with dissatisfaction. *Don't be a prude,* she snarls.

I chuckle. *I am simply determining family dynamics to better understand the inner workings of your mind so we can more effectively reach our goal.*

She scoffs. *You're a poet, not a scholar. You best know your place or else you might just find out how dangerous Faeus can be.* Her empty threat falls flat as our amusement sends a thrill through the room.

I'm trembling in fear. I pick the nonexistent dirt out of my nails.

Why do you have to be so negative? She gives up on her search and makes her way to the door, flinging it open with more vigor than required, and I move to follow her out. She whips back around stomping toward me with her finger trained at the space between my eyes. *Stay here or else I'll find a way to gouge your eyes out.*

I would like to see you try, darling.

Such a penchant for violence indeed.

DEX

CHAPTER NINETEEN

The hot water laps against me as my fingers glide across the surface covered in thousands of tiny bubbles. The warmth almost takes away all memory of our journey and the existence of a 'weapon' that specializes in the art of irritation. Lathering my hair in Saeya's shampoo, I become grateful for the lack of hair washing that has occurred in the past eight days. The red is still vibrant, though a shade lighter than my 'blood moon hair'.

Tapping the necklace against my chest, I wonder what it might feel like to let my powers really course through me and find out just what kind of damage I can cause. I need to be more careful now that we're so close to Hinixsus's border. There isn't a doubt in my mind that Aywin knew who

I was, and there's no telling if one of the other soldiers did, or even if the callpaith somehow figured it out. This means that there must be absolutely no trace of moon magic on me.

Worst yet, at that moment, I didn't even think about the book. I was so stricken with fear that I didn't even consider that they might have forced me to empty my bag just as the Black Bloods did. My people may not be as cruel as the Black Bloods or the Paragon Dawn, but a lot can happen in eight years. People change as soon as power or money is involved. If Gideon is 'the secret of kings' like he alleges, as a trusted advisor of the king, Aywin would know exactly what the book is.

Another daunting thought crosses my mind; what if they were heading for Zarlor because they knew that the book had been unlocked and they could somehow locate it back to the waterfall? I shudder to realize that I owe Gideon my life for waking me up when he did. Beyond the sound of the rushing waterfall, I would have been dead to the world, only to wake once blood had stained the waters.

The light padding of footsteps against the creaking wooden stairs draws my attention away from the mountain of bubbles dripping off my bent knee. A soft knock rattles the door, and Saeya says from behind it, "It's just me. I'll put the dress in your room."

I stir upright, picturing what would happen if I walked into the room—where Gideon is likely waiting—while I'll be completely naked. "Actually, just bring it in here."

She pauses for a moment. "Um, are you sure?" Guilt crams over me because I know that the request will make her uncomfortable and she's too nice to say no.

"I just thought I'd be cold, but I just remembered that I brought a robe in with me." I curse under my breath for the terrible lie because it isn't cold in this house, and I left the robe lying somewhere in my room.

"Okay, I'll leave it in your room for you." The volume decreases as she heads into my room, and the sound of the stairs creaking vibrates through the house.

"Thank you!" I yell before she gets out of earshot.

Rinsing out my hair, I let my own powers seep into the tub, warming the water to somewhere near scalding hot. I sigh with contempt, sinking back into the tub as I try to cover as much of my body in the water, savoring the moment for it may be the last time I have a proper bath for a long time.

Having Gideon and the book around places more of a target on my back, and every second that he continues to be linked to me could be my last second of freedom. They'd kill me just for being found in possession of the cursed thing. Gods, I can't imagine the uproar if anyone were to discover that I'm fated to end the war, cursed to bring back dead gods, and apparently, I've unlocked the door that unleashes the kaliaks—and apparently every second that I waste is another second that allows for more of those beings to come into the realm.

With that morbid thought, I haul myself onto my feet, already missing the warmth of the bath. I wring out my hair before wrapping myself in a threadbare towel.

Gideon, are you there? I hold onto the tether that has started to ignite every time he spares me a glance.

Silence.

I dry myself as much as possible, slathering my skin in a berry-scented lotion that soothes my aching muscles. I start mumbling profanities for not thinking the whole process through.

I'll wrap the book in one of Vencen's shirts. If he can actually hear me, then this will surely get his attention.

Silence. Again.

Surely if he's in the bedroom, he will be able to hear me?

Heat rises to my cheeks as I slowly open the door, creeping out into the hall and tiptoeing across into my bedroom. It would make more sense if I move about in a ruckus to warn him of my arrival. Yet on the flip side, maybe it's better if he isn't alerted to the fact that bath time is over.

Pulling the towel tighter around my torso, my hand wraps around the brass door handle, turning the knob and rushing inside without a second of hesitation. As soon as I'm inside, I feel his presence.

"Saying you're in nothing but a towel is a far more effective summons." His warm voice crawls down my back along with his gaze, and my cheeks flush an even brighter red.

I'm of the mind to stay in my position so he doesn't have a view of my front. Just like the time by the waterfall, I don't want to give him the satisfaction of thinking that he's capable of making my confidence falter. I've been through too much to feel vulnerable by what clothes I'm wearing, or lack thereof.

I shift on my feet, turning to face him with my arms folded firmly across my chest. Sizing him up and down just as I've done many times before, while in the back of my head, there's a little voice saying, 'I can take him' despite how untrue it may be.

"You were wearing far less in the forest, little elf." His chuckle stirs that need inside me that begs to be touched.

If you were a gentleman, you would have turned away, I snide, somehow offended by the very factual accurate nickname.

"I have never claimed to be a gentleman," he says darkly, taking another step towards me.

My breath hiccups in my chest, and I fight back the urge to turn away from the heady taste of mulled wine and the fervor in his gaze. *You never claimed to be insolent either. I suppose not everything needs mentioning. Now be a dear and turn around,* I say like there is a breeze in my voice as I eye the delicate black and silver fabric laid atop the chair.

"And if I were to say no?" he asks in the same casual tone as my own, taking another step forward. His chin juts out as he looks down at me with a barely noticeable devious smirk. "What will you do then?" He takes a step closer. "What is it that you said you'd do?" Another step. "Gouge my eyes out?" One last step until his chest is inches away from my own, and I stop being able to tell the difference between my irritation and an insatiable need.

Every corner of his body radiates heat like he may as well be a furnace, and it's as if I'm about to melt. I close the distance until only a whisper is between us, teasing the line between satisfaction and frustration.

I think the book might need an extra layer of protection. The mischief that dances on his lips moves to mine as his turns into a thin line. *Now turn.*

"Witch," he grumbles, walking backwards before turning to face the wall.

The disappearance of his closeness makes me feel a loss so profound that I almost lose my balance. My soul feels like it needs some kind of relief, as if the tether has been pulled taunt and my muscles have followed suit.

Smartass, I retort.

Barbarian.

Inconvenience. I try to keep the smile out of my voice. I feel like a child.

Say another word, and I'll turn back around, he growls darkly.

I bite the inside of my cheek. Shrugging the feeling off, I try to focus on the dress. Taking the few short steps to it, I marvel at the way the silver threads glisten beneath the fae lights. The longer I stare at it, the more enchanting it becomes as the black threads seem to act as a show of the silver.

Glancing at Gideon to make sure his eyes are on the wall, I let the towel fall to the floor and rush to pull the dress over my head and slip into my undergarments. The chiffon caresses my shoulders in a sigh as it cascades down onto the floor, leaving the sides of both my legs exposed from high splits. A silk rope crosses over my exposed hips, crisscrossing over my back in elaborate twists and turns, moving to climb over the folded chiffon on my shoulder that drapes over my chest in a way that leaves my sternum bare.

Adjusting the dress to fit properly, I grunt as my shoulder contorts at an unnatural angle to do up the back of the dress. Inching closer to the mirror, I crane my neck and attempt to see how to fit the minuscule button into the minuscule hole.

"Cough once if you're dying. Cough twice if you're being a nuisance." In the reflection of the mirror, I just catch the remnants of his shoulder shaking from hiding his laugh.

And what if I cough three times? I straighten my head so that I look directly at him.

He turns. "Three times means..." The sentence hangs in the air as he takes me in, his lips slightly parted, apparently unable to move. Cocking my head, I meet his gaze with a triumphant grin, noting the red that now stains his cheeks in a gentle blush. "You look," he starts, running his gaze over me like he's trying to imprint every inch into memory.

It's okay, I know I look good. I try to hold onto the confidence as my arm twists once more to button up the dress.

He clears his throat, fixing his collar which was never out of place. "Apologies, I mistook you for a kaliak." I roll my eyes, continuing in my attempts to button the dress. He sighs, taking another step closer. "It's painful watching you do that. Let me, please." He walks behind me before I get the chance to refuse.

Breathless heat spreads from my chest when his finger skims over the soft part of my back, leaving goosebumps in its wake. For a man with no physical form, his hot breath lingers heavily on the back of my neck as he does up one button after another. I try to stay perfectly still as I swallow the lump in my throat, holding firm so not to sway into his touch.

We both pull away as soon as the last button is done and practically jump to opposite sides of the room like a magical force has pushed between us.

Thank you, I mumble, pulling out the chair and starting to apply makeup as quickly as possible. Even in the silence, his heavy gaze is on me, still studying, still imprinting the sight into his memory.

After swiping kohl along my eyelids and tapping rouge on my lips, I move on to the next step. Using my magic to warm my hair as I brush through my strands to leave behind waves and bouncy curls that likely won't last the night. I start picking rings and bracelets at random, piling them on like I'm desperate to convince someone of my status when the reality is that this is the only place I can wear them without worry. As a final touch, I put earrings in every pierced hole until a row of silver climbs up my ears, catching the light each time I move.

Letting my necklace fall proudly on the front of the dress, I take one last look in the mirror with complete admiration. After everything my parents did to me, after they killed my sister, after I've been brought to death's door more times than I can count, a smile still finds its way to my lips. My skin still radiates with an impenetrable glow. I can still laugh until my stomach aches just as I can cry until I have no more tears to shed.

I don't know who Devereux is anymore; she's a myth. Maybe she once existed and became a shadow of a memory, haunting the world with a crown on her head and hatred rooted deep in her soul. I won't deny that I still do hate, but now I also love—and I love freely. Never in my wildest dreams would my younger self so much as believe that this is the woman we've become. She would be proud. My sister would be proud.

Tying my shoes on, Vencen's voice faintly travels through the walls, and I groan internally. I just know that one day I'm going to slip up and call him Venison now. I ignore Gideon's continued stare as I run down the stairs towards the sound of laughter. Vencen has always been Ama's favorite, gods know why. She almost treats him better than she treats Faeus, her own son. But I put that down to the fact that Faeus is a hundred years older than Vencen and he's still living in his mother's house.

The whole family is gathered in the kitchen. Kselia leans on her cane that she only uses at night when she wears her floor-length cotton nightie. As usual, Vencen's arms swing wildly as he boasts about escaping a 'legion of Paragon Dawn' and how he single-handedly got us out of our interrogation by the Crystal Spear.

He doesn't know when to stay silent, Gideon growls as I start tasting herbs.

Hush now, little one. No unsolicited comments, I coo, enjoying the heightened taste from the flare of his annoyance.

Pride streams through me when I look at Saeya. She may be older than me, but I've always looked at her like she's my little sister. Gold bangles climb up her wrists, bringing out the golden detail of her saree. The vibrant crimson-colored silk drapes over her dress, complementing the textured turquoise blouse beneath that matches her bindi. A golden chain hangs over her cheek from her nose ring to her hair, flowers woven into her braid.

She leans ever so slightly against Mirya, who dresses like someone who should not be messed with, in her red lipstick and fitted white dress that has leather paneling throughout. She meets my eye and shoots me an apologetic smile, which I return in kind. She always feels responsible for Mirya.

None of us held back when getting ready tonight. Even Vencen has thrown on his most expensive navy suit and white tunic that has lace sewn into the fabric.

He stops mid-sentence, turning his full attention to me. He gasps dramatically, holding a hand over his heart as he bows deeply at the hips with his wings tucked neatly behind him. "Your Highness," he says breathlessly as he straightens back up, stretching his hand out to me. I narrow my eyes at it, and the taste of whiskey and ginger returns as it does every time Vencen is involved. I take his outstretched hand out of spite to Gideon, only to regret it immediately as a wet kiss lands on the top of my hand. Snatching my hand away, I stare at him with unfettered revulsion when he says, "You look dashing as always, Princess De —"

Kselia smacks him in the back of the head with a rolled-up newspaper that magically appeared in her hand. "Are you stupid? Don't say that out loud," Kselia hisses.

That's her one rule; our real names are never to be uttered. She'll look after us, as long as we look after each other, which means that we will do whatever it takes to keep each other's identities a secret.

Despite it, the light air in the room remains the same.

I never did say that I'm against violence, Gideon chimes in after Kselia's loud whack. I glance at him to find him smirking until days end.

"I'm told we're going to Icoden's tonight." Vencen's tone sets me on edge. "Might this have something to do with the quill you're looking for?" There's an air of mischief around him like he knows something that I don't.

"It's for a job," I say casually so as not to arouse anyone's suspicion.

"Is it really?" He narrows his eyes, grinning from ear to ear.

"Do we have conflicting interests?"

"I guess we'll find out."

DEX
CHAPTER TWENTY

OUR HEELS CLICK ALONG the pavement as our giddiness echoes along the busy street. To say 'our' giddiness is a lie when the only ones truly laughing from the heart are Vencen, Saeya, and Mirya. My own joy stops short of a snort and chuckle here and there all while Mirya's snakes stand on end like they're attempting to find Gideon.

A cloud hangs over my head, stopping me from truly living life in the moment like we would always do. Maybe it's the fact that I can taste the uneasiness in Gideon, or maybe it's the fact that it feels like I'm counting down my days until something bad happens. Gods, or even the fact that I might find myself at a dead end with the whereabouts of the quill.

But I keep my head up, attempting to ignore the storm that tries to bring me down.

We need to talk, Gideon's voice stirs in my mind as he sidesteps another pedestrian.

I give him a sideways glance as he walks next to me at the very edge of our group. Another step away, and we'll both be on the streets in the way of the carriages. *I'm busy.*

No, you aren't. You don't want to be part of their conversation, he says knowingly. *Let's talk.*

Their conversation about Kselia's latest laughable comment floats in the air as I try to drag myself into their conversation. *How would you know? I'm having fun.* I try to say the words like I mean them, but even I'm not convinced.

Because I can feel all of your emotions.

I freeze in my tracks, whipping my head around to face him. I shouldn't be surprised, after all I can taste his, though I don't know what half the tastes mean. *What?*

The snakes react to my abruptness first. Mirya cocks her head at me and stops walking as well. "What's wrong?" A smile still plays on her lips like she doesn't read the shock on my face.

"I just forgot to do something. I'll catch up with you at Ico's." I walk backwards before they can ask more questions.

"Alright," she says suspiciously before laughing at something Vencen says.

Ducking into an alleyway, I grab onto the sleeve of his perfectly pressed overcoat and tug him toward the shadows behind a rundown staircase.

"Careful, darling, you don't want to know what I get up to in the shadows." His deep voice bounces against the walls and tears a shiver through me that starts at my core. A threat lurks beneath the surface of his words, one that has many meanings.

My mouth goes dry, and in the darkness, the harsh shadows across his face and the darkening glow in his eyes are all I can see. Pushing past the swirling desire in my core, I drop my hold on his jacket and take a big step back.

What do you mean 'you can feel all of my emotions'? I blurt in an attempt to distract from the lingering heat of his words, and the tipsy taste of mulled wine on my tongue.

"Exactly what it means." He follows me in my steps until my back hits the wall and has my head almost in the crook of his neck. My breath catches, and I try to push myself further back into the red brick wall to get away from the heat emanating off him and the sparks that seem to fly when he draws near. "Just as I know that feeling that's coursing through your veins is from the realm of the wicked." He leans down until his lips are shy of touching my ear, and his fingers trail fire down the side of my neck, moving the hair off my shoulders.

All I can seem to think about is how badly I want him closer, to be consumed by the smell of sage and become engulfed in his warmth. Energy thunders through me like wildfire when soft lips press against my ear, and I become deaf to everything around except for his steady breaths.

"Admit it, you love the feeling, and it drives you mad." His hoarse breath brings another wave of need that makes me turn my head away from his touch to give those lips the freedom to explore my neck.

The invisible tether thrums around us, sending perverse signals that my body wants to obey.

Then its reminder sets in: who we both are and why we've come to be. More specifically, *why* the tether comes alive when we touch.

My body objects as I place both hands on his chest and shove. It does nothing but cause his fingers to wrap around my wrist and keep them locked in the place above his heart. My soul sings alongside the tether like it's finally getting what it's always wanted.

This isn't right. Souls aren't meant to react this way. Getting a shadow shouldn't make me feel like this.

"What are you?" My breath comes out as if I've just ran up and down the street a thousand times.

"Oh, little elf, you do not want to know what I am." His thumb moves agonizingly slow up my wrist like it isn't something he's in control of, and all of my focus goes to that single motion.

With all the energy I have, I push past thoughts of the need settling in me.

He pauses, and the taste of rosemary stains my tongue. I can't for the life of me figure out what the taste means, only that he looks down at me with such fervent concern. "I felt your fear when he called you princess, why?" An edge of danger sharpens his words.

Fear rises in my chest, and I force myself to think of anything but the answer so he doesn't find out the truth. He might not do anything with the knowledge of who I am while he's bound to me, but what about once he's free? If someone has the ring that controls him, could they not force the answer out of him?

"Come on, lass, stop pissing around." Vencen swoops in from the sky, landing unsteadily and righting himself with a hand on his hips.

"As soon as I get my physical form, I'll kill him just for interrupting." Gideon's eyes darken as his hands stay wrapped around my wrists.

Don't you dare, I'll end you if you do, I bite. *No one kills him but me.* I snatch my hands away and take a step to the side so I can see Vencen properly, and say, "You're meant to be drinking the night away."

Gideon chuckles softly, lowering his head to the point on my shoulder, and I shudder. "I can *smell* the lie on you, little elf. You couldn't hurt me if you tried."

Pushing him aside, I ignore the comments of both men as I quickly walk in the direction of Ico's tavern. As I move through the city, an almost empty taste sours my tongue. I can feel Gideon following at the very edge of the tether, and Vencen jumps from roof to roof, flapping his wings in between and making it to the bar first.

I can't shake the feeling that there's something within the tether that will answer all of my questions, I just need to look deeper or think harder. And I do just that as I walk, but all I see is a need to wait for him to catch up—the man who tried to kill me not so long ago.

I thought my breath would loosen when Ico's tavern comes into view, but my shoulders only coil tighter. Fae lights make the drawing of a rabid dog glow while the words 'Once Bitten, Twice Shy' illuminates even brighter.

Loud jabbering and laughter streams through the air as a lunar elf goes stumbling out of the door with the handle of a broken jug in hand. He spots me and I roll my eyes, preparing my knee for impact if he steps too close.

"Hello," he slurs, raising the handle at me and tossing it close to his mouth as if it were filled with ale. He slumps down against the steps staring at the handle with deep rooted confusion.

Shaking my head, I walk over the drunken elf. Just as I'm about to reach the door, it swings open, and I jump aside. A short woman with thick features and partially invisible wings drags out a drunken male twice her size by his collar.

Nessa's auburn hair turns crimson beneath the sign as she awards him with a back handed slap across the ear. "Yer lucky ye've still got yer cock on ya after that stunt." She shoves him down the steps and we both watch as the male trips over the elf's legs.

She bends down to the elf whose eyes go wide as her plump chest comes into his line of sight. Smacking the elf in the head, she points directly at his forehead. "Watch yer eyes, lad. Now get off me steps, or I'll be gettin' yer suckin' me feet yer damn gremlin." The elf struggles to get up, only to give up and crawl away in a hurry. She spins, pointing her finger at me as the matching crimson crystals along her brow catches the light. "Control that winged boy of yers or ye'll be picking his remains off me street too." She pulls me into a tight hug, keeping my arms hostage in her embrace.

"I missed you too," I laugh, even though deep down what I'm thinking is 'please don't throw me down the steps as well.'

"Now get in there." She slaps my backside. Whiskey and ginger ignite on my tongue, and I leap forward as she holds the door open. Every time I meet her, I begin to understand more and more why she's Icoden's significant other. She's probably one of the few people in existence that could boss him around.

Scurrying inside to avoid another slap, I am greeted by the high-pitched squeals of women congregating around Vencen as he shows off the diamond rings on his fingers. Searching the crowd, I spot Saeya twirling in Mirya's arms, and just as I expect, I find Ico behind the bar whisking around another barmaid as they serve patrons.

Sensing my gaze on him, he grins widely and yells for me to come closer. I can spot beads of sweat coating his umber skin as he works. His clawed hand with scales climbing up the arm expertly navigates the jugs and ale without missing a beat. For a brief moment, I wonder what's different about him, then I realize that he's finally changed his earring from a boned point to swirling black talon to match his horns.

About time, I think to myself. I've started getting bored of seeing him wear the bone that Kselia gave him when she first took him in years before she took any of us in.

My gaze lands on a fae with forest green hair and eyes to match, leaning against the counter as he looks me up and down.

"What are you looking at?" I hiss.

His eyes round but he doesn't back down. "Let me get you a—"

"Another sound from you, and I'll have your tongue as a snack."

He grins, thinking it's an innuendo, only for his face to fall when Ico places a knife in my hand. I hold it up, looking at the black blade, then at him with a sensual smile. "Tell me," I say slowly. "Do you want to play?"

He shakes his head quickly and scurries off to another corner of the room.

Ico's powerful laugh shakes the wooden counter, and I hand the weapon back to him. "I ain't afraid of usin' my claws if the other pretty boy starts harassin' the maidens." His silky voice wraps around me when he speaks, motioning to Vencen, and a warm smile tugs at my lips.

Nessa plunks freshly cleaned jugs onto the counter. "Oi, less talkin' an' more workin'," she snaps, then yells a list of orders for all the barhand to hear. I stifle a laugh watching her snap her fingers at the tavern owner.

"Aye, your grace," he chuckles, pulling her in to place a kiss on the top of her head. She sinks into his touch for the briefest moment before continuing with managing the patrons. He turns to me, softening his smile while passing a jug of ale into another patron's hands. "Feathers says you're after somethin'." He nods his chin toward Vencen again.

I nod stiffly, feeling Gideon appear behind me, and suddenly the room feels overcrowded. Ico considers something for a moment before extending his clawed arm to its full length, just long enough to hook around Vencen's trousers. He whips around, starling the women around him.

"Man the bar," Ico orders, releasing Vencen now that he has his attention.

Vencen's gestures disarmingly, shaking his head furiously. "Absolutely not. I came here to—"

"I'll tell em' where you got them rings." Ico's eyes glimmers with excitement. He wants to tell them regardless of what choice Vencen makes.

"Alright, alright, no need to be unreasonable." Vencen holds his hand up in surrender, taking position behind the bar, and I follow Ico to the corner of the room where it's quieter, all while Vencen curses under his breath.

I'm painfully aware of how protectively Gideon stands while eying Ico with unchartered suspicion. *Calm down, he won't hurt me.*

I don't trust him. He runs with bad people.

I'm his people.

Gideon doesn't stand down like I asked. The almond taste of his protectiveness only compounds when an elven clan member stumbles out of the washroom, with some form of weapon strapped to every inch of his body.

"Do you have any books for me?" I'm not giving up on my search just because Gideon is here.

Ico shakes his head. "Nah. Heard you've been actin' strange since you got the last 'un."

Ignoring the way his response makes my skin prickle, I focus on the fact that Vencen really doesn't know how to keep his mouth shut. But I'm impressed with how quickly he managed to unload everything to Ico.

"What do you know about that book?" Maybe he has information that Gideon has conveniently withheld.

"You got a dud." He shrugs. "That ain't what you're 'ere to talk about though. Out with it, lass."

Of course it isn't. If there's ever something I need, Ico will know where it is. Or he'll at least know someone who knows someone who knows someone that knows where it is. Just like Taravene, Ico is neutral. He doesn't pick sides in any political or clan wars, which is how this tavern came about. Rather, he gives them both the arsenal they require, and he lets them have at each others throats. But, there's more to this place than meets the eye.

I lower my voice and say, "I'm looking for Hell's Quill." My muscles stiffen as I watch the blood drain from his face. Vencen told him everything and conveniently left that out?

Ico looks around quickly and drags me to the kitchen. The pounding in my chest makes the fae lights brighter than it actually is. "Whatever you think you know, you don't. Stay away from it." His gaze pleads with me more than his hushed whisper.

I'm willing to admit that I probably don't know the whole story, but I've stopped concerning myself with knowing everything so long as I find out what I actually need to know. "It's for a job," I say, hoping he'll give up what he knows in the name of business.

"Don't matter. Cancel the job." He glowers at no one in particular.

"I can't."

"It ain't your business. Don't get involved."

"What is it? Why is it so bad?"

Gideon shifts his weight, which only makes me want to find out more. Could it be to do with what exactly he is? Or does it have to do with kaliaks being freed with the book—well, by me.

"I mean it, Dex, stay away from it. Stay away from the book, the quill, the ring, all of it." He grasps my shoulders, squeezing it tightly in urgency.

"This isn't getting anywhere. Let's go," Gideon says.

"Tell me everything you know about it," I urge. This is my chance to find out what it is that Gideon is hiding—it could be the missing piece to the puzzle.

"It's a game o' kings. They'll be comin' for you for that as well. Everyone will," he warns.

My heart thrums louder and I become dizzy with the unanswered questions. "I know it's a weapon, but what kind? Why is it so dangerous?"

Ico pulls me towards him, glancing around for any prying ears. "What's in that thing can flatten the whole fuckin' realm. It ain't no bedtime story, he's a bloody nightmare. If he's out—you know what kings will do with that kind of power? If your *father* or the False God had that kind of power? He'll kill everyone. Me, Nessa, Saeya, Ama. Everyone you love," Ico hisses. His grip on me grows painful and he stares at me like he's coming unhinged. "Stay away, Dex. Please. Be smart."

I wish I could. I so wish that I never touched that damn book or been so obsessed with looking for spells. I wish I was content with simply being free from my father. I could help Kselia sew or help Faeus with his food stall, or even become a jeweler. I'd never be any of those things, but I could if I wanted to.

I had to be greedy and ask for more than what the world was ready to offer. A prophecy *and* a fucking curse? I'll only be able to escape that in my dreams. Now, this *creature* that has the power to kill every single person that I love is my shadow—a shadow that pushes me against the wall and makes me feel things I shouldn't.

My skin starts to feel too tight for my body. It tingles, raising my hair on ends as a wave of nausea rips through my stomach. I feel unclean—dirty—that I let him get into my mind like that and fool me into believing that there was some semblance of kindness in him.

Don't listen to him, Gideon starts, moving to stand behind Ico so I can see his pleading expression.

I shake my head, pulling away from him as the walls start to close in. "If you don't tell me where it is then I'll try to find it myself." I speak the words with a steady ease that I don't feel. It feels like my life is crumbling and I have no way to catch the falling pieces.

"You don't want the attention."

"I've already got unwanted attention," I say, looking Gideon directly in the eyes.

DEX

CHAPTER TWENTY-ONE

THE FAE LIGHTS DIM as we travel belowground and into the reason that *Once Bitten, Twice Shy* is known by the criminally minded in Taravene. It's the only tavern in Taravene where quarreling clans and rival assassins leave their weapons and their war at the door, only to be resumed once they're off Ico's property. And like any good meeting place involving people that can commit murder on a whim, there are plenty of exits.

We enter through one of the many doors, and all eyes turn to assess us as they always do whenever someone walks in. We may be in neutral territory, but no one here trusts each other. A callpaith comes up to me with a basket for me to drop all my weapons into, so I start unarming myself: the knife in the shank of my shoe, the pin hidden in the folds of my revealing dress, my ring that opens into a needle tipped with poison.

The fae lights change color from blue to purple to orange and red, complementing the red skin of the callpaith woman. She looks down at me in question; she's seen me enough times to know that I'm well versed in the process.

"All of the weapons that I carried into the building are in the basket you hold. There are no more weapons on my person hidden or otherwise," I chant like it's muscle memory.

She nods, accepting that I haven't lied, and she walks into a private room.

My gaze floats over the familiar faces and up to the ceiling where magic blocking runes are carved. Knives and poisonous objects aren't the only weapons we have. I can still feel my magic, and though I can't feel the block that's been placed, I know that I won't be able to summon my powers if I try.

The worst part of me silently prays that the runes stop Gideon from entering. Like every prayer, it goes unanswered as Gideon walks ahead with his fists curled tightly and his stance ready to kill. I don't need to taste the whiskey to know that he recognizes some of these people, and they didn't end up on his good side. The better half of me feels a sliver of sadness for him that he watches people move about the world freely while he's stuck with me.

It's telling me to abandon our search for the quill, because it's better if he never gets out to kill everyone. Still, the other half of me is a selfish woman, unwilling to sacrifice everything for him. But, either way, who's to say I won't die as soon as he's free?

We walk in the direction of the chameleon woman on the platform who dances in time with the band at the front of the room. Her hair and skin change in time with the lights, and she nods at Ico when we pass.

He pulls out a stool at the bar, nodding to the waiter to get me a drink. "Stay put. I'll be back." He pats my shoulder, and I watch him stroll toward a group of fae men that fills the red couches in the opposite corner. I recognize them from Saori; they're a clan of fae, looking to overthrow their leader. If memory serves, the clan practices magic so naturally, they hate the Black Bloods. But they also hate the Paragon Dawn because they don't believe in the Divine or royalty—a rowdy bunch of people, really.

The bartender hands me a glass of wine, and I down it without a second thought, relishing in the way it burns my throat and distracts me from *him*. The same *'him'* that walks through the counter to stand on the opposite side of me.

"Don't listen to him," Gideon says again.

Why? Was he wrong? I sneer, turning my head away so that I don't need to look at his face.

"I'd never do anything to hurt you or your family."

But with the ring, you won't have a choice in the matter. I say it like a question, though I already know the answer. When he doesn't respond, I scoff. *That's all I need to know.*

"Everything I've told you is true. You must believe me." A slight flicker of desperation waves in his voice and it almost makes me break my resolve. And then he hesitates, like what he just said is a lie.

Really? Everything? And what about everything that you haven't told me?

"Dex, I—"

I don't want to hear it.

If I'm being truthful, I'm more enraged at myself than I am at him. He told me that he is a weapon. He told me that he's dangerous—he was locked up with the kaliak, for gods' sake. How did I not piece it together sooner that he's capable of truly despicable things—to my family no less? How did I think that my family would be safe from harm? All the information was right in front of me, and I dove in anyway.

A new taste tips my tongue: cinnamon. Deep and warm, leaving behind the same burning sensation on my cheeks as after tears are shed.

"You don't need to do this. We can find the quill through other means," he pleads.

Please, you want your freedom, and so do I. Don't try to stop me.

"One wrong step and they'll kill you."

There it is, I think to myself. *The truth comes out again. His care about my life is only to the extent of his.*

"Dex," Ico calls from across the room, and the group of fae doesn't so much as spare me a second glance; a sure sign that they think they are superior to me. Sometimes that kind of thinking is in my benefit, they underestimate me and I, therefore, get away with more. On the other hand, it's nothing more than another obstacle I need to overcome to get what I want.

I say a silent prayer to my dead goddess as I jump off the chair. Only I'm not sure if I'm thanking her for getting me out of the conversation with Gideon or if I'm begging her for luck. As my feet hit the ground, I let my 'stage persona' sink in: shoulders rolled back, head tilted up ever so slightly, hips swaying with each step, and a bored expression on my face. If I add a smirk to this walk, they'll turn the closest object to them into a weapon because all they'll see is a deranged woman—that is, of course, dependent on what I wear. Smirking and swaying my hips in this dress? They'll think I'm a lady of the night.

I don't need to turn around to know that Gideon is watching me walk to the group of men. Whiskey, cinnamon, mulled wine, almond; too many varying tastes build on my tongue, and I have the urge to gulp down a whole glass of the strongest liquor just to get rid of the taste of his emotions. And my own.

Gideon comes into existence through a cloud of smoke right before the men, walking around each chair to eye every one of them up with a scowl on his face.

The first fae makes eye contact with me: a male with velvet-like horns curving out of his forehead. He holds himself too rigid and too brazenly to be the leader of their group. Through his partially ripped brown tunic, I can just make out a scar that curls around his muscles. A pattern of swirls is tattooed on his head, which only serves to exaggerate the emotion written on his face. The only question is whether they think that I'm a witch or a human. Because luckily for me, I've managed to keep that answer outside of public knowledge.

I pick up a spare seat on the way, and a scaled male shifts in his seat to look at me down his snout with an eye of interest. Instead of looking at him in his eyes, the carved rune in the center of his forehead calls to me like a song.

"It senses lies," Gideon says, noting my attention. "He's the muscles." He nods at the first tattooed fae.

This isn't my first fae meet-up, I snap, instantly regretting doing so. He's just trying to help, and frankly, I had no idea what the rune meant. *Thank you,* I mutter tensely.

Setting the chair down in front of the men, I lower myself onto it with the same grace I've seen my mother use many times. All seven men's eyes are on me. The way they look at me varies between indignation, criticalness, and apprehension, except one of them who looks at me with a mixed cocktail of disinterest and intrigue—the man in charge.

He's far more relaxed than any of the other men. And he's the best dressed, though the bar is low on that front, seeing as he's the only one without a stain or rip of some sort anywhere on his attire.

Ico stands back with his arms crossed over his chest. "Rhistel, Dex. Dex, Rhistel of the Hollow Cry." We nod at each other tersely as Gideon moves to stand behind me like he's one of my goons. "She can get you what you want." I look up at Ico, who gives me a warning glance just before he leaves.

I quickly weigh up my options and consider exactly how I want to be perceived by these men. If I come off as meek, they'll double-cross me or lose faith that I can get them whatever it is that they want. If I come off too poised, they'll think I'm mocking them—which I'm already doing to an extent in this dress. If I come across too confident or stand-offish, they'll take it as hostility. *But* these kinds of men respect brutality.

"It isn't too late to walk away, Dex," Gideon mumbles.

Uncrossing my legs, I slouch so my elbows rest on my knees. "Let's get to the point then, shall we?" I start, and any trace of disinterest disappears from Rhistel's face. "I believe you know the whereabouts of something I want, and by the sounds of it, I can get you what you want."

"You're a thief?" He forms it like a question but means it as a statement.

"Trader," I correct.

"I have enough of those. None of them is quite as pretty, though," he laughs the type of laugh that tries to gain a rouse from his men. They all snicker and laugh dramatically like it's the most hilarious joke they've heard. I don't let it phase me the way it's phasing Gideon, whose rage burns my tongue.

I glance at the scaled man's head and consider testing out a lie on him. Callpaiths are born with the gift, but he's simply borrowing it. *How does he tell if a lie is told?* I question Gideon while the men have their moment.

It will glow.

I consider his response for a moment, letting a plan unfold. *Will we be able to see it?*

Yes.

Convenient.

Slumping back into my chair, throwing my arm over the back and crossing my legs, I blink at him boredly. "Information in exchange for an object. That's the trade."

The laughter dies in an instant, but Rhistel cocks a brow. "Go on."

"I want Hell's Quill."

"No."

I grit my teeth. I've never been the best at negotiating like this. "Do you know where it is?" It's the question I should have led with, there's no point entering into any deal when they won't be able to fulfill their end.

"Yes. We have it," he says simply.

It takes every ounce of energy I have not to let the excitement seep onto my face, or they'll see my hand and just how desperate I am. "Are you willing to part with it?"

"No."

My heart drops, and it takes even more energy not to show them my disappointment. The smirk that corners his lips tells me that I've failed in my attempt. If I break into their stronghold to steal it, they'll know it was me, and Ico will inevitably be dragged into the mix. But then, from the corner of my eyes, I can see something glow.

"Then this conversation is over." The chair skids back as I stand. It's a game, of course. If they aren't sharp, they'll interpret my leave as a lack of real investment for the item.

"Unless for the right price," Rhistel says with nonchalance, and the glowing disappears. Taking a slow breath, I lower myself into my seat, patiently waiting for him to continue. "The Mirror of Dracon."

I can't breathe. *Is he fucking kidding me?* He might as well say that I should steal one of my father's crowns. It's been in the Lodaxian royal's line for generations—a mirror that shows you your greatest enemy, and the location of where they are.

"You expect me to break into a palace?" I say calmly, keeping the bewilderment from my tone.

"He don't say it if 'e was fuckin' jokin', now would 'e?" the tattooed male growls, and Gideon steps forward like he's about to hurt him.

"Steep price for an equally steep item." Rhistel's face is a full-blown smirk at this point. He leans onto his knees, his eyebrows cocked in challenge.

"You're a pawn, not a king. Your games mean nothing. I need faith that you will fulfill your end." I'm impressed with my ability to sound so confident given the circumstances, but I have my desperation to thank for getting me through.

"Walk away. It is not worth it," Gideon pleads.

"Smart girl," Rhistel teases. "Our chief wants that mirror. He gets what he wants. Right now, I speak for him and his interest."

"Does he know that?" I'm poking the bear, but it's the language his type understands.

"How 'bout we seal the deal the fae way then, aye?"

"Don't do it, Dex," Gideon warns.

I ignore him, forcing my curled fingers to straighten. Breaching the terms will result in death. I've managed to live my entire life without getting into one of these—without tying myself down by a bloody fae and some contract. I'm breaking one of my many rules of survival, all to free a man that could kill everyone I love.

Rhistel opens his mouth to speak, but I stop him before he can. Entering into one of these contracts is bad enough, letting him define the terms of the trade is even worse. It's time I put all my experience eavesdropping on Father and his meetings into good use. "I will acquire the Mirror of Dracon—"

"Don't." I can feel Gideon's eyes on me, but I don't dare to look at him in case I change my mind.

So I continue. "—on the grounds that you are in ownership of Hell's Quill. Contemporaneously upon the handing over of the Mirror of Dracon, you will personally provide me with the sole and unfettering ownership of Hell's Quill. The trade is to occur within six weeks, if not, the deal is off and not considered breached."

The fae's nostrils flare as I speak, seemingly displeased with the terms of the agreement. Though, at the same time, his smirk remains, as does the amusement in his eyes. "Two weeks."

"Five."

"Three weeks."

"Four."

"Three and a half."

"Done." The back and forth makes me dizzy, and my chest squeezes with worry that it isn't enough time to travel to Lodaxo and back, as well as plan and execute a heist. I wave the worry off for now. I can panic once the doors are closed.

I hold out my hand at the same time the fae does.

Dex, you're going to get yourself killed, Gideon's voice is urgent in my head.

Luckily, we both have a mutual interest in keeping me alive then, I bite back, clasping the hand of the fae and feeling the magical effect of our deal thrum through my body. The tether seems to tug uncomfortably, but I try to ignore it.

"It's a pleasure doing business with you. *Dex.*"

DEX

CHAPTER TWENTY-TWO

THE ROOM SWINGS AND blurs, turning faces into nothing but a haze. My body moves by itself, navigating the bar under the blaring lights. I grab my weapons and mutter my thanks to no one in particular.

Three and a half weeks. Ten days to Lodaxo. Four days to plan and execute a heist from the most protected place in their kingdom. Ten days back. It isn't doable for *real* thieves, let alone one whose only experience comes from breaking into the safes of nobles and people with more wealth than they deserve.

If I don't make it on time, then what? I can't very well walk into the clan's territory and take the quill. And if I get caught stealing the mirror?

Well, that makes matters much worse. Unless King Haemir has changed his mind, he's one of the kings who would tear my heart from my chest and raise the Divine back from the dead. I remember hearing Father mention that Lodaxo's allegiance only goes as far as the crops the Volducan brings into their city, and they'd bring the gods back at the drop of a hat.

In essence, if I get caught, I'll die. If I fail, there's no way to get to the quill without more people I love dying. It's a suicide mission, that's what it is. It doesn't escape me that I don't have proof of its existence. It also doesn't escape me that this could be a set-up. If only I had time to verify its existence. The only faith I have is in a volatile contract. All I can hope is that there's no loophole that I've opened myself up to.

I don't react when the cool air stings my skin or even when a deep voice that stirs my soul calls out my name. I keep walking, one foot in front of the other, head held high with an emotionless gaze. Left foot, right foot. I don't feel the way the balls of my feet ache from my heels, or the ever-present oils that live beneath my nails, or even the single strand of hair down my back that would otherwise make me a menace to society. I just need to get out of here.

My feet turn me down a street that doesn't lead home, and suddenly, I feel it all. I feel the way the rope scratches against my skin, the way the fabric is *too smooth, too slippery*. I feel my muscles scream, winding up tighter and tighter. I feel the weight of my impending nightmare. But I don't cry. Not yet.

My heels scrape uneasily along the gravel while air gets stolen from my lungs, burning just enough to distract me, even for just a moment. My hands shake, finding coarse brick. I drop my head down and wince when the rough material rubs at my skin. My chest heaves and scrapes for breath that disappears while I inhale. I stumble along, weight still against the wall, tearing my flesh with each rigid movement. Each step becoming more difficult than the last and the desire to let the true extent of my emotions come out teeters close to the edge.

"Fuck it," I hiss, yanking my heels off without bothering to untie them first, leaving a harsh red mark on my skin in the process.

My fingers wrap around cold metal and I pull myself up a ladder before I think it through. And for the briefest moment, with my hands and mind preoccupied with climbing, it becomes easier to see, easier to breathe, easier to *think*. It's a blissful silence that I want to hold onto and never let go of, but as I reach the top the voices in my mind reel again.

My knees scrape along the brick roof, crawling to the spot just above the jutted window.

I can feel *him* blink into existence near me. And the taste—too much fucking taste. I'm done with tasting. I don't want to know what he's feeling. I don't *care* what he's feeling. I swear I don't. I swear it. I shouldn't care—I can't.

The night turns gray as the fabric starts to stick to my skin, and off in the near distance, drunken patrons laugh and cheer, breaking glasses and starting bar fights. The first drop of rain hits the top of my nose, and my unshed tears take it as a sign to let the first one fall. It rolls down my cheek along with the next raindrop, heating it to the point that it feels like it's burning. Blood prickles along my knees, but I do nothing to address it. Let it bleed. I won't be able to hide forever.

I drop to my elbows at the point where the roof protrudes over the window. And I let the pain thunder up my arms, into my shoulders and savor the feeling.

And I cry.

I let it all out.

I sob without care that someone might hear, or that Gideon watches me helplessly. My tears fall onto the moss-ridden surface and stain my dress. But I can't bring myself to think about anything other than *them*: Father, Nodisci and Gideon.

A warm hand drops on my shoulder, and I jump back. "This is all your fault!" I point my trembling finger wildly at him. I know it isn't true, I know that it's harsh, but my lips refuse to speak reason. "You've ruined *everything*."

Pain spears his face, but he doesn't move. He doesn't say a word. He just watches with an almost pitiful gaze. He studies me—always fucking studying me. Always fucking tasting like something.

Even if none of this business with Gideon had happened, how long would I have lasted before my fate caught up with me? Months? Years? This is just speeding up the inevitable. I was never meant to be free—not completely at least. The only freedom that I will find is in death. When I am finally reunited with my goddess in the heaven beyond the Divine Lands.

"Leave me and my self-pity alone," I choke as I try to gulp down air, staring at the pinpricks of blood on my hands from the jagged edges of the brick roof.

I look up again, and my heart sinks to my feet as a whimper releases from my chest. The space where he once stood is cold and empty. He's gone. He actually left. He did exactly as I asked. Of course he did. I can't blame him for it. The only reason he is miserable and stuck living in my shadow is because of me. Maybe it's time to accept what I have never wanted to accept before in my life. I've shifted the blame every step of the way; it's the witch's fault that I'm cursed; I've only been prophesied because my father is a king; my sister died because my parents are deranged.

The reality is that I'm the common denominator. I'm the problem.

I've accepted blame for little things like what happened with the book and other misfortunes along the way. But I've never truly accepted that I'm responsible for everything else, and how I acted afterwards will forever be on me.

Even Gideon is to blame for who he is, *what* he is. Callaia had the power to destroy the whole realm, but she chose to use her powers for good; healing those who asked, and sacrificing her love so that everyone can have a rest from the sun every single night.

Gideon is a product of his own choices. *I* am a product of my own choices. I just so happen to make the wrong choice each time.

The rain caresses my skin as my breath becomes a gust of wind rather than a storm, and my wounds close over. Still, the tears fall. This time, it is not out of hysteria or sadness or anger toward Gideon or myself for landing us in this mess. No, this time the tears shed because I'm mad at myself for not realizing my part sooner.

Soft purring breaks through the laughter from down below, and I turn my head toward the source of the noise. Gideon walks toward me with something cupped carefully in his hands, and the sound grows louder as he nears. I pause my sniffling, letting my curiosity control my movements as I twist to see what it is that he's holding.

He lowers himself down onto the empty space next to me, and I wipe my tears off my cheek with the back of my hand, trying to pretend that they were never there. Peering over into his hands, the big, round, brown eyes of a kikii stare back at me with a lopsided smile, and I can't help but smile back at it. It lies on its back with its big striped belly up in the sky, purring happily from Gideon's soft belly rubs. Its brown cashmere tail drops down from the small gap between his hands, swinging about in a gleeful rhythm as its eyes flutter close.

"Unfortunately, I'm unable to get you more of those buns that you like, however, I believe this may be the next best thing," he says softly, lowering his hand to gently place the creature in mine. It's heavier than I expected, and I have to adjust my hands as it wiggles around to get comfortable. My finger glides along the top of its head, and the kikii starts to purr even louder, snuggling into my touch. "I found her in the kitchen of one of the restaurants. She wasn't all too pleased that I took her away from her midnight snack."

We both chuckle, staring down at the harmless creature with no sense of self-preservation. I continue patting it as the silence stretches on between my unsteady breaths. "I shouldn't have yelled at you. I'm sorry," I finally sniffle once the kikii starts to snore lightly.

"You needn't be sorry. You're right."

I shake my head. There is no excusing my behavior. "No one deserves to be spoken to like that. I just..." I look up, blinking away the tears that threaten to fall again. "I just wish things were different, and I wish that I would stop screwing things up all the time."

"None of this is your fault, Dex. The book—"

"This only happened because I pricked my finger on a gods damned thorn while picking berries," I interrupt. It's utterly laughable, but I can't bring myself to laugh. "I was mad at an inanimate object for not getting what I want, and now you're forced to stay by my side, and—"

"Let me finish." It's his turn to interrupt. I snap my mouth shut and nod my head begrudgingly as I meet his intense stare. "You should never have been able to open the book, Dex. The greatest powers the realm has ever known bound me to that book. Though the spell weakens with time, this should not have happened. It is not your fault. Do not blame yourself for it."

I open my mouth to respond, but nothing comes out.

"It isn't a bad side to be on either," he mutters quietly like he doesn't want me to hear what he's saying.

I stare at him for a moment, trying to make sense of his response. Then I remember the words I said, *now you're forced to stay by my side.*

I turn my attention up to the moon, feeling her tease my veins to let her in. "We almost got caught in Zarlor because I decided to dye my hair. You were almost dragged back into that bloody book again because I almost died. The kaliaks are—"

"Dex," he interrupts forcefully. I jump slightly when his hand touches the side of my cheek, scattering goosebumps over my skin. "You can hate me as much as you want, blame me for every wrong that has ever happened. You can scream your hatred for me into the sun and crumble mountains in my name. You can pierce a dagger into my heart a thousand times until my blood stops pouring. You can do it all as long as you promise me one thing."

I swallow the lump in my throat, wanting and hoping that I could do exactly that: hate him. "What?" I whisper.

"You promise me that you will not hate yourself." His words crash down on me far harder than he realizes, and a single tear breaks free from my hold.

"I won't make promises that I can't keep," I mutter beneath my breath, unable to face the heat in his eyes.

In my own eyes, I may never be good enough. Just as Saeya thinks that no one could possibly like her, and just as Mirya thinks that no one could ever love her and her snakes. But we don't need to see everything, there's a reason we aren't mirrors that can see outside and in. We may never see ourselves as anything more than dust, but to someone else, we could be their whole universe.

I won't see it today, I may not even see it tomorrow. I'm still learning and growing every day, but I know that one day I will see it. And that is all anyone can hope for.

But I don't need to love myself to know: My name is Dex. I am a thief, I am a killer, and I will not break under the hands of men. I am the lost princess, and the one they call Savior. But no one is getting saved. They're getting damned instead.

"Shall I make that promise for you?" he says.

My brows furrow and I turn to look at him and the silver light that kisses his smooth skin. "You'll hate yourself?"

"No," he chuckles softly. "I promise that I will never hate you."

"Don't make promises you can't keep." The kikii sighs in my hand, turning onto its side with a groan.

"When Ico spoke of me, you were scared." He hesitates before saying, "Are you scared of me?"

I consider for a moment. "I'm afraid of the future," I correct. "There are too many uncertainties, and that frightens me." I stop there, but he looks at me to explain further. "Greed changes people. It destroys one's moral compass, and when push comes to shove, who knows how either of us will react? You may not wish me harm now, but that will change when someone has the ring."

The muscles in his jaw ticks. "Then once I'm free, run far away from here. Hide where I can never find you. Then, and only then, will you be safe. I won't be able to live with myself if I ever harm you or your family."

I start patting the kikii with more fingers to distract myself from the storm brewing in my mind. "Then once we've broken the binding spell, we split ways and never see each other again." It shouldn't make me sad to say it, yet it does, and I wonder if he can taste cinnamon on his tongue as well.

He nods once. "Then you will have your life back."

I don't know what that means anymore.

I feel grounded now that my feet are on solid pavement.

The kikii scurries through the bush in the direction where the smell of food is the strongest. My heart aches as I watch it leave, never to be seen again, and in that moment, all that I can think about is my desire to settle down. I can almost see it: Every day, I would wake up a few hours past sunrise, I'd run an antique shop of magical objects and things that shine. I'd live in the apartment above it, and have an old dog that followed me around wherever I went, keeping me company during the day and acting as a warmer at night. I'd pick a kingdom where Black Bloods and Paragon Dawns hardly went, and I'd stop looking over my shoulder every few minutes.

"What are you thinking about?" Gideon's voice wraps around me like a warm blanket, and for a second, I stop feeling the cold air hiss against my skin.

"It would be a blissful life staying in one place—having real stability." Gritting my teeth to stop them from clattering, I wrap my arms around myself, squeezing rainwater from the fabric in the process. He pulls his coat off and wraps it tightly over my shoulders. Instantly, the remaining heat soaks into my skin and my jaw relaxes ever so slightly. "Thank you," I mutter.

"And yet boring is not a word I would associate with you." He casts me a sideways glance as I stare at my reflection in the window of one of the buildings lining the street and wipe the black streams of kohl running down my face. I glance around, taking in the fact that the world seems so much smaller than it did on the roof.

"Not boring, *safe*. Call it 'stable' if you must." I don't bother talking to him in my head. The only people walking along the streets are intoxicated by one means or another. Wiping the last drop of kohl, I start walking, holding my heels by the strap, swinging them in time with my steps.

"Do you think it will make you happy?" His line of inquiry has me questioning every moment of my life. Have I ever been happy?

I jump up onto the edge of the sidewalk as Gideon continues to walk along the street. Despite the extra step, his height still exceeds mine. I think for a moment longer before finally answering, "I think there have been times where life has been more... more *acceptable* than other times. Maybe I felt some happiness playing in the garden with my sister? There was a period of time when I was giddy from my newfound freedom. But happy? I'd like to meet someone who's truly happy."

Whiskey tips my tongue, and I look around to try to locate the source of his anger but see nothing but his darkening eyes on me. "It's a story parents started telling their children at night to prevent nightmares," he says. "It doesn't mean that it isn't something you can't strive for."

"On the off chance that I become completely free, maybe I'll try to become one of those stories," I mutter softly.

"You know, the Divine—"

He stops when the blood drains from my face. A burst of distinct laughter crashes through the air as the door to the tavern across the street swings open.

"Shut your ugly mug," the male laughs. Playful white eyes look back at his friend and long silver dreads tangle at his back two shades darker than his skin. But that isn't what makes me certain that it's the elf that used to be assigned to guarding the hallways of my bedroom; it's the five jagged scars on his neck that mars his dark skin. Avin.

"You suck at darts. I bet you fair and square," the elf with green skin grumbles.

I turn, trying to find some alley to hide down, but nothing comes into sight. *Shit, shit, shit,* I think as their footsteps make their way toward me.

Kneeling, I force my hair to fall over my face as I pretend to tug my shoes on.

Who is he? Gideon growls, bringing with him a wave of almond and whiskey.

Someone from my past.

"Your mom plays better darts than you," Avin taunts.

Yes, continue being an idiot, I think to myself, slowly tying the laces as they walk parallel to where I am. What frightens me is that he's a great soldier, which makes him a smart idiot.

"Get my mother's name off your tongue," the green elf hisses, which only makes Avin laugh harder.

As soon as they have their backs to me, I yank the shoe off and walk calmly in the opposite direction just as I hear a battle cry followed by a punch. I break into a run with Gideon next to me, matching my pace as exhilaration rattles through me. I almost feel lightheaded from the sensation. We both drop back into a brisk walk as soon as we turn a corner and they're no longer in sight.

I expect my heart to be riddled with anxiety from another near slip-up, but for some reason all I feel is relief. Maybe there's some level of peace in knowing that even if I'm taken, I won't actually be alone, because Gideon will be right there by my side. Not willingly, but at least he will be there.

I catch the reflection of the gray sky as I step over a puddle. But really what I notice in the reflection is his look of grief. I've been so consumed by my own needs that I have completely forgotten all about what he wants, and it isn't just freedom. He wants to see his family too.

"You've never asked me about my past," I blurt. Of course he hasn't. Why should he? I haven't asked him either.

"I know you will tell me once you're ready."

"You've never told me about *your* past." I've been so fixated on *what* he is that I forgot to remember that *who* he is, is more important.

"There are not enough days in your lifetime to answer that one, little elf."

Heat creeps into my cheeks from the nickname that I once hated. "Then tell me about your family."

His husky laugh melts my inside, sending a fluttering feeling to the tips of my toes.

"My mother was very motherly, and my father was less than fatherly."

"So you have daddy issues too?" I grin at him as he narrows his eyes.

"Like Kselia, my mother was a mother to many of us. None of us are related by blood by any means, but some of us acted like we're siblings." His tone is calculating, like he's being strategic in what information he wants to present to me.

"The siblings that you're close with, tell me about them." I want to know everything about the way this man ticks.

"The one I saw as my brother never stopped trying to challenge people. He had to be the best at everything he did or else his destructive tendencies would come out." His words are even more calculated, like talking about it makes him uncomfortable.

"I know children like that." I wink, and he levels me with a glare. Even though the wine has long since worn off, I feel tipsy. And I don't want the mood to sour. "I'd wager that I'm a better fighter than you," I bite with a confidence so fake that it makes me laugh. The tension releases from his face in an instant, and something bright lights up in his eyes as vanilla coats my tongue.

"Don't start something you can't end," he warns, trying to hide the light in his gaze.

"Oh, we both know how this is going to end."

With me hurt.

DEX
CHAPTER TWENTY-
THREE

"I'LL MISS YOU," SAEYA whispers into my freshly dyed hair, squeezing me tight. "I wish you could stay longer."

I hug her even tighter. She didn't ask any questions when I told her that I have to do a big job in Lodaxo within three and a half weeks. She just nodded reluctantly and continued to cringe as she sipped her hangover remedy. I was grateful Mirya was still in bed, or else I'd get an earful about what a bad sister I am. She wouldn't be wrong, either. I haven't seen her for months, then she sees me for all of ten minutes before I leave again. It breaks my heart to see that she has become used to it, seeing me no more than a few days at a time, then leaving when something else comes up, constantly chasing this dream that every job I do will get me one step closer to ending the curse.

"This will be the last job, I promise." I can feel her body tense up beneath my touch, and I hold my breath waiting for her to call me a liar, but she doesn't.

I guess my conversation with Gideon about happiness called to me. The more I think about it, the more I realize that there's no reason I should seek to end the curse. What's the worst that could happen if I accidentally trigger it? The gods come back to life and bring back peace and order to the realm? At this point, I'm not sure why I haven't actively tried to bring them back; everyone's lives would be better for it. Maybe I'm just so selfish that I'd risk everyone's lives for my own sake.

Except, in all my years of searching for an end to my curse, I've found nothing to tell me how I'd trigger it. Unfortunately, the witch did not grace me with an instruction manual to follow, nor did she tell me how to end a war in the process.

Even then, how will my heart win a war like it said in the prophecy? Maybe the prophecy is metaphorical in the sense that 'everyone' will win if the gods are brought back? It makes more sense if they go hand in hand like that.

"I've done this for long enough, and I'm not any better for it," I add, becoming uncomfortable by the silence.

She pulls back, staring into my eyes with disbelief. "But you love this?"

"I do, but there's enough danger in being who I am. Plus, I never said that I will get my stock ethically." I glance around, making sure Gideon has kept his promise of giving us space.

"What will you do instead?" I pull her to the seat in front of the mirror.

Parting her hair into three at the top of her head, my hands start to braid by muscle memory alone. As I move, my dark brown, almost black hair drops onto my face, and a whiff of the sage hair dye I used this morning assaults my nose. "Maybe I'll follow in your footsteps; find myself a nice lady, take up sewing, make boys cry." I wiggle my brow.

Her cheeks flush crimson. "I did that *once,*" she says like she's trying to convince herself.

"Three times," I correct. "They all deserved it."

Her cheeks turn an even darker red. She may look the definition of innocent, but she's as much a snake as the ones living on Mirya's head. "They looked at me the wrong way." She looks up at me in the reflection through her lowered lashes.

I chuckle in response, checking to make sure I've gathered all the hair from the base of her neck. "I think I could see myself living in Saori. They actually have decent weather there. Lodaxo is too cold, there are too many elves in Taravene, Zarlor is out of the question, and there are too many Black Bloods in Ealgate."

"Ama will refuse to visit if you live there," she adds.

I bite the inside of my cheek. It's just the way it will have to be, and Kselia will have to be fine with it. "So long as you visit, I will go anywhere." I wink at her, tying off the end of her hair with a rope. I walk backward, slumping onto the bed to relish the feel of it because it'll be the last time I'll lay on one in a few days. "Just imagine it, Saeya: me owning a shop full of antiques and jewelry."

She scoops up the jewelry and knickknacks on my dresser with both hands as she gives me a knowing look. "You'd refuse to sell any of it."

"Point taken. *However,* I will have a 'for sale' pile and have a pile just for me." I can't help but feel excited by the thought that it might become a reality. The 'for me' pile will likely be bigger than the 'for sale' pile, now that I think about it.

Saeya stands, shaking her head, and I perk up, watching her with curiosity as the bed dips under her weight and I sit upright. She reaches into her pocket to pull out a small black leather bag. "I got you something."

I edge closer, resting my chin on her soft shoulder. My eyes widen with excitement as she pulls out a simple golden band that catches the light. She drops it onto my hand, and from the center of my palm I can feel small tendrils of power radiate from it, stretching far beyond my hand.

"What is it?" I slip the cold metal band onto my finger.

"The merchant said that it tells the wearer when danger is coming."

"I'll be hearing from it quite a lot then." I give her another sideways hug, wrapping my arm around her shoulders and pushing my face next to hers. "Thank you, I love it. It couldn't have been cheap."

I can feel her grin against my cheek as she says, "Remember when you said that I only made three boys cried?" I pull away, narrowing my eyes at her. "Make that four boys instead."

Silence stretches between us before we break out into a fit of giggles until our stomachs ache. She leaves to let me get ready. We're edging close to late morning, but we couldn't leave without getting my affairs in order; dyeing my hair to fit in, locating a horse to take us to Lodaxo, and asking Kselia to make another winter cloak after I lost the other one in a knife fight.

Strapping on my leather harness, I sheath the two swords at my back. Shoving the book into my already full sack, I pause, considering whether to bring the Hinixian blade. I'll have to continue pretending that I'm not a lunar elf, which means that I can't risk having it on me. Lugging the heavy bag over my shoulders, I start wishing that I owned a bag like Vencen, where I could fill it up with as much as I want without it ever getting full.

Perhaps that's the next thing to put on my endless wish list. Fortunately or unfortunately, we all agree not to steal from family.

Running down the stairs, I head to the bottom floor. In between rolls upon rolls of different colored fabric I find Kselia in the workshop whispering a spell under her breath as she sews fur onto the inside of the cloak.

"So much trouble you are," she tsks when I enter the room. "Here." She starts to clean her station as she holds out her hand for me to collect the item. "Lose it again and I'll have you scrubbing the kitchen floors."

I grab the gray garment quickly, rubbing my fingers against the wool. "Not lose, *misplace*." I know full well 'back talking' will rile her up.

She snaps her attention to me. "I'll undo the warming spell on that cloak of yours." She holds up a pair of large fabric scissors threateningly. I throw my hand up in surrender, and she points the scissors to the corner of the room where my snow boots lie. I head toward it when she says, "You're taking my horse."

I whip around to face her. "What? No, Ama, I have enough coin to buy a horse." I don't, I only spotted one that I'm interested in stealing.

Actually, Rhistel was right: I am a thief. There really was never any denying it.

"Already decided." She waves her hand dismissively as she shuffles with a limp to a shelf on the other side of the room.

"You need it more than me." Pain lances my heart every time a mother figure is nice to me. Especially when said figure's age is ancient.

"It's not like I can ride it." She touches her hip.

She's seen many kings come and go, and even lived through the fall of a kingdom. She refuses to tell us kids how old she is, but we've at least guessed that she's in her thousands.

"You need her to carry your supplies." I hate when she puts our needs before her own. We already owe her the world for giving us a family and somewhere to live when we were at our lowest. Even once we've found our footing, she still keeps providing for us.

"My boy will let me use his horse." There's almost a touch of endearment in her tone, which tells me that she's referring to Vencen and not her actual boy.

"I dou—"

"He doesn't have a choice," she says in the type of innocent elderly voice that makes you weak in the knees and ready to serve at her beck and call. I don't think Vencen knows of this yet, but it very much sounds like a problem for him to deal with—which is a preferable situation to be in compared to my predicament.

"For you." She throws a black bag into my hands. I fumble around to catch it as tin containers and bottles jumble in my hold.

I give her my most grateful smile, already knowing what the containers are: endless food. Spelled to always be filled with the food or liquid that's been placed in there. I just pray that Vencen didn't decide to swap it out for something I don't like.

"Thank you." I hug her despite her protests.

She shoos me away, disappearing behind another shelf before I walk outside to where Kselia's chestnut shire horse waits patiently for me with its winter blanket already strapped onto its saddle. Liu whinnies as I approach, and I have to stop to make sure she doesn't bite me. She's one of the best horses I've ever come to know for the simple fact that Kselia took her in when her original owner got sick of her biting men and children.

Frankly, I don't blame Liu. I'd do the same.

I strap everything onto the saddle, from the blankets and tent, to the containers and my clothing, adding a bow and arrow at the top as a finishing touch. This is one of the many things I dislike about traveling to Lodaxo: It's hard to pack light.

I stand back, wincing at how poorly I've tied everything onto the saddle; it will be easy for anyone to steal from. At least it would be if it were any horse but Liu. Behrman loves people, she'd let anyone get near her and knick something off her saddle so long as she gets a treat. Liu, on the other hand, isn't afraid to kick someone even if they breathe around her the wrong way. I suppose that's what makes her perfect for Kselia, as they are completely alike.

Going back inside, I bid farewell to Saeya and Kselia. Only then does Gideon come back into existence and the giddy fantasy I've been living in all morning disperses.

It's time I get rid of my shadow.

I wince again from the feeling of the sun battering down on my skin. It was blissful being up late into the early morning when the moon was at its highest last night. Even though I blocked myself off to her powers, she still lifted my spirits. Unfortunately, that also meant that I got less sleep. Compounded with the fact that the heat has started to turn my skin a burning bright red, wincing is the only thing that I can do to cope. Fortunately, the cool wind keeps the sweat from prickling my forehead, making it only slightly more bearable. Looking up, I groan internally because the moon is nowhere in sight despite the cloudless sky.

"It would be faster if we traveled at night," Gideon says after rolling his eyes the same way he has every time I've winced.

Liu's ears point rigidly, and her head raises high when he speaks. She steps over another tree trunk as we continue to follow the small stream that leads in the direction of one of the few settlements between here and Lodaxo.

"Yes, but everyone will know I'm an elf, and I might as well take my necklace off if that's the case." If it weren't for Liu, we'd probably get to Lodaxo in eight, maybe nine days assuming the weather holds. With the longer nights and shorter days, I could probably run the whole way and not get tired. But if anyone were trying to track me, they'd likely follow the scent of my powers all the way to Lodaxo.

"This whole 'travel by foot' is tedious. I did not stop walking for eight days while you sat the whole time."

"That's not true," I gasp in disbelief. "You got to rest at night."

I grin at him, which he returns with a tight-lipped frown. "If I had my wings, we would be there already."

"Someone's overselling their capabilities," I mutter under my breath just loud enough that he can hear.

He halts in his steps. "Stop the horse."

I squeeze my legs to get Liu to jump into a trot. She resists, and finally by the fourth attempt, she does as I ask and I turn back around to his slowly shrinking figure. "No thanks!" I yell behind me.

As I turn my head to stare straight ahead, my entire body jolts to a stop, and I just make out smoke from the corner of my vision. I throw my hand out to catch Liu's tangled mane to keep from losing balance as something tugs at me. My lips part as I stare at Gideon whose hand is gently placed on Liu's chest.

"Maybe you didn't hear me, *little elf*." His voice is nothing more than a dark whisper that snakes through me. His hand moves around Liu, slow and steady with his steps. They wrap around my ankle, moving up my leg until they firmly grip my calf. "I said *stop*."

I swallow the lump in my throat in a useless effort to buy time to find a response.

"I listen to the orders of no man." His eyes darken sinfully, like it's a challenge, as I attempt to tug my leg out of his solid grip. "How did you stop her?" I doubt he'll fall for my attempt at changing the topic, but he chuckles all the same, sending pinpricks of warmth all over me.

"There's a monstrous side to every creature." His grip on me relaxes, and he moves closer, trailing his finger up my leg as I start to feel the warmth from his other arm by my back. My heart pounds against my chest as my gaze follows his hand that slowly drags up to my thigh before grabbing onto the horse's mane.

In the blink of an eye, he pulls himself onto the horse. His arm wraps around my waist, pulling me against his chest. The whole motion makes my breath stutter in my chest. Suddenly, the sun no longer feels like it's my mortal enemy, and I almost forget about our suicide mission. I want to lean back or pull his other arm around me. But I shouldn't. What I'm feeling right now is wrong. Once he's free, we'll go our separate ways and forget any of this ever happened because nothing can happen without there being some kind of risk to my family. They're far more important than whatever my heart may feel.

"You're taking up too much room," I force myself to snarl. I beg to the Divine that he'll agree and go back to walking which will force me to stop thinking those kinds of thoughts about him. Especially thoughts about what might happen if his hands lowered.

His chest vibrates against my back as he hums. Liu starts to walk again, and my fingers dig into my palm with how tightly I grip the reins.

He chuckles darkly running his fingers over my middle. "That's not anger I sense," he whispers, leaning even closer. "You can't fool me, darling."

His breath warms the side of my neck as his arms drop to my leg and his large hands squeeze my thigh—a barely noticeable squeeze, but one I feel with my entire body. With his other arm, he hugs me tighter and his thumb grazes the underside of my chest in the process.

I suck in my cheeks as a way to keep myself from gasping. "Whatever you feel, I assure you that it is completely misplaced." Dropping the reins, I peel both his hands off me despite my body's protests and sit upright, scooting as far forward as I possibly can until my back bends at an unnatural angle.

"I don't bite, little elf." He chuckles. "Unless you want me to, that is."

My eyes widen, and I shuffle forward until the horn of the saddle pushes into my stomach. "Absolutely not. There is to be *no* biting. Remember what I said about unsolicited comments? That is going to be extended to include all points in time," I snap, hating the way my core leapt from the thought of his mouth on me, his teeth nibbling my skin.

He tenses behind me, and from the corner of my eye, shadows flicker in and out of existence, taking Gideon with them before I have the chance to wonder what is happening. A sickening wave prickles over my skin, lifting my hair on end. I can feel him on the very edge of our tether, but I don't know what emotions brew within him.

My gaze jumps from tree to tree, waiting to see signs of movement or attack, yet not even the bugs dare flap their wings. Even the humming within the pixie hive has become devout of sound. Nothing but death fills the air; an eerie void of silence consuming any sign of life.

Liu starts to grunt, stomping with each step like she's prepared to either fight or sprint away at the first sign of danger. Burying my fingers into her soft coat, I try to soothe her anxieties, rubbing in circular motions as each step becomes more hesitant than the last.

The leather hilt rubs against my palm as I slowly draw one of my swords, careful not to make a single sound. With the other, the leather reins dig into my hand that is wound completely tight with the sharpened edge of the air.

Then the smell—the gods awful smell. Putrid, metallic, and acidic, like poisoned bodies have been left in the woods for the creatures of the forest to feast on. Ash coats the back of my throat as a gray tint covers the trees like the aftermath of a fire.

The sound of the stream creeps back into existence.

The stream that leads to the village.

~~GIDEON~~
CHAPTER TWETY-FOUR

THE DEAD MORTAL'S ENTRAILS lead out from the hut, where it is left splayed all over the garden. The green leaves and vibrant fruits have become blanketed in droplets and chunks of murky brown. Every five steps, another shredded body lays, and the limbs of some have been torn from their bodies, leaving ivory bone jutting out of sockets.

All signs point to the kaliak.

Their clothing have been ripped apart by one creature or another, leaving behind chewed up chunks of meat. Rats have begun feasting on the carcasses, huddling over the dead and tearing into the flesh. Other animals have taken to dragging their meals into the wilderness to eat in peace or feed their young.

My shadows lurk in every corner, laughing, screaming, crying. They all say the same thing: "You did this."

I know that I did. But I've long since been fazed by such a sight. Wars between mortals and the mortal's war against the creatures always ends the same: with a sight that will cause nightmares in even the strongest of individuals. Bloodshed is not for the faint of heart, while carnage caused by the beastly urges of a monster is only for those whose heart holds nothing but chaos and destruction.

I walk to the very end of the thread that is quickly moving with her pace and I make faster work. Nausea builds deep in my stomach as I touch ghouls, hellhounds, and other creatures of darkness to make fear thunder through them, causing them to run back to where they came from. A ghoul hisses, scurrying in Dex's direction. I reach it before it can get far, wrapping my hands around its saggy skin, and I squeeze, crushing the skull beneath my fingers in a crack that gets all the other monstrous creatures' attention.

I can't let her see any of this. I felt the blame she carried on her shoulders when she saw the travelers in Zarlor, I'll be damned if I let her feel that way again.

Tugging on our rope, her silver thread glows, bringing me before her. A sword stops short to the base of my throat, and I stare down at her.

In all my years of existence, she is the first person to hold a knife to my throat, and she has succeeded in doing so twice.

I might be annoyed or amused by her besting of me, but the creasing in her forehead and the guilt that already lines her face has me thinking of nothing but all the different ways I will stop her from seeing the massacre.

She drops her sword with a huff. "Give me more warning next time," she seethes, glancing at the feline creature prowling around us. "What did you find?" she says grimly.

"We go around." I don't leave room for argument, cornering her so she gets back on the unhappy horse.

She ducks under my arm, jumping away from my arm as I reach out to stop her. Her lips twist with rage, yet her eyes darken with endless sadness. "It's the kaliaks."

I consider denying her statement so as not to add to her rapidly building guilt. I've led her to believe enough false things about me and my purpose, and lying now will only harm her. "It is not your fault. They were never meant to leave the book."

"Why were they in that book to begin with?" Her voice jumps higher, and her animated hands move around like startled birds.

I focus on controlling my breathing that threatens to shorten. I want to tell her about everything that has happened leading up to this moment: the spells mother and father cast, the truth about who I am and all the lives I've destroyed. Yet anything I say will only complicate matters further. We are to part ways and I am to force myself to live the rest of eternity watching from afar, tearing down any person who wishes to cause her harm. If she knew, it would only make it harder for her to forget.

One thing has become undeniably clear to me: I will never be able to stay away from her. She has become my sun and moon and the space in between. Filling me with a darkness so intoxicating that all I want is more. She is a light so bright that her smile can silence even the most violent voices inside of me. And yet I could spend another lifetime walking in her path, but I will never become worthy of her.

"It was for a spell."

"What is that book?" she asks cautiously.

Tell her the truth so she leaves you forever, the chaos laughs. I strain my mind, forcing the voices back down.

This could be my chance to tell her who I am—what I am. But what if she decides the realm is better off without me living amongst them? Until she takes her last breath, she'd remain bound to me against her will, looking at me with nothing but hatred. That isn't a life that she deserves to lead. She's to own a shop or maybe continue living life on the edge as a procurer. Whatever she does, so long as she's happy.

The weightless effect she has on me comes down to more than companionship. She has no idea who I am. She does not look at me in fear, or hold her tongue in my presence. Her words are not calculated or intended to deceive. Every relationship I have had has some element of manipulation and scheming. Nothing has ever been truly pure.

Until her.

She sees me, not as an obstacle or a stepping stone or something to control. She sees me for who I am.

"Gideon," Dex growls, and the need inside me to lay the truth bare teeters on the edge of insanity. Stepping forward as her knuckles turn white from her grip on the weapon. "What is that book?" The power in her voice could bring a god to his knees.

If I don't tell her, I may lose her. If I do, she may figure the truth out. Taking a deep breath, I settle for the truth—on this one matter at least. "One might call it a portal to another world. When the gods were creating the realm, Aditi and Pater kept it with them as a way to keep balance. As the light in the realm began to dwindle, darkness rose to fill the gaps. Eradication of a species only creates more darkness because purification is hardly ever pure. The kaliak were placed in the book to restore balance and let light grow." I brace myself, knowing exactly what her next question will be.

"And why were *you* put in that book?" I try to read her—feel her—but I can't through that of my own racing heart.

"Because I, too, can be a vile creature." I hold my breath, waiting in pain for her response, waiting for her to figure out what I am. But it never comes. She spins on her heels, drawing her other sword and marching to the village. "They are all dead. It is not a pretty sight," I call out, grasping her arm.

She yanks free without speaking or looking at me, continuing to the bloodbath. My heavy conscience sways, unsure whether to stop her. In a single breath, I admit to myself that I was wrong. This is something she needs to see.

Cursing, I pull myself onto Liu and direct her to follow Dex, who has started to run. She stops at the clearing, and the cloud of my emotions crashes under the weight of her guilt, sorrow, anger. Her lips quiver, and I want to pull her into my arms and tell her that the worst will pass. It's what I wish I did last night, only, last night I was an element in her tears.

I drop onto the ground in complete silence, moving close to her. Confusion flickers in her chest before a sense of realization kicks in. I try to figure out what it is that she saw that makes the pieces fall into place. She breaks into a sprint, and we follow suit, leaping over collapsed buildings and the holes in the ground from where the kaliak's feet once sank. I disperse into a cloud of smoke, appearing ahead of Dex to kill another ghoul.

Skidding around a corner, she drops to her knees before an elven male, and her swords fall at his side. Tugging on the rope, I appear beside her to stare down at the male with a gash across his stomach and small bites taken out of his leg.

Dex may be a lunar elf, but without Callaia, the moon can't bring a man back from the brinks of death. His sputtered breaths stutter when she leans over him, touching his cheek. The milky hue over his eyes stares up at her as he coughs up blood in his attempts to say something.

"Shh." She caresses his cheek slowly. I walk around, making sure none of the monsters get close enough to her. "You're okay. It's going to be okay." The softness of her voice makes me look back at her.

A single tear falls from the male's eyes as he opens up his mouth to speak once more, only to choke on his words. I resume my walk, monitoring the feline creature from before as it stalks toward the dead fae.

Dex starts to hum a lullaby, awakening something inside me as I edge closer to her as if she's singing the song of sirens. I watch as her other hand inches toward her thigh, silently unsheathing a blade. Her humming turns more pained as it grows louder. There's a slight quiver in her hands, barely noticeable unless I pay enough attention. The blade touches the base of his neck. With a sharp inhale, she glides the blade across his throat. Blue blood gushes from the slit as he starts choking and twitching, but still she continues humming and caressing his cheek, staring straight into his eyes.

She doesn't stop humming until he takes his last breath, and she swallows before closing his eyes with her shaking fingertips. Pulling away, she drops her head to the dirt before leaning back to look up at the sun and whisper, "In the shadow of the light, and the tides of the deep. Through sundown shall you find peace."

She stays there for a long moment, guilt riddling her inside. As she sits there, I stop the ghouls and hounds that try to get near her, crushing bone and penetrating hearts. A rat tries to climb up Liu's leg, but she kicks it back with a threatening grunt.

Eventually, Dex rises, gripping her sword as she charges toward a ghoul sucking on a child, cutting its head off with a clean slice. More monsters start to charge for her and Liu, and she swings her sword again like she was born to wield it.

"Let's go."

I nod. Whatever she says, I will do. Because she has quickly become my greatest weakness.

It has been five days since we passed through the slaughter. Which means it has been seven nights of protecting her as she sleeps. Five kaliaks have perished under my hand since. My guilty conscience weighs down on me because it is another secret that I have come to keep from her. If she knew, she'd insist on traveling through the day and the night to get her hands on the quill.

Getting our hands on it will mean nothing for the likes of the kaliaks unless I have the ring as well. Only then will I be able to guide them back into the book and seal the door shut while I wait to fulfill my true purpose. She doesn't deserve to have that weight on her shoulders, because Ico was right: Pursuing the ring or the quill will only result in more attention that she doesn't need.

Back in Taravene, I roamed the street as she slept in search of the one true person who is meant to release me from the book. But I haven't heard a single word uttered about them.

Liu's hooves sink into the snow with a crunch as we navigate the rocky terrain. The further we travel, the more the snow blankets the mountains, and from it the gray rocks jut out, dripping down the mountain as if it were melting.

We haven't seen any parties bringing carriages of supplies to Lodaxo. The one building we have passed was completely abandoned save for the littering of rubbish from other travelers and the few creatures that have made a home there for a night. Here, I'm more concerned about mortals approaching in her sleep than I am of any monster. At night, the blizzards do a far better job at keeping away the danger.

We've spent the entire evening ignoring the cliff beside us, and how one wrong move made by any of us will send us toppling over the side and down to the rocks that lie below.

After seven days, she has finally started to lean against me, letting go of the reins and entrusting me to direct Liu. Dex claims that it's because we have entered Lodaxo's territory, that the harsh snow turns her skin white and her nose bright red, so she is merely keeping her hands warm.

She shivers, adjusting her legs to tuck the cloak beneath her. She slumps into my hold, only to sink deeper when I hold her tighter. Though the weather doesn't affect me, I'm cold everywhere that she doesn't touch.

Why didn't I ask Kselia to spell me a flask of hot water? she grumbles when the wind gets too loud for us to speak. Though conversation hasn't stopped flowing all day, we haven't heard each other's voices since we started gaining altitude this morning.

Because beggars can't be choosers.

Are you calling me a beggar? she snaps playfully as another violent shiver goes through her.

You would be the most high maintenance beggar if you were. I tap on her silver bracelet from over the cloak.

I do hope that you don't expect your coat back anytime soon. I have claimed it indefinitely. A gust of wind tugs the hood off her head, and she pulls it back up, tightening the scarf that covers the lower half of her face.

And it brings me great joy every time I see you wear it, is what I want to say. Instead, I settle for saying, *I expect you to hand stitch a new one for me instead.*

I think I have one of Vencen's spare coats lying around back at home.

His arms are much too small to fit. We can make a day of burning them instead once we are back.

Anxiety taps on her chest, and her shoulders tighten against me. *How are we going to find the mirror?* I can feel her start tugging at her clothing underneath the cloak.

Without thinking, my thumb moves around her arm in slow circles. *I have been in the palace before and have sensed areas where the magic is darker. So long as we prepare, we will get it.* I don't underestimate her skill. My only concern is locating where it is while planning an entry and exit strategy with only days to spare. If there is a blizzard or a storm, that will set us back a day, if not more.

She nods against my chest.

Turning my gaze to the navy sky, I try to look ahead, but we can barely see more than a few feet in front of us. *We should break for the night.*

Agreed. She reluctantly pulls her hands out from the comfort of the cloak to grab onto the reins. Dex steers in the direction of the rock wall where a section of it partially dips into the side of the mountain, granting us some reprieve from the battering snow.

Jumping down first, I wrap my hands around her waist to pull her off the horse and set her gently onto the ground.

I'm well capable of getting off a horse myself. She tries to sound annoyed when she says it, but she fails to hide the mischief that lurks in her tone.

I know, but I want to do it, is what I want to say. I settle for remaining silent instead as she fixes Liu's spelled coat to protect her from the elements.

Untying the tent off the saddle, she throws it onto the ground, where it pops up in an instant. Despite the wind, it stays perfectly in place. It's no taller than her hip and does not appear long or wide enough for anyone to sleep lying down. With shivering hands, she ties Liu up to one of the rocks and unbuckles the saddle. Then she drops onto her knees with the saddle clutched tightly against her chest and makes quick work of opening the tent and crawling inside, shutting it tightly behind her. Crouching down, I crawl through the walls and into the spelled tent, moving back to my feet once inside.

With the assistance of the fae lights floating in the middle, I watch as she tugs off her boots and drops her snow-covered cloak next to the entrance and grabs the black bag before walking the few steps to the pile of pillows on the mattress tucked neatly in the corner. It's by no means large inside the magical tent, but four people could sleep inside it with room to spare.

She drops onto the cushion and starts to devour Faeus's food without another word, swallowing it down with her endless supply of tea. "I never want to eat another pork bun again in my life," she grumbles between mouthfuls as color starts to return to her features.

Dropping onto the fur beside her, I watch with unparalleled fascination as she licks the sauce from her fingers.

She catches my gaze and closes the lid on the container, extending her legs to lie on the fur blanket as well. "Do you ever miss the taste of food?"

I chuckle at her question, lying down to stare up at the ivory ceiling. "It isn't simply eating," I start. "You've sat down at the restaurant, eying every server that walks into the room with a plate of food thinking that it might be yours. Then, you take the first bite that always tastes better than every bite thereafter. And when the last crumb is cleaned off the plate, you lean back into your chair feeling both pleasure and content."

There was a time when my brother and I challenged each other to eat at every single restaurant in Taravene. After two years, we gave up and decided it was better to eat at the favorites.

"Stop it, or you'll make me hungry again," she snickers.

"Do you miss the days before you were on the run?" I turn my head toward her, lying in a similar position, though her forehead is now creased deeply in thought.

"I don't miss the constant expectations to act a certain way and be a certain way. Nor do I miss not having the freedom to move around as I please. Have a guess of the two things I do miss." She props herself up to look at me, and I turn to face her. Her eyes are bright as she offers me a lopsided grin.

She's close enough for me to reach out and touch, but I stop myself before I do. She does not see me the same way that I do her. I suppose it is better that way. Whoever it is that holds her heart will be the luckiest person alive, and they better not do anything to hurt her.

I look just above her like I'm thinking considerably. I click my fingers. "The food."

"Actually, that's the third thing I miss." She grins. "I miss the glamor of the highlife: the shoes, the jewels, the pretty dresses and the unlimited supply of trinkets." Her intoxicating smile softens slightly. "But most of all I miss my sister."

"Tell me about her." I reach for her hand, giving it a comforting squeeze.

She perks up, moving to a seated position. "Boy, do I have some stories."

DEX
CHAPTER TWENTY-FIVE

THE BLIZZARD PICKS UP just as the Kingdom of Lodaxo comes into sight. Pinpricks of light peek through the dreary gray stone buildings that climb the mountain overlooking the roaring ocean. It's now the tenth night of our journey, and all journeys to Lodaxo are tedious no matter how you look at it. You're cold, hungry, bored, and worried the elements may find a way to kill you. But for the first time, I actually enjoy it to some extent.

I wrap my cloak tightly around me, reveling in the warmth the spell provides. The feeling in my toes and nose has long since vanished, and who knows when I'll get it back?

As we enter the city, the buildings do very little to stop the raging snow as Liu trudges us up the ice-covered pavement. Carriages, caravans, and cartons stamped with Hinixsus and Volducan's symbol sporadically line the street. I pity the poor souls that are tasked with traveling to and from Lodaxo every month just to deliver supplies.

Despite the blizzard, taverns are packed to the brim with patrons. Through the condensation covering a window, I can just pick out silver hair and pointed ears. Every time Vencen and I would visit Lodaxo, we would always spend most of our time in the taverns, drinking as a way to stay warm.

Someone stumbles out of the door dressed completely in fur. For a moment, I forget that no one can see Gideon, and I groan as I pull myself away from him and stick my gloved hands out into the cold to hold onto the reins.

Patting Liu's fur, I say, "Don't worry girl, you'll have somewhere warm to stay for the next few days."

We both watch as the patron all but runs out into the snow and down some other street. But apart from him, the streets are deserted. *We'll scout the palace now while everyone is inside,* I say to Gideon.

We start tomorrow. Tonight, we rest, he replies, grabbing my hips to pull me back and close the space between us until everything from our heads to our hips touch. A forbidden thrill resonates from my core, and I adjust myself on the saddle to find a position that feels less scandalous.

We don't have time to waste. I have to find a way into the palace undetected, I object.

And we will. Tomorrow. He must sense that I'm about to protest further, because he says, *I advise that you remember* who *it is that can steer Liu with their mind.*

Jerk.

Witch.

I find myself smiling at the insult despite myself. It almost feels impossible to believe just how far we've come since the night we met. Given, there are many times that I want to put a knife to his throat and fight him, but I can appreciate that we are now beyond the realm of wishing each other dead.

The higher we climb, the louder the wind gets and the tighter Gideon holds me. When we start nearing the palace at the very top, we search for the closest stables. I can just hear the sound of hooves clapping against stone as we walk past a side street. Riding toward the sound, a rundown stone building comes into view, and the faint smell of horse manure and hay makes it through my scarf.

We both jump off Liu, and my feet sink into the snow that reaches my knees. Gideon walks through the stable walls as I bang on the flimsy door. No response.

What are they doing? I question Gideon through our bond.

He's taking his merry time.

I huddle closer to Liu, who side-eyes me with a look that I can only assume is of complete animosity for dragging her through this. I bang on the door again, straining my ears for the sound of feet.

The door swings open, and a mop of blond sticks out. "Wha'?" snaps a brutish boy no more than fourteen years old with three little horns sticking out of his forehead. He scowls as he sizes me up and down like I've just stolen his toy.

Oh, this won't do. Not only is he a male, but he's also a child.

"I was after—"

"It a bit fockin' fat innit?" He juts his chin toward the horse.

Never mind, let Liu have her field day. "She's big boned," I correct.

"Aye, me grams say that 'bout me. 'N me ain't just big boned." His look is even more sour than before. I suppose it makes me a child for continuing with my request for a stable despite my knowledge of Liu's bias towards children and males. But I've never claimed to be the bigger person. "Right." I nod uncertainly, handing over the reins. The boy grabs it, and Liu starts jerking her head and flaring her nostrils. *Here we go.* "Well, make sure she's kept fat, fed, and warm for four nights."

He spits, holding out his hand. I bite my tongue to stop from commenting on his manners and dig into one of the bags on the saddle. Dropping the coins into his palm, he looks down and back up at me.

"You're joking. This is more than what I'd pay in Taravene." I already added extra to cover any damages.

"Premium se'vice, late check in, palace right there, fat horse..."

"Okay, okay." I drop another coin into his hand. "You best be feeding her gold at that price."

He shrugs, not bothering to help me as I untie my snow-coated bags and weapons from the saddle and throw it over my shoulder.

"Her name is Liu," I say, flustered from the effort required to remove my belongings.

"'ll call 'er horse." He turns his back to me and drags Liu into the stables.

I turn to find Gideon with his arms crossed and an amused smile on his face.

What are you looking at? I challenge.

I think you've found your match.

Rolling my eyes, every muscle in my body strains as I lift my leg up high enough over the snow just to take a single step. Trudging through the snow and in and out windy streets, my muscles scream louder and louder with each step. Ten days of riding up and down deadly terrain does horrendous things to the body.

If this is what the weather is like on the day that we carry out the heist, I'm not sure how we will be able to make a clean getaway, especially if we're facing creatures specifically bred to thrive in this climate. I shake my head to clear the thought away. I need to focus on things that I can control, one of which is how I am getting into the palace: disguising myself as a maid. I would have more freedom as a guard, and less people will question my movements, but one thing I've learned is that there is unquestionable comradery between guards, meaning that they'll recognize anyone new or out of place.

We skirt around the outside of the palace, moving from inn to inn trying to open the door until finally one swings right open. I wouldn't normally stay near the place I'm about to rob, but Gideon's invisibility is a commodity that we need to take advantage of.

Ice gathers on my stray hairs, turning them into sharpened blades that constantly try to attack my face. I hiss when one wins. Throwing my hand up to my face to touch my numb cheek, I can tell that any bloodshed will freeze against my skin in an instant.

I all but stumble inside, no longer used to walking without lifting my knees up to my chest. The snow that piled against the door falls inside the dark and musty room, stopping the heavy wooden door from swinging back shut.

"Bloody hell," I groan and hiss as I attempt to use my feet to push the snow back out, but all it does is fall back in.

The snowflakes whistle past as it finds its way to the empty counter, flicking through and dampening the pages of logbooks. I throw my belongings to the side and lower myself in an attempt to kneel down, but my thighs burn in protest refusing to listen to my command. Straightening, I bend over instead where the steady ache in my lower back turns into an uncomfortable pain. Scooping up the snow, I try to throw it outside as fast as my muscles will allow, but the snow tumbles and piles inside faster than I can toss it out. Giving up, I press my back against the dry side of the door and let my power trickle into my muscles to give me enough strength to force the door closed—but not so much power that it leaves behind a trace.

Breathless, I pull myself off the door and look down to see the remaining clumps of snow and melted ice covering the floor. Something soft hits my chest, and my hands snap up to the site of impact. Pulling the item off my chest, I avert my gaze between the hunched fur-covered woman and the towel.

"You made the fucking mess, so clean it," she snaps, crossing her arms over her chest.

Lodaxo and their hospitality, Gideon chuckles in my mind.

Not having the energy to argue with her demand, I unfold the towel and drop it onto the floor. I start shuffling around the area with the towel under my boots, all while the woman taps her foot impatiently against the wooden floor.

With my thumb and index finger, I pick up the sodden towel from the floor, contorting my mouth from the black and brown patches that now stain the towel. I try to erase the image from my mind, because I don't want to think about the bedrooms' level of cleanliness.

She nods to a basket in the corner for me to discard the towel before showing me to where we're staying. As I enter the room, I bite my tongue. Sometimes it's a curse to always be right. Dust piles along the windowsill and on the mantle of the empty fireplace. It isn't too different from Brewer's Boot in Zarlor, and at least this place doesn't smell like piss and ale.

Admittedly, the tent almost seems preferable to the questionable brown stain on the pillow.

Dropping my bags in the corner, I go through the process of peeling off all the different layers of clothing before heading to the equally questionable bathing chamber. Gideon has gone off to do whatever it is that he is doing, leaving me to defrost in my own time.

By the time I'm finished in the bath, I come back to the room to find him staring out of the window that faces the palace. Swallowing the lump in my throat, I take the space next to him. Edging as close to the window as I can, I squint like it might somehow clear the blizzard and reveal the palace to me.

"Gideon," I whisper, and I start to taste turmeric—a taste I've become increasingly familiar with over the past few days. I want to say that it tastes like guilt, but I can't be certain. "What if we can't find it?"

"We will," is all he says. But I can sense his reservations.

"What if we don't make it back in time?" I wrap my arms around myself, except I'm not sure if it's to warm myself up or to give me some sense of comfort.

"I believe in you. I know you will find a way." This time he sounds so certain that I almost believe him.

I nod, swallowing the lump in my throat before leaving him to his own devices. I sink in between the sheets just as my teeth start to clatter. Wrapping the blankets tighter around me, the chill from the cotton sheets seep through my clothes, raking a shiver up my spine. I tell myself it's from the cold and not the fact that what I plan on doing in four days could potentially cause a war, and if not a war, then my death. And frankly, there's nothing Gideon can do to stop any of it from happening.

Worst yet, I know Rhistel believes that he has the quill, but what if someone else swaps it out for a fake?

I never usually have trouble sleeping, but nothing about this plan feels right to me. There are too many variables that can go wrong, and there are too many questions that I don't have the answers to. It isn't just the fact that I don't know how to get in and out of the palace, it's the fact that it's a palace to begin with that sets me even further on edge. I made a promise to myself when I left Hinixsus that I would never step foot in a palace ever again. Yet here I am plotting how to do just that. What if I run into the king and queen? They've seen my face enough times from all the balls and parties that have been held. With enough time to plan and another corporeal person involved, maybe then I'll be able to pull it off.

The only thing I can recall from the last time I visited the Snow King's palace is the dreary ballroom and the guest chambers that were filled to the brim with furs and a fireplace that never extinguished.

"What's wrong?" Gideon whispers, taking the empty space in the bed beside me.

I shake my head. My teeth stop clattering when his arm skates over my shoulder and my entire body tenses under his touch. He nudges me back. Against my body and soul's wishes, I push against his hold, moving forward instead until I'm at the very edge. If I move any further, I'm guaranteed to fall over the side. Still yet, his arm stays on me, bringing with it forbidden thoughts of all the things that could occur on this bed should his hand move further down.

I clear my throat, wiggling underneath him. "Don't you usually scout the area?"

His fingers tap gently against my arm like he's considering his next move. "That's much too boring."

"People watching is far more interesting than watching me sleep." My breathing catches because of my pounding heart when a single finger starts trailing letters up and down my arm, drawing with it a fire that starts deep in my core.

"Protecting you as you sleep is a very noble duty." The bed doesn't move as he shifts closer to me, yet it feels as if a hurricane has flipped the mattress upside down.

His hand crawls lazily down my arm, barely stopping short of my hands that rest rigidly just below my belly button. I start seeing double from the proximity of his hand to the area that yearns to be touched. Even once he moves it back up to my shoulder, my breath still doesn't return to me.

"You can protect me from over there," I nod at the window, even though I know my soul will screech if he leaves my side.

His fingers move up higher, running through my damp hair with utmost tenderness and care, making my heart squeeze as a shudder works its way through me. "From there I watch the sleepy city and the frown that creases your forehead as you pretend to sleep. Over there, I can do nothing but watch as the chill of the night holds you hostage." His fingers trail down the bottom of my jaw, and I wonder if he can feel how hard I'm gritting my teeth or how frozen my fingers are. He wraps his arm around my waist, and I become helpless to his will. "From here I can protect you from the cold and the thoughts that plague your mind."

"I'm not cold," I mutter, ignoring his other comment.

Smoke and shadows appear before me as Gideon takes up the narrow space that I once occupied so there's no gap between us. I almost whimper when his arms disappear from around me, only to gasp when the heat from his cupped hand warms my face. I can feel the crimson climbing to my cheeks as I fight the urge to turn away and avoid his consuming gaze.

I stop breathing when his focus moves from my eyes to my lips where his thumb dances over the soft skin. The blood rushing to my ears and the explosion of flavors on my tongue makes it hard for me to breathe. I curl my fingers, tucking them closely to myself to stop them from straying over the dip in his cheek and the strong line of his jaw before making their way to his wet lips that glisten in the dark room.

"Look at me," he whispers darkly, tilting my chin up so my eyes meet his and I can feel the heat of his breaths caress my lips. "If there's anyone that can pull this off, it will be you. Believe in your own power, and the whole realm will fall before your feet."

If only he knew what the realm already thinks about me.

His hand leaves my cheeks to run down my arm until he finds my hand that clutches onto my tunic for dear life. He uncurls my fingers for me, grasping my hand tenderly in his and sending my soul reeling and begging for me to hold his hand as well. Bringing our hands up to his lips, he presses down. My world tilts on its axis, like a thousand mountains have come crumbling down around me, destroying cities and sending an avalanche right to my doorstep. Yet I don't want it to stop. I want to pull on that tether and let him unravel my whole world.

When this is all over and the quill is in our hands, there is a question that I don't know the answer to: Will I be able to part with him? I don't want to know the answer, because the truth is never easy to accept.

"I believe in you, Dex."

"Devereux," I want to say. But if he knew the truth about who I am, would he still say the same?

DEX
CHAPTER TWENTY-SIX

THE TOP LAYERS OF snow have melted away, so I only sink to my ankles as I stand across the street from the inn, holding my travel bag like I'm waiting to be picked up. Behind me, the palace towers over the rest of the city. I've always thought it the most ugly of all the palaces that I've been to; naturally Taravene's palace is the most beautiful with its white walls and golden columns. Even despite my bias, I still think the lunar palace is stunning. From the outside, King Nodisci's palace is dreary, but the inside is breathtaking in its own morbid way.

This palace, on the other hand, is disappointing in its own special way. The ice-like silver and white barrier separating the city from the palace matches the gray accent walls of the palace. The pointed pitched roofs twirl like a spear. Icicles drip down from the fascia almost strategically making it appear like the place is made of ice. The outside shows a lot of promise. I remember as a child I thought the furniture inside would be made of ice, or maybe everything inside will be completely white. Unfortunately, other than King Haemir's throne, everything in the palace is disappointing. I've broken into homes owned by clan members with nicer interiors.

I tighten the scarf around my face, breathing warm air into it in an attempt to defrost my nose. People filter by paying me no mind, riding their horses and pulling their carriages this way and that with urgency. Blizzards are plentiful in Lodaxo this time of the year, so it would make sense to take advantage of the break in weather while they can.

A lunar elf walks by, and our gaze locks. *Don't react. Your face is covered,* I have to tell myself as more and more followers and Hinixians filter pass, each one appearing as unhappy about their existence as the last. However, the followers seem to always have slightly more light in their eyes, I've always assumed that it's because they believe they're serving some kind of higher purpose.

From the corner of my eye, I can just make out guards walking in and out of the side entrance, while the only maids that have walked through it have gone out for some type of supplies only to return shortly after. Gideon said that he saw all the maids file into the building before the break of dawn, just after the changing of guards.

A slight tug on the tether tells me that Gideon is about to appear next to me. I throw my sack over my shoulder to head along the side of the barrier in the direction of the main entrance.

What did you find? I question as soon as Gideon appears.

I could not sense the object. There wasn't enough range for me to move around. I believe there is a vault beneath the palace going deeper into the mountain. He speaks like he's not used to being the one making reports.

Every villain needs an underground lair, I mumble before saying, *Which direction should we go to give you the most range?*

He shakes his head. *We will resume later, or else people will notice you milling around.*

Noted.

We cross the street when there's an opening in the traffic. He starts walking in the direction of the inn, and I tug his sleeve, turning him in the opposite direction.

Where are we going? he asks, and I can't help but smile from the turn in tables. Now it's him asking all the questions, and I'm the one with the information.

Business, is all I say, grinning to myself when his eyes narrow.

We walk down the winding streets until we're halfway down the mountain, well past where Liu is. I wonder if she's successfully bitten the kid yet or if someone else has stepped in to handle her—another male for her to bite perhaps?

As we walk, I study every woman and male wearing something cerulean in color, noting what they carry and what shops pique their interest. The servants I've seen leaving the palace this morning all carry the same cerulean color, be it a dress, cloak, or gloves. Some walk straight into a tavern while others walk into various bakeries and sewing houses.

When we reach the very center of the mountain, I look for the brown wooden sign that says 'We Sell Furniture.' Frankly, it is one of the most unfortunate store names I've heard of, only because they've missed out on naming it 'Ice-credible Homeware.' The more I think about it, the more

I realize how fitting the name is for Lodaxo. It's only understandable that they'd have such a straightforward name for such vulgar people.

When I push the door open, the smell of cedar and pine fills the air, bringing with it a gust of heat that washes the chill off me. Pulling my hood down and tucking the scarf beneath my chin, I make my way over to where an earthen elf hunches over a station, carving something into the side of a chair.

"Are you lost?" they bark like I've just interrupted their very important business. They've met me twice already, but I won't hold it against them for not remembering me.

"Maybe I'm looking for some furniture." I drag a gloved finger along a table and collect sawdust in the process. I scrunch my nose, wiping it off on my cloak.

"Leave the attitude at the door," they snap. Clearly, years of being in Lodaxo has taught them how to fit in with the locals.

I blow out a breath, returning my hands back inside my cloak. "Straight to business then. Tell Ta'nola that her favorite procurer is in town. I'll be at Xonas' at seven."

They grunt. "Close the door properly on your way out." They return back to their carving like I was never there.

I grin in response, walking backward, careful not to bump into any furniture before spinning right before the door. I pull it closed tightly behind me, just as the shopkeeper said, in case they have some reservations about passing my message. The last time I came here, Vencen broke their coat stand, and who knows if they remember?

Is this a way inside that you haven't mentioned? Gideon's voice edges towards annoyance.

She's another procurer with far better connections. I start walking the same path that we took here, careful not to make any wrong turns and end up lost.

You're outsourcing the mirror? This time, he almost sounds disappointed, like he wanted to see our mission through.

While that would be a preferable option, no, she's connected all around the realm and should have information that might help us both. She also happens to be Ico's ex-girlfriend. It was a rather toxic love affair, or so I was told.

The ring.

I nod. *You deserve true freedom as well, Gideon.* Turmeric once again coats my taste buds, and I turn to him with a frown.

I'll be free when it's time.

As we walk, I look for cerulean once more. Only this time, I search for it in the shop windows, even a smidge of fabric poking out of a basket or draped over a desk. My legs ache from walking uphill by the time I spot the shop that I saw one of the maids walk into.

I tuck myself into an alleyway, and Gideon follows suit.

There's that look in your eye that you get when you have a plan. Crossing his arms, he shifts his legs to a wide stance and looks down at me.

He arches a brow expectantly, waiting for me to elaborate as he watches me shove the scarf into my bag and throw my hood back down.

It's all about my disguise.

I start to unwrap the leather strings tying my braids together, running my finger through my hair to undo it. Flipping my head down, I shake my hair to turn it into a disarrayed mess that sticks out at all angles. Standing back upright, I pat my hair down to make it appear like I've tried to control my hair without any luck.

The bottom of your hair is red, Gideon says, and I freeze.

I should be counting my lucky stars that it has taken him this long to notice, but still, I don't feel very lucky. I know that he's keeping parts of his identity from me for whatever reason he believes is fit. And maybe it does frighten me a little to find out why it is that everyone is after him. I believe that he has more reason to keep the truth from me, while my excuse is purely selfish and less than reasonable. Why? Because I'm worried that he'll think of me differently for running away from a war I have the power to stop.

But another more grueling thought enters my mind; if he can see it, just how washed out is my hair dye?

I grin, hoping that he didn't sense my momentary shift in mood. *It's fashionable.*

I can tell my response doesn't answer his question, but I continue getting into my disguise all the same: pulling the cloak so it droops down more on one side, shoving my visible weapons into my bag then hiding it underneath a broken table.

Every part of me wants to pull my hood back up to keep my ears warm, but I force myself not to. I have to sell the act that I'm somehow immune from the cold from living in Lodaxo.

I head toward the seamstress's shop with my shoulders hunched slightly and my head hung low—not so low that I appear weak, but not so high that it's above the status that I'm trying to appear. The current aim is to look tired and at my wits end—which isn't too much of an act to put on.

And who are you becoming today? Darkness lurks in his tone, adding another layer of excitement to my plan. He has caressed me with his words and filtered thoughts into my mind in ways that would make a priest cry. He forgets that I too can evoke such carnal emotions.

I'm pretending to be a lady of the night. I wink.

Whiskey and ginger terrorize my tongue in a violent wave, and the whole city becomes a blur of movement. His hands are around my wrist in an instant, tugging me back into the alleyway firmly but not painfully. His form towers over me as his eyes thunder with chaos and destruction. But in the darkness of his gaze, all I can hear is the sweetest melody that I can't get enough of.

The shadows in my core that I haven't felt since the inn returns. I can see them at the corners of my vision. They scream and hiss and cry, telling me to pull my knife and plunge it into him. Telling me to gouge the eyes out of men who dare look at me. Telling me to destroy the whole city.

His face lowers to mine, and his breath comes out hot and ragged against my cheek. His tremoring breaths match my own, and the hand around my wrist starts to shake like he's struggling to hold back something primal. It emits from him in waves, crashing against me, pushing me away to the shore before pulling me into the storm.

"If you—" he stops himself short, and I watch the muscles in his jaw tick violently as he squeezes his eyes shut like he's reconsidering his words. Until he finally opens his eyes, holding me in place with his stare alone better than his hands ever could. "If *anyone* touches you, I will summon an army of monsters to feast on their entrails until there is nothing left of them for their family to mourn," he growls.

I can't speak. No words dare to form on my lips that feel worthy of such power. My knees threaten to buckle beneath me, to worship the ground that he treads and obey his every command. But mostly, all I feel is an insatiable hunger that only he can quench.

The thought of a man doing something so *deranged* in my name ruptures something within my morals. Because for the briefest moment, I yearn for that to happen. I crave it.

He pulls himself away, and the shadows recede, letting the light take its place. Still, the hunger remains. He shakes his head, shock fresh in his eyes, curling and uncurling his fist as he attempts to control his labored breath.

"Forgive me." He takes a step back. "You may do what you wish. I know many powerful women who have done so. Just know that you needn't do that to help me." He speaks like every word is tearing him apart.

A heavy weight settles on my chest as he takes another step back from me like he's afraid that he might hurt me. "I'm sorry." I take a step to get closer to him, wanting to do something to take away the pain in his eyes. "I was only joking."

He shakes his head, unable to look at me as warm cinnamon coats my tongue. "I apologize, something came over me. Please, continue." He holds his hand out in the direction of the shop, and I hesitate, unsure if I should go. "Please, Dex. I'll be right behind you." His voice is strained like he's holding something back.

I nod, uncertain about what to do in the situation. "Stay here. I won't be long," I say before breaking off into a fast walk to the shop.

I try to pull myself together as I walk. If this is the power he possesses in this form, I can't imagine just how dangerous he is once he is fully restored. Despite it, I didn't feel afraid of him. No, I want to feel it again, learn everything there is to know about what makes his powers tick. Learn everything there is to possibly know about him. But I can't. He'll slip through my fingers soon enough.

The bell above the door chimes as I enter, and an elderly woman who wears dark bags beneath her eyes tilts her chin down to look at me from above her glasses. The room is packed to the rafters with the same cerulean color ranging from wool to cotton. Her brow arches in question as she looks at my flustered face.

I clear my throat. "Me friend said to come 'ere to get me a work uniform." After years of listening to Nessa and Ico speak, I only hope the accent I've layered on sounds at least somewhat believable. She looks at me like I haven't given her enough information, so I continue, "Just got a job up at the palace. Housemaid of sorts."

"What're ya?" she grumbles, returning to her stitching.

What does that have to do with my need for a uniform? I let my eyes rove over the room to engrain it into memory should I find myself needing to acquire a uniform without politely asking for one. "Me mum's a human, bu' me dad's a fae. Coward done walked off. He didn't want no half breed."

She grunts in approval. "Ya don't look like ya're from 'ere." She snatches a measuring tape off the table like this is the last thing she wants to be doing today.

"Aye, Taravene," I say. It's the safest answer seeing as every species but Black Bloods migrate there. "Yer don't either."

"Ya don't know shit about me girl," she snaps.

I bite my tongue. I was wrong, with manners like that, she's definitely from Lodaxo. She motions for me to take my coat off, and I do as I'm told.

She starts muttering under her breath in a language I don't understand as she measures me. I suck in my breath, hoping she doesn't feel the weapon in my pocket as she measures. The woman leaves the room, coming back out with a cerulean dress in hand. Throwing it at me without another word, she shuffles back to her spot to continue stitching.

What is with Lodaxians and throwing things at me?

I don't bother saying my thanks before dropping coins on the counter, slipping out the door, and making a beeline through the snow to the alleyway. I grip the dress tightly, ready to show Gideon my success, but there's no sign of him anywhere. Frowning, I grab my bag and shove the dress inside. I make quick work sectioning my hair into three to braid my hair off my face and avoid any more incidents where my hair turns into a weapon that cuts my cheek. Righting my cloak and covering my mouth with the wrapped scarf, I throw my bag over my shoulder.

You can run, but you can't hide, Gideon. I try to make light of the situation that unfolded despite my better judgment. Maybe it should have bothered me that he felt so strongly about my comment. Maybe it should have bothered me that I didn't see any light or goodness in his eyes as he made such a vile threat. Maybe it should bother me that he would spill blood in my name. I suppose not all monsters are villains.

I should be scared of him. Not now when he's bound to me, but of the force of darkness he will inevitably become once he's freed.

The invisible tether tugs at me, and I take a deep breath before turning to find him standing at the very end of the alleyway, where it would still take seconds of running to get to him. His hands are clasped behind his back at attention like I've seen soldiers stand.

I step forward, and he steps back. "You'll be safer if I keep my distance," he rasps, still wearing the same look of pain from before.

I take another step forward, and he takes another step back. "I feel safer with you around."

He stares at the ground and his fists drop to his side while his lips twitch into a sneer. "Chaos lives in me. And chaos wants to come out and play."

Out of the corner of my eye, I can make out faces within the darkness that unfurls from the shadows, and I can just hear them whisper, "You'll never be worthy."

Swallowing the lump in my throat, my feet stay put this time and I drop the bag. "There's a monstrous side to every creature," I whisper, using his words against him.

"And I am a monster," he declares in a tone that could bring down mountains, tightening his fist until it turns white. He's trying to make me afraid of him. "Once we get the quill, I'll make sure you're safe from me."

I don't answer, letting the silence stretch for as long as it needs to until he finally looks up at me. The force of his gaze almost makes me stumble. His gaze is a whirlwind of sorrow and longing, mixed in with deeply rooted need. I blink, trying to douse the thought that the need he feels is for me.

His eyes stay on me, and I start walking. This time, he doesn't move. His knuckles are no longer a ghastly shade of white. It isn't pain that I see in his eyes now, it's something I can't quite place. I keep walking until he's little more than two steps away.

He has very quickly become the face that I search for in any crowd. But he is nothing more than a passing phase, one that would never look at me as anything permanent. I don't want to be just a distraction to him, or just a means to an end.

"You know the emotions I don't even admit to myself," I whisper. "So tell me, Gideon, what did you sense?" He doesn't answer, so I take another step. "Did you sense my fear?" Still, he doesn't answer.

I close my eyes and breathe in deeply, taking in the smell of the crisp snow and sage, attempting to gather my thoughts. Opening them, I see the world in a new light; the soft dip in his chin, the slight crinkle in his eyes, the way his skin seems to glow when he's surrounded by snow.

"I'm not frightened of you—nothing could ever make me fear you. If you are a monster, you're the most beautiful monster I've ever seen." I take another step until our chests almost touch, and I look up to stare at his silver eyes. Every fiber of my being is on fire from his nearness and still I want more. "I've seen darkness before, and your darkness? It's the night sky dusted with stars that glow even in the darkest hour."

Before I can say another word, his hand cups the back on my neck and pulls me in. My entire being comes alight when he tips his head down, dragging his lips softly against my ear, down to my cheek. "It is you, my little elf, that is a master of words." His hand snakes around my waist, pulling me against his. "But know this, darling," he rumbles. My heart hammers against my chest, making everything feel light as his lips caress the side of my face, a trail of silver heat that makes me forget how to breathe. His breath heats my skin and moves my soul as his lips land a whisper from my own. "I could show you things that would make ladies of the night blush."

My core turns into molten lava at the knee buckling thoughts that rampage my mind.

He pulls away, walking down the street with a slight sway in his step. The fire that burns through me this time is the same type of fire that could burn a city to the ground. "Come along now, witch. We best get moving."

My teeth grind as I stare at his receding figure. "I take it back," I yell, gaining the wary glances of people walking past the entrance of the alleyway. "Kelpies are much more beautiful."

DEX

CHAPTER TWENTY-SEVEN

As it turns out, Liu has tried biting the Lodaxian boy seven times, and his father two. They called her a demon on four legs; they thought it fitting that a witch such as myself would own such an unruly creature. So rather than spend the afternoon scouting the palace, we had to find another stable with at least one female stable hand.

Now, the moon rests perfectly above Callaia's gray statue head, leaving shadows that curve over the goddess' soft features. The falling snow tucks along the folds of her dress and piles on top of the moon she holds in her hands.

Moving onto the next statue, I crane my neck up to admire the pride in Mediel's eyes as he holds his sword up to the sky in victory. I remember reading about how annoyed the other gods would be by the God of Sport's competitive nature.

To my left, guards who adorn half their uniform stumble through the street with their arms hung over the other's shoulder. I guess happy hour has started. Behind me, the laughter of children fills the air followed by a mother's string of curses as she yells at them in a language that I don't understand. My lips curl into a scowl. Gods, I hate children. Even when they're happy and silent, they make me uncomfortable.

I block my ears and turn to the next statue that depicts a god with dragon-like wings spread out beside him and a vicious snarl engraved on his face. Hadeon's hands are at his side, fingers contorted in a way that makes it look like they're dancing along to his power, and he looks off in the distance like being bound to such a form is the last thing he wants. It's almost as if the artist knew he'd disappear.

Next to him, Satrina looks down her nose at the square while dressed in sheer lace that hugs her curves. Her pointed tail curls around her leg, and her bat wings tuck closely behind her like they're a mere accessory. Hadeon and Satrina; the two lovers that have been on and off for centuries. Apparently, most of the volcanoes in Renlork are just the aftermath of one of their lovers' spats.

How any of these statutes have stood the test of time and survived through Lodaxo's weather is beyond me. I almost feel angry at the statues and their continued existence. It's like they're taunting me, laughing at my fate. I wonder how they'd feel knowing that their own fate rests in the hands of a runaway princess turned thief. Would the artist return just to fit a scowl to all their faces?

I turn around, making a mental note of the lack of followers and priests in the square in front of the palace. I snicker to myself, recalling what I overheard back in the palace when I was younger. Father was complaining that King Haemir refused to tear the statues of the twelve gods down because his late grandfather commissioned them. Truthfully, I think it's only to keep the followers of the Paragon Dawn from milling about in the square to keep tabs on the king.

I move to the next statue, Kriotz, the Goddess of Trickery and Satrina's part-time lover when Hadeon leaves upset about one thing or another. Before I can scuttle on to the next, the back of my neck prickles like I'm being watched. I let a whisper of my power flow to my ears, heightening my senses to see if I can hear the swishing sound of my stalker's tail. I close my eyes, letting the sounds come to me as I slowly pick them apart; someone chewing, children giggling, snow crunching beneath boots.

I open my eyes, and turn in a slow circle, ingraining every face I see into memory. None of them look my way and none of them look familiar in the slightest. I shift my weight, glancing across the court as my hairs continue to stand on end.

Nothing.

I'm just stressed and helpless, I tell myself, shaking my head. I've been letting Gideon take the lead, and I just feel like I'm not doing anything. But beyond watching the comings and goings of people from the palace and the timing of all the shift changes, there isn't more I can do without revealing my plan to steal from King Haemir.

I wouldn't drag anyone that I actually like in to help me execute my plan for fear that they may get burned. On the flip side, I wouldn't trust anyone that I don't like with my secret plans. No, I'm alone on this one. Alone with Gideon.

Shadows flicker next to me, and I turn just in time to see Gideon eyeing the statues with vehemence. My heart stutters when I lay my eyes on him, washing away my anxieties and feeling more intoxicated by him than the moon has ever made me feel. My fingers itch to reach out and run my fingers across the smooth surface of his lips.

I clear my throat, bringing myself back to reality. I arch my brow at him, expecting another debrief as we wait for the clock to tick by before we meet Ta'nola.

He shakes his head as almond and blueberry starts to lather on my taste buds, a taste that I realize I haven't stopped tasting for days. "Next time you're shivering, you call me immediately," he bites, pulling my cloak together after the wind blows it open.

I'm fine. I slap his hand away before anyone sees my cloak move of its own accord. *What did you find?*

"Nothing," he says through gritted teeth. "We will go to Xonas' early, and you will order a proper meal. Eating nothing but snacks will not take your anxiety away."

Spinning on my heels, I stomp in the direction of the bar. *We're going there now, not because you said so, but because I want to scout the area first. Make sure it's safe.*

He inhales sharply behind me as he matches my pace, and like always, the sound turns my insides into molten lava. "You will soon learn, little elf, that I am always right."

I don't answer. My stomach groans loud, making heat rise to my cheek. *That still doesn't mean that you're right.*

His snicker has me light-headed, and I trudge through the snow with newfound vigor when the door to a restaurant swings open and the smell of steak and roasted potatoes fill the cold air. I picked Xonas' because it's never packed and it's close to the square. Now it feels like it may as well be at the very bottom of the mountain.

I have never seen you move so quickly, Gideon says as he strolls along several paces behind me.

Ignoring him, I take advantage of the freeing feeling of letting my legs move on their own as I run down the hill. My braid bounces against my back, and the harsh wind stings my eyes, making them water. I keep running until I skid to a stop before a darkened alleyway. *Xonas' Roast & Ale House.*

The tether tugs, and he appears next to me as I make my way down the narrow street. *One would argue that a rational person would not dine in such an establishment,* he remarks, nodding to the mischief of rats feasting on a carcass.

It merely adds to the ambience of the place.

Gideon huffs.

He isn't wrong. There's a reason this place is never busy, and it isn't because the food is bad. Quite the contrary, Xonas cooks the best steak in the kingdom: rosemary infused meat, drizzled with garlic butter and a trickle of rich red wine, served with home-cut potatoes. Their problem is the unwanted visitors out front and the fact that the owner is part Black Blood. Still, I admire Xonas for abandoning their kind to pursue their passion in the culinary arts.

The smell of garlic curls around me in an embrace as soon as I walk inside and ogle at the sight. It's the busiest I've ever seen the place; almost every single seat has been taken, and the barmaids run from one table to the next, taking orders.

I start the chore of taking off my snow-covered coat and crisp scarf, draping them on the hooks by the entrance and watching as the snow trickles down to become sludge on the wooden floors. The raging hearth is a welcomed guest that roars against the back wall, acting as the primary source of light. I make my way to one of the few tables available: a brown booth tucked against the corner wall with a single oil lantern hanging above it. Slumping into my seat, the cushion behind my head dips as I lean back, closing my eyes to suck air into my lungs.

I have three days left until I need to break-in, which only means that there can be no room for errors with getting back to Taravene. We're going to find the mirror and give it to the Hollow Cry clan regardless of what they plan on doing with it. I'm not responsible for their actions.

If Callaia were still alive, I doubt she'd let my soul ascend to the moon to spend an eternity in peace and harmony. At this rate, it's looking more likely that Satrina will drag me screaming and clawing all the way down to Hell. Not only am I willingly freeing a being capable of flattening kingdoms, but I'm also giving a clan known to hate their king the resource to locate their enemies. I wonder if Father would be proud that I've become as selfish as he is.

I open my eyes only to become startled by Gideon who sits on my side of the booth, blocking me in. I blink, expecting the image before me to change. I didn't pick up on it last night when he lay on the bed, but now that I realize it, I don't know what to make of it.

How are you sitting on furniture? I'm of no mind to ask him to move, too focused on the fact that he isn't falling through the chair.

You sleep for too long. I've been practicing, he says with indifference, like he is past being impressed by his own abilities and this was simply expected.

And you didn't think to tell me?

That you sleep for too long? I thought you already knew. I narrow my eyes at him, and he looks at the crowd in subtle satisfaction. *Now tell me, my moonlight, does it appear 'safe' to you?*

I grind my teeth. I may no longer want him dead, but he still vexes me.

A server meets my eyes, and my attention pulls to him, studying every inch of him. His pointed ears are decked out in an array of silver and gold studs and rings, matching the bar in his brow, the ring on his nose and the center of his lip. In an instant, his ruby eyes light up pale gray skin, and he starts walking over while wearing a flirtatious smile that could melt any man or woman. My lips curl to give him a smile of my own.

Ginger and whiskey fill my senses as Gideon's shadows start to creep in from beneath the tables. The sound makes my skin crawl and sends a shiver tearing up my spine. They're whispering something, but I can't quite hear it.

The elf looks down at me through his thick brown lashes, throwing his braided red hair back over his shoulder. He licks his lips before saying, "What can I do you for? I can show you what's on the dessert menu after your meal." He winks.

Gideon's flavors sear my tongue, making each breath hot and distracting. Gideon's power starts to pulse off him in waves, turning the room smaller than it actually is. But the male is completely unaffected, grinning wide so his teeth show even though another meaning lingers behind his words.

"This *mortal* needs to be taught a lesson on professionalism," Gideon growls.

The chaos starts to make its noises: singing, screaming, crying, laughing, and I can finally make out what they're saying. When I look down to see them, I notice that they aren't speaking to me at all. Each head is turned to Gideon as tendrils of darkness climb up the male's legs like claws. They want him to kill the elf.

I try holding on to my smile and pretend the taste isn't there and that the shadows aren't all averting their attention to me. I clear my throat. "Just the rosemary steak." My voice comes out hoarse and breathless.

His grin stays firm as Gideon moves to his feet in front of him, blocking the elf from my vision. The chaos grows louder in their noises and the power rolling off Gideon starts to suck the air out of my lungs. I can hear them all, they all say the same thing: *kill him.*

The shadows are rather morbid. It's getting a bit old.

"Well, if you change your mind about dessert, you know where to find me," the elf says, and without seeing the look on the elf's face, I nod slowly.

He walks away, maneuvering between tables before going into the kitchen. Gideon continues standing in the long stretch of silence, and all I can do is pull one of the blades from my pocket and twirl it between my fingers to not feel *or look* so awkward. With each heartbeat, the shadows recede back to where they came from, taking with them their morbid sounds. I stare down at the blade, feeling it flow in between my fingers as it catches the light for the briefest moment before the light moves across the blade like a shooting star.

Why does it bother him so much that other men look at me in such a way? I want to say that the taste of ginger is just his jealousy, but I'm hesitant to say that he cares about me more than what is expected of a... friend? Acquaintance? Travel companion?

The voice at the back of my mind begs to be more than any of those things. It is whispering fantasies that could never be, because *we* could never be. Still, I can't help it. His presence makes me feel richer than I ever did living as a princess.

After a long moment, he lowers himself down onto the empty space beside me, grim determination firmly on his lips. He doesn't look at me, gripping the end of the seat with his new talent. "I don't trust him." I can't make out what it is that I hear in his voice when all I taste is the residue of whiskey and ginger. Now it's a concoction of something unknown to me, and the only thing I can pinpoint is the blueberry. *Odd.*

"Is there anyone that you do trust?"

He turns his head to me, and I suck in a sharp breath. I want to look away, but his gaze keeps me firmly in place. "I could ask you the same question, little thief." The remaining darkness in his voice curls sweetly into my core.

"Trust is a finicky thing."

"As finicky as it may be, I find myself trusting you completely," he breathes heavily.

My heart seems to stutter, and I'm acutely aware of how close his hand rests beside my leg and how quick my breath has accelerated.

His eyes darken like he's noticed the same. He knows it isn't fear that has made my hands freeze, no, I worry that it might stumble from his nearness. His gaze flickers over to my frozen fingers and he turns his head to mine.

"Keep going," he whispers as he moves his hand onto my thigh.

And just like that, the world melts away and it's only him and I in this little booth. I bite my tongue, forcing myself to concentrate on the hand movements and stare at the dancing lights on the blade, forcing myself to ignore the electricity that sparks through my veins or the ecstasy that stirs to life in between my legs from a single touch.

"Well done," he croons, drawing his hand up higher up my thigh. My soul feels like it's swaying, I'm completely lightheaded from Gideon's skin on me. My hand stumbles momentarily, lost in his touch before I catch myself. "You're doing so well, darling."

Heat rushes to my cheeks as his hand continues to travel higher and higher. I swallow the lump in my throat and stop myself from squirming in my seat. *We're in a tavern. Everyone can see*, I say breathlessly, gripping the seat beneath me with my free hand.

I yelp when his finger touches the place where I ache the most. Suddenly, my leather pants feel too hot and all the layers covering my skin feel like they're too much as sinful heat explodes inside me. I grip my blade, trying to regulate my breathing as his thumb starts to move in slow circles, making the room spin and shrink until all I feel is him.

His lips caress the soft skin of my neck, traveling up until they find the spot just beneath my jaw. His teeth graze my skin, and I lose the fight against myself as I start squirming underneath him. He chuckles darkly in my ear, and I have to stop myself from groaning for more.

"Tell me to stop," he whispers, adding more pressure to the site of my need.

My soul feels like it is screaming in bliss, threatening me not to answer him. He starts to trail soft kisses along my jaw, stopping just before his lips meet my own. My grip on my blade starts to shake as it takes everything in me not to turn my head and come undone with a single kiss.

"Tell me you don't like it," he breathes beside my lips, nuzzling his nose against my own. I try to stay perfectly still in case anyone glances my way to see me completely flushed.

"I don't," I whisper, not believing my own words as any hope of resuming my movement with the blade evaporates. He presses harder, and my breath catches in my chest as I grip the seat like it's my only vice.

"I don't believe you." He drags his thumb against me and grinds his knuckle against my center. Leaving my hold on the seat, I slap my hand over my mouth so as not to make a sound. "No one can see what I'm doing to you."

He kisses my neck delicately, completely at odds with the vigor of his touch below. I suck my bottom lip as my breaths turn short and sharp. A cold sweat breaks on my brow, as it becomes near impossible to keep any sense of self-control.

Everything about this feels so wrong and so right at the same time. I don't want it to stop. My body aches for whatever it is that he's offering. I want every inch of him. I want everything that he's willing to offer. His forbidden touch and wicked whispers—I didn't realize he is what I was craving. But the most deadly thing of all: It isn't just my body that wants him.

The smallest whimper escapes my lips when his thumb stills for the briefest moment before his fingers take the lead. "Tell me, if I get on my knees before you under the table, and feast on such a... delicacy, would you be able to hide it from the whole room?"

"Gideon, please," I whisper, shaking my head slightly despite how badly I want—no, *need* it to happen. "We shouldn't." The second those two words leave my lips, I wish I could take them back.

The heated air around us evaporates and he withdraws from me without another word, throwing us back into the silence. I give up on the blade and resort to twisting the ring from Saeya in circles, wishing for something else to fill the space between us and the aching hunger that he started consumes my mind.

No one is stopping us from stumbling into the inn in a heated frenzy, but I know that it won't stop at one night beneath the sheets. I'll want more of something that neither of us are in the position to give, not when we'll split ways right after. And especially not when we will be the most wanted pair in the realm: the Daughter of the Blood Moon and the weapon.

Gods, where in the hell is Ta'nola, I hiss to myself, glancing over to the clock ticking just past seven.

I clear my throat, trying to think of something to say when the voren walks in with her ivory tusks held high. Despite the freezing temperature, she adorns nothing but a leather vest to show off her bulky muscles and the tattoos that cover them. Her green fringe bounces against her forehead with each swagger filled step as she shoots me her winning smile. I almost see the humor in the weapon strapped to her back; the axe perfectly decorates the side of her head like a halo. Yet she is nothing but unholy.

She slams her axe onto the table, and some of the people around jump up with their hands going to their weapons. She grunts in response, showing them her long canines. She drops herself onto the seat, kicking her legs up onto the bench.

"Long time no see, girlie." Ta'nola smirks before yelling across the room for an ale. Her brutish and careless demeanor sets me at ease, and I finally feel comfortable enough to let the ring go. "Have you finally taken up my offer?"

Gideon side-eyes me, and I shake my head. "As much as it would be my pleasure, I'm a lone wolf nowadays."

"Is that why I don't see blondie around?" she snorts in distaste.

"I have him hog tied outside for you to take home." I grin, relaxing more into my seat as my hand finds the leather handle of the knife and spin it through my fingers like a dance.

"He won't come back in one piece if you do that." Her laugh rattles my bones as she hits the top of the booth, startling the people in the next cubicle.

The jug of ale lands on the table in front of her, and I look up at the elf from before who no longer smiles like he wants something perverse. Instead, his face is pulled taunt, glaring daggers at the voren.

She returns the stare, only hers is one of bored intrigue. "Your mommy still owes me money," she says calmly, folding her hands over her stomach. "She best make payment before she discovers firsthand what happens to people who cross me." She pulls out a blade from the strap at her thigh and begins picking her teeth with it. My gaze skirts to the elf while I'm on the edge of my seat waiting for the next move. "Tick tock," she says.

The elf walks away, scowling at her, and I watch as he pushes the kitchen door open with a fuss. Ta'nola laughs again, vibrating my bones with her loud crowing. Still, I join in. My chest shakes along with her, but it doesn't feel genuine.

"Now, girlie, onto business," she says seriously, putting her feet onto the floor as she leans her elbows on the table. "What can I do you for?"

"I'm after a ring." I sound foolish as soon as I say it. After all these weeks, I have no idea what the name of the ring is.

"Don't tell me you're getting engaged with blondie," she groans.

I chuckle, shaking my head, trying to buy time as I say to Gideon, *What's the name of the ring?* I extend the chuckle awkwardly before saying to her, "No, I'm after the..."

Ring of Destruction, Gideon adds quickly.

"Ring of Destruction," I repeat.

Her face turns grim, making my heart drop once again from just how serious my mess is. "Who's asking?" she says carefully, lowering her voice so that only I can hear.

I consider lying to say that it's for a job, but she'll see right through it. My clientele are less inclined to go after an object that will cause mass destruction as opposed to the list of vicious clans that have her on their books.

"It's for myself," I settle on.

"What do you think someone like you will do with it?" She skulls her ale. "That ain't no plaything," she says once she reaches the bottom of her glass.

I sigh. "I guess you could say that I have a bone to pick."

"Well, you're picking the same bone as King Rhaelson."

I know I shouldn't be surprised, but the blood drains from my face all the same. Of course my father is after it; King Nodisci probably is as well. Does this mean that they have her looking for it? What if I come across him in my acquisition of the quill?

Gideon's hand drops to my knee, rubbing it softly in comfort. I'm grateful for the grounding effect it has on me, it reminds me that she said something. "Does this mean that you know where it is?"

"Beats me." She shrugs, leaning back in her seat. "I don't fuck with kings."

I glance at Gideon, hoping that he can be a source of guidance on what to do next. "What about Hell's Quill?"

"Fuck if I know." She starts licking the froth left on the inside of the glass. "All I know, girlie, is that whatever that thing does, it ain't none of your business. My advice is to keep your nose out of shit to do with politics and the gods."

Wait, what does Gideon have to do with the gods?

DEX
CHAPTER TWENTY-EIGHT

It's time.

We've spent every waking moment since preparing for this day. I've woken every day when the moon is still high and the sun is about to stir awake. Then we'd hide in the shadows with Gideon following closely behind the maids to learn from them. He has scaled every inch of the palace that the tether will allow from my spot outside—even pretending to sell newspapers I sold to passersby just to hang as close to the palace's barrier as humanly possible to give Gideon more range. We've narrowed down the floor that the Mirror of Dracon is on, along with the path to take to get to said floor.

I've gotten little to no sleep since we spoke to Ta'nola. I'm about to go on a suicide mission, Gideon refuses to answer my questions about his connection to the Divine, and I have no way of knowing if the quill is going to be a fake. Added to the fact that the feeling of eyes on me haunts my every step, it's a miracle I get any sleep at all. The only thing I have is some semblance of assurance that if the palace suspected that I was about to break in, they'd have stopped me already.

Patting my chest where Saeya's ring hangs on my necklace, some sense of ease ebbs into me knowing that no one knows what I am and that my secret is hidden beneath the cerulean collar. My hand grazes over the white buttons running down just off the center of my dress, and I hug myself tightly both to stop the cold from raking my body with shivers, as well as to give myself some pretext of comfort.

Gideon's hand touches my elbow. I look up at him, just realizing how I've gotten used to only hearing my footsteps crunch in the snow and not his. "I will be right here," he assures me.

I don't have the heart to tell him that however grateful I am of the assistance he'll provide if things go sideways, truthfully, I can only rely on myself to get us out of there. Unless he's magically discovered how to touch a human, I'm on my own.

I nod instead, turning my focus back to the opening in the barrier as I blend in with the rest of the servants filing into the palace. We'll be with the first wave of maids to arrive, which means that the palace will be at its quietest. It also means that it will be nearing its busiest when we leave. Going in with the night servants wasn't an option, as they all know each other, and they'll spot me from a mile away.

My teeth start to chatter as I begin to lose feeling in my limbs, missing my spelled cloak that waits for me, strapped onto Liu's saddle. That is, if

I ever see Liu or the saddle again, of course. The stolen cloak does next to nothing to stop the harsh wind from seeping in, and the snow soaks into the material.

I keep my shoulders hunched and hustle along with everyone else so as not to stand out. All I want to do is run to the open wooden doors and get this over with, but I can't. Rushing any of this could get me killed. I glance over at Gideon, expecting to find an answer for the rosemary flavor on my tongue, but his assessing eyes drag over the area, and I can see him calculating all the threats in place. I'm grateful for my small mercy when goosebumps don't prickle my skin from the feeling of being watched.

The muscles in my shoulders tighten when we cross the barrier, stepping right into King Haemir's home. One way in, one way out. Going through the front door isn't an option. Going through the guard's doors isn't an option, either.

Our boots squeak on the concrete floors as we spill into the servants' entrance, and I'm careful not to be obvious in how uncertain my steps are. I've been in places I shouldn't be hundreds of times, but it feels different now. If I didn't complete a job, the main repercussion was a disgruntled customer. If I got captured or arrested? Well, I was stealing from small fish compared to today.

Everyone's hoods remain on as we adjust to the temperature, and I tell myself that Callaia is watching over me. I know that she isn't, but it still gives me some false peace of mind.

Like everyone else, I brush the snow from off my shoulders before I follow the line of people, sifting through the narrow walkway that leads to another opening. I keep my head down and my ears open as some people mumble their hellos to each other and hang their coats and cloaks on rusted hooks screwed onto rotting wooden walls. In the other rooms I can just hear people say their name followed by the sound of something scratching on paper.

Follow me. Gideon's voice does nothing to calm my nerves.

I follow in the other servants' lead, heading for the tenth hook from the entrance, letting the tiredness show in my shoulders as I shrug the cloak off. My careless braid falls down my back as stray hair falls onto my face. I throw the cloak lazily on the hook, righting my dress before heading through one of the seven doors in the room.

If anyone asks, you report to Albert, tasked with the upkeep of the guest rooms, Gideon adds.

And if it's Albert that asks?

Then you report to Marion.

I clear my throat again, grateful that he did more than figure out the whereabouts of the mirror. Before we enter the next hallway, the dress suddenly feels thick and uncomfortable. The fabric is clammy against my skin from nervous sweat.

Gideon looks back, watching me carefully before offering a comforting smile like he did when he tended to my wounds. All it does is make me suck in a sharp breath. Any failure by me today won't just affect me, it'll impact him too, my shadow.

The squishing sound of our shoes slapping the puddles of melted snow is too loud, echoing through the dark hallway like an endless cave. But the hallways feel too narrow, closing in and making it hard to breathe. Gideon's hand finds mine for a brief moment, and he gives it a wordless squeeze before we move into the next room.

The heat of the room starts to prickle against my cheek, and I avoid the woman standing in the corner with a clipboard as everyone seems to go straight to her as they step in. Neatly folded linen lines the walls, but still the room feels sparse with people. The room is too empty for me to go through undetected, so I instantly feel her eyes snap to me just as I'm about to leave the room.

Fuck.

"Oi," she snaps.

Gideon tenses, and we both turn to her at the same time. I let my instincts take over, so I turn calmly. All the eyes in the room fall on me, and I let a glimmer of my anxiety shine through to my features. "Yes, marm." The accent falls off my tongue just as easily as my nerves do, and I say another silent thanks to Callaia.

"Yer lazy or somethin'? Pick up the basket," she orders, and I jump into action despite having no idea where one is. "Oi," she barks again, and I spin around for the second time waiting for her to tell me that I don't belong here. But I breathe a sigh of relief when I notice her eyes aren't on me. "I told ya yer on toilet duties after that stunt," she seethes at another woman who tried to sneak down another hallway with a basket in hand.

She drops the basket on the floor with a huff, leaving the room through the hallway I came in through. I pick up the basket she dropped before the woman says anything else to me.

"Get goin' yer lazy shits," she snarls at no one in particular, and everyone starts moving in a flurry, making the room feel smaller than it actually is.

People reorganize the shelves, fold the freshly cleaned linen, and I eye one of the males holding a basket as he stumbles to a clipboard hung on the wall, running his hands over the words before leaving through the other door. I do exactly as he does, flipping through the pages without actually reading it, pausing on one page and then departing. I force myself to somehow look like someone who knows where they're going as I follow Gideon out of the room, turning right down the servant's hallways.

I balance the basket on my hip like I've seen our maids do back in Hinixsus, and I start thinking about how this is the perfect prop. I sewed on an extra layer to my dress to hide the mirror, which seems idiotic in hindsight. Gideon seems to think it's only a handheld mirror, but my own fears bog my mind, warning me that it's the same height as the ceiling. If that's the case, then we are most definitely screwed.

We continue down the hallway as I follow Gideon blindly down whichever path he takes. The only comfort I have is the fact that he is confident in his steps. He doesn't waver at any fork in the passage or hesitate before picking which turn to take. We pass other guards and servants rushing this way and that, and my heart hammers in my chest each time they pass, expecting one of them to point out that I don't belong here, that I don't really belong anywhere.

For a moment I consider hiding a weapon between the sheets but decide against it in case someone searches or takes my basket. Gideon wordlessly stops in front of a door, and I push it open and stumble into the main hallway, coming face to face with a guard. The woolen navy uniform and silver chainmail matches his deep blue eyes and the silver flecks within. The fae's eyes twitch slightly like he's trying to place me. His forehead starts to crease, and I lower my chin with a soft smile and look up at him through my lashes. He blinks in confusion.

I sidestep him, and say sweetly almost to the point of a giggle, "Excuse me, sir."

Ginger and whiskey roll on the tip of my tongue, and I continue trailing closely behind Gideon who walks at the same pace as all the other servants do before the fae gets the chance to say anything.

Dragging my gaze along the hallway, I take note of the simple chandelier and the worn rug. Sconces jut from either side of the wall every few steps, casting a golden hue over my cerulean dress—a color I've grown to despise. Every once in a while, a painting hangs between the panels of the dark mahogany walls of the otherwise barren hall.

We're exposed out here. I worry my bottom lip when we turn down an empty corridor. *We need to get back into the servants' corridor.*

He shakes his head, making me tense up even more. *That's the only way into the mountain. Only the maids with higher status go down there.*

Panic rises in my throat as I lose my character and snap my attention to the male. *You didn't think to tell me this* before *we went inside?*

I look up and down the empty hallway. He slows down his steps to match mine, and my soul jumps excitedly from his proximity. His warmth seeps through me, but still the chill in my bones remains. *I didn't want to worry you.* There's no emotion in his voice, but there's a finality to his words like he would make the same decision if given the opportunity.

I feel it prudent that I knew this, I hiss. *We could have planned accordingly.* I try to remain calm, while my sweaty palms fidget with the basket, wanting to twirl a knife between my fingers.

There is nothing to plan. Trust me.

I scoff in my mind for him to hear but nevertheless accept his answer. I want to say that I don't trust him, but that would be a lie. Even if I knew, what would that change? How would we have figured out a way down within four days when we still haven't even figured out exactly where the mirror is? This had to happen regardless of how little or how much we plan. I would much prefer spending months working up to this; getting a job as a servant and properly scouting the area without our whole plan hinging on Gideon's limited access to the palace and my ability to slip in and out without getting noticed.

Our odds aren't good, but I've hidden and strapped on enough weapons to get me out of here. Plus, I doubt there's another elf in here with some of Callaia's pure blood coursing through her veins because of her lineage. I can still feel the moon high in the sky; would any of the lesser elves feel it too? I've never done it before, but I'm sure the Daughter of the Blood Moon could blast a hole in the side of the building if push comes to shove.

Ruffle the linen, Gideon says quickly as we approach another turn.

What?

Mess up the sheets in your basket.

My brows scrunch, but I do as he says, turning the contents of the basket into a disorganized mess, shifting the basket to hold it with both hands.

We turn a corner, and Gideon's arm links with my own. Instead of tugging away, it takes everything in me not to lean in closer to his touch. *Don't look around, just head straight down the stairs,* Gideon says, and I instantly see why he'd say so. Two guards stand on either side of spiraling stairs that lead downward. I force myself to keep my labored breaths under wraps as I start worrying that somehow the guards will hear how rapidly my heart beats.

Tell him that Marion wants you to empty out the chuckles. He hesitates for a moment. *Do not smile at them like you did the other mortal.*

His added comment almost tugs at the corner of my lips, but I focus on keeping my shoulders soft as I approach one of the males. Neither turns to look at me, and the wheels in my head start turning in debate of whether this character I'm playing would look up at them or stare at the floor.

Pulling away from Gideon's touch, I buff my shoulders out so I appear bigger than I actually am and stand directly in front of the closest male who's brutish and looks like he hates his existence. I clear my throat.

He looks down at me with a sneer. "Scram. This floor is off limits to you."

I hold out the basket. "Huh? You wanna clear out the chuckles? 'll tell Marion 'ta get ya a job cleanin' it," I grunt, laying on an accent that doesn't sound natural. I neither know what the chuckles are or what type of person Marion is, I just hope that they're both awful.

This isn't blending in and staying hidden, Gideon warns.

This interaction will only mean that he remembers the stray that went below ground. The guard's sharp eyes tell me that he'll laugh at the appearance of meekness, while his perpetual frown means he'll want as little disruption as possible. Either that or he'll seek chaos.

I'm trusting you. Now you trust me, I tell Gideon, though I don't even trust myself.

The brutish fae scowls and the other guard steps in. I turn to look at the lanky elf as he says, "Marion, aye? I spoke to her just this morning, and she didn't mention you."

I try to dispel the anxiety from my mind, letting my instincts take hold. I grumpily shift the basket onto my hip like his further questions irritate me. "She tells you every mornin' that she's cleanin' the chuckles?"

"She usually—"

I roll my eyes dramatically, cutting him off and letting my gaze fall on the disgruntled fae for a brief second. "Are ya gonna help me clean or not? This is holdin' me up 'nd I'm 'bout to be elbow deep in Taravenian shit right after." I recall the note on the clipboard saying something about the Taravene guest rooms clearing today. Gods, please be correct.

"Come back when—" the tall elf starts.

"Just go," the fae interjects.

I huff, muttering curses under my breath as I shoot the elf a dirty look before stomping down the stairs. Exhilaration rips through me, making my hands shake as I grip the basket tightly. My blood roars in my ears, and my breath is labored, but I made it. I know they said something else, but I'm too focused on the steps to figure out exactly what they said.

I apologize for doubting you, Gideon says with pride shining in his eyes.

The day is still young, I retort as I skid to a stop just before I reach the bottom of the stairs. I strain my ears, trying to locate the sound of footsteps echoing down the hall before running down and in the opposite direction of the footsteps.

His fingers wrap softly around my arm, directing me down hallways and behind turns as we both look around skittishly for any sign of people. Other than the padding of feet and clanging of chainmail I heard, the hallway is completely deserted. That should ease my nerves, but the silence only heightens it. People will be able to hear me coming.

Please tell me any of those servants can go down to these levels.

He doesn't answer, and I notice the tick in his jaw that drains the life from me. He takes me down another flight of stairs, and I flatten myself against the wall as he heads on forward first, checking left and right to make sure no one is there before I follow. Then another set of stairs, and another. Each level we go down is barer than the last, slowly losing the paintings, then the rug, then the wooden walls disappear leaving gray brick walls and stone floors. The only thing that remains is the bluish hue of the fae lights.

How many fucking more? I gasp.

I lied. I don't know what floor it's on. I snap my gaze up to him. His confession only makes my palms clammier, and the desire to scream into my hands becomes overwhelming. *I feel it, though. We're close,* he adds.

Putting his hand on my chest, he stops me from taking another step. He pushes me against the wall. I flatten myself without hesitation. The moisture from the brick wall seeps into my dress, dampening it and fueling my cold sweat. He steps out, lifting a finger to his lips as his eyes turn predatory and his fingers curl into a tight fist. I can't even taste his emotions over my own as I silently balance the basket on my knee while my hand lowers into my pocket to draw my weapon.

We wait. And wait. And wait. But whoever it is doesn't move. I can hear their breathing and the weight that they shift from foot to foot. Gideon lifts his hand, like he's getting me ready to move. His hand signal changes, and I move in an instant, creeping through the hall with quiet steps. The eerie silence of the floor amplifies the sound of my boots, making it louder than it already is. Too loud.

"Hey!" a gruff voice calls, chainmail clanging with his fast approach.

Tucking the knife beneath the basket and my hand, I spin around saying, "I was just looking for—" A raised axe comes down on me, and I swerve out of the way, discarding the basket and leaving it to skitter along the ground. "That wasn't very nice."

He comes running again, and I jump out of the way, dropping to the floor and kicking my leg out with the help of my powers. The voren stumbles but rights himself. My dress hikes up and I unsheathe the dagger strapped to my thigh. I come back up and he charges, axe raised, shaking his head to try and catch me with his tusks.

Again, I avoid his lunge as the axe severs the air where my head was a moment ago. I kick his side, and pain thunders up my leg from the solid muscles covering his body. He smirks, catching the sleeve of my dress with his tusks as I lunge to get away from him.

This is too loud. I need this to end. I need to kill him.

I drop to the ground as he swings his axe at me again. I spring on my knees to appear behind him and uppercut with my dagger in hand. A suckling sound fills the air, and he gasps his last breath. Then he drops to the ground.

Maybe I'm a monster for killing without remorse. But this is just business.

The metallic smell of blood trickles into the air a moment later, and a sharp pain pierces my gut from the rancid taste. Fuck. Dragging the bloody blade along the woolen fabric, I drop to my knees next to him, covering the hole at the base of his head with my hands. The green blood starts to seep between my fingers, and I push down harder, stopping anymore from going through. I squeeze my eyes shut and start to mutter an elven healing chant, focusing solely on closing the skin. Using the moon will be faster, but someone will be able to smell it. I can't use my blood moon magic. Not the moon's magic either. No, we stick to simple elven magic.

The bleeding starts to slow, and the wound slowly knits together. The smell of magic is hot in the air, and I can only hope that it overpowers the smell of blood. I continue muttering the chant until the wound seals completely.

Wiping my bloodied hand on him and jumping to my feet, I run to the door closest to us, turning the knob to check if it's open. *Small mercies*, I think to myself when it swings open with a loud creak. Grabbing the voren by his boots, I let my power trickle into my muscles to pull him into the room. Shutting the door behind me, my breath fogs in the cold air. I snatch the basket off the floor, hiding the unused dagger in the sheets and sheathing the knife in my pocket.

Gideon nods sharply, grazing his eyes over the sheen of sweat on my forehead.

How much further? I bite, padding along the stone as we descend another flight of stairs and stop at the very bottom.

It's on this one.

Keeping my feet planted firmly on the steps, I peer around the corner, looking left and right. The smell of dark magic is all around, burning the air with its putrid power, making my stomach churn. My entire body is stiff, begging me just to go back up the stairs.

Where? He looks at me but doesn't answer. *Have you even been down here?* My voice has turned high-pitched as I search his emotionless face frantically.

Our bond is not long enough, he answers simply.

DEX

CHAPTER TWENTY-NINE

I STAGGER BACK. WE have no plan. Absolutely no fucking plan. I thought we had some semblance of a plan. We've both gone in this absolutely blind. We're going to die down here. This is suicide. I *knew* this would be suicide and yet I still went with it. Now someone is dead, and they're going to smell elf magic. *My* elf magic.

He holds my chin in his hand, angling it up to look at him. *Trust me.* His heavy gaze bores into mine, making my breath catch for a completely different reason. *I won't let anything happen to you.*

I nod tensely, knowing that the voren just now could have very well done something to me and Gideon would have been powerless to stop it.

I follow him through the corridor—blindly like I have been all morning. I trust that he would never intentionally lead me astray, but now all we are doing is trusting that his sense holds true. Senses that weren't used for hundreds of years. No, I have to trust this. I have to trust that we will find the mirror and bring it back to Taravene. I have to have faith that the mirror is in fact small and can be smuggled out of the palace undetected.

Open the door, he says softly, nodding to the one across from us. I do as he says, opening it slowly so it doesn't alert the whole floor. My eyes adjust the instant the door opens, and I can clearly see potions and jars of fetuses of various creatures lining the shelves. *Leave the basket. It's too loud with its squeaks and is slowing us down. We'll come back for it,* he promises like I've become emotionally attached to it.

I leave it there, feeling naked without it as I grip the dagger firmly. We start going in circles, turning down one walkway or another trying to find the source of the smell of magic, sticking close to walls and keeping our footsteps silent. It isn't 'this floor' because it isn't even a fucking floor. The path is no longer flat, it angles up and down, ascending and descending back up the mountain. But he isn't wrong, I feel it too, the dark magic. It lingers in the air like a stain.

Gideon walks ahead, looking around corners before I near. Dread builds in my stomach that what we're feeling is just the darkness emanating from the room, and not the mirror itself. For all I know, it's sitting somewhere in King Haemir's chambers, and he looks at it every morning when he wakes.

But I feel it before I see it—the area from which the darkness originates. Gideon does too, because he runs even further ahead. We've found it, in the very core of the mountain where the fae lights are sparse. If I listen closely, I can hear the waves crashing against the side of rocks.

I edge closer to where Gideon stands still, staring ahead with a calculating look on his face. My hand is frozen in its grip around the dagger, and I've lost all feeling in my limbs. Three guards lean casually against the wall on either side of the silver rectangular door. A wolf-like man picks at his nails with his teeth, a voren woman reads a small book, and the last woman slumps on the ground with her eyes closed. But her, the resting woman, I can smell her power from here, I see it, a purple light in the darkness. It vibrates through me, making me convulse with the cold.

There's too much room between me and them to have the element of surprise, and I don't like how powerful the woman is. Even if I try to fight them, how do we get in? What kind of magical protection will there be on the vault? How will we get out?

I turn to Gideon, hoping he has some bright ideas on the next step. He closes his eyes for a moment, concentrating on something before tugging at our tether to appear right in front of me. I lean into the touch of his warm hand against my cheek as I stare up at him with a questioning look.

Stay here, and don't try to fight them, he orders before disappearing with another blink.

I push myself against the wall, staring at the ragged stone stacked on top of each other and I start questioning every mistake I've made to end up here. This is it—my last job. I'm not dealing with this type of shit anymore. I'm not going to stumble on another magical object and accidentally find myself cursed and on a mission to end it. Maybe I don't deserve peace because of the choices I've made, but that doesn't stop me from wanting it. I want nothing more to do with clans or black markets or procuring. This is it. I'm done.

Every fiber of my body runs cold as a scrape sounds from inside the vault, followed by a high-pitched screech. *A kaliak.* The guards move to attention, and I move closer, peering around the stone wall to see. The sound of tearing metal sends pinpricks covering my skin as I watch two of the guards draw their weapons.

The human-like woman stands in front of the vault, holding up her index and middle finger up as she starts chanting ancient words. She's a witch. The guards raise their weapons higher. I grip my dagger, holding it up as well as bile starts to rise in my throat. Gideon tugs on the tether, appearing inches away from me, grabbing my wrist he holds them to my side shaking his head.

What did you do? I steel my spine, trying not to let my fear show.

Found us our key, he whispers, pressing his body into mine and encompassing me with his warmth. The cold wall at my back pierces my skin, but I'm far too anxious to complain.

The sound of the vault doors creaking open fills the air, followed by a deadly silence. At once, havoc unfolds. I can hear it all. The sound of metal flying through the air, their screams, her hopeless chants, its screech, their gargled breath as the kaliak tears through their armor. Then again, silence.

I can hear it—feel it creeping. Stalking. Searching. Gideon pushes against me, tucking my head into his shoulder, and my mind flashes back to Zarlor.

I want to see, I urge as I retch from the smell of the rotting flesh of the kaliak.

He untucks my head, letting me crane my neck so I can watch when it comes around the corner. My free hand intertwines with his as I hear its pointed feet click along the rock getting closer and closer and closer. It casts a long shadow on the ground, hulking the entire wall, and I hold my breath.

It's like it's tiptoeing because it knows that I'm here. It's taunting me, setting me on edge for its own monstrous pleasure. Its bloodied sharpened hand shows up first, and I battle the urge to squeeze my eyes shut and look away. But I hold firm. I need to see. I need to remember exactly what all this is for, and it isn't just for my own freedom.

My nails dig into Gideon as the rest of its body comes into view and he tenses up as well. I stop breathing altogether, afraid it'll smell me. It's unlike the kaliak I've seen—almost double in size, with ten arms sticking out of it in random places. Green ooze drops from it as fresh blood and voren entrails spill from its stomach. The witch's blood.

A fully grown kaliak. It's been in the chamber for a thousand years. The Divine missed this one. Gideon's voice is a welcomed comfort compared to the squelching sounds still ringing in my ears.

Fully grown? So the ones roaming the realm are only babies and already that deadly? How is it not dead? Guilt starts to burn my insides. It's going to be unleashed on Lodaxo. More people are going to die because of me and my brigade to freedom.

He squeezes my hand. *I'm not leaving you. They'll be able to stop it.* Part of me doesn't believe him. It took down a powerful witch and two guards in a matter of seconds. What chance do a servant or lone guard have? It's starving, and it won't let anything get in the way.

It pauses, and Gideon's power starts to roll off him like he's ready to stop the monster from getting near us. Over his shoulder, I can just see the kaliak cock its head before it takes off. Its pointed steps screech against the rock, echoing through the halls and reverberating down my spine.

When its steps are little more than a whisper, we stir into action, scrambling to the vault without hesitation. I don't pause to see the discarded bodies, jumping over them and straight into the darkness. The kaliak is a distraction, but they'll know there was foul play. A dead voren in a closet and a kaliak freed after one thousand years is no coincidence.

I jump over the sigil carved into the floor, inactive because of the witch. I pause as soon as I enter the vault; my body tries to shrivel up on itself from the weight of the power in the room. Goblets, bones, coins, paintings, spelled furniture—everything—is piled in the room, at the very back, a cage with the door flung wide open. I can just see another symbol within the cage and the part of the floor where the stone has strategically lifted, breaking the sigil that has kept it imprisoned for centuries.

I run my eyes around the room, forcing myself to ignore all the jewelry and crystals strewn about. All of which could be cursed. Most of all, books; they're everywhere. I can feel the power radiating off the spellbooks that stare back at me, knowing that I want to take a peek and find the answers I seek. Maybe they hold something about my curse? I force myself to avert my gaze to anything but the book. There's no time. We might hear footsteps any second now.

We both run around the room searching for a mirror—any mirror. Sweat starts to soak my back as I scatter furniture around the room, digging through coins, rummaging through shelves.

It's not here. It's not fucking here.

I groan in frustration. We're running out of time. They're going to know. They're going to come running down here and that'll be the end. Throwing open a chest, I start piling children's art and toys and heirlooms all onto the floor, moving onto the next and repeating the process.

"I think I found it," Gideon calls. I drop everything and run over to him, spotting a mirror the size of my torso with silver swirls encasing it.

How do I know if this is the one? I say quickly, turning the mirror over like I'm expecting it to be labeled. With all the magic in the room, I can't tell just how dark this object is.

"Ask it who your greatest enemy is."

I look up at him, hesitant for a moment before deciding that there's no time for pause. I stare down at the mirror, repeating the question in my head. Out of everyone I've encountered in my life, there's no telling who hates me most. The mirror ripples like water, flowing and changing the colors. We both stare intently, waiting to see who will appear. Finally, an image flows of an older man with snow-white hair biting down into his meal with a silver goblet encrusted with diamonds in his hand.

My father.

That's enough, I hiss, and the image floats away. I jump to my feet, holding it tightly in my hands and heading toward the door. *Shit. Shit. Shit.*

They're going to sense the mirror, Gideon, I say frantically, searching the room for something that looks like it could counteract the magic.

His hand covers my own. My soul calms momentarily, and I focus on nothing but him. He pulls me lower on the ground, and I let go of the mirror. *Do you trust me?* He holds both my hands in his.

I don't think anymore, I just nod. There's no time for confessions of trust. He moves my hand that holds the dagger, angling it so that it is parallel to my other. *I'm sorry, this will sting*, he says, and I nod, uncaring of how much pain I'm about to feel.

Inhaling deeply, I wince when the blade slices open two of my fingers. Without waiting, he starts drawing on the mirror, something similar to the symbols I've seen in his book. *You have a goddess' blood in you, so this spell will work.*

I don't know what the symbol means, and at this point, I don't care as long as we get out of here. I've left enough of my own magical residue in here that it doesn't matter much that now the scent of my blood fills the air. No hound will be able to track it if there is a blizzard.

He places the last dot and lets go of my hand. My blood on the mirror glows silver and red for a few heartbeats before it settles down into blackened dried blood.

Let's go. I jump to my feet with the mirror in hand and run out the door and over the dead guards. Who knows if the spell worked? Right now, who cares? If the kaliak is causing hell, the scent of dark magic will be the least of everyone's concern.

My boots slap loudly on the stone as I try to navigate my way through the labyrinth, and I follow the trail of blood left behind from the kaliak. I follow the faint sound of screams. Gideon disappears ahead, sending mental messages that the passage is safe.

We finally make it to the potion closet, and the smell of elven magic tints the air. I swing the door open and shove the mirror into the basket, grimacing at the way it juts over the whicker. Throwing a sheet over it, I send one last glance at the closed door containing the dead voren and we run again. Sticking to walls, hiding in shadows, clutching my dagger against the basket.

The higher up we go, the louder the cries become. Nausea climbs higher up my chest from the shrill screams of men and women. Yelling ensues, chainmail clanging, explosions vibrate through the mountain. All because of me.

The ground floor comes into sight as we fly up the steps. My dress is stained with sweat, and everything moves in a blur. Everything aches. Everyone is screaming. My feet catch on the last step, and Gideon's hands steady me without missing a beat, touching the small of my back to urge me on. The air is stained with blood and the smell of magic from people trying to defend themselves. The mirror in the basket feels too heavy, like

I'm carrying the weight of the mountain within it. My arms rage against me, my fingers threaten to give way. Everything is begging me to stop.

This whole morning has been nothing but a string of destruction and chaos. We did it, but at what cost? How many will die because of me today? Will they recognize the smell of my blood in the chamber? How many people will come after me for what I've done?

Blood drips onto the stone staircase and at the very top, the severed head of the lanky elven guard stares down at me, his mouth open in a silent scream. I swallow down bile as my feet struggle to find their rhythm despite the adrenaline burning in me.

I summon the moon's power to my muscles as I leap up the last step, missing the pools of blood as Gideon directs me in a different direction than the one we came in. Every hallway we turn down reeks of magic and blood. Everywhere we turn there is chaos: blood splattered on the walls and dripping on the floor, people running in every direction desperate to escape, severed limbs that appear out of nowhere. The kaliak's scream rips through the air and I wince, wanting to cover my ears from the sound, but I stop. Completely. Frozen in time. The sound grows louder, building to the point that the liquid in my ears boil.

There are three of them.

How the fuck are there three kaliaks? Gideon tugs at my arm trying to get me to move, but I'm not finished. *I'll find a way out. Help them!*

He breathes in, staring at me for a heartbeat before nodding his head and disappearing out of sight. My legs start moving without a second thought. They are stiff at first, and then they don't feel like legs at all, just wheels that turn without control. Stuffing the weapon into the basket and yanking the door open to dash down the servants' corridor. Everyone races in the same direction—even guards—all with one thing in mind: getting the fuck out of the palace. Most of their hands are empty, some with weapons drawn, some clutch another person. But not a single one holds a basket.

The kaliak's scream reverberates again, and everyone turns thinking the monster is behind them. But the scream stops abruptly. I don't spend time considering whether it's Gideon or if the tether is long enough for him to linger and kill them all.

The people in front push each other aside trying to run through the narrow hallway first and I fall back, letting them wrestle through before following closely behind. We spill out into the locker room, and most don't bother grabbing their cloaks before running out. Sprinting to the tenth hook from the entrance, I yank at a cloak that isn't mine. Using the cloak and linen I wrap it around the mirror, clutching it tightly to my chest before pushing ahead of everyone else to make it outside. Everyone is too busy focusing on saving themselves to notice my escape and the object I hold in my hands.

The sun has just passed the horizon, and the falling snow stills. The tether tugs, and Gideon appears, sprinting beside me along with all the other servants.

The full-grown and its child are dead. They can handle the other baby.

Child? Is that why I saw ten arms? I shake my head, not caring about the monster's reproduction. Gideon said that they can handle one baby on their own, and I'm choosing to believe it.

Thank you, I wheeze, exhaustion nipping at me.

Skidding down one street and then another, he turns his head to me saying, *I'll check on Liu.*

I'm too exhausted to even nod, and he knows that too. I don't even blink when he disappears, focused on whether any guards follow behind me. I keep sprinting with the moon's help until the stables come into view and an impatient Liu stomps her hooves with my bags already tied securely to the saddle.

Yanking her reins from the post and shoving the mirror onto the saddle, I strap it down. My fingers wrap around the horn, propelling my leg up and over and kicking her to a canter before I even settle on her properly. With one hand, I hold the reins, with the other I rip the cerulean dress off, popping the buttons and tearing the fabric, exposing the dress I wear beneath. Hurling the servants' garb away I watch as it floats down onto the snow covered with Liu's hoof prints.

Tugging my cloak from where it's tied down, I yank it over my head, not bothering to unclasp it. The wind catches on the fabric, blowing it behind me as we descend the mountain. Then I feel it; the eyes on me. It's everywhere but nowhere. I search the windows and the alleyways, but I can't see anything. I wave it off, putting it down to paranoia. Every few seconds, the tether tugs, but Gideon doesn't appear and I'm too fueled by my own fear to notice where he went.

People scurry out of the way, cursing at me as we avoid stalls. Only when we make it to the middle of the mountain do we slow down to a trot, blending in with the carriages and the other horse riders. As time goes by, more people start to file onto the streets, and I have to pull the reins to stop Liu from biting people's raised hands that hail for a carriage or to get people's attention. She fights my hold as we near a fruit stall, and I give in, dropping more coins than necessary in exchange for an apple.

Gideon appears behind me during the brief pause, wrapping his arms around my waist. I don't let myself think about it, still adamant that eyes are on me, but I have nothing to prove it. Neither of us say a word until we're outside of the city, well beyond its view.

Then we ride, and we ride hard with Lodaxo at our back and the mirror strapped to the saddle. We ride through the night using the moon's magic to fuel Liu and I.

I wrap my fingers around Gideon's hand, squeezing it tightly. He pulls me back against his chest, whispering, *"You did it, Dex. You will set us free."* Though, he doesn't sound pleased.

I shake my head. "There are still nine days left."

DEX

CHAPTER THIRTY

THE CUSHIONS MOLDED AGAINST my back cave under my weight as I stretch before going limp on the soft fabric. The mirror's intricate silver detailing peeks through white linen, strapped tightly against the saddle. All that I can think when I see it is that *we did it.*

We broke into a palace with no real plan in mind and came out unscathed. I traveled into the heart of a mountain and came face to face with a fully grown kaliak and lived to tell the tale. At this point, what we did trumps every single one of Vencen's stories and I won't be able to tell a living, breathing soul about it.

I thought I'd always look upon the mirror with fear or hatred, for everything that occurred to get to it and for showing me the truth about my father—a truth that I always knew deep down but didn't want to accept it. Now, I stare at the mirror and pride blooms in my chest, making me ignore all the death that came with reaching our goal.

I sigh with contentment, leaning back to stare at the skeletal outline of trees hitting the tent in time with the pattering rain. Dropping my hand to the tent floor, I dig my fingers into the tough material, feeling the snow and dirt beneath sludging around my fingers.

We're still five days ride from Taravene with only hours to spare before time runs out. But at least tomorrow, we will watch the snow dwindle as we ride until there's nothing but grass beneath our feet. Still, my heart pinches at the thought, because it will all be over in five days. We'll get the quill and part ways, never to see each other again, never to irritate each other or share heated breaths in the shadows. In five days, it will all be over, and somehow I'll have to figure out how to go back to 'normal' when being around him is the most normal I've ever truly felt.

Other than my true name, I haven't needed to hide from him or choose my words carefully in fear of judgment. He's been the support I never realized that I needed. I'm not sure if I want to wake up in the morning, and not have him be the first thing I think of. Or turn to him and blurt out whatever random thought crosses my mind. Or not have someone who knows my every need without so much as a curl of my own lip. I didn't think that it would hurt this much, having a thorn at my side turn into the air that I breathe. Now, without the thorn's poison seeping into my mind, the world will be nothing but gray.

I don't want to lose him, but I'm afraid that he is prepared to lose me.

Rolling onto my side, I admire the golden glow of the fae light kissing his skin and the golden flecks in his silver eyes that rest comfortably on me.

"What's wrong?" His deep voice snakes around my heart, making it ache more than it already does.

"I'm just thankful for all your help, that's all," I lie through my teeth. Thankful doesn't begin to explain half of how I feel.

The softness of his finger dances across my cheek as he tucks a stray strand of gray hair from my face. "Tell me the truth." There's no smirk on his lips, not when he can feel my heart being eaten up inside.

I take a shaky breath, playing with the soft fabric of his coat. "I'm thinking about what happens once we get the quill." I want to hide my blushing cheeks from him. I don't know if he'll understand the way my soul sings whenever he's near. He looks at me in silent question, and I grab my necklace and twist it between my fingers. "I mean once we're no longer bound to each other."

His gaze drops to my fidgeting hands, and my heart pounds in anticipation. "You'll open your antique store." He stares at my hands like it isn't what he wants to say, but what he should.

I nod stiffly, feeling the same way he does. "And you can go home."

My breath catches in my chest when his gaze flicks up to meet mine, and I can't help but lose myself in the longing deep within his gaze. A longing that reflects my own. "I have never truly had a home before, not until I met you."

His finger trails my lips, stealing unspoken words from me. My fingers move on their own, letting go of the necklace to touch the curve of his jaw. He sucks in a sharp breath, shutting his eyes to lean the rest of his face in my hand. His own hands gently curl around my wrist, planting a long kiss on the inside.

The room around me goes light. Each drop of rain becomes a vivid sound in my ear, and each of his heavy breaths turns my own heavier. Pain lances through his eyes, and I want nothing more than to take it away, to tell him that I feel exactly the same. So I do.

"Hinixsus was never my home." My voice is a whisper, but still, it feels too harsh for my own ears. "Kselia's always felt temporary, but..." I hesitate, searching for the right words to say when it feels like my world is on the line. My fingers find themselves tangled in his hair as I get lost in my own thought. Swallowing the lump in my throat, I say the words that scare me. "Even if whatever is between you and I is only temporary, I'd give it all up. Even for just a day with you."

His lips crash into mine, pulling me into his arms like we'd be torn apart at any second. It's like everything in my soul is snapping into place—like this was always how it's meant to be. I kiss him back with everything in me, meeting each brush of lips with the full force of my emotions. The stars could fall and the moon could shatter, but none of that would matter. I claw at him, not wanting a single inch of space between us, even though our bodies are entwined like the gods designed us for each other.

He draws back, touching my nose with his, holding me only so far that our foreheads still touch. "When the sun sets and when the sun rises, all I want is you." His lips meet mine again, only for a moment before he pulls back. "Even after all my years in the darkness, you are the only light I see." He holds me away from him, still grasping me tightly like he wants to see my face, staring intently at me. "There is nothing I wouldn't do for you. If you want a palace, I'll build one with my bare hands. If you want the world to burn, I'll ask you what color you want the flames. But if you want my heart?"

"You'll give it to me?" Pinpricks of tears gather in my eyes.

He shakes his head. "I'm afraid you already have it."

This time my lips move to his, wanting to taste every inch of him that I've been hungry for. Nothing can describe the way my entire being lights up from his touch; I feel like I'm shining brighter than I ever have at night. Our tongues dance together, exploring and searching for more.

"Gideon." I place a hand on his chest. He breaks away, concern written all over his face like he fears that I might regret what is happening. "I think I love you."

They're words I can't take back, and I'm not sure if I know what they mean. Is that what love is? When it feels as if two hearts are in sync, beating and vibrating together. Or is it the kaleidoscope of stars that paint the night sky whenever our souls collide? This must be more than an infatuation, right? This has to be more than boredom and lonesome, right?

The soft frown on his forehead melts away, leaving behind only light in his eyes that fills me with more power than the moon ever has. "It is no longer a thought for me." His fingers trail blazing heat across my collarbones, making me shiver with lust and anticipation. "It's a fact."

I can't breathe, can't move. He loves me. He *loves me.*

Slowly, he tugs me underneath him. His forearm makes the cushions beneath dip, his other hand pulling my tunic up, and he pushes my legs apart with his knees. I oblige because I don't think I'll ever know a day where his wish isn't my command. Maybe that's what love is. Maybe that is what made those words slip from my lips.

He places a soft kiss between my collarbones as his hand molds to the curve of my neck, as his thumb gently caresses over my throat. My core tightens under his touch as I silently wish for his hands to move lower and satisfy an almost primal craving. My hands move into his obsidian hair, tugging him down—any part of him—but he stays unmoving, staring at me with awe.

"Please," I whisper, not knowing what it is that I'm pleading for when there are so many things that I want; his lips on mine, to fill the space between us, to feel him between my legs, to scream his name until the whole realm tremors.

He continues to say nothing, as his eyes stay focused on me, following every bend and dip on my face. "You are my home, Dex," he says, "I love you even when you ignite an anger in me that could tear apart a kingdom." He drags his hand down my chest as he speaks, bringing a gasp from my lips as he jerks at the string holding my blouse together.

"Kiss me, please, Gideon," I beg, clawing at his tunic to bring him closer.

A deadly smirk spreads across the face that once held nothing but passion. "Oh, little elf," he purrs, dragging his finger along my jaw, over the center of my neck and down between my breasts. I fist his pristine tunic like it's my only link to sanity, feeling the fabric wrinkle in my grasp. "I would destroy a kingdom at your wish. However, your wishes will fall on deaf ears when you're whimpering my name."

He feels it too. That need. That feeling of falling onto his knees, blind with hunger. Because I feel it too—for him.

He doesn't move from his position above me as air gathers between us, prickling the middle of my chest where my blouse has left me exposed. His hand skates over my skin before pushing against my center, making me buckle to his touch. His hand rubs against my need as something starved inside of me starts to rage because of the fabric left between us.

Our lips meet just as I'm about to move. The kiss is heavier, needier than it was before, and the speed of his fingers grows with each pant. The arm keeping him up moves, embracing my head and fisting my hair. My fingers fumble at his tunic, reaching for his waist, tugging it up to his shoulders. But he doesn't move, keeping his lips on mine and the fabric between us.

He clicks his tongue. "So impatient darling."

"I am not a patient woman," I rasp, using my powers to push him off.

He chuckles, and with one swift movement, the tunic lays discarded on the floor next to us. "Your turn." He moves with certainty like every move up to this point has been calculated. I'm putty in his hands as he bends me to his will, slipping the blouse over my head.

The night chill sends goosebumps over my skin, but I don't let myself shiver. I want to reserve that for him and only him. His mouth descends on my breast, grazing his teeth over the point and raking a shudder from me. Hands grip my backside with careless vigor, and a strangled moan leaves my lips. He starts massaging it like he's pleased with my reaction, which only makes me moan even more.

My legs squeeze around him as his length presses against my center and I fumble with his trousers so I can wrap my hand around him. There's still too much fabric between us. He snatches my hand in his own, pushing it above my head as he growls, "Wait." I push against his hold, which only makes him tighten his grip nearing the point of pain. "I said wait," he hisses.

I narrow my eyes at him as he returns his attention to my breasts while keeping my hand held above my head and his hips just out of reach of mine. He lets go, running his hands down the sides of my body, leaving blazing heat behind as he tugs down my cotton pants with a single movement. I gasp, feeling the cold air bite at my exposed skin.

He rises to his knees. The light casts dark shadows across his abdomen, highlighting every inch of muscle that has been honed to deadly perfection. My eyes lift to him as I get drunk on the taste of mulled wine—on the taste of his lust. He owns me, he owns my heart, he owns every part of who I am. He looks every bit the danger that he is, the perfectly formed muscle built by the heavens and the chaos in his eyes that threatens to swallow me whole. He looks like a god.

He licks his lips, dragging his gaze over my body, pausing on my bare chest and center with an expression that can only be described as a primal hunger. "You look like a goddess."

He withdraws from between my legs, and I move to my elbows as the growing fear that he'll leave chews at my heart. Only for a strangled scream to leave my lips when his head buries between my thighs.

My breathing is labored, hiccupping, moaning, crying with complete bliss in time to each flick of his tongue. My hips roll against his mouth, taking my pleasure with each hungry lick. He works his tongue like he's been starved his whole life and his hands are continuously moving, sending my mind into a flurry of desire that stops me from knowing what is up and what is down. He feasts like he's a man starved and I am the best meal he's had in all of the eight kingdoms. His hands move from my hips, to my thighs, to breasts, to my hands, constantly moving like he's searching for something more. Needing more. And I let him.

I can't help but stare at him. He is feared and desired by kings, a weapon capable of annihilation, and yet there he is: a weapon, on his knees and between my thighs.

His eyes look up to meet my own, and red rushes to my cheeks from getting caught staring. "You needn't ingrain what you see into your mind, darling. I intend to be on my knees for you every day until you know me in no other form." His tongue drags languidly up my center as if he has all the time in the world and he never wants to forget the taste of me. "This," he growls, and his hot breath fans my center, fueling my desire. "This is where I am meant to be." His tongue slides in me, scraping my soft skin with his teeth and drawing my pleasure higher. "A worshiper that has finally found his altar." A wicked grin spreads across his lips. "And I intend to pray all night."

I moan from his words alone rolling harder, faster as pleasure builds in my core. I need him, I need more. This isn't enough, I don't want his tongue, I want *all* of him. I want every single inch of him that he's willing to give. "Please fuck me," I whimper, digging my nails into his shoulders.

His fingers slide into me, and I scream, trying to arch my back but his hand holds me firmly in place. "I've been wanting you for weeks. Do not rush my meal, darling. I will have my fill," he growls, taking my center in his mouth as his fingers start to press against my walls as he pumps inside me.

I buckle with each move, grinding my hips and arching my back, wanting more but overwhelmed with the explosion of sensation. Overwhelming pleasure builds in my core as my ragged moans and screams shake the tent wall. As my pleasure grows my screams only grow louder and my hands claw at the furs beneath us.

"If you can't take my fingers, then how can you handle my cock?" Gideon snarls, inserting another finger inside me. I scream, slapping the cushions and the blanket, incapable of containing myself. "Now come for me, my moonlight." He hooks his fingers and pulls a shrill cry from me.

I start to smell colors as the pressure builds and builds until the world shatters into a million pieces, except Gideon is there to pick it all up. My chest heaves as the heavy feeling in my body starts to dissipate, slipping on the edge of readiness for sleep. He moves up so his hot breath tangles in my hair as he whispers in my ear, "Good girl, now you get what you want."

My eyes widen as he starts undoing the buttons of his black pants where a heavy dent presses in the middle. My body reawakens, ready for more, ready for him. I suck in a sharp breath once his pants lay discarded on the floor. I can feel myself tighten as I squirm beneath him; he's larger than anything I've seen, and I want every last inch of him.

He lowers himself on top of me, propping himself right by my entrance. The unhinged hunger in the air is gone, and the look on his face is one of blind worship as his lips meet mine in a tender embrace. We meet each other's movements as I drag my hands over his face, wanting to engrave it into my memory.

I pull back just as he did, nuzzling my nose against his. "You're my home too."

A thick moan curls from me as his tip pushes into me, and his lips capture mine, stealing the moan away from me.

Slowly, his hips move, plunging deeper inside of me with each thrust. "*Fuck*," he growls.

My nails dig into his back as my desire soars higher than it has before. A scream breaks through me when his hips flatten into mine, filling me with all of him until there's nothing on my mind but the thought of pleasing him.

My lips find his neck, dragging my teeth over the soft skin, kissing and sucking as his groans fill the air, calling to my desire. He starts thrusting into me faster as his hands grip my hair, pulling it so that my head touches his chest.

"Watch me fuck you," he snarls into my ear like a primal switch has just turned on, and the air all around becomes dense, laden with our combined pleasure. "I want it burnt into your memory so you know nothing but how perfectly we fit."

I whimper, watching the light dance as he pounds into me, drawing my pleasure as his fingers start to rub the delicate skin of my desire.

"Oh gods!" I crumble beneath him as my core explodes with pleasure once more and his hands move away as he groans from my tightened hold. I start to see stars as he continues pounding into me.

"They aren't listening. Scream it louder." His hand returns again, rubbing faster and harder and pulling pleasure from me, I didn't even know existed.

With my powers I push back against his grip on my head, slamming my lips against his as I moan a string of curses. I've never felt anything like this with anyone that I've been with; none have ever taken me this high. Not many times has someone made me reach my climax once, and this force of nature is bringing me to another.

"Fuck, Gideon," I let out a throaty groan cut short by another scream as he thrusts the whole of him inside me.

"No, call me your darkness," he breathes, thrusting faster and faster, building up the ache in my core until I don't think I can stand it anymore. I claw his back, I slap the cushions, I pull the furs. "I need you to come, my little elf." His voice is raw, strained, like he can barely contain himself.

Without a moment of hesitation, I come completely undone, and with one final thrust he roars into the mountains before falling in a heap next to me.

DEX
CHAPTER THIRTY-ONE

THE LINGERING REMNANTS OF our desire clouds the tent as our languid bodies press closely together. His hand spreads over the span of my back, and he plants a tender kiss on top of my head as our legs tangle and lock together. My finger trails over the expanse of his chest as I try to ignore my visceral thoughts that plague me. I can feel his tenseness too, yet our lips stay sealed like neither of us wants to be the one to ruin the moment.

Something about our tether feels different as well; I just can't place what it is. But that isn't what plays on my mind. He said, "I love you, *Dex.*" Not Devereux, Dex. Worry gnaws at my seams, like his words won't ring true unless I lay it all bare for him. Goosebumps prickle over the skin that he touches as if my body is telling me that I've deceived him into giving himself to me when he doesn't know the whole truth.

There's a little voice inside my head telling me that it isn't rational to think that way, and his feelings toward me stem from who I am and not just a title. But the voice that calls me a liar speaks louder than the one trying to calm my racing mind. And those who speak the loudest are always the ones most heard.

Bringing up the truth will only ruin the moment, however the moment won't be real unless he knows. The truth has been a weight on my shoulder for long enough, and I need to set aside my fear that he'll see me in a different light. We haven't talked about the 'what's next' in our road ahead or how exactly our profession of love changes anything. He deserves to know so that he can make a conscious decision on how he wants to move ahead.

"Gideon," I say slowly, and he winces like I struck the wrong chord. His reaction triggers the cowardly side of me that wants to close my mouth and pretend that I didn't just speak. Avoiding the truth won't make it any less real. "I have something to tell you."

He breathes in a staggered breath as we both sit up at the same time, keeping our legs entangled but our chests apart like we need to study each other's faces. "As do I."

I search his eyes hoping to see that he already knows the truth, but all that stares back at me are desperate eyes. "Please, let me go first." My voice is heavy with plea as I take his hand in mine, squeezing it gently. He nods, and I breathe deep before continuing, "I don't care about who you are or what you are. I know what you are like deep down, but I think you deserve the truth all the same."

He stares at me, and written on his face is the wavering belief in my words as the cowardly side of me starts to speak louder. I take slow breaths, one, then two, trying to find the courage.

"My name is Devereux Selino of the Kingdom of Hinixsus, I am the first in line for the Throne of the Moon."

He stares at me as I fidget, twirling and curling my fingers as if I might open a portal to run from his reaction. Or lack of reaction. His heavy eyes are on me as a war turns behind them. I'd settle for yelling or even a snarky comment at this point because the silence is too loud. "Say something," I beg.

"I know." The weight of his response removes the one sitting heavily on my chest.

I blink once, twice, expecting him to elaborate, but he never does. "How?"

He shifts his weight uncomfortably, but something tells me that it isn't because of my question. "Once I got my bearings and my senses slowly returned, I started smelling the royalty in your blood. Then your family reacted strangely to Vencen's 'princess' comment. My thoughts were only confirmed when Rhaelson appeared in the mirror. Most of all, you walk like someone born to command an army," he lists, voice full of meaning as he strokes my waist.

Yet I can see as clear as day that there is something bothering him.

He continues, "I have not been truthful about my name—"

"There's more," I interject as my hands start to shake. If he says his piece, I don't know if I'll find the strength to say mine. He reaches out for me, but I move away with more force than I intended. The louder voice in my head is telling me that I don't deserve his comfort, not yet. "This is all my fault," my voice breaks as I shake my head. "You're bound to me because of the magic that taints my blood to keep me hidden from my father."

He sighs, softening his gaze on me as he reaches for my hand again, and this time I don't move it. I let the comfort seep from his hand, acting like liquid courage. "None of that matters. Don't think that any of this is your fault."

Part of me wants him to be angry at me for not admitting it and keeping it a secret for so long, like his rage is what I deserve. My own mind wishes for my downfall. "I have other names as well," I start carefully, and his brows crease like he didn't expect me to have more secrets. I wait for the anger to shine in his eyes, or even disappointment in me for keeping so much a secret. But still, nothing comes. I dig my nails into my palm. "I am the prophecy of the crescent moon, and I am the Daughter of the Blood Moon."

All semblance of life and light sucks out of the air as color drains from his face. Only it isn't rage or disappointment; it's unparalleled horror followed by something that I've never seen on his face before; fear.

"What did you say?" he breathes, untangling his legs.

"My heart will win the war and I'm the one fated to bring back our gods." My voice breaks and shakes as images of him wishing for my death flicker in my mind.

The images only get worse by the morbid tone of his voice when he says, "You're the Daughter of the Blood Moon?" He moves to his feet like he's physically frightened by my presence.

My heart sinks deeper and deeper, and it feels like I won't be able to breathe. I want to say no and take it all back, pretend that I'm Dex, a retiring procurer. But I can't take back what has already been said. I can't change who I am—and I've tried. For years I've tried pretending that I'm not who

I'm fated to be. I kept pretending that if I don't say it out loud, then maybe there's hope that it won't be true and somehow the curse will go away by itself. Maybe I'll stop needing my necklace; I'll stop glowing when the moon is at its peak, the crescent moon will just disappear, my hair will be plain silver. But it never happens, my fear only grows stronger.

I swallow the lump in my throat, watching as he turns his back to me with my heart sinking further. "Yes, I am," I stutter as something else starts to boil within my blood: anger. Anger at myself for falling so carelessly, and caring about the perceptions of a man who made it clear that he is capable of destruction. Anger at him for reacting like I'm the one who has destroyed him. He starts pulling on his pants, pacing the short distance of the tent, back and forth, back and forth. "I'm sorry, if I knew you'd be so upset about it I would have told you sooner." A lie, but one that I won't admit to myself.

He kneels, and I push back into the cushions, afraid of his approaching touch. "No, it's not that, I—"

He recoils like I've set his skin aflame. Standing up, he continues his pacing and with each turn the tent seems to shrink, taking the air with it. He runs his hand through his hair, his eyes consumed by endless horror. A string of curses leaves his mouth, and I curl deeper into the furs, this time not angry, but scared of the power rippling off him. Scared of the faces creeping through the shadows. Scared of losing him completely.

He kneels back down across from me, every muscle in his face is pulled taunt like it pains him to even exist with me in the room. "Dex, I need you to listen to me very carefully, okay?" I don't miss the quiver in his voice and the plea in his eyes as he tries to comfort me. Only I don't feel what he wants me to feel.

Panic creeps in, sinking its teeth into me as I nod my rigid head.

He touches my hand and only then do I realize that I'm hugging my knees like a frightened child. "It wasn't just your blood that bound us. Stumbling upon that book was not an accident, it was fate."

I retreat from his touch, replaying every moment. No, it was an accident. Vencen was the one that got hired to procure the book. He's the one that brought it to Zarlor. I only got it because the Satyr refused to pay. It was all an accident. "What are you talking about?"

He tries reaching for my hand again, and I pull away, moving to my feet and putting my clothes on as well. Desperation burns in his eyes, but I can't begin to comprehend why. Everything in me is screaming to run, like something is about to happen and I'll be the last to find out about it.

He gets to his feet, his chest rising and dropping nearly as fast as mine and the fear in my heart is written all over his face. "You unlocked the door because you are the Daughter of the Blood Moon. We are bound together because I cast the spell that ends in your death."

Everything goes silent. The rain seems to stop pouring, the wind has stopped singing, all that's left is the thundering roar in my ear. I stumble back as far away as I can from him. No. *No.* That's not true. He's joking. He has to be joking. A witch cursed me. Not him. Not whatever *he* is.

"This has to be some sick, twisted joke." *No, no, no.* He's just trying to rile me up. He's trying to make me laugh or something. "Well, I'm not laughing." I shake my head, trying to put even more distance between us, pressing against the tent canvas.

"This is not a joke, Dex." His voice is stern as his own mask starts to crack. Emotions thunder to every corner of my body as pain pierces my heart. "My sole purpose of becoming confined to that book is to one day find you, and together we can free the gods. I was meant to be freed with the quill."

It isn't just fear that I see, it's pain. This pains him? *Him?* I am the one forced to live every day on the run. *I* am the one fated to perish one way or another. No, this isn't his agony to bear. This is *mine*. And it's all his fault.

"None of this was real." Each breath is strained, rough, broken. Nothing between us was real. It was all him. He doesn't really love me. He tricked me—cursed me. The only reason for my alleged love for him is because he decided it. That's why my soul sings when he's near. That's why he's bound to me. There's no connection more powerful than that between a cursed and its caster.

He's right. He is a monster.

"Everything has been real, Dex." He reaches out to me, and I snatch my hand away, moving to the other side of the tent as something on my hand starts to buzz.

A snarl rips through my throat. "No. *No*, get my fucking name out of your mouth. It doesn't belong there. Not anymore," I hiss, watching as the light drains from him. I grit my teeth, pointing my finger at his face as his chaos starts to come awake inside me. I can hear them, their cries and laughter, egging me on, telling me to use my powers, telling me to try and kill him. "You said sweet words and made me fall into your hands, all the while it was *you*. You ruined my fucking life. I can *never* be free because of you. Never. Every single king on this gods forsaken land wants me—dead or alive. Because of you, Gideon, because of *you*."

The buzzing amplifies on my hand as red corners my vision. I hate him. I fucking hate him. My necklace hums as power rips through me at the chaos's demand. I want to kill him. I want him to feel my pain. I want him to know what betrayal truly feels like. The worst part about it is that I can't. I can't bring myself to hate him. I can't bring myself to bury a knife through his heart. Because I still love him.

"My name isn't Gideon," he says like it's meant to mean something to me.

"I don't give a shit what your name is." I want to forget about his name forever, erase it from my memory and pretend this was all a bad dream. But it isn't a bad dream for everyone who died because of the kaliaks. Because of us. All this running was for nothing. All the death and heartache was just to land me right in the curse's hand. I don't want this. I don't want any of this. I can't do this. I need to be left alone. "I have to get out. I have to find a way out. Away from you." My mouth struggles to keep up with my thoughts. "*Get away from me,*" I roar.

He disappears in an instant, engulfed by shadows and leaving the tent bigger—too big. "Coward!" I clutch my chest as each breath pains me. I repeat the words over and over again. He left. He actually left me. He said that he'd do as I ask, and he did. I asked him to, but I didn't think that he would. He cursed me, he fucked me, and he left.

He cursed me.

He cursed me.

He cursed me.

I need air. Fumbling with my pants, I tug them on, carelessly buttoning them before crawling into the night. Rain soaks my hair in an instant, the wind screams in my ears and cold seeps into my skin. But I don't feel it—I don't care about it. The slush and dirt squelches beneath my weight, hissing and screeching as I run through the forest.

I can't see him anywhere. I grab onto our tether but all I feel is empty space. It's gone. I can't feel it. Where is he? What is happening? I need him to tell me what's going on. I was wrong, I shouldn't have pushed him away, I should haven't told him to leave. He holds the answers, he holds the key. I need him, and still, he cursed me. Still, he leaves me frightened and alone.

Gideon, where are you? I scream and scream, but he doesn't reply. He doesn't appear.

A sharp burn sears my finger, and I wince. Holding my hand up, I watch as the golden band glows red with heat—Saeya's ring.

A hand darts out of nowhere, covering my mouth with a cloth drenched with a putrid smell.

Gideon! I scream one last time before everything goes black.

The jolt and bumps of a carriage stirs me, and I peel my heavy lids open for a brief moment only to see a woven pattern of fabric before I succumb to the darkness once more. I sink deeply into the lulling melody singing at the back of my mind. A soft string plays peacefully, haunting me with its spelled melody, keeping me prisoner in my own body.

The carriage comes to a halt, and hushed whispers sound all around me, but I can't make out the words that they're saying. The breath is forced from me when something bony digs into my stomach and the blood rushes to my head as my hair drops to the top of the sack tied firmly around my head from being hurled over someone's shoulder. My upper body sways, helpless to the melody, and I can just make out shadows of legs striding along a marble floor.

My hands twitch and something burns around my wrist. A cold and sharp ache squeezes my chest as I fight the hold on my mind and body. I try to summon my power but that, too, is just out of reach.

My body swings against a person's back as energy slowly filters back into my system. The melody quietens and my mind reels, trying to piece together a pictureless puzzle, only the pieces don't fit. Gideon, a forest, Saeya's ring. They're nothing but meaningless words to me.

We start to near the sound of whispers, and the sound of the person's boots against the floor rings in my ear. Silence fills the air at once as I slide down whoever has carried me to slump down onto a cold floor that seeps through the woolen material wrapped loosely around me.

Calculating hands touch the back of my head, undoing the tie before yanking the sack from me. My eyes squeeze shut, blinded by the crystal chandelier hanging above. I squint to adjust to the light and get my bearings.

Shoes click against the floor, piercing my ear drum. I try to angle my head to the sound, try to prepare myself for what's to come. I can't move. Frozen and poisoned in place, left to stare at the intricate patterns carved into the white marble ceiling as the clicking comes closer until it stops just beside me.

A tall male stares back down at me, the blue light of the candles reflecting in his silver hair. A sadistic curl twists on his lips as his pale blue eyes bleed with victory.

Eyes shaped as mine.

Everything slams into me at once.

The curse, the hand, the burning ring, the tether.

His chin juts forward as he looks down at me. "Welcome home, daughter."

BOOK TWO COMING 2024

ABOUT THE AUTHOR

Born in Indonesia, and raised in New Zealand, Zian Schafer has a love for the world of make believe and stories based in a fantasy world. She has two dogs who wants constant attention, and two rabbits that will chew every cord in the house, if given the opportunity. You can visit her at zianschafer.com or on Instagram @zian_schafer and TikTok @zianschafer.

Printed in Great Britain
by Amazon

23106404R00218